LOST ISLANDS

Part Two

The Lonely Seeker

C.A. OLIVER

Book's cover and portraits:
Virginie Carquin - Brussels, Belgium

Heraldry, genealogy and maps:
Sylvain Sauvage - La Tour-de-Peilz, Switzerland

Editorial correction:
Thomas Bailey - Oxford, UK

Editorial review:
Laurent Chasseau - Paris, France
Eric Train - Biarritz, France

SONGS OF THE LOST ISLANDS
EXISTING PUBLICATIONS

Songs of the Lost Islands #1 – An Act of Faith (2019)

Songs of the Lost Islands #2 – The Lonely Seeker (2019)

Songs of the Lost Islands #3 – The Valley of Nargrond (2019)

Songs of the Lost Islands, First Trilogy – Odes to Dusk (2020)
(Includes *An Act of Faith*, *The Lonely Seeker* and The *Valley of Nargrond*)

Songs of the Lost Islands forthcoming publications

Prelude (2021)

Songs of the Lost Islands #4 – Two Winged Lions (2022)

www.songsofthelostislands.com

ISBN: 978-1076079657
Legal deposit: April 2020

BIOGRAPHY

C. A. Oliver was born in 1971 and spent his youth between Oxford and Bordeaux. From an early age, he was an avid reader of both the English and French canons, and it was J.R.R. Tolkien and Maurice Druon who would come to influence his writing above all others.

In his teenage years, Oliver and four friends began a tabletop role-playing game. Fifteen years later, after 3,500 hours of discussion, imagination and strategy, what began as a game had developed into an entire universe. As gamemaster, Oliver documented the gargantuan campaign's progress.

This fantasy world lay dormant for several years. Then, in 2014, after witnessing uncanny parallels with real-world politics, Oliver began to forge *Songs of the Lost Islands*, a fantasy series that draws heavily on the fifteen-year campaign. He started writing the first trilogy at Sandfield Road in Oxford, the very street on which Tolkien once lived. It was concluded at Rue Alexandre Dumas in Saint-Germain-en-Laye, where Dumas composed *The Three Musketeers*.

C. A. Oliver now lives between Paris and Rio de Janeiro, having married a Brazilian academic. *Songs of the Lost Islands* has been above all inspired by what Oliver knows best: the ever-changing winds of global politics, the depth and scope of English fantasy; and the fragile, incomprehensible beauty of his wife's homeland.

ACKNOWLEDGEMENTS

It has taken me five years to write the first three instalments of *Songs of the Lost Islands*. But developing the world that is the basis for these books was an even longer process.

It is now thirty years since I first joined forces with four of my closest friends to devise the world of the series. It began in the summer of 1989 with the creation of an RPG wargame campaign, in which different Elvin civilizations fought for the control of a distant archipelago. The arrival of Curwë and his companions in Llafal, an Elvin port on the island of Nyn Llyvary, marked the starting point of a story that would go on to last decades.

For the first twenty-three years, we had no intention of sharing these myths, legends and adventures with anyone outside our tight-knit group. It was a secret garden, or perhaps rather a dragon's lair, rich with treasures built up over 3,500 hours of gameplay. No intruder ever broke their way into our various dungeons: the garage of 37 Domaine de Hontane, near Bordeaux; a cramped bedroom in Oxford; and a flat in Arcachon, with a beautiful sea view we never found time to enjoy.

After the campaign had drawn to a close, the years went by and I found that I was missing the thrill of those night-time gatherings: the smell of smoke, the taste of wine and, above all, the noise of the rolling dice.

I therefore eventually gathered the material accumulated over all those years of frenetic creativity, and soon realized that I possessed enough content for twelve books. The distinctive nature of this story lies in its genesis: characters, embodied by players, interacting with plots and settings developed by the game master. Outcomes were decided by applying a set of specific wargame rules, the authority of which was unquestionable.

The result was quite stunning: a fifteen-year long campaign

made up of dozens of characters, whose destinies were determined by both the roll of the multifaceted dice and the choices made by the players.

Much to my surprise, the first readers of *An Act of Faith* were very enthusiastic in their responses, and eager to discover what would follow. Some were fascinated by Roquen or Curwë, others resonated naturally with the more reckless Irawenti, while the more aesthetically minded readers were attracted to the Llewenti.

My mind was made up. I embarked on a quest to complete the *Songs of the Lost Islands* series.

When I started, I had no idea how complex it would be to forge *Songs of the Lost Islands* from all the material I had before me. I now look in utter fascination at the copies of *An Act of Faith*, *The Lonely Seeker* and *The Valley of Nargrond* sitting on my desk and feel relatively confident that the remaining tomes will follow. The debts of gratitude that I owe are therefore very significant.

Firstly, I must thank my beloved family: Mathilde, Marion and Agatha, who probably think me mad, but who nevertheless continue to provide their unwavering support.

I am enormously grateful to the scholars who have helped me negotiate the pitfalls of writing fantasy: Eric Train and Laurent Chasseau read the first drafts of the *Songs* and provided me with their insightful responses and suggestions. Their feedback was invaluable, not least because their passion for the Lost Islands dates all the way back to 1989.

The series could not have been written without Thomas Bailey, a gifted poet who studied at Oxford University, whose expertise and enthusiasm turned a manuscript into the finished article.

I am also extremely grateful to Virginie Carquin and Sylvain Sauvage for wonderfully designing and illustrating the Lost Islands, that last refuge of the Elves. Their prodigious efforts gave me the strength to push ahead, at a time when I was finally waking up to the full scale of the challenge before me.

Virginie is illustrating all twelve books of *Songs of the Lost*

Islands. She has produced a series of twenty-three portraits of characters in the novels. Her work also features on the covers of the collectors' editions.

Sylvain has served as chief concept designer for the Lost Islands' world. His achievements include creating the maps of Oron, the genealogy of the clans and houses, and all their emblems and insignia. His overall contribution to the project is even more far-reaching; it includes, among many other things, designing the series' website.

Lastly, I must thank the readers of *Songs of the Lost Islands*, for already making it through more than a thousand pages of stories and legends about the Elves. As Feïwal dyn puts it:

"The quest for the Lost Islands is a journey that cannot offer any hope of return. It is a leap in the unknown. It is an act of faith."

TABLE OF CONTENTS

ELVIN NATIONS

High Elves *(Hawenti)*

Gold Elves *(Halwenti)* — 2 royal houses *(Dor)* / 16 noble houses *(Dol)*

Silver Elves *(Harwenti)*
Night Elves *(Morawenti)* — Guild of Sana *(Dir)*

The High Elves accepted the gift of the Gods and became immortal.

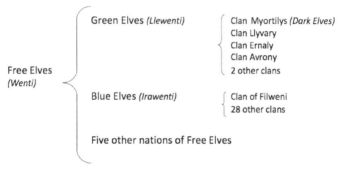

Free Elves *(Wenti)*

Green Elves *(Llewenti)* — Clan Myortilys *(Dark Elves)* / Clan Llyvary / Clan Ernaly / Clan Avrony / 2 other clans

Blue Elves *(Irawenti)* — Clan of Filweni / 28 other clans

Five other nations of Free Elves

The Free Elves refused the gift of the Gods and remained mortal.

Anroch
Desert

Essawylor

Nen

Austral Ocean

Atolls Fadaluḃ

Sea of Cyclones

Lost
Islands

Sea of Isyl

ANTIPODES

200 Leagues

Sea of Cyclones

Nyn Llyvary

Nyn Ernaly

Nyn Llorely

Main
Land

Sea
of
Llyoriane

Nyn Avrony

Gwarystan

Gwa Nyn

Sea of Isyl

Nyn Llyandy

LOST ISLANDS

50 Leagues

NYN ERNALY

20 Leagues

* Eïwal Vars Lepsy peak
** Moka Kirini peaks

Austral Ocean

Strait of Tiude

Mentolewin

Arob
Chanun

Tios
Lly

Strait of Oymal

Llanely

Hageyu
Falls

Sian Ningy

Llatya

Wood of
Silver Leaves

Tios
Sian

Tar-Andevar

Sea of Llyoriane

CHAPTER 1: Dyoren

2712, Season of Eïwele Llya, 78th day. Nyn Ernaly, Hageyu Falls

The tree was about to fall. Axes from both sides had hacked their way towards the centre of the great trunk, and the ancient oak was creaking forward over its newly formed hinge. The Men dropped their tools and threw themselves out of harm's way.

"Move!" shouted the chief slaver.

The thick lower branches of the oak crashed into the humid soil below, obliterating every plant within their reach. When the tree fell, a loud howl tore through the air, as if its soul were fleeing its ruined shell in terror. The moment the great trunk lay motionless across the earth, the rain ceased. Midday approached. The forest, indifferent to the loss of one its oldest inhabitants, was suddenly gaining new life. A light breeze carried the murmur of a distant waterfall. Birdsong emanated from the bushes. Scampering squirrels rustled between the tree branches overhead, and even an unseen predator added its low growl to the melody of the woodland.

"Marshal the Giants," ordered the chief slaver, eager to win back time now that the rain was over. "Move faster, you lazy scum!" he barked.

The chief of this site was a Westerner from Nellos, that faraway maritime realm whose main island lay beyond the Sunset Ocean. The Men of his unit came from various barbarian tribes of the Mainland, whose loyalty was now sworn to the Westerners. The slaver frowned; his face made pale by his lack of sleep. As he looked about him, he stroked his beard, to conceal his worry.

"Get those beasts to work immediately, or this won't be a day you'll forget," he warned.

The cold hatred in his eyes guaranteed the sincerity of his threat. Then came the screech of steel grinding against steel. A score of slavers, escorted by a dozen soldiers, led three chained Giants to the site of the fallen tree. The scene was overseen by a dozen guards, led by a mounted commander. These soldiers were covered in plate armour and equipped with halberds and lances. The weary and weatherworn Giants were constrained by enormous chains which bound them all together. The slavers relished in reminding their captives who their true masters were: whipping, beating and administering all manner of cruel and degrading punishments.

At the site of the felled great oak, the sun was already high in the sky, and sweat poured from the Giants' bodies as the summer's day reached its hottest peak. One of the three Giants began to express his discontent in wild yells. Its simple language was as rough as the rocky quarries from which he had emerged.

"JURK, BOTA! JENKCHE! KRABAK! ORKY SU AKAGO LAKBRAR?"

The chains that ensnared Old Gamo, as was his name, to his unfortunate companion, who was now completely motionless, were severely slowing him down. Fear of punishment soon flooded through Gamo's mind. The second Giant, who had been named Big Bota, did not seem to hear these complaints. Every ounce of his limited intellect was focused on something else: something invisible, odourless and soundless. Giants of Chanun, natives of Nyn Ernaly, were usually short and stocky in comparison to others of their kin. But Bota was much larger, towering above his two other companions from a height of fourteen feet. He was also extremely muscular, capable of hurling huge boulders. The comparative shortness of his limbs made his thick arms look even more fearsome.

"TUK FOMEK?" Old Gamo asked, guessing that Bota must have been suffering from the same hungriness that tortured him.

Giants of Chanun needed a great quantity of food. These colossal beings would devour almost anything, and they were not averse to eating humans. The lash of a whip suddenly interrupted their exchange, and Old Gamo felt the pain searing across his back. The slavers' punishment had come but a moment after they had paused their work. Now Gamo was angry with his companion, who still seemed absorbed in his inner torment. By stopping, Bota was paralysing the progress of all three Giants, endangering them all. In their society, betraying one's tribe was the worst possible evil, and though the hierarchy of Giants was determined by a combination of physical strength and appetite for food, solidarity was the cornerstone of their relationships. Big Bota's refusal to move would lead to retribution.

"TEN KE ANKAR!" ordered Old Gamo.

The stress in his voice indicated that his limited patience was already spent. The only answer he could extract from his companion was unintelligible. A horn blew, and soon guards were reaching for their spears and halberds. The impending punishment promised to be severe. Suddenly, Big Bota started to move erratically, his hands reaching up to cover his ears. His huge, muscular body was convulsing violently. He then began shouting ferociously, as if possessed by a wild spirit.

"Can you hear the music? Can you hear that evil sound?"

Most surprisingly, Big Bota was expressing his anguish in lingua Llewenti, the tongue of the Green Elves. The two other Giants of Chanun looked at each other in total disbelief. There was no sound around them but the loud orders the commander was giving to his troops to begin the punishment. A dozen guards, their weapons raised high, started to encircle the three wretched slaves. The air grew tense with the promise of imminent bloodshed. The slavers, whose sole duty was to supervise the Giants' work, chose to retreat cautiously, knowing that their whips and short swords would be of no use in what was to come.

"Do you hear the music; do you hear that Elvin song?" Big Bota roared.

He gestured chaotically, driven to madness by some unknown soundless witchcraft penetrating his mind.

"The music must stop! Do you hear? It must be stopped!" he cried, now totally lost.

Bota pulled at his chains, and the third and smallest Giant was toppled over violently. Rushing towards him, Big Bota started to beat the fallen slave with his huge fists, still shouting out in that Elvin tongue that was not his own.

"Ogo! Stop the music! Do you hear? The music must stop!"

But Young Ogo could do nothing to help him. He had been surprised by the sudden violence of his companion. His meagre resistance to the series of blows crashing down upon his head soon faltered. Before long, Ogo was nothing more than a bloody, motionless corpse, his brains seeping out from what remained of his skull onto the humid forest floor below. Old Gamo was terrified. He decided to flee. But the chain linking him to Bota soon became taught, and its sudden steel resistance knocked Gamo to the ground. In a heartbeat, the mad Giant was on top of Gamo, raising a large boulder high into the air. With all the strength that only madness can produce, he hurled it down at his helpless companion.

"The music must stop!" he repeated incessantly, his horrible voice degrading the Elvin words.

Not content with the devastating wounds inflicted upon Old Gamo by the boulder, Big Bota set upon the now defenceless body of his companion. The unrelenting blows of his fists soon crushed Gamo's head into the earth.

Until that moment, the guards had observed the bloody scene, keeping strictly to their ordered, defensive formation. An encircling wall of their large shields denied any hope of flight to the mad Giant. At the bark of their commander, the soldiers aimed their lances forward, forming an even closer deadly circle around the Giant. Behind their iron visors, their gaze showed resolution mixed with no small anxiety. They had heard similar stories in the taverns of their city, tales of Chanun Giants who, bewitched by Elvin sorcery, had savagely killed soldiers before the rebellious slaves met their own bitter end.From atop his horse a few yards from the melee, the commander of the Westerners was coordinating the final assault.

"Form ranks soldiers of Nellos! Let us show that beast who we are!" he shouted.

Everything about his attire demonstrated his high status: the glistening plate armour, the navy-blue cloak around his broad shoulders, and the golden helmet bearing the insignia of Nellos, a wide sun setting over the horizon of the sea. Safely positioned a few yards behind his troops, the commander could never have anticipated what was about to occur.

Bota rushed towards the charging guards, dragging the corpses of his two former companions by his chains. Ignoring the stabs of the lances and the cuts of the halberds, the Giant broke through the circle. After smashing three soldiers to the ground, he grabbed two other guards with each of his big hands. With his unnatural strength, galvanised by the pain still pounding through his head, he threw the desperate Men, one by one, across half a dozen yards away towards their commander.

The first human projectile hit the horse's front legs, nearly causing it to topple. The second crashed into its head and ensured its fall. The commander was caught. Failing to remove his heavy iron sabatons from the stirrups, he came tumbling down with his mount on its left side. His leg was snapped and crushed in several places, and the searing pain left him just enough consciousness to hear, rather than see, the continuing bloodshed around him. One by one, his soldiers fell to the wrath of the mad Giant, as they tried in vain to bring him down with their weapons. The last four guards, abandoning all hope of defeating the monster, decided to flee, casting their shields and weapons down onto the forest floor as they ran. Though he desperately tried, the commander could not free himself from the weight of the dead horse that was trapping him. He heard the thudding of the great Chanun Giant approaching, still dragging behind him the heavy corpses of Old Gamo and Young Ogo.

"The music must stop!" were the last words the commander heard.

He caught only a glimpse of the madness in Big Bota's gaze before the Giant ripped his helmeted head from his body.

*

Some distance away, up the grassland at the edge of the forest, the Elf Dyoren, wrapped in his long brown cloak, was almost invisible. He was hiding behind a broad oak which, though gnarled and weather-beaten, was still living. Dyoren's long, thin blond hair was fading to a golden white. His gaze was clear and focussed.

Dyoren stopped his soundless chant, ending the powerful spell that had drawn away much of his forces. Recovering his senses, he peeked out from behind the oak, chancing a look at how the situation was evolving at the slavers' site below. A single Chanun Giant, the sole survivor, was just now contemplating with horror the carnage he had wrecked.

Indifferent to the numerous dripping wounds about his own body, the Giant began to cry over the corpses of his two former companions. Spurring himself into action once again, Dyoren darted towards a nearby pine, which rose towards the heavens as straight as an upward arrow and started to climb.

"What will be their next move?" he wondered aloud as if talking to the bare blade of his broadsword.

Now a hundred feet above ground, Dyoren orientated himself by looking to the tops of the Arob Chanun Hills on the distant horizon. The tips of two twin mountains towered above the rest. Hawks and falcons circled around the slopes, barren of trees and vegetation. Only birds of prey such as these could use those peaks for their hunting ground; the sheer cliff edges kept other predators at bay.

Drawing a long flute from his satchel, Dyoren began to play a strange tune. The instrument, carved from rare wood, emitted no audible sound. Dyoren played his instrument for a long time. Though he kept an eye on the wailing Giant below, his attention was mainly focussed on the flight of the birds of prey to which his silent music seemed destined. They soared through the air above the mountains, perhaps more than two leagues away from him.

'I cannot be certain they could hear my call,' he regretted.

At last, Dyoren stopped his strange flute's song. Something was happening below. To the south, down the path along which the surviving soldiers had fled, a dust cloud appeared. It likely signalled the arrival of a troop of riders. Dyoren did not have to wait long before his theory was verified. Indeed, two entire units of Nellos cavaliers were riding swiftly towards his position. The group was fifty strong, mounted on sturdy war horses and covered head-to-toe in plate mail. They were no doubt part of the elite army who served directly, the lords of the Westerners, the sea hierarchs. The charging soldiers proudly carried the banner of the setting sun behind a golden tower: the emblem of Tar-Andevar, the capital city of the island of Nyn Ernaly.

'To arrive this quickly, fully equipped for battle, they must have been waiting nearby,' thought Dyoren. 'Someone has positioned these cavaliers anticipating I would strike again. This may be a trap.'

He then made out, among the navy-blue cloaks of the soldiers, one particular man mounted on a great black steed. This confirmed Dyoren's fear. Now that the riders had approached the site of the fallen oak and the surviving Giant, the dark horse was galloping to overtake the rest of the cavalry, eventually positioning itself at the front. The cavalier who rode it was no ordinary Nellos commander. Dyoren recognized his order immediately from his headdress: a ruby-red cloth wrapped about his face and head, masking everything but his eyes. His plate armour, covered in a large cloak the colour of blood, was of the finest quality. He wore a gauntlet upon his left hand, a golden hand of rare design. The gauntlet had six fingers.

"Find the Elf! Find the Elf!" the knight of the Golden Hand ordered, his growling voice rising above the stomping of hooves as they spread out from the dirt road towards the edge of the forest.

None but the knight seemed concerned by the fate of Big Bota, the mad Giant who now stoically awaited his end, standing tall and proud at the centre of the battlefield. The navy-blue cloaks continued charging up the hill towards the trees at the forest's edge, carefully circumnavigating the Chanun Giant. But he who appeared to be their commander stopped his black steed thirty yards from the rebel slave he now intended to dispatch. Slowly, without a word, the knight of the Golden Hand drew from his saddle a heavy war hammer that had hung by the flank of his horse.

The weapon's handle, as long as a halberd's, was of a hard,

dark wood, and the weight of its fearsome head could be sensed from a distance. Wielding it with his covered left hand, the knight started swinging the fearsome weapon high above his head. Dyoren was amazed at the quickness of the movement given the hammer's size and weight.

Seeing that the end was near, Big Bota charged. For the final time, he dragged forward the chained corpses of his two companions. But the Giant of Chanun did not get far, and his attack was soon thwarted. The terrifying war hammer flew through the air. It hit him directly in his head, tearing off the left side of his skull. The Giant faltered, his hands reaching for his forehead. Blood and brain matter covered his gnarled fingers. As he let out one last cry of pain, the war hammer began circling back towards its master's outstretched gauntlet. The knight spurred his dark stallion forward, before releasing his weapon again. The full force of the hammer hit the Giant straight in the chest. Big Bota fell backwards, defeated.

'The Golden Hand is looking for me,' Dyoren suddenly realized.

Still in shock after the demonstration of power he had just witnessed, the Lonely Seeker knew he had to move. Reaching out to a nearby branch, he then slid down the pine's trunk to ground level, concealing himself with the thick lower branches. Without looking back, Dyoren started to run, his broadsword Rymsing dangling on his back with its blade bare. Multiple thoughts rushed through his head.

'If this is a trap, if that fallen oak was the bait, then other knights of the Golden Hand with their own units will be positioned in the woods all around here. I must withdraw quickly to the falls. I can make it to the Hageyu River and escape.'

But soon, with the steepening slope, his breath grew short. The dense vegetation was slowing his progress. So, he started to sing. Dyoren intoned the war chant of the trees that he knew so well. His mother, a powerful matriarch of the clan Ernaly had taught him those sacred lyrics long ago. As he sang louder and louder, he ran faster and faster. A path was continuously opening before him as he fled, as though the small trees, wild plants and thick shrubs wanted him to escape and survive.

"Find the Elf! Find the Elf!" the knight's orders rang out throughout the forest.

The hunt had commenced and, this time, Dyoren was the prey. Dyoren kept running through the forest. He was concentrated intensely on which route to take. His objective was to reach the Hageyu River, which flowed down in waterfalls from a large lake up in the hills. Once he reached this haven, he would be safe, for no man knew the old paths of the Elves beyond the Hageyu Falls. Obsessed with maintaining speed and afraid to find his route blocked, the Lonely Seeker opted for short cuts, meaning ever rougher terrain and even steeper slopes.

'This is getting too dangerous," thought Dyoren. "This errand has become ineffective! I will have us leave this dreaded place and return to Nargrond Valley. Our quest calls us there, not to these old woods. The island of Nyn Ernaly is lost.'

A few hundred yards downhill, a group of Men were pushing though the wild vegetation and ancestral trees with difficulty. Their skin was dark and shone with sweat. Wearing rough brown tunics and walking in tired mountain boots, they carried with them scythes of gleaming iron. With them were a pack of ferocious hounds, barking and grunting, straining to be unleashed to follow his scent.

Dyoren moved forward up the hill, putting as much distance as possible between him and the hunting dogs. He drew from his pocket a small vial and, still running, sprinkled its powder onto his clothes, shoes and hair. Its powerful scent would confuse the hounds. The matriarchs of the ancient clans had been preparing such potions for centuries, and no animal in the Lost Islands had ever been known to elude its effects. Dyoren accelerated his pace, controlling his breath, his blade beating reassuringly upon his back. The colour of his cloak blended into the woodland, making his progress almost undetectable.

"I must be less than one league away. I am almost there," he murmured.

The thick bushes before him finally opened out into a small glade, bathed in sunlight. A rapid, furious torrent cut through the clearing.

"Finally, I have reached the Hageyu River!" the relieved Dyoren exclaimed. "Though I must be way downhill, I am not safe yet."

He saw a movement in the bushes beyond the river. It was a Man on foot, an axe in his hand, hacking his way through the foliage of the forest. The short barbarian, bearded and filthy, was attired in rough leather clothes. The Man was thrashing at the vegetation as if possessed by rage. Each blow swept away entire sections of wild vines. Dyoren recognized him immediately as a scout: an H'ontark, one of the barbarian woodmen that the sea hierarchs employed to track Elvin outlaws in the wildest parts of Nyn Ernaly.

Dyoren hesitated and eventually decided to hide. His anxiety grew when he discovered that the man was not alone. He was leading a full pack of barbarians; whose purpose was to open a path into the thick woods that surrounded the Hageyu River. Soon, some of the woodmen were on the near side of the stream. Dyoren had no choice. If he wanted to reach Hageyu Lake, it was essential that he crossed the water and made it to the woods on the northern bank. Sweat pearled on his forehead. Twisting his head and snorting like a fierce wolf about to attack, he reached for his shining broadsword.

"I need you now," he muttered.

Now that he held Rymsing in his hand, Dyoren began his war chant, his voice clear and loud. Despite the perilous fight to come, his heart was filled with hope, and he leapt forward to meet those who dared challenge him in his own land. Immediately, a dozen raised axes glittered in the rays of the midday sun. The combat began with all the ferocity of opponents who are enemies twice over: Man versus Elf, and bounty hunter versus outlaw.

Dyoren fought with calmness and strict technique. He quickly dispatched his first adversary, the broadsword piercing his enemy's heart. Then, with a swinging blow as fast as lightning, Dyoren stretched out a second opponent upon the grass with a wound through his thigh. This scout put up no further resistance, so he moved forward. Dyoren forced his third adversary back so vigorously that, after retreating several paces, the woodman soon took to his heels. Against the fourth, he fought purely on the defensive; when Dyoren saw his adversary tiring, the Elf sent his axe flying with a vigorous side thrust. The disarmed barbarian stepped back in retreat, but in so doing slipped backward into a crevasse. Dyoren was over his fifth opponent in a bound, surprising him by jumping over the tumultuous stream before pushing him to the ground. He screamed at the scout to yield, his sword at the man's throat.

"Miserable barbarian, you should have never come to this place…!"

But Rymsing, as if acting out of its own rage, wrested itself from Dyoren's control. The shining blade ripped open the barbarian's stomach, thus sentencing him to a slow and painful death.

Five of his dozen enemies had died in the blink of an eye, taken aback by the quickness of Dyoren's movements and the power of his shining glaive, which he wielded as lightly as a mere dagger. The morale of the remaining troops started to wane. These Men were barbarian scouts; though sworn to the service of the sea hierarchs, they were not defending a cause, still less their own self-interest. Abandoning the glade to the victorious Elf, they began to regroup beyond the wild stream, clearly intending to run away. But they were stopped by the arrival of a second group of woodmen as the sky suddenly darkened, as if clouded by a swarm of locusts.

"Find the Elf! Find the Elf!" Dyoren could hear throughout the forest.

Drawn by the cries of war and the clashing of swords, another unit of barbarian scouts was joining the melee, rushing out from the depths of the woods. Flocks of birds were plummeting from the sky into the forest, darting downwards between the branches. Horns were blaring, and no doubt other units would soon converge upon the glade. If any of the surviving members of the first group were still tempted to flee, they soon thought better of it; a formidable knight rode forward, holding in his golden gauntlet the severed head of their unfortunate fleeing companion. This knight was unnaturally tall and strong for a man, towering above his soldiers from a height of over seven feet. His muscular body was naked but for his tanned leather breeches, boots, and a red headdress that masked his features. As for his torso, his scars seemed to be the only protection he required.

"Kill the Elf!" he roared and, like a wild cat pouncing on its prey, the fierce warrior ran towards Dyoren, marshalling his Men as he did.

He drew a long scimitar from his scabbard and launched the severed head through the air, throwing it with incredible force towards Dyoren, twenty yards away. The Lonely Seeker swiftly sidestepped the improvised missile.

"Another knight of the Golden Hand!" he deplored. "Now is the time to flee."

The multitude of birds cried out in support, as they simultaneously took flight from the lower branches of the forest around the glade. Dyoren looked around; attempting to deduce the quickest way to the river.

"To the north! Up the hill!" Dyoren decided.

Then, just as he was leaping from a large boulder, flocks of vicious birds of prey lashed down upon his enemies like torrents of hail pouring from a stormy sky. Their impact was as deadly as it was sudden. The air was filled with a blizzard of darting birds, a swarm of hawks and falcons swooping down onto the Men: tearing and piercing flesh, pecking at eyes and ears with sharp beaks, slashing skin and armour with their knifelike claws. Men screamed out in pain, struggling vainly against the onslaught. They floundered through the bushes, striking out with their axes at random, and before long the barbarians were scattered far and wide.Dyoren looked back. He saw briefly the knight of the Golden Hand emerging from the whirlwind of birds. His body was dripping in blood, with fresh wounds adding to the myriad scars that already covered his exposed skin. He had lost his headdress in the fray. His head was bald, his eyes small and mean; everything in his face betrayed his unthinking violence and base desires. Now, the knight of the Golden Hand was on Dyoren's heels, a mere twenty yards behind.

"He won't let me go!" Dyoren feared.

The chase began. They ran for a long time, each of them failing to gain much advantage over the other. The wood of Silver Leaves echoed with the sounds of their passage. Leaves rustled, dry branches cracked, water splashed, and small animals hissed, all to accompany the great battle of wills that was playing out between Elf and Man.

Dyoren, who had been cutting a path through the branches and vines with his enchanted blade, now ran out of ground to cover. He found himself rushing towards a steep cliff overlooking a large pool of clear water, fed by roaring waterfalls. Without hesitation, without even slowing his momentum, he leapt head-first from the precipice. He dove into the water thirty feet below like a meteorite striking the ocean. When the knight of the Golden Hand reached the cliff edge a moment later, all he could see of Dyoren was the centre of the impact and the rippling waves across the surface of the water.

Dyoren had to swim underneath water for some time. He finally managed to cross the width of the pool, remaining invisible in the basin's depths. When he found enough strength to get out of the water, Dyoren could no longer see where his pursuer was. He then passed through the dangerous passage where the falls cascaded onto rocks, before finally reappearing behind the cover of the waterfall. Dyoren could now pull himself out of the water. Still breathing heavily, Dyoren first made sure that Rymsing was still securely fastened to its rope.

"You are still here!" he exclaimed "Always with me!" and the Lonely Seeker kissed the silvery blade.

Bruises and flesh wounds covered his body, but he did not linger to tend to them. A dangerous climb now awaited him. In the cave behind the waterfall, there was a narrow passage, known only to Elves, which led to a higher plateau of the wood of Silver Leaves, near the Hageyu Falls. The way up was slippery, treacherous and unpredictable, for the structure of the near-vertical tunnel was constantly changing with erosion.

Dyoren approached the tunnel, scrambling over the rough terrain of the cave and pushing aside rocks as he went. He then began his ascent. The Lonely Seeker climbed the first few feet very slowly but then, curiously, as his pace accelerated, he closed his eyes, relying on the touch of his hands and his feet. Dyoren felt a kind of lightness, as though a higher power were drawing him upward. He once again felt hope. In his mind, he was no longer climbing, but rather gently flying towards his sanctuary ninety feet above. Dyoren felt so light that he decided to try another path, this one steeper and more direct. When he finally reached level ground without further injury, Dyoren rolled with relief onto his back. Suddenly he was laughing. It was a genuine kind of joyous laughter, as clear and honest as the mountain water he could now see cascading down into the pool below. Dyoren marvelled at the broadsword in his arms kept laughing aloud.

"Rymsing, Rymsing! With you I feel invulnerable!" he exclaimed through his laughter.

Looking down at the wall he had just climbed, Dyoren shivered, only now comprehending the feat he had achieved. Finally processing the reality of the peril he had just escaped; he was seized with severe vertigo. At that very moment, Dyoren knew, he could easily be lying crushed upon the ragged rocks a hundred feet below, his body reduced to broken bones and seeping flesh. But he was still alive. To make sure of it, he feverously ran his hands over his whole body.

'I am alive. For that I must be thankful,' he thought, smiling now at his broadsword as if it were a Deity he wished to honour.

Dyoren decided to rest a while, unburdening himself of his cloak and satchel. He stood just a few yards from the dangerous cliff that looked out over the pool. The day was hot, and the few pine trees dotted around him did little to protect him from the sun. As he dug into his satchel to retrieve some food, Dyoren suddenly heard heavy breathing, the sounds of someone straining in extreme physical exertion.

"What is this?" he cried.

Dyoren then looked in horror as a clawed human hand reached up over the cliff's edge, clinging onto the rocks. A second hand, wearing that same gauntlet with six fingers, found another hold on a nearby outcrop. Dyoren shivered, so stunned he could not move.

The bald Man let out a strange battle cry before hauling himself up and leaping to his feet. He hesitated only for a moment, judging how best to reach his prey across the boulder-strewn ground. Then, the bald Man started running. His big size did nothing to impede his agility across that rocky terrain. He was upon Dyoren in an instant. But that precious moment of hesitation had spared the Lonely Seeker. Dyoren had reached for his enchanted blade. Or was it Rymsing who had flown to him?

The broadsword slashed through the air quick as lightning, reaching for the Westerner's head. The bald Man avoided the deadly swipe, but his right ear was cut clean from his skull. He cried out in agony and withdrew a couple of paces. Rymsing sprung forth once again and disarmed the knight of the Golden Hand as he was reaching for his scimitar. The shining blade then danced through the air, driving the Man closer and closer to the cliff's edge. Seeing that his end was near, the knight suddenly ducked and rushed forward, with the strength of will that only fear of imminent death can procure.

"Die! Miserable Elf!" the bald Man yelled.

With savage ferocity, he head-butted Dyoren, elbowed him in the face, and bit his shoulder like a rabid animal. He then tried to grab hold Dyoren in the hope of pulling him to the ground, but then suddenly stopped. He had been impaled by the sharp blade of his enemy. The knight staggered back and looked with disbelief at the blood spurting from his stomach. Even then, the bald Man bent down to draw a vicious-looking black dagger from his leather boot. He took a few more steps back, but before he made any use of his weapon, the knight slipped backwards off the cliff.

In shock after the sudden violence, and bleeding from several new wounds, Dyoren kneeled down, to catch his breath and recover his strength. Then, with some hesitation, he peered down over the cliff's edge. His enemy was nowhere to be seen: disappeared into the haze of the crashing waterfall below. Still kneeling by the cliff edge, both hands clutching his sword;

Dyoren became lost in his thoughts, looking out at the landscape before him. The Lonely Seeker looked at his enchanted blade with renewed awe.

'Once again you have saved my life. Without you, I am nothing.'

At last, Dyoren could continue his journey. He turned away, inland, towards the Hageyu Falls and the Arob Chanun Mountains beyond, but with a profound sense of loss. In those enchanting surroundings, the rocks and waterfalls could have been the converging essences of the heavens and the earth. The cascading currents had carved the stone and soil, leaving countless curious and fantastical shapes. Long ago, secret walkways had been built by the Elves along its canyons. Dyoren knew them well, so he could now walk freely around that place of natural beauty and power. He wandered without fear, finally reaching a natural pool that the wild waters of the torrents had carved into a most unexpected location; between a thicket of trees and an abrupt cliff.

Dyoren looked down at the northern trail he had taken the day before, which climbed steeply across a wide, rocky slope before disappearing into lush woods of aspen and pine. Then, in places, large meadows, speckled with vivid flowers, interrupted the green canopy of the forest. Glistening waterfalls too numerous to count spilled from the grey mountains above into green highlands, feeding the many brooks that formed a silvery network of waterways connecting the many lakes.

Dyoren finally reached the path of the matriarchs. A wooden figure of Elvin design marked the secret entrance to the trail. It was a statue from long ago. It showed an armoured High Elf.

The story went that, in one of the battles of the so-called wars of Ruby and Birds, this knight saw a matriarch of the clan Ernaly escape into the knot of a great oak tree. The High Elf had tried to wrench the oak apart, but he overestimated his might and his hands became trapped. The matriarch reappeared at his back;

the knight was now helpless against she he had pursued. She ordered the wild beasts of the woods to devour him.

Before starting out along the secret path, Dyoren examined the beautiful statue. He could not suppress a shiver.

'It is no surprise that Ernaly artists chose scenes of violence as their inspiration. The Elves of my clan have a fierce nature. When pushed, they relish in cruelty. My two half-brothers are the epitome of the violent Ernaly nature,' regretted the Lonely Seeker.

But Dyoren considered himself to be very different. Although his mother had been a renowned matriarch in the clan Ernaly's history, and one of the most feared, his father had the clan Llorely's blood in his veins. His parents had not been together for long. Theirs too was a troubled age; the fate of the Lost Islands had been wrested from one conflict to another, as incessant as a mad torrent cascading from the hills. His father had been lost to that violent flow, never to reappear. Dyoren believed his solitary, artistic nature came from that father he had barely known.

'Such is the secret of my lonely fate and the mould for my musical compositions,' he confided to his shining blade.

Dyoren came up to a rocky passage, as narrow and treacherous as ever, piercing the sheer face of a mountain wall and winding downwards. He followed the passage until its walls to either side opened out into a little vale, tucked between the encircling rocky cliffs, thick with tall trees and wild plants. Dyoren heard water drilling along the rocky slope, then saw the little silvery stream coming down through the vale. The air was dense with the sweet odours of the mountains: evening flowers, humid earth, and pines.

Dyoren had chosen this vale as his lair. He believed it would be impossible to locate him here, for there was only one narrow path leading into it, beset as it was with winding gorges, slippery rock walls, and false trails to deter the uninvited. The whole place was a kind of wild walled garden, where the full beauty of nature was displayed in delicate balance. The music of the gurgling stream echoed all around. At the centre of the vale, beyond the little stream, was a grove of clustered pine and cedar trees with a few aged and weathered oaks.

Night came, and the Lonely Seeker smiled, as if he had been waiting eagerly for darkness to come.

"At last, we are home" he rejoiced.

Dyoren headed towards the cliff's wall and removed foliage to unveil a secret passage, which opened out into a small cave which served as his own private chambers. This place was Dyoren's refuge, the haven to which he could always return. The cavern's walls were covered with hundreds of rare books, ancient scrolls and dusty parchments. It was here that Dyoren would read, study and cross-check the tales of old, ever seeking out the smallest details, the tiniest morsels of information that might help him in his quest. Whenever he was away, he always felt anxious to return here and continue his research. Dyoren knew that what he was looking for was there somewhere, amid those unlikely piles of paper, leather and ink. But that night, another priority was haunting his mind. Dyoren reached down and pulled up an old cask he had safely hidden an inch or two below the cave's soil. Without pausing, Dyoren filled and refilled his cup several times, rapidly swallowing long gulps of that golden nectar he cherished so dearly.

'How sad that drinking is the only comfort I can find...' he murmured, before rising to his feet ceremoniously, in order to propose a toast to himself.

'I shall drink so that my heart is ever young, and ever filled with songs. I shall drink myself into oblivion.'

He looked out at Rymsing, which lay bare on the grassy soil of the glade, before continuing.

'Hope is born of desire, and desire must be rooted in memory. You, Rymsing, are my only memory and my only desire. You are my first and unique hope. I know you; you are mine. You give me my energy, like a morning breeze carrying the fresh ocean spray. You are the only one.'

Before continuing, he helped himself to another glass of the golden liquor.

'I remember the day I first held you in my hands. I was brought forth before the Arkys of the Secret Vale. It was the hour of day when the light changes most. The sun was slowly sinking while the moon was opening out into its full beauty. The majesty of the Arkys filled me with awe. I remember bowing low, in deference before their thrones. The Arkylon then said to me, 'Rise, son of Ernaly, for the Secret Vale is glad of your coming. If you have found our dwellings, your heart must indeed be filled with the desire to serve.' I answered as though awakening from a deep reverie: 'I have no memory of what strange paths I have walked to reach the Secret Vale. I followed a stag, a great one, unlike any that have ever roamed the Lost Islands.''

Dyoren reached for the oboe that was stashed in a corner of his little cave. After playing a few notes, he remembered.

'That day, I composed this piece of music.'

It was a simple and vibrant hymn, paying reverence to the ideals of loyalty and respect. It was powerful, poetic and heartfelt: the kind of music that can tame savage souls. The sublime melody rose from Dyoren's oboe: a fragile and pure love song. It produced an almost divine harmony, which mixed irresistibly with the sweet fragrances flowing in from the grove.

As he played, Dyoren's face was all compassion, his poise one of noble grandeur; but his eyes were burning with an intense inner fire. His mystical music was building an ethereal bridge between his own spirit world and the magnificent natural environment that surrounded him. Now remembering the melody in full, the Lonely Seeker lay his oboe on the ground and picked up the tune with his rich, mournful voice. Dyoren sang out his finely crafted verses with exquisite nuance. He continued with his song until well after the sun had disappeared over the far side of the mountains' peaks.

At last, the moon went down too, sinking behind the highest peaks of Nyn Ernaly that stretched up towards the starlit heaven. Dyoren brought his hymn to an end. He was exhausted in body and mind. He lay down on the grassy soil of the grove, hugging his precious sword close into his chest.

*

The next day, early in the morning, the sun was just rising above the peaks of the Arob Chanun Mountains, its rays pouring down through the pines, while clouds of violet and turquoise emanated up from the undergrowth. Nature was shaking itself back to life. A thrush started to sing. The sun, in celebration, sent a single ray of light through the oscillating branches to illuminate the slumbering face of Dyoren. Curiously, the current of the grove's small stream suddenly began spraying up and over its banks with surprising force. The straying droplets slowly began to soak Dyoren's clothes. Eventually it reached his hair and face, wrenching him awake from his dreams. The startled Dyoren got quickly to his feet. Immediately, intuitively, Dyoren knew he was in danger. He looked down at the broadsword in his hands. The colour of the blade was unchanged, but its usually reassuring presence had somehow ceased to comfort him. Yet, there was no sign of the emerald glow the blade gave off in times of peril. Dyoren was perplexed.

'No Man or Giant has ever found their way to this hideout. Even if anyone identifies the passage in the rocks, he will have a hard time facing the spirits of the forest that guard the entrance to the grove!'

This new threat was therefore of a different nature. Looking up, Dyoren was shown a kind of answer. The morning sky was filled with hawks; their flocking in such great numbers was highly unusual. While falcons were numerous in the mountainous parts of Nyn Ernaly, they were seldom seen in the Hageyu maze, for it was located close to the waterfalls: the realm of herring gulls and cormorants. Dyoren held his breath. He now felt scared. Dark memories were rushing through his mind: images of frantic flights from horrible violence in the night.

'I need to flee immediately!' he realized.

Dyoren quickly gathered the few possessions he had brought with him. Dropping down his blade, he rushed inside the cave to grab some food. Soon his travel bag was filled with supplies that would be indispensable for the journey ahead. Finally, Dyoren turned back to his broadsword and reached out to seize it, but it slipped out of his grasp. The emerald stones that were incrusted along its pommel scratched the skin of his fingers. Surprised by his nervous clumsiness, he took a breath and then picked the magic glaive up from the grass.

His eye was caught by movement in the foliage. He could just about make out a lurking silhouette, shifting and shimmering, which he then discerned as a brown and green cloak blending with the gleam of leaves and lower branches. Others followed this first scout. They were walking in formation down the matriarchs' path.

'It is too late to flee!' Dyoren understood.

And he stood still, his sword in hand, its blade cold and bare. He soon recognized the intruder leading the group. It was one of his half-brothers.

"What are you doing here, Voryn dyl? And why travel with such a heavily armed escort? Are you afraid of walking alone in the woods of your childhood?" Dyoren asked.

There was no warmth in his words. Dyoren despised his youngest half-brother, who he had always called 'the Ugly'. Though they shared the same mother, their fathers were very different Elves, and had been renowned as fierce opponents.

Indifferent to Dyoren's words and gesture, Voryn dyl 'the Ugly' was progressing slowly along the rocks. The dreaded archer held his bow in his left hand, while his right hovered over the string. There was menacing intent in his posture and gait. He could fire that bow at any time.

Many other Elves of the clan Ernaly now appeared amidst the vegetation of the grove, creeping between the trees and climbing down rock walls. Dyoren knew them personally, for he had fought many battles by their side. They were seasoned fighters of clan Ernaly, dedicated to the service of his other brother, Mynar dyl. Like some harrowing ballet, they slowly positioned themselves at regular intervals, forming a semicircle around Dyoren, closing off all escape routes. He counted them: two units, or fifty fighters in total. Prospects were grim.

The encirclement was soon complete; Dyoren was now isolated at the edge of the glade. He instinctively stepped back and threw a glance behind him. Dyoren shivered; thirty feet down the sheer cliff face, the wild and cold waters of the Hageyu River were rushing madly towards the falls, whose thunderous roar could be heard from a league away. Dyoren, now anxious, turned back towards the newcomers to question their intent. Suddenly, his face froze.

"You have also come, Mynar dyl..." He could barely utter the words. "These must be grave times indeed."

A slim, elegant figure emerged into the light, like an actor stepping onto his stage. He was dressed with great care, as if he wanted to capture the attention of his numerous spectators, all waiting in anticipation for what was about to happen.

"What you mean is: I have returned," said Mynar dyl drily.

His face expressed calm determination. His beauty had earned him the name of 'the Fair,' and indeed Mynar dyl was blessed with a magnetic physical appearance.

"Remember, brother," he continued, "this island used to be our homeland."

"Your mission must be pressing, for you to have travelled far, and left behind the comfort of your chambers," said Dyoren, trying to establish some authority as the elder brother.

"Indeed, I have..." replied Mynar dyl. His tone almost had a noble sadness to it, like a king looking over a realm overflowing with strife.

He was interrupted by the sound of rocks tumbling down from the steep slope above. Dyoren turned his head to find the source of the noise. A mighty stag had loosed the stones as it walked up a rocky promontory overlooking the glade. The animal was unnaturally large: the size of the largest war horse he had ever seen. But the creature was also blessed with a rare nimbleness. Like a quick mountain goat, it moved swiftly along the ridge to gain the best vantage point over the scene below.

Taken aback by the sudden presence of this legendary creature, Dyoren then understood the significance of the moment. His features became tense and sweat drilled down his temples. His face was illuminated by another ray of morning sun, as if he were being picked out as the principal character in the drama about to unfold. Dyoren hesitantly sung out an old chant of praise.

"O Eïwele Llya! O Mother of the Islands! I praise your glory, for if the Archipelago is vast; your realm is even greater."

The presence of the stag seemed to inspire confidence in Mynar dyl. With a booming, authoritative voice, well used to giving orders in the heat of battle, the fair warlord ceremoniously spoke.

"We have come to excavate the tombs. We shall convey the remains to the forest of Llymar. They will there be safe from the defilement of Men."

"No! That cannot be done," Dyoren responded with vehemence. "It is too dangerous. The knights of the Golden Hand are watching in wait. The servants of King Norelin have surrounded the Hageyu Falls with many spies. They are using fell magic! You will not be able to leave the wood of Silver Leaves unnoticed, especially if you are transporting the four coffins."

Still very calm, Mynar dyl brought an end to the debate. "I did not come here to discuss strategy. I am following orders."

"This is unwise. This is ridiculous! Do you know what is kept inside the most sacred tomb of them all? Do you realize what is at stake? It is the one relic we must preserve, at all costs!" insisted Dyoren.

Mynar dyl remained impassive, as cold and distant as the silver diadem that crowned his head. He ignored his brother's questions and continued.

"Those are not my only instructions."

The livid Lonely Seeker said nothing in response. His eyes widened in realization. A silence followed, during which Voryn dyl indicated to his combatants with the slightest nod of his head. He wanted them on their guard. The clan Ernaly's fighters began stretching out the strings of their bows.

"Dyoren the Seventh, I have come to terminate your charge."

Mynar dyl's clipped declaration hit Dyoren with all the force of an avalanche crushing everything in its path. Dyoren could barely believe what was happening and tried to appeal to his half-brother's better nature. His gaze went from Mynar dyl to the great stag, unable to take in the very scene that was centred upon him. Finally, Dyoren protested vehemently.

"Do I need to remind you who I am?"
"We all know who you were. I can say no more," replied Mynar dyl, laconically.

That cold, heartless tone brought the Lonely Seeker's anger flooding back to him.

"I am Dyoren the Seventh; the honours accorded to me tower above any clan warlord. I am the great bard whose lyrics have woven the history of the swords of Nargrond Valley. I am serving now as the knight sent forth by the Secret Vale. My errand is of unmatched importance."

As he was speaking, Dyoren started to feel like he was merely throwing words into the wind. Mynar dyl kept silent for a moment, giving his speech, when it did come, all the more strength.

"The situation is critical, and action is urgently required. My brother, your quest ends here. The time has come for the Arkys to appoint a new Dyoren," commanded Mynar dyl.

His detached intonation suggested he had received his instructions from a higher authority.
To illustrate the power vested in Mynar dyl, the stag jumped from its high promontory and came sniffing and snorting into the middle of the glade. The majestic animal then hovered by the water's edge to drink. Driven to despair, Dyoren looked at his blade, Rymsing, which he still held in his right hand.

"You would betray me?" he asked, barely audibly, overwhelmed by anguish and denial.

Dyoren took two steps back and disappeared off the cliff, without a cry.

CHAPTER 2: Nyriele

2712, Season of Eïwele Llya, 94th day, Nyn Llyvary, Llafal

"The three sister Deities, Eïwele Llyi, Eïwele Llya and Eïwele Llyo, have dwelled about the Lost Islands for millennia, long before the coming of the Elves. Together, they have cared for the Archipelago, through its flourishing summers and its freezing winters. To carry instructions, deliver favours and settle the inevitable conflicts, Eïwele Llyi would send forth 'The Veil', a vast congregation of butterflies. Its flurry of intense colour could instil hope into the hearts of lowly creatures, and its enveloping cloud could protect many a helpless doe. Eïwele Llya planted giant trees, the Eïwaloni, so that she and her sisters could breathe the vivid air of the forests from their great subterranean sanctuaries. Eïwele Llyo created lakes, like the great Halwyfal we know so well. From all those placid pools of clear water scattered across the Lost Islands, the Deity of Dreams and Fate could watch the Archipelago grow and strive."

"Matriarch Nyriele, may I ask a question?"

With a gentle smile, the young high priestess responded.

"Please do, Mayile."

"You have not mentioned the Daughter of the Islands. Is she not the servant of Eïwele Llya?"

"Indeed, she is, Mayile, you are correct. The Daughter of the Islands is the messenger of Eïwele Llya, who we also call the Mother of the Islands. But this came later, much later, after the Green Elves reached the Archipelago's shores."

"Tell us about that, Matriarch Nyriele! Oh please!" her audience begged unanimously.

The young high priestess gave in with pleasure.

"Our clans came from across the Austral Ocean, from the tropical forests of Essawylor on the Mainland. One day, a very long time ago, our white ships finally reached the shores of this Archipelago. News of our coming spread rapidly. The three sister Deities were so overjoyed that, for a time, they would leave their hideouts and walk among our ancestors. They said that the Green Elves had been summoned to the Lost Islands by Eïwal Ffeyn, who had delivered them from the tyranny of the Gods. They warned that because of their jealous nature, those Gods feared the Elves' power would grow too great to be governed, and thus encouraged the Giants to populate the Archipelago and put them in place to rob the Elves of their rightful kingdom. Following the advice of the three sister Deities, our clans claimed the Lost Islands as their own, destroying all those who stood in their path."

"And the Deity of War and Hunting, Eïwal Vars, taught our ancestors how to make steel swords and spears! And also, strong bows and enchanted arrows," said Melyne, a radiant maiden with shining eyes and long curly hair.

"Yes, I learnt about that too!" added Megyle, another young apprentice. "Eïwal Vars also made shields for them, and the Deity of Storms, Eïwal Ffeyn, emblazoned them with images of the birds he had created. That's how the arms of our clans were made."

Nyriele could see that her pupils wished to know more about this ancient period of history, dating back more than twenty-five centuries. She went on.

"Indeed. That is how the Green Elves were so well armed in what we would later call 'The wars of Birds and Stones'. The Giants and other creatures marshalled their forces and took to the land, forgetting their origins in the mountains, spreading across the Archipelago in great number. War wrecked the Lost Islands for many decades. This was the time of Aonyn dyl Llyvary; it was during these wars that his great spear was forged. The Giants were eventually driven out into the farthest corners of the isles where they could be watched. It was in those days that Eïwele Llya chose one of the Elves to become her envoy, to speak out and give warning to those who did not abide by the laws of nature."

Mayile was at this point getting excited.

"I saw her!" She could not help but exclaim, her eyes blazing like two magnificent sapphires. "Some years ago, I saw her, after the great ship of the Blue Elves washed up on our shores. I crossed her path, near the temple of Eïwal Ffeyn in Llafal."

A discontented murmur ran through the temple's classroom, as the other pupils of Eïwele Llyi's cult expressed their incredulity at what Mayile claimed. The large, high-ceilinged room, made of white stone from the nearby mountains, was adjacent to the main shrine. The grumblings of Mayile's fellow pupils echoed throughout the vast classroom. It was as if all the heroic characters, whose images decorated the numerous stained-glass windows above, were muttering in disbelief along with all the maidens. Mayile raised her voice to make herself heard.

"She's an Elf like no other! She is part-animal and part-statue. I remember her eyes; they looked like they were made of shining stone, like emeralds, and she had tall antlers like a great stag of the forest."

The general murmur turned to open dissent, and Mayile almost had to yell the proof that would guarantee her story.

"I saw her, I did! My friend Marwen will tell you. She was with me that day. Marwen is now a priestess. She serves Matriarch Lyrine. No one would dare doubt her word."

Nyriele finally ended the tumultuous debate. As soon as her clear voice was heard, she had her students' full attention and calm was restored. She looked at them with love and pride. The young matriarch was standing in front of a dozen apprentices of Eïwele Llyi's cult. One day, they would become priestesses of the Deity of Beauty and Arts. Nyriele knew what influence her teachings would have on their futures. She continued, conscientious of the effect her words would have on her audience.

"Mayile speaks the truth. And I have a very good reason to believe her. She is referring to one of the few meetings my mother and I had with the Daughter of the Islands."

A profound silence fell; all were astonished that their beloved tutor had been present at such an important event. Some of the apprentices looked to the marble statues that adorned their classroom, like as many heroes who could suddenly spring into action. The statues all showed legendary figures performing their immortal deeds.

"The Daughter of the Islands is indeed no common Elf. In the old days, she was known as Lore, the eldest matriarch of the clan Ernaly at that time. Her power is still immense; try as one might to erect fortresses to escape her grasp, is no use, for she can take any of the various forms with which nature has endowed her. She is often seen as a mighty stag, her resplendent antlers flashing through the fields and forests. Some say that the Daughter of the Islands can change herself into a giant hawk and fly across the straits. Indeed, she has been known to roam across all of the Lost Islands."

Nyriele wished to say no more. It suddenly felt as if a shadow were passing before her, like the lurking, distant memory of a cruelty from long ago. Just as she was turning away, to hide her distress from her students, there was a knock at the classroom door. The young high priestess gestured for Mayile to go and open the door. The blond maiden, always spirited and willing, soon welcomed in a beautiful lady, lightly dressed in a white robe. All the apprentices immediately recognized Fendrya dyn Feli and rose at her arrival. The Blue Elf, somewhat embarrassed, addressed the room, her words coloured by her exotic accent.

"I am deeply sorry for interrupting your class, Matriarch Nyriele. If I had known…"

"We were just coming to an end, Fendrya; you have arrived at the perfect moment."

The young matriarch turned to her class and dismissed her apprentices before continuing.

"I must thank you, on behalf of all of us here, for the gift you made to the temple. These sea pearls will be treasured forever, as indeed they deserve to be."

The two ladies exited the classroom to walk about the temple's nave, as the murmur of the chattering young Elves faded into the distance. Reaching the centre of the nave, Nyriele and Fendrya stopped in front of the main altar of the shrine. They took a moment to contemplate the unique sculptural masterpiece. It was made entirely of black marble. Eïwele Llyi's, main commandment was carved into the marble: 'Pysa argola', meaning 'give yourself to art'. Fendrya resumed the conversation. She was excited and spoke quickly, though she had not yet fully mastered the Llewenti tongue.

"I believe we discussed the calendar of the Blue Elves last time we met. Do you remember? It would give me great pleasure to explain it in further detail. Do you know what's most amazing about it?" Fendrya began.

"No, I do not. But I look forward learning everything about it," Nyriele politely replied with her most beautiful smile.

"Our calendar divides a year into forty-four 'solar terms'. It sets specific dates to mark important changes. The wisest among my people understand that seasonality has a great influence on our mood and health, and consequently we adapt our diet according to the solar terms to limit the impact that changes to weather might have upon the body. If you look at this chart, it might become clearer."

Fendrya unfolded a beautiful piece of embroidery she had herself created. She was very skilled with her hands and was particularly gifted with a needle. It required both patience and perseverance.

"How remarkable, this is state of the art!" exclaimed Nyriele as she marvelled at the work's complexity.

But suddenly she remembered a conversation with her mother, and her focus on the calendar waned. Nyriele remembered that Matriarch Lyrine had warned her of the Blue Elves' cunning, of their ability to manipulate. They could easily utter nice words and offer precious gifts, but there was little chance they would honour their side of the bargains which had been made.

Since their arrival on the shores of Nyn Llyvary and their heroic defence of Mentollà against the barbarians, the Austral Ocean's castaways had been granted many honours and privileges. First, land had been handed over to the new warlord of Mentollà, Feïwal dyn Filweni. He now was also a member of the council of the forest. Nyriele knew how important it was to stay vigilant around these refugees from distant lands. Though gentle and friendly, they did not share the same values, beliefs or ambitions. Her mother's words echoing in her mind, Nyriele suddenly felt cautious and cold-hearted. She turned to Fendrya abruptly.

"Is it also for calendrical reasons that your shipwrights are having such difficulty completing the work they promised to carry out? For how long now have they been tarrying in Penlla's shipyard? These delays in the construction of the new warship Feïwal dyn Filweni pledged to the clans of Llymar are causing frustration. A seat on the council of the forest does not only grant privileges and procure advantages; it also entails duties to the community."

Fendrya was taken aback by the sudden severity of Nyriele's tone. The young lady hesitated for a moment, but the look in her eyes was one of wisdom. She was no ordinary Elf. Fendrya was a cousin of the dyn Filweni. As such, she exerted a certain authority within the community of Mentollà. She considered her answer carefully before replying.

"No, it is not so. To speak true, delays in building the ship are caused by our discontent."
"Discontent?"
"I am not calling our friendship into question, but it is sometimes a friend's duty to speak their mind. The clans of Llymar welcomed us and gave us aid after the battle of Mentollà, and we are grateful for that. But the council of the forest now seem to consider that it is the destiny of the community of Mentollà to dwell forever in this island. I believe we made a significant contribution to Llymar when we fought and won at Mentollà, and yet we have not been dignified with a new boat of our own, and the routes of the seas remain prohibited to our kin. Our unique shipbuilding craft we learnt from the God of all Seas himself. I doubt that Feïwal will allow the Green Elves to benefit from the skills of our shipwrights until we have been granted what we so much desire. Is it fair that sails woven with our own hands shall be snatched away, never to be used by us? I think not."

A long silence followed. Nyriele contemplated her interlocutor. She saw only benevolence and kindness in all Fendrya's gestures. She was wrapped in simple white robes which did not fully mask the fullness of her form. Her dangling, colourful earrings and bracelets from Essawylor brought the sensuality of her feminine beauty to life. The softness of her tanned, delicate skin was remarkable.

Fendrya had joined the temple of Eïwele Llyi shortly after she discovered the teachings of the Deity of Arts and Beauty. The cult Nyriele headed had been honoured to welcome such an influential Elf into its order. The young matriarch was not going to change her mind now because of the rude sincerity of the Irawenti lady's words. She adopted a more diplomatic tone.

"I thank you for speaking your mind, Fendrya, and for advising me of what troubles the guide of your clan, Feïwal. I am surprised he did not make his position clearer."

"The Blue Elves tend not to swim against the tide. They will never directly refuse a request if they anticipate that their protest would be of no avail. It is part of our nature. We learnt to conduct ourselves in this way from the teachings of the God of all Seas."

"I understand. As you know, none can oppose the will of the council. In the case of these restrictions, you cannot deny that their purpose has been to protect you from our enemies at sea, be they the ships of the king of Gwarystan or the great galleys of his human allies. But I will nevertheless plead your cause, so that more freedoms might be granted to your kin. I wish you a safe trip back."

Fendrya understood that she was now being dismissed. Bowing respectfully, she took her leave. For a while, Nyriele observed her leaving the temple's nave. She gazed around the architecture of the ancestral columns, the colours of the wall paintings, and the elegant marble statues.

Nyriele decided to set out for a walk around her beloved city of Llafal. As she exited the temple, six guards followed her in formation, dressed magnificently in white cloaks and silver mail, bearing the symbol of Eïwele Llyi's cult, a jasmine flower. Nyriele walked alone along the terraces of Temples Square which overlooked the vast pond below. Her figure was full of grace, and her face was blessed with unreal beauty. Her long, golden hair was held back by a headdress of white flowers. When she reached the open esplanade, the setting sun illuminated the fine silk cloth of her cloak, creating a shimmering light all around her.

Nyriele looked out across the landscape, slowly taking in the air, seizing that brief moment of respite to commune with the nature she so loved, and to replenish her own inner strength. But that evening, the young matriarch was troubled by a persistent sense of resentment. Nyriele shivered and flinched as she felt her body growing numb, not from fear, but from a distant and wistful sadness. At first, she took little notice of the remote sensation. Gradually, however, Nyriele recognized the numbness as the dire threat that it was. Her day's teaching had brought back a painful memory. Flashing through her mind repeatedly, almost obsessively, was her last encounter with Lore, the Daughter of the Islands. That unexpected meeting had now been a few years previous, just after the battle of Mentollà. Lore had revealed her much to her that day. Nyriele, ever since, had feared for her freedom to choose her own path.

"Nyriele, you are the one the Mother of the Islands has elected. You are the chosen one, for your child shall one day replace me by Eïwele Llya's side and join the Arkys in the Secret Vale. So be it. Be thankful for this grace bestowed upon your womb," the ancient matriarch had sternly announced.

Taken aback, Nyriele had tried to decline. "I never asked for this honour..."

"None of us freely choose our destiny. Your fate was decided before you were born. I myself prepared the decoctions of plants that blessed the fertility of your mother."

A tense silence had followed. Lyrine's daughter, with her independent nature, had refused to submit to that command.

"I will not accept this. I am a matriarch of the clan Llyvary," Nyriele had responded vehemently.

But the resolution of Lore had proven strong.

"Hear me well: there will be a day when my time upon the Lost Islands will come to an end. I must find a successor, she who will become the powerful servant that the Mother of the Islands has at her side to do her bidding. You have come of age and your power is growing. You must find the ideal father, from among the clans' dyn, he who would be capable of giving you this mighty child."

Ever since that day, the despotic decree had troubled Nyriele's mind, for she knew that there were powerful figures who had very different visions for her future. The young matriarch anticipated she would have to confront the will and prejudices of her kin if she wanted to live up to her own higher principles. As she remembered the encounter, Nyriele's blue eyes expressed malaise and solitude. With an effort, she forced herself to stir.

'Thinking too much about forces beyond our control can be dangerous,' she knew instinctively.

From the handrails of the majestic temple banisters, Nyriele was now looking down at a large wooden construction, slightly downhill, on the outskirts of the city. The Halls of Essawylor, as it was named, had been recently built to honour the castaways of the Austral Ocean after their courageous defence of the tower of Mentollà. The centre of its structure resembled a large, upturned ship, while from the multiple sides of the building sprung what looked like the oars of a powerful rowboat. The great wooden hall was a place of entertainment and leisure, with recreational facilities, decorative plants and flowers, and a decidedly jovial atmosphere. It had rapidly become Llafal's most popular venue, for it regularly staged musical performances and held contests.

'That evening, a gathering of Llymar's artists is programmed,' Nyriele remembered. 'The city is teeming with excitement,' she noticed.

A cheerful, colourful crowd, primed for the evening's celebration of music and wine, converged and headed up towards the Halls of Essawylor like an invading army. Nyriele became absorbed in the pleasant spectacle, hoping to rid her mind of the disruptive influence that the Daughter of the Islands' words still had upon her.However, Nyriele's attention was distracted by a strange and unpleasant feeling that disturbed the calm of her surroundings.

'I can sense the suffering of a troubled heart: some inaudible complaint of a desperate being. It is somewhere around me. Danger could be at hand,' she feared all of a sudden.

Nyriele possessed a high sensitivity, which allowed her to pick up on the emotions of those around her. Not only could she see into the hearts of the Elves she conversed with, her expanded awareness could also perceive the troubled thoughts of those at a greater distance. Nyriele immediately scanned the numerous crowds gathered in and walking through Temples Square. She strained her ears to distinguish individual voices amongst the general babble and scrutinized the most inconspicuous-seeming Elves to see through any potential disguise. A moment later, she found him.A figure had walked out of the covered arcades that led to the sanctuary of Eïwal Vars and was now coming up to Temples Square. She did not recognize the mysterious Elf first. He was poorly dressed, though his stature was imposing. His abundant blond hair was flowing over his shoulders and masking his features. Realizing that his odd gait had given him away, the tall Elf changed direction, heading directly towards Nyriele. The young matriarch was about to call to her guards when she recognized the newcomer.

"Oh, Dyoren! It is you! What has happened?" she exclaimed, shocked by the distress she perceived in him.

The Lonely Seeker came right up to her and quickly whispered, almost inaudibly, like one possessed.

"We cannot talk here. Let us meet in the Halls of Essawylor. I am in desperate need of your advice," and he was gone, disappearing into the crowd that flocked down the slopes towards the great wooden hall.

Nyriele stood there for a moment, puzzled. She realized something unusual was going on. Her first instinct was to inform her father, to seek his counsel and protection. But Gal dyl was away at sea, commanding the swanships on the whale hunt. While Nyriele could have called upon her mother, curiosity for what Dyoren had to say soon prevailed. And, more than that, her heart was full of compassion for the fabled bard. She did not know him personally, for the wielder of Rymsing lived alone in the wilderness, dedicated to his own mysterious quest. Occasionally he would make a sudden appearance in Llafal, or in another of Llymar's cities, to share the tales of his journeys, what he called the 'Songs of the Islands'.

Dyoren was renowned as the greatest bard ever to have walked the passes of the Archipelago. A legendary figure among the Green Elves, the eldest scion of the clan Ernaly was also held up as a symbol of creativity. Now that he needed her assistance, there was no way the young high priestess could refuse him. Nyriele covered her head with a light shawl to hide her face. She turned towards her guards to dismiss them.

"You may leave. I will not require your services tonight. I am going to the Halls of Essawylor, to dance."

She spoke with the lightest, most joyful of tones, in the hope she would convince them. The guards hesitated before finally resolving to depart. Nyriele found their presence unnecessary and embarrassing. She suspected that their primary duty was to spy on behalf of her mother, rather than protect her from some unknown threat. In any case, it would not have been the first time she had participated in one of the great hall's festivities.

Soon afterwards, Nyriele entered the Halls of Essawylor. A

great murmur of the many high-spirited conversations echoed throughout the large reception room. Amid exotic plants and tropical flowers, the vaulted room was decorated with colourful tapestries. A crowd of over four hundred Elves milled carefree about the room, surging in particular around the generously furnished buffets. A swarm of young Elves were circulating among the crowd, carrying jars of cider and jugs of wine, dependably refilling the glasses of the revellers. Elves of all origins and races mingled in the gathering throng, amazed by the sheer magnitude of the festivities.

Nyriele set off towards the furthest side of the great hall, ostensibly managing to hide her identity from the partygoers. The audience were all smiles as the next song began; two Elves from Mentollà, sat around a large wooden table, were skilfully plucking at the strings of their exotic harps. The crowd cheered and clapped along to the rhythm of the new piece. Nyriele then saw another musician, a High Elf with brown hair and gleaming clothes, who joined the musicians at their table, his lyre in his hand.

'This is the bard Curwë,' she immediately recognized.

Curwë was the undisputed master of this music from Essawylor known as Muswab. He began playing, and seamlessly the notes of his instrument mixed with those of the harps. His playful melodic line would accelerate, rebound and dance around the lightly textured layers of the harps. Curwë had entered into a state of perfect communion with his art; he was not simply playing his lyre, but rather helping the strings to laugh and dance of their own volition, so as to celebrate freedom and joy.

One by one, other musicians came to sit around the table to join in the Muswab. Another High Elf from Essawylor struck his tambourine to accentuate the contagious rhythm of the song, adding a new drive to the piece. Nyriele saw Gelros, the dark-featured scout from Mentollà; settle down with his large drum, bringing depth and power to the Muswab with its low-pitched beat. More than a dozen musicians had now taken position on the stage, and began to play, improvising verses of their own. The crowd continued to sing in chorus. Over the course of this celebration in music, the hearts of the players had returned to their homeland of Essawylor, across the Austral Ocean, and they had transported their audience with them.

Nyriele was just coming up to the main crowd, dancing despite herself, when Dyoren finally joined her. He had taken the precaution of hiding his face with an azure mask. Many guests had adorned colourful disguises to lose themselves more completely in the feast. Here, just like celebrations held in the kingdom of Essawylor, the masked and costumed revellers could fully indulge their desires to become someone else. Dyoren was the first to speak. His voice, altered by anxiety and despair, contrasted dramatically with the scene that surrounded him.

"Noble Matriarch, I come to seek your advice. You hold my life in your hands, for I dare not speak to anyone else. I fear the charge of treason."

Nyriele, now more concerned than ever, replied.

"Why would you fear such a thing, Dyoren? And why not directly seek the protection of Matriarch Lyrine?"

"I have been betrayed. I cannot trust anyone anymore. They want… they want to take her away from me."

"Her?" Nyriele asked, now committed to help him.

"My sword, my beloved Rymsing…"

"Tell me plainly, Dyoren: who would dare attempt that?"

But the Lonely Seeker's distracted mind had lost its train of thought and was now jumping from one memory to another.

"I have not rested since. I cannot sleep. I am in danger, grave danger. There's madness upon me, a madness I cannot shake… or perhaps it is lucidity? One thing I cannot stop asking: was it my own family who betrayed me or… was it her? Yes, it could have been her… she has been different, changed, ever since the siege of Mentollà… as if she no longer trusts my abilities…"

Nyriele took hold of his hands in an effort to placate the violence of feeling that tortured his soul. She uttered a few words of prayer to Eïwele Llyi, and soon Dyoren found a certain peace and composure.

"Matriarch Nyriele, you are a high priestess of Eïwele Llyi, you are a servant of the Deity of Love and Beauty; you know the secret of hearts."

"How can I help you, Dyoren?" prompted the beautiful maiden.

"Can the one you love betray you? When you have dedicated your life to her, when you have sacrificed your own fate for hers, is it possible she could betray you and leave you by the wayside?"

"Love is not an oath," Nyriele started gently, compassionately; "It is not an eternal commitment."

But Dyoren had lost the thread of his thoughts once again. He began muttering feverishly, like one digging around in the depths of his soul.

"Your beloved, your clan, your very brothers, might one day turn their backs on you and condemn you to your doom. I cannot, I will not survive…"

The desperate Elf was about to faint. Nyriele decided to act. She laid her hands upon his head.

"The grace of Eïwele Llyi be bestowed upon you; may her strength calm your torment and soothe your soul. May you find peace!"

Dyoren was so weak that he could no longer stand. Nyriele took hold of him, guiding him into a chair against the wall.

"I had to swim the strait of Tiude to flee them... I could not rest for days... I can no longer think..." he murmured, before sliding off his seat onto the ground.

Nyriele pushed the chair aside and leaned over him. In the happy confusion of the feast and the music, no one had so far noticed the dramatic scene taking place. The young matriarch was looking around to find help when she saw him: a tall, thin Elf, with dark hair and lunar-white skin, dressed without ostentation in a black tunic. The left side of his face was covered by a metal mask, shadowy green in colour. But this disguise was no ordinary costume; it was a necessary protection, for this Elf had lost his eye at the siege of Mentollà. She knew him to be the second master of the Halls of Essawylor, a close companion of Curwë. But she could not remember his name.

"May I offer my assistance, Lady Nyriele?" proposed the pale Elf curtly. The gaze of his single eye was sharp and piercing, as if he were extracting the truth from her veins.

The young matriarch hesitated; she could perceive an enigmatic sadness in the gaze of this newcomer: the cold flame of a deeply buried anger. She knew immediately that her powers to charm would be wasted on such an icy heart. But Nyriele did not have the time to be overly cautious. Some Elves from the crowd had already turned in their direction, intrigued at the strange scene unfolding at the side of the hall. Nyriele decided to accept his offer.

"This Elf needs immediate assistance. Could you kindly take him to one of your backrooms? You are one of the masters of this house, I believe?"

"My name is Aewöl, and I am at your service, my lady."

Aewöl bowed respectfully, and then immediately set about aiding the helpless Elf. Then a look of recognition swept over his face.

"Ah! This is Dyoren... the fabled Seeker," he whispered to Nyriele. "I thought I recognized him as he entered the Halls of Essawylor. I know him well; Arwela, the seer of the clan of Filweni, faithfully tended to both our wounds after the battle of Mentollà."

Aewöl's hand involuntarily reached for the mask which covered his left eye, the remembrance of his severe injury inducing a distant pain. After shaking Dyoren with some force, Aewöl lifted him to his feet and put his arm around his own shoulder. The music was still playing, but this disturbance had broken the concentration of many Elves in the vicinity. They were looking angrily at those who had distracted them, until one guest let out a gasp of wonder. He had recognized the young matriarch of the clan Llyvary.

"Nyriele is here! She has come to dance! Nyriele is here..." The rumour spread across the great hall as swiftly as an ocean breeze through the coastline's woods.

Nyriele knew that she could no longer hide her presence. It was just after nightfall, and the voices of the bards were joining a new song. They were united in their effort to probe the mysterious beauty of Essawylor music. There was a powerful wave of excitement through the crowd. From the threshold of the room to its besieged buffets, one name was now on everyone's lips.

"Nyriele... Nyriele will dance..." the murmur rippled.

Just as the song was building, and the musicians had once again captivated their public, the young matriarch made a sudden entrance onto the stage. Her simple light dress, white with brightly coloured patterns, sculpted around her perfect body with a boned bodice. Her shoulders were beautifully naked and her now-unveiled hair was remarkable. Like some mythic divinity, it was pushed back by a diadem and then cascaded elegantly over her shoulders and down to her hips.

Ignoring the swell of praise from her admirers as she walked on stage, the beautiful maiden began to perform her first movements. The crowd yelled, cheered and applauded widely. They were immediately taken aback by Nyriele's style, a succession of unusual gestures that paid little heed to formal rules, using her entire body as she went unpredictably but fluidly from one unconventional move to the next. She was unconsciously adapting her body to the music's twists and turns.

After a time, the pleasure of seeing soon mingled with the joy of listening because, of all the musicians, the renowned bard from Essawylor, Curwë, stepped forward. As the song and the dancing gradually drew to an end, his lyre emitted a low swell of noise, indistinct and muddled, but nonetheless pleasant. Nyriele ended her sweet movements and stood in the middle of the stage. She looked as if she were hypnotized. The bard's music became increasingly clear and intelligible. Curwë, sat up on a raised wooden level, was working his lyre with great virtuosity. Like in a strange spell, its music bewitched and delighted the audience. Curwë's fingers were doing more than playing. They were developing an exotic musical structure, a magnificent architecture of heavenly notes. The crowd applauded, their spirits lifted and ignited. Bewitched, Nyriele listened with fond recollection, until Curwë extinguished the final echo of his instrument. Applause spread throughout the great hall with tumultuous fervour.

"Our gift from Essawylor! The music of the Five Rivers! You interpret life's beauty like no one else!" the audience shouted with fervour.

Curwë gave a stylish salute to the crowd, who continued to cheer feverishly long after the end of his incredible performance. He then gently offered his hand to Nyriele and, as the other musicians started up again, the two Elves stepped offstage and became lost in the crowd.

"You play the lyre with such beauty," Nyriele said, somewhat shyly, hesitant to immerse her gaze into the mysterious emerald eyes of the charming Curwë.

"Firstly, this is not a lyre. We call it an Ywana in Essawylor. It was fabricated by the best luthier," replied Curwë with assurance.

He continued with the same confident tone, apparently undaunted by the bewitching beauty of the young matriarch's smile.

"Secondly, it's not the way I played which charmed you. It was, I believe, the music itself that you enjoyed. I could tell by the way you were listening, the way you were moving. But I agree with you! The music was magnificent. I am particularly proud of this song."

Curwë then explained how he had composed the piece, and why it sounded so different from anything Nyriele had heard before.

"I just performed a traditional ballad; its movements are set out with all the precision of a full musical score, yet it is full of elusive gaps and evocative silences. The Ywana travels free, like the sound of the wind at temperate dusk. It imitates the lute song, but its arrangements are stratified, played consecutively rather than at the same time. Its overall structure is that of a descending arpeggio. It's this that makes all the difference."

"Ah!" she muttered, now openly smiling.

Nyriele did not follow the full meaning of what Curwë had said. He understood from her lost expression that his explanation had been unsatisfactory, so he went on.

"In other words, this tune was particularly pleasing because its chorus was composed according to the old standards of consonance, as established by the Silver Elves of yore. This is how I infused the delicious trace of exotic melodies into my composition to bewitch my audience. Wasn't I clever?" he concluded, visibly very happy with himself.

His green eyes were sparkling with self-content and genuine pleasure. Nyriele listened to Curwë talk with sincere attention. She let the handsome narrator lay out his ideas without daring to stop him, without having even the idea of interrupting. He spoke with animation and passion, as if his life depended on each detailed explanation of his art. Instinctively, Nyriele knew that now was the moment to plead her cause. She spoke softly, with an appealing voice.

"I need your assistance... I need your assistance... now..."
"I beg your pardon, my lady?"
"I said... I need your assistance..."
"If it concerns the art of music, I am the most trustworthy servant you could ever find."
"No, Master Curwë, this is very serious."
"Oh, I apologize! I see now that you look distraught."
"This is not the proper place to discuss this matter... perhaps..."
"Come, come with me. There is passage out of here where the air will be cooler. What can I do? How can I help you?" Curwë asked. He could hear himself; he knew he was speaking with a pining anxiety. "I'll do anything to assist you."
"Your companion, Aewöl, has rescued a friend of mine who is in dire need of assistance. They must now be in one of the backrooms," Nyriele finally confided.

The two Elves escaped the clamorous crowd by a side door. They soon reached a large room at the very back of the halls. It was Aewöl's dwelling. Reaching up to this vast chamber's high ceiling were enough species of plant to fill a wild, dark forest. Bookcases were loaded with ancient manuscripts. A stock of phials filled with wine was displayed openly, as if the bottles were a fine piece of sculpted glasswork. The fine wood floor and sophisticated decor conferred the place with a striking air of exotic elegance.

Dyoren was sat in a large, comfortable armchair, busy examining the contents of his crystal glass. He seemed to have recovered from his faintness, and his gaze was utterly changed. He looked somewhat uneasy and upset, however; the concoction he had been given had energized his body but impaired his mind.

"What is that he's drinking?" Nyriele inquired offhandedly, hiding her worry and suspicion that some toxic substance had been administered.

"A liquor from Essawylor," replied Aewöl, "a decoction of lime and the leaves of Bronyel. Sailors use it to ward off evil sea spirits. It is a very powerful restorative, but in no way should it replace a long period of rest. Dyoren is exhausted."

"I have no time to rest. That which hunts me will not allow me any respite," interrupted Dyoren abruptly. "I'll be on my way in a few moments, but I have much to tell you before then. Please listen carefully."

Then, looking at Curwë with fascination, Dyoren added with a distant, dreamy tone.

"We meet again, Elf with green eyes. How is it that you cross my path each time I am about to fall?"

Curwë ignored the comment and curtly gestured for Nyriele to sit down. Meanwhile, Aewöl filled four elegant crystal glasses with a refreshing-looking wine, the colour of blackberries. All eyes then turned to Dyoren. After taking a few sips of the precious beverage and relishing every stage of a ceremonious tasting ritual, he began. His speech was slow and hesitant.

"We used to live in Nargrond Valley. My quest invariably led us to that dangerous place, full of perils…"

"Nargrond Valley is at the centre of the main island of the Archipelago, Gwa Nyn," explained Nyriele. "It is protected by high mountains. The territory has been disputed for centuries by the king of Gwarystan's armies and the clan Myortilys' units. It is a land of legend, home to many monstrous beings: Giants living by the fire of its volcano, Gnomes seeking to extract its precious metals. Very few Elves have dared set foot in that valley for a long time."

Dyoren continued with the authority of an Elf who had.

"Legends say the Nargrond Valley was created when the fabled Star fell from heaven and hit Gwa Nyn. Its mighty impact split the earth asunder. Molten lava and poisonous vapours flooded down across the region from the great volcano of Oryusk, where the meteorite had completed its destructive course. The very heart of the mountain melted, and stone poured down its western side like liquid fire."

"It is said," Nyriele added, "that the meteorite's impact was felt across the whole Mainland."

The four Elves remained silent for a while, their minds wandering in that distant glen and their imaginations set ablaze. Eventually, Dyoren continued his tale, more confidently now, as if he had been granted the need to speak by an unknown power.

"A few years ago, I received evil tidings from Nyn Ernaly, my homeland. The pernicious influence of Men was growing beyond control, leading us all to fear irreparable consequences. After the Century of War, the Pact granted governance of Nyn Ernaly to the Westerners, and they chose to establish their main city upon the ruins of Mentobraglin. They renamed it Tar-Andevar, and in a few decades that human town had swollen to great proportions."

"It is said that Tar-Andevar is now three times the size it was when ruled by the High Elves," said Nyriele.

Dyoren went on. "Indeed, the Westerners are Men of craft. They are builders who tirelessly strive to extend their dominion. For decades, they have fuelled the growth of their fortified town with timber from the wood of Silver Leaves. It is a sacred place up the hills and a few leagues north of the great human harbour. The Westerners worked tirelessly to mine the hills, divert the rivers and fell the trees."

"I know what the trees represent to the Green Elves," Curwë interjected, full of compassion. "It is your belief that you will eventually be reincarnated by your Deities into the flora of the Islands."

"It is not a mere belief, foreigner from across the ocean! It is our fate. You still have a lot to learn," Dyoren spat back harshly.

His sudden aggression surprised his interlocutors, though it then reminded them that the Lonely Seeker was in a state of little self-awareness. For a moment after his outburst, Dyoren's gaze became lost, as if his soul were sensing the pain of his ancestors' spirits as each tree was struck down. After a while, he continued, saddened.

"But there is worse to come. The Westerners are destroying the wood of Silver Leaves not just to feed their new town with timber. I have come to realize that they are set upon its devastation for a different purpose."

Dyoren's interlocutors were hanging on his every word.

"A long time ago, the wood of Silver Leaves was chosen to shelter the secret tombs of Rowë and his followers. They hold the testament of the Dol Nargrond lord: The Forbidden Will."

Nyriele could not help but flinch at the news. She stepped back unintentionally. Aewöl's one eye widened, filled with curiosity. He leaned forward. But it was Curwë who spoke first.

"What is the significance of that holy scroll?" he asked feverishly. "Why is so important to you?"

Nyriele immediately intervened. "That answer, Dyoren will

not give you," she insisted, "Know only that Rowë Dol Nargrond was the greatest Elf ever to set foot on the Archipelago. The best scholars and artisans of all Elvin races flocked to serve him in Yslla, the city at the centre of Nargrond Valley. Rowë and his followers left us the mightiest of legacies: first, the legendary swords forged from the metal of the Fallen Star and, second, a testament, the Forbidden Will, that none shall read until the time comes."

Swept up in her own agitation, the young matriarch had revealed more than she had intended. She became quiet, her closed expression making it clear that she would say no more. But then, to the surprise of all, Dyoren continued, impatient to reveal what he knew, and perhaps eager to rid himself of a burden now too great to bear. He poured himself another glass of wine and turned to the others, his speech now slurred.

"When I was entrusted with Rymsing, one of the legendary swords of Nargrond Valley, I became Dyoren the Seventh. Other Seekers had preceded me, and all had failed to complete our noble quest. Rymsing is the last blade of Nargrond Valley that we still possess. Its wielder's task is to find the five other swords... Until now, I too have failed in this mission... though I have learnt a great deal."

Nyriele tried to comfort him. "But you were also charged with defending the secret tombs of the fabled bladesmiths, those mighty Elves who made the swords of Nargrond Valley."

Dyoren looked away, his concern and dismay were visible. Nyriele added.

"Those four Elvin tombs are the only ones in the Archipelago, for the tradition of the Green Elves dictates that bodies of the dead be returned to Eïwele Llyo's care. Priests of the Deity of Fate will normally place bodies into pools or lakes, which are thought to be part of Eïwele Llyo's domain... The High Elves, however, cremate the remains of their dead upon funeral pyres. Rowë and his followers, one of them of Llewenti ancestry, are the only exceptions I am aware of. They were buried in tombs."

"It is said their bodies were wrapped in shrouds soaked in the perfume of Eïwele Llyo, so that their remains would stay unaltered," Dyoren explained.

"For what purpose, I do not know," Nyriele confided.

"I do not believe that anyone knows," said Dyoren. "But that purpose must have been of considerable importance; such extensive resources have been deployed to hide the four tombs in the depths of the Silver Leaves Wood. This is why I have spent these last few years trying to delay the progress of the Westerners."

Curwë expressed his compassion.

"And you have been alone, for all that time?"

"To hold Rymsing is to never be alone. There is nothing comparable to her presence and influence. She loved me, and I gave her my life. Now I see that my efforts were vain."

Dyoren regretted, like reciting the words of an improvised poem.

"How did it come to this?
How is it that I now must run like a hunted deer?
How is it that her touch is now cold as ice?
How is it that her gaze is full of resentment, and that she looks at me as if all my pride were depleted?
How is it that she no longer visits me with her dreams?"

Dyoren became overwhelmed with despair; he was speaking faster and faster, the words flying out like a thousand birds fleeing a stormy sky. Was he talking, or was he singing? He rose from his armchair and faced Nyriele, forcing her to witness what he felt.

"My love for her, my love for Rymsing pains me! It spits upon me!"

Dyoren was half-singing now in his agonising fever.

"She has broken her vows!
She has run me into the ground!
Do not wonder why the strings of my harp are broken!
Do not wonder why my vocal chords are wrecked!
The music... has ceased."

For a time, a frozen silence reigned. The three Elves around Dyoren were overwhelmed by the sheer depth of feeling carried by these few quasi-verses. Each listener remained quiet, paying homage to the suffering, artist. Aewöl was the first to speak.

"Where is your sword now?"

Once again, the room fell silent. Seeing the extent of Dyoren's pain, all feared the worse for the legendary blade.

"None will find her until I decide it can be so. There are some who desire her for themselves. Some believe they shall win her favour more than I ever could. More still have condemned me as a criminal and, worse, their enemy."

"You must free yourself from your pain," encouraged Nyriele with the utmost sincerity.

"They claimed that my quest was over, that my duty towards the Elves had been fulfilled. They wanted to transport the secret tombs to Llymar, to snatch them from the grasp of the Westerners. But I could not believe them, for I saw in their leader's eyes what his true purpose was. He had come for my sword, Rymsing... to take her from me. He said to me, with his polite voice, that the time of Dyoren the Seventh was over, and that an eighth Seeker would need to be appointed to persevere in my quest. Listening to his melodious voice, it seemed obvious, it seemed right, that I should submit to his will, that I should kneel to surrender my only companion, the object of all my devotion. But I could not accept such an arbitrary sentence. I chose… I chose to jump into the void…"

"The void?" murmured Curwë.

"Such is my bond to Rymsing. I would do anything to safeguard her… I fell from a great height into the wild torrent below. How I did not perish, I do not know. I can see it only as a sign of Gweïwal Uleydon's favour. He is the Lord of all Waters and, for a reason I cannot fathom, he decided to spare me that day."

Another long silence followed. Nyriele remembered Dyoren had claimed that he had swum across the strait of Tiude to reach the shores of Nyn Llyvary. If that was true, the protection of the almighty God of Oceans must have been upon him. She shivered. The calm voice of Aewöl broke the silence.

"You refer to your enemies as 'they', as if you dare not name them. Who are 'they'?"

For a moment, it looked as if Dyoren would not answer the one-eyed Elf. His gaze went excitedly from the emerald gaze of Curwë to the blank features of Nyriele. When he finally spoke, he did so quietly, though his inner rage was palpable.

"By 'they' I mean: my brother Mynar dyl, my brother Voryn dyl, the entire clan Ernaly, and, worst of all, the great stag of the Secret Vale. It is they who declare me their enemy."

The defeated Dyoren ended with a sad smile.

"What have you done, Dyoren?" Nyriele exclaimed, now feeling afraid. "Do you not know the significance of the great stag's presence? It means, it means… that what Mynar dyl was doing was legitimate. It must have been ordered by the Arkys in the Secret Vale. There is no greater authority for us than those ancient figures! They are the closest disciples of the Deities.

Even Matriarch Lyrine bows before them!"

Sad, weak, Dyoren continued.

"I know the significance of the great stag's presence, Nyriele… but I could not bring myself to obey. I was not given a chance! No one was willing to listen; despite the years I have dedicated to protecting the tombs. Moving those graves would be a fatal strategic mistake. The fools would fall into the very trap our enemies have set to locate them! Fighting them for so long, spying upon their servants, I have come to understand their stratagems. They have planned for this very move."

"How did you know this?" asked Curwë. "What makes you think your brothers are in danger?"

The green-eyed bard had naturally sided with the Lonely Seeker, overwhelmed by his show of desperate heroism. He admired this great artist and felt profound sorrow for his solitary fate.

"A few years ago," Dyoren explained, "just after the battle of Mentollà, the king of Gwarystan decided to send some of his most fanatic followers to Tar-Andevar. The new ambassadors that King Norelin appointed at the sea hierarchs' castle were chosen from among his most trusted servants. It was they who would enact the ruby crown's new diplomatic approach: pursuing their dreams of grandeur alongside the Westerners."

"You mean those who call themselves 'The knights of the Golden Hand'?" asked Aewöl.

"Yes, indeed. Such is their influence at the royal court in Gwarystan that they are known as 'The Fingers that hold the Sceptre'. King Norelin elevated those six miserable plunderers to the rank of knight sorcerers. They are a powerful force; some of them are Westerners from Nellos, but they also count among their ranks a powerful High Elf of Dol lineage," explained Dyoren.

He took a few sips of the precious wine Aewöl had just served before continuing.

"There is now no doubt in my mind: the dreaded servants of King Norelin have been sent to find the secret tombs of the bladesmiths of Nargrond Valley. Scattered across the wood of Silver Leaves are metal statues of obscure origin, and with strange powers. The knight sorcerers are waiting for us to make the fatal mistake that will unveil the tombs' location. They are using powerful sorcery. Mynar dyl does not know the enemy he faces. My brother does not understand the magnitude of the risk he is taking. Instead, he has chosen to betray me and claim my sword for himself."

"But they must be alerted. It is of vital importance," Nyriele insisted firmly.

She thought for a moment before adding.

"What does Matriarch Lyrine know of this expedition?"

"Your mother is already involved, Nyriele. When the units of the clan Ernaly reached the shores of Nyn Ernaly, they disembarked from swanships of Llafal. I learnt that the clan Llyvary's fleet shall be transporting the tombs across the strait of Tiude. Your father, Gal dyl, commands those ships."

Nyriele was suddenly anxious for her father's safety.

"Someone needs to warn them of the peril they are facing! Someone needs to go to Nyn Ernaly!" she repeated several times, her gaze eventually fixing on Curwë, as if she wanted him to act as a witness to her distress.

Curwë was about to offer his services, but then hesitated, unsure of how best to answer such a request. Before he could make up his mind, Aewöl intervened, his voice unemotional.

"Noble Matriarch," he began, "we need to slow down and

think of a solution. Rest assured that we will support you as best as we can in this ordeal."

But his look of scepticism made it clear that he thought the challenges ahead would prove difficult. Aewöl shared his thoughts aloud, detailing each step of his reasoning with the young matriarch.

"We must indeed depart immediately for Nyn Ernaly… but our community of castaways from Essawylor does not possess a ship that could sail the seas. The council of the forest denied us the right to build a new vessel. You must know this!"

The accusatory tone of Aewöl's argument crept into Nyriele's subconscious, leaving her somewhat unsettled.

"I am aware of this restriction… it was my mother who ordered it," the young matriarch conceded, her own tone implying she had not been partisan to that pronouncement when it was made.
Aewöl concurred. "This discriminatory measure was indeed unfortunate. But one can always reverse that which is wrong," he stated, somewhat evasively.

The pale Elf's one eye then widened in sudden realization.

"I do believe the answer lies in the question. If we were given such a boat, we could quickly provide our assistance in the events to come. Our Blue Elves' friends would be an invaluable asset. As navigators on the open sea, they are unequalled."
Nyriele was disconcerted. "I understand your plan, Master Aewöl. But I have absolutely no authority to donate one of our swanships."

Seeing an opportunity, Aewöl pressed on.

"A ship would also be an invaluable asset to the commerce

we are currently establishing from Mentollà. Curwë and I dream of establishing a naval trading company. We have plenty of ideas that would benefit us all," stated the former counsellor of House Dol Lewin.

His only eye began to shine like a dark amethyst.

"Master Aertelyr and the Breymounarty are certainly making the most of their profitable arrangements with us. It is their large vessels that must transport our goods across the Lost Islands. At the moment, therefore, only Master Aertelyr can benefit from our resources and know-how."

Nyriele could sense that Aewöl wanted was complete emancipation: trade routes, merchant ships and lucrative commerce. These assets weighed heavily in Nyriele's mind, like the crucial components of a vast game, where power was the prize. She could feel that behind the one-eyed Elf's soft tone, there lurked ambition, perhaps even greed. She began to find the conversation embarrassing.

Meanwhile Curwë, uninterested in his companion's opportunism, had his gaze fixed on Nyriele. Each change in her attitude, each emotion that flickered across her face, was a chance for him to uncover another facet of her exquisite beauty. The bard was captivated by her unrivalled charm and sincere kindness. Unexpectedly, Curwë intervened with excitement.

"Aewöl is right."

The others turned to him in surprise.

"Aewöl is right... We could use Aertelyr's merchant ship to reach the shores of Nyn Ernaly. That guild master is a smuggler as much as he is a trader; I am sure we can come to some kind of arrangement with him. Against a higher percentage of our next shipment, he could have us discretely dropped off on a remote beach. There is our solution. As we speak, his vessel is anchored in Mentollà creek, being loaded with the summer's harvest."

"You would do that? You would do that for me?" Nyriele asked with infinite gratitude. "Though I rank highly in my clan, my influence is little. The assistance of loyal friends will be a vital support."

Curwë bowed ceremoniously. "You now have knights to do your bidding, my lady Nyriele, brave servants who will do anything to help you, for you are indeed the incarnation of Eïwele Llyi's teachings."

Aewöl had remained silent during this exchange, astonished by the commitment his friend had undertaken. The one-eyed Elf looked at him impassively... At last, Aewöl joined his bard companion. He bowed in turn, before drawing his two black swords.

"Noble Matriarch, you have kindly listened to the plight of the community of Mentollà. It gives me great hope that such a caring ear has been leant to our just demands. For this, I thank you. My blades will not rest until your father is returned safe."

Nyriele stood up, seized with emotion. For the first time, she was experiencing the absolute loyalty she could inspire. It felt like a glimpse of royal authority. It felt like power.

"And I gratefully accept your help, noble Elves," she acknowledged, her voice confident and clear. "May the Deities protect you and grant you fame."

Indifferent to these outpourings, Dyoren had opted to continue enjoying the residual aroma of Aewöl's wine, emptying the crystal carafe of all its precious content. It was as if the exquisite beverage's soothing properties had somehow waned, for the Lonely Seeker's mood was once again growing anxious and aggressive. He gathered his few possessions, visibly eager to be on his way. Before departing, Dyoren offered them a word of caution.

"The task before you is beset with perils. The knights of the Golden Hand are supported by the sea hierarchs' army. They have the territories around the wood of Silver Leaves completely covered, with dozens of units patrolling day and night. They also dispatched many spies. Most are not even living beings, for the knights of the Golden Hand are powerful sorcerers... I fear for you, but I admire your bravery... You have my blessing. Remember, saving the secret tombs from the grasp of the knights of the Golden Hand is a lost cause. All who persist in that vain quest will perish. Only the Forbidden Will, the testament of Rowë, can be saved."

And with those final words, as though he were expressing his last wishes, Dyoren left the room through one of the windows, disappearing into the night. Curwë turned to Nyriele.

"My lady, is it wise to let him go? After all the hardship he has only just overcome, he is weak and vulnerable. Despair is obscuring his mind. I feel guilty that I was not of more assistance."

Nyriele looked at him with kindness. "You have a noble heart, Curwë, and your sentiments do you much honour. I am proud to have you henceforth at my side."

She took a breath before continuing. "Dyoren the Seeker does not answer to any of us; he will not bow before the council of the forest, nor even before the matriarchs of the clans. Dyoren answers only to what he called 'the Secret Vale,' but that high authority is shrouded in mystery. It is not for us to judge him. It is not for us to assist him. His role in the order of things goes far beyond my knowledge."

Aewöl was curious, eager to know more.

"Noble Matriarch, what became of the Seekers before him? I understand that several knights, each in turn, previously took the oath and were entrusted with the sword Rymsing. What was their fate?"

Nyriele hesitated. She then decided that Aewöl and Curwë deserved to know more if they were to risk their lives in this expedition.

"Little is known about this unique order, even by the matriarchs. In the Secret Vale, which lies hidden somewhere in the Islands' mountains beyond the reach of all, those we call the 'Arkys' divine the wishes of the Deities. At times, they will call upon a hero to pursue a quest. We believe that their aim is to return all the swords of Nargrond Valley to the Arkys. Legends say there is no task harder than the honour of wielding Rymsing; when it loses hope of finding its sister blades, another wielder, younger stronger, must be chosen."

"A cruel destiny for a hero who has devoted his life to others," judged Aewöl with some bitterness.

Nyriele tried to comfort him. "I'd like to think those brave Elves who are left behind will be shown the path to the Secret Vale, and that thereafter they will enjoy a life of peace in the hidden garden of the Deities, among the chosen ones. This is what I wish for the seventh Dyoren once the pain of his dishonour has diminished."

Aewöl chose not to dwell any longer on the fate of the Seeker. He turned his attention to the mission ahead.

"We all know there is little time. I will ask Gelros to prepare our horses. We will set off for Mentollà at dawn. It will take us several days to reach the tower of the creek." Aewöl bowed respectfully, before taking his leave.

Curwë immediately offered to accompany the young matriarch home. The festive celebration was still in full swing within the Halls of Essawylor. Indifferent to its now distant murmur, the two Elves wandered through the city streets, up towards Temples Square. They admired the night's tremendous starry sky. The discussion focused anew on the legendary bladesmith who had forged the fabled swords, and who had left behind the Forbidden Will. Nyriele was explaining.

"Rowë, first son of Nargrond, was the wisest of the exiled High Elves in the Lost Islands. After the army of King Lormelin disembarked upon Gwa Nyn's shores, to invade the main island of the Archipelago, the clan Myortilys were defeated and the High Elves seized the heart of their realm. It remained a dangerous place, threatened by the raids of defeated Myortilys, and further attacks from darker beings. Its custody was therefore entrusted to Rowë and his house. It was known thereafter as the Nargrond Valley."

"It seems everyone covets the Nargrond Valley," Curwë muttered to himself.

"The valley has been the ultimate object of desire since the Star fell from the sky and the meteorite hit Gwa Nyn, which awakened the volcano of Oryusk."

Nyriele and Curwë walked in silence, overpowered by the beauty of the surrounding scenery. Along the citrus orchards that bordered the sandy walkways, the scent of orange flowers mixed to those of jasmine petals. Below them, the bay was resplendent in its finest natural garb. The moonlight picked out the outlines of sandy islets, exposed in the low tide, tracing the design for ephemeral new archipelagos. They finally reached the steps of the matriarchs' hall which was Nyriele's home. The two Elves were reluctant to part company. Curwë once again renewed his pledge to support the expedition to come. Suddenly, his voice rang out, clear and vivid. He had been overwhelmed by the beauty that surrounded him, and he began to sing.

"Lost in the Ocean, we had given up our fight,
So, I read the tales of Llyoriane through.
I dreamt of being the Llewenti Queen's knight,
Now I walk in the moonlight with you.

I was purposeless and vain but will now march straight,
I was stooped and feeble but will now stand strong,
For I do your will and entrust to you my fate,
I serve you, Nyriele, sovereign of my song."

These words came out hesitantly as the bard improvised the rhymed verses. The fact that he was expressing his feelings unselfconsciously, without fear of failure, made the performance even more moving. Nyriele smiled and, all of a sudden, handed him her silver necklace.

"Take this, take this with you. It will prove to my father that you have come on my behalf."

Before Curwë had time to refuse the precious gift, or even to thank his benefactor, she was gone. Nyriele breathlessly reached the upper quarters of the great hall where the matriarchs resided. Her heart was beating furiously; whether it was from the steep stairs or the intensity of this new, unknown feeling, she did not know.

"Good night, Nyriele," said Lyrine, standing in the entrance of her own room.

Nyriele was taken aback by the unexpected encounter. The young matriarch often felt guilty and embarrassed in her mother's presence; any show of initiative from Nyriele somehow always felt like a challenge to Lyrine's authority. Nevertheless, she managed to put up an innocent front.

"The sky is beautiful tonight!" she said, marvelling at the multitude of stars that illuminated Llafal like as many heavenly lamps.

Lyrine responded, her tone somewhat matter of fact.

"Indeed, it is; this summer's night is a gift from the Deities…"

She paused before continuing enigmatically.

"It is odd… I was reading an old scroll tonight… beautiful poetry that charts the sundering of the Elvin races a long, long time ago, during that night when the stars were so bright. Like other Elvin nations, the Green Elves and the Blue Elves were unwilling to bow to the Gods, refusing their summons. They chose the perilous corners of the Mainland over divine protection… and over their gift of immortality. In ancient songs of our people, some echoes of which are still remembered in the Lost Islands, we hear that our ancestors parted from the High Elves and chose a different path… We became independent and also… different. We grew into another race… and were never meant to meet again those who made a different choice. From the beginning of times until today, our bloodlines were not supposed to comingle…"

There was a pause. Nyriele was hesitating before responding to her mother.

"The seer of the clan of Filweni," the daughter began, "that noble lady they call Arwela, once told me, 'Gweïwal Uleydon plays music for all Elves. The sound of the sea on our shores is his attempt to enlighten our hope.' Perhaps she was right. Are not all Elves enamoured with the Ocean? Is it not strange that we all joy in the elemental music of breaking waves? Maybe we are not so different."

Lyrine was visibly displeased with this answer.

"Daughter, I know how much you like listening to sweet music, ¬¬but just remember," she now warned, "this it is not merely the lyrics that matter. Listen to the resonance of the voice that sings them. This will tell you more about the true intent of the charming singer... I wish you a good night, Nyriele. Tomorrow will be a different day."

CHAPTER 3: Camatael

2712, Season of Eïwele Llya, 95th day, Tar-Andevar, Nyn Ernaly

The day was fine. It was unusually quiet aboard the merchant ship as it bobbed in the gentle swell. The air was rich with the mingling smells of wet wood, iodine and sea spray. Intense rays of sunshine poured into the small cabin, chasing the shadows from its seldom-seen corners. Camatael moved the scroll further up his desk and continued reading with care.

"..., the Sea Hierarchs have overcome all dangers that have thus far been presented them. But such achievements have not quenched their thirst for discovery.

Let me warn you. No further conquest will fill the emptiness that haunts their souls. Beware, for that day will come sooner than we might think.

House Dol Nos-Loscin predicts that, when this time comes, the Westerners will turn against their allies, commit them all to servitude and impose tyranny. Their eagerness to accumulate power and wealth shall know no bounds.

It is strange, is it not, that these dark omens concerning those who call themselves friends of Elves and vassals of King Norelin should come from a house that is currently facing innumerable deadly enemies.

The barbarian tribes under the command of Ka-Blowna are ruthless. This warrior's fury is without parallel. His deeds are so demonic that his fanatical troops have come to believe that a Dragon God is marching at his side. Nevertheless, House Dol Nos-Loscin and its allies are holding out. We will not let the principality of Cumberae fall. After all, despite our pain, suffering and fear, our current struggle is of little importance in the greater order of things. The blows you are preparing to inflict upon the proud Westerners, on the other hand, may well resonate throughout history.

Those days we studied side by side at the Ruby College are not so long ago. I am glad that time and distance have not eroded our friendship and mutual esteem. I feel proud when I consider the path you have chosen. I hereby renew the alliance between Llymar and Cumberae and provide the Council of the Forest with all guarantees of the Prince's support.

Alton of House Dol Nos-Loscin, Herald of the Principality of Cumberae."

Camatael Dol Lewin dropped the scroll onto the desk of his small cabin and paused for a moment. Only the sounds of the swelling sea and the teetering ship could be heard. The young lord was dressed simply, in traveller's clothes. He possessed a natural essence of power without seeming to desire its trappings. His icy blue eyes held both intelligence and learning.

This was the third time Camatael had read through that scroll. The diplomatic missive had reached him onboard one of the merchant ships from Cumberae, a vessel that Aertelyr, the guild master of Breymounarty, sailed to Llafal twice a year. Reading it over and over strengthened his determination. Undoubtedly, the message was strongly supportive of the dangerous move that Camatael was about to make.

Alton Dol Nos-Loscin's latest letter confirmed that their existing partnership, currently founded on trade, could gain an entirely new dimension. Now that the principality of Cumberae was willing to back the forest of Llymar's move against the sea hierarchs, those powerful allies of King Norelin, it was possible that the two rebellious Elvin realms could soon form a defensive alliance.

'This is a significant development,' thought Camatael. 'Confronted by two new bastions of resistance to the north and the south, the king's real influence will be limited to the Sea of

Llyoriane. His rule is confined to those provinces at the heart of the Archipelago. Norelin has completely lost the control of the south and the trade routes across the Sea of Isyl. Conflicts are raging across those regions, between House Dol Nos-Loscin and the bloodthirsty barbarians. Norelin's control of the west is fragile; he is now fully reliant upon his Westerner allies to keep the peace on the islands of Nyn Avrony and Nyn Ernaly, where barbarian tribes are constantly rising against their authority. In Gwarystan and across his kingdom, the young sovereign is abhorred by most of his subjects. He has closed their temples and outlawed their ancient faiths. He can no longer afford to blindly support his Westerner friends. Now is our chance to strike. The time to send a clear message has come. The faithful Elves of the Islands, shall not tolerate the abuses of Men indefinitely.'

Camatael, feeling confident and serene, turned to the west and whispered a short prayer to Eïwal Lon, the Demigod of Light and Knowledge.

"Without wisdom, the world would be chaos, and only wisdom
is worthy of worship.
I am thankful for the knowledge it brings, blessings to we who
abide by your law.
Let wisdom's influence among Elves be without bounds."

His cabin was small and cramped, and he was having some difficulty getting used to the rocking boat. To distract himself from the discomfort, Camatael decided to take some fresh air and join Curubor, his mentor, who was also travelling aboard. Accessing the ship's deck was far from straightforward; he struggled to find his way amidst the various crates and sacks of merchandise stored inside the ship's dark bowels. This merchant vessel was transporting heavy cargo: principally barrels of wine and casks full of fruit. It was sailing under the flag of Tios Lleny, one of the dominions of the Gwarystan kingdom, located in the province of southern Nyn Llyvary, a region fabled for bountiful orchards and excellent wines.

When he finally reached the upper deck, Camatael was surprised by the strength of the sea wind. Otherwise, all was quiet. The crew was busy contemplating the influence of the steady eastern gale, which was gently inflating the boat's only sail. Looking to the north, Camatael noticed with some apprehension that Nyn Ernaly's shores had already become visible.

Curubor Dol Etrond looked old and severe, his lips were thin and his eyes cold. He stood at the edge of the deck, pondering the waves below. His hair, an unusual snowy white, fluttered in the sea wind. He wore leather gloves, and his azure gown was completely covered by a large ochre cloak of common fabric. Curubor was abruptly brought back to reality by his companion's arrival.

"I hope you are not thinking of throwing yourself overboard, my lord..." started Camatael, with a sarcasm that sounded foreign in his mouth.

Serious, focused and dedicated, the young lord Dol Lewin was not known for his sense of humour. Curubor smiled. His face, until that moment grim and concerned, had regained its friendly and open composure.

"On reflection, I think I would prefer the warm waters of Penlla Bay," he responded cheerfully, before continuing with an enigmatic tone. "In fact, I was thinking... I was thinking about you, and the risk you are taking by agreeing to support me in such a dangerous endeavour."

"I know where my duty lies, my Lord. Many were the glorious deeds of those who served under the banner of the White Unicorn. I should not like to stand apart," replied Camatael boldly.

"These are proud words that do you much honour. Though your strengths differ significantly, the blood which flows in your veins is indeed that of Lewin."

"Thank you, my lord. Believe me, I have no fear. I know the

importance of our task, and I am convinced that we have devised the best plan possible."

"I appreciate your confidence, Camatael. You are an Elf with rare gifts. I praise your patience, my young companion; it is an invaluable attribute. I know the high standards you set for yourself. I must acknowledge that, since the day you chose to join us in Llymar and abdicate your high position by the side of the king, little progress has been made. That day was four years ago. Others would have expressed impatience by now or worse, their discontent."

"Since then, I have been entrusted with the temple of Eïwal Lon in Tios Lluin. Dozens of Elves of all origins live under the protection of my banner; I am responsible for the fate of hundreds of followers. This is a most noble task and one that satisfies my sense of duty. I am filled with the Demigod of Wisdom's love; it inspires me each day," Camatael replied modestly."I know how seriously you consider your new role as high priest of Eïwal Lon's temple in the City of Stones. Your commitment to restoring the ancient shrine to its former majesty can only be praised. But I sense that your ambition is greater."

"What do you mean?"

"I remember a certain claim you may once have made. You desired to lead the High Elves from Essawylor."

"What you say is true," admitted Camatael. "This formidable unit is worth hundreds of fighters. Their commander, the one named Roquendagor, is a valuable knight who some say can hardly be defeated in open battle. I heard that, back in Essawylor, those High Elves were honoured guards of the White Unicorn."

"That is correct," confirmed Curubor. "I know it for a fact. These fierce fighters used to be servants of the elder branch of House Dol Lewin in the kingdom of Essawylor. But nowadays they follow a knight, who is committed to serve only the new warlord of Mentollà, Feïwal, the clan of Filweni's guide."

"That arrangement is most odd. To think that the strongest troops of our realm serve a chief of the Blue Elves, a mere navigator! I believe that such able fighters would be better employed as guards of the temple of Eïwal Lon in Tios Lluin," said Camatael, somewhat harshly.

"Ah… I sense disappointment, and perhaps also disdain, in your words," commented Curubor. "It is as I thought yet, until now, you have not spoken out. These past four years, you have followed my advice without uttering a single complaint."

"Indeed I have not, my lord, and I am sorry to speak out now."

"My dear Camatael, I owe you an explanation. You deserve to know why I have asked you to stay away from them, as I did. Let me tell you, my young friend, this is enough of a connection to have with that cursed community."

Visibly surprised, Camatael could not refrain from asking more.

"Cursed? I thought you have been fighting for their rights! I have seen you plead the cause of the clan of Filweni's guide, that Feïwal. Were you not the great architect of his admittance among the council of the forest as warlord of Mentollà?"

Curubor nodded, fully his own master, and continued with his usual professorial tone.

"I know what you are thinking. I can sense the bitterness behind your words. You mean that I have failed to advocate the cause of House Dol Lewin with the same fervour. You mean that, despite your great contribution during the battle of Mentollà, you were not rewarded with a seat at the council of the forest."

"I did not utter a single word along those lines," noted Camatael curtly.

"You thought it. Yet you controlled your just ire… 'He who is slow to anger is mightier than the mighty. He who rules his spirit is a greater victor than he who wins the battle,' or so Rowë Dol Nargrond used to say. That legendary lord knew the teachings of Eïwal Lon."

Curubor paused, looking at his companion with care and affection. Eventually he went on.

"Camatael, I agree with that which you will not say. You must have known, however, that if I acted cautiously in this regard, I would have had my reasons. It is too early for House Dol Lewin to join the council of the forest. I am afraid that you will need to work harder, and for longer, if you truly wish to earn the respect of the Llewenti clans, most of all their high priestesses. Trust can only be earned over time, but it can be lost in an instant, especially when one deals with a figure such as Matriarch Lyrine."

A silence followed. Despite being disappointed, Camatael agreed with his mentor about the cautious strategy which had so far been followed.

"You described the castaways of Mentollà as cursed. What makes you say this? You are not accustomed to superstition, my lord."

"Mark my word, Camatael: a powerful oath stands before them, no less than the vow of a king."

"How can that be? For centuries, until very recently in fact, those High Elves have lived thousands of leagues away from Gwarystan and its kings. How could they provoke their ire?"

Curubor took a sharp intake of breath before going on to explain, a tremor in his voice.

"Those castaways who now live in Mentollà have no idea; it is that which makes it all the more frightening... King Lormelin's oath dates from long ago, from the beginning of this Age, a time only your forefathers knew. He who would become known as 'the Conqueror' had just been crowned by the assembled Dol houses. I still remember that day, on the sandy beach of Essaweryl Bay, when I took my vow of obedience to the new sovereign... Fleeing from the north of the Mainland, the

High Elves had finally found refuge in Essawylor, the land of the Blue Elves. War was raging between the royal houses of the High Elves; two pretenders were fighting for the crown... Aranaele insisted on settling in Essawylor, whereas her royal cousin Lormelin wanted to cross the Austral Ocean and find the legendary Lost Islands of the Green Elves... I fought in what was later named the war of Diamond and Ruby, Camatael. I saw with my own eyes how Aranaele sought to destroy Lormelin."

Curubor's eyes were glowing with the vividness of his memory.

"I know all about this war of old," Camatael interrupted, "the kin-slaying conflict between the Ruby and the Diamond. It led to the rupture of my very house! My forefathers, of the second branch of House Dol Lewin, were right to part from their elders. Lormelin was our lawful king; he had been crowned according to our ancient traditions. History has proved him right. He led our houses across the Austral Ocean and became the conqueror of the Lost Islands. For that feat we must always remain grateful and respect his memory."

"Lormelin was doubtless a great king," Curubor concurred, "and one that will always be remembered as such, but the blood of his grandfather flowed in his veins... His dark temper pushed him to pronounce a dreadful vow against those who had defied his authority. A royal oath is a fearful evil, Camatael... I would rather not to repeat those dreadful verses... That oath will endure until the king's bloodline is spent, bringing chaos, misery and woe to all who confront it, regardless of their guilt or their innocence... The High Elves of Mentollà are direct descendants of those who mercilessly fought the royal banner of the Ruby. They are therefore cursed upon these islands; there will be no refuge or escape from the vengeance of Lormelin's heir... This is why, my young friend, I ask you to stay away from them. See them as a dangerous weapon that must remain secret, that must be kept safe and far away from us. This weapon we shall use to our advantage when the time comes. The community of Mentollà have no allies. They are doomed, with no recourse except for us. But we must keep them at bay until the time to unleash their power comes."

"I see," Camatael concluded simply, and he turned his gaze towards the shores of Nyn Ernaly, determined to conceal the tumultuous thoughts that raged within him.

There was, in Curubor's words, such rationality, such cold heartlessness, that the young Dol Lewin felt hurt, and deeply so. For the first time since Camatael had known him, the ancient Elf was expressing a darker side of his personality. It surprised Camatael. It felt as if the foundations of the values he had learnt at the temple of Eïwal Lon had been shaken. Somehow stung by that recognition and eager to demonstrate his independence and strength of will, Camatael decided to change the topic of the conversation.

"What we shall attempt in Nyn Ernaly is a most perilous task," he announced unexpectedly, almost brashly. "This shall be the second time I have risked my life in a few short years. If I survive, I have decided I will marry... I now know my life's higher purpose, and therefore have the strength to become one with my beloved."

"You are too young for such a decision!" exclaimed the ancient mage, taken aback."With all due respect, Lord Curubor, the High Elves have always wedded in their youth. We have very few children, and it is my duty to ensure a future for House Dol Lewin. The time is right. I shall make sure that my family is held together by a profound sense of kinship. I will cherish my heirs."

Surprised by this genuine conviction and already anticipating who the bride would be, Curubor now knew he must fight back more harshly.

"We, High Elves, wed only once in our lives, when we are sure of our love. Once we commit ourselves, our fate is changed forever. We are no common Elves. I do not believe that any of our countless ancient tales glorifies deeds of lust, which is all your absurd proposition would amount to."

"I am no child, my Lord; I know that marriage is the natural course of life for High Elves, though sometimes that course is disrupted by strange destinies. Early in my youth, I chose Loriele Dol Etrond; I have always secretly desired to marry your beloved grandniece. I have waited patiently for us to reach an appropriate age. Despite losing everything with the fall of Mentolewin and the death of all my family, I have ever since been moving up the ranks of power, to prove myself worthy of her bloodline... Four years ago, I followed her into exile in the forest of Llymar. I left behind all I had built in Gwarystan."

"We all know your deeds, Camatael. Rest assured that every member of House Dol Etrond praises your valour."

"Naturally, I respect that the betrothal must be approved by her parents. Therefore, I have decided that, should I survive the task before us, I will gather the houses of Dol Lewin and Dol Etrond, and appear before Loriele to offer her the silver ring, proof of my eternal commitment."

Curubor was caught off guard by Camatael's implacable resolution. His young companion was ready to risk his reputation to win his heart's dearest prize. Camatael risked a humiliating dismissal if Loriele or her father Almit, the lord of House Dol Etrond, chose to return his silver ring publicly. Such was the law, though such embarrassing situations had seldom occurred in the past, for High Elves did not choose their eternal partners lightly. Camatael, seeing that his bold declaration had proved successful, exploited his advantage further.

"I am a priest of Eïwal Lon. My spirit is master of my body, and I will never be swayed by simple desire of the flesh. I know Loriele will return my love and that she wishes deeply to celebrate our love in marriage. She has prepared her silver ring too, and has assured me that, one day, we will exchange those slender rings of gold, to bind us together for eternity."

Curubor had difficulty breathing. He refused to accept that such feelings had developed so quickly between his two protégés. He did not like it; the prospect of their union felt like a threat to the special relationship he had developed with his grandniece. He tried one last cunning attempt to dissuade Camatael.

"There is something I must warn you about, my dear Camatael, and none but I can assume this responsibility. You know how fond of you I am, and the great ambition I place upon your future…"

The ancient mage suddenly looked grave.

"Have you ever considered," Curubor began, his tone serious, "Almit's fate after he lost Nuviele, Loriele's mother?"

"I know she came from House Dol Ogalen. I remember that she died in her daughter's youth. Many tales recount the despair of Nuviele's lover."

"She did not die, so to speak. She disappeared. Almit was devastated."

"She disappeared?" asked Camatael. "Did nobody try to find her?"

"She was captured but… not ransomed. We looked for her across the Lost Islands, summoning all our influence. But, after a few years, Almit knew that she had died. Their bond had been broken. It almost drove him to madness. Though it did not kill him, the trauma destroyed much of his spirit. Almit will never be the Elf he once was; his future achievements will never be worthy of his bloodline's valour."

"It's true that Almit is cold and heartless," admitted Camatael."I have entrusted you with my family's secret for one reason: I am warning you. Forging an eternal bond with your beloved spouse will give you a sense of accomplishment. It will also give your enemies a new way to harm you."

The ancient mage was becoming insistent. Though he almost never talked about himself, he decided to make an exception. He used the third person to accentuate his point.

"You may wonder how Curubor survived all those struggles, how he still enjoys that which is best in life despite all the trials across the centuries. His secret is simple. Curubor has no bond, he has no tie, he wonders freely. Long ago, he grieved for what he had lost; knowing that those he loved had died in vain. Nothing can affect him anymore, for his time of mourning is over. His bereavement ceased when his father chose to die in a hopeless fight, after failing to save his mother in the final upheavals of the First Age."

What the ancient mage had confided made a distinct impression upon Camatael's mind. Curubor, cunning as ever, thought he'd won the case.

"Look to your own future, Camatael. If you are to live up to the high expectations the world has of you, your strength will not be enough. You need to be untouchable."

A long silence followed, but Camatael had already made up his mind. With a low tone that left no doubt as to the resolution of his will, he spoke.

"I thank you for your advice, my lord, but I have made my decision. If I survive what is to come, I will gather our two houses and offer my silver ring to Lady Loriele."

Curubor, defeated, had to change his position. He did so as quickly as a fox that chooses a second prey, once he understands the first has escaped.

"If this is so, you force us to seek a swift victory in Nyn Ernaly, for I see now that there will be a grandiose feast to prepare …"

"Thank you, my lord, you honour me greatly."

Camatael's gaze became lost in the sea, as he tried to master the flow of his emotions. He remembered the day he first laid eyes on Loriele Dol Etrond. In that moment, he had almost forgotten to breathe. He remembered how the light of the setting sun was diminishing in the king's palace chambers, back in Gwarystan. From the great hall in the highest tower above the cliff, one could fully embrace that incomparable view of the Sea of Llyoriane. Through the crowds of courtesans and nobles, ladies and knights, artists and musicians, he had seen her.

Loriele was tall and slender, with jet-black hair, her pale skin marked with a tiny mole above her charming lips. Her posture was majestic; upright with a beautifully arched back. She knew no rival. Irresistibly drawn to her, the young lord Camatael had managed to utter a few awkward words of introduction to her. Their discussion soon demonstrated that she was highly educated, deeply cultured and had a rare knowledge of art. But it was the intensity of her gaze which struck him. He had seen, in the sapphire of those eyes, a thirst for life, a hunger for power and for all the pleasures it brought. It contrasted sharply with the childish, almost naïve way in which she held herself. That day, he decided that the heir of House Dol Etrond was born to be a queen: his queen... Curubor, already focused on their more immediate objective, interrupted Camatael's thoughts.

"Look, we are approaching the mouth of the Sian Ningy. You can already see the walls of the Westerners' city."

Camatael turned around, clinging to the bow. Suddenly, he could see the tower of Braglin, the city's beacon and its tallest spire. For a long time, he kept his gaze fixed upon the great edifice. The sun was now high in the sky. The fresh southern breeze of the morning had cleared the sky above, and seagulls and cormorants were gracefully soaring through the air, embracing the curves of the wind and letting out furious cries. The fortified town of Tar-Andevar, known as the city of

Mentobraglin when the High Elves had ruled all the Lost Islands, was the largest city of Nyn Ernaly. Its imposing buildings were surrounded by high walls, which loomed over the mouth of the Sian Ningy. A fabled wonder of the island stood imposingly upon the hilltops above the populous town. The castle of the sea hierarchs had been built in white granite, its gleaming walls surrounding the ancient Elvin tower of Braglin. The rich houses of the Elvin guild masters, the legacy of the town's golden age, bordered the western bank of the river where most of the trading port's activity was concentrated. These facades formed an architectural phenomenon, which majestically overlooked the vast quay where dozens of ships of all sizes were anchored.

The coaster, with its banner of Tios Lleny openly unfurled, passed the southern tower of the sea hierarchs' castle, which oversaw the mouth of the river and protected the bay, where several great galleys from the realm of Nellos were anchored. Camatael took care to examine the formidable vessels.

'For a long time now, the great galleys of Nellos have done little fighting but they remain the supreme symbol of the Westerners' power and of their ceaseless ambitions,' thought Camatael.

As the small merchant ship approached its destination, all those aboard could see a flurry of activity on the docks. Curubor could not refrain from expressing his astonishment.

"Many years have passed since I last came to Mentobraglin, but I never imagined that such a change as this could be possible. The Westerners have built a great harbour for their galleys, a harbour like we have never seen in the Islands. They have also made strong towers to defend it. This demonstrates their true nature. They truly are conquerors at heart, rather than the fair companions they pretend to be for the moment. They are preparing to seize and loot the entire Elvin kingdom."

Camatael agreed. "I recall how the Westerners took delight in our masonry. After the Pact was signed, their craftsmen often came among us, in the masons' guild of Gwarystan. I noted at the time how they were being taught precious skills, especially those which required fineness of handiwork. No wonder they now surpass their teachers. Look to the northern embankment. That is where they have concentrated their guilds, to smith a great hoard of weapons and construct their galleys."

"I can only imagine the fear that shall fall upon the Elves of Gwarystan when they next see this formidable fleet emerging out of the sunset, its colourful masts covering the sea like a field of flowers," Curubor replied thoughtfully.

"Wherever they dwell," Camatael explained, "the Westerners strive to prosper. First, the cunning Men engage in trade, offering gifts to their hosts, wishing to be seen as benefactors. It is, however, a wicked strategy, by which they gain crucial knowledge from their partners. Their wealth grows and grows, thanks to their efficiency in organization and the new skills they have acquired. At first, all will benefit. The Men of the West always devise new techniques, improving the crafts of their hosts. But, eventually, when they have been admitted into the circles of power, they will inevitably demand positions of great authority. When they are given such power, they reveal their true nature: fierce tyrants and Men of war, who had always planned to subdue and, eventually, to enslave. This is how they built their maritime empire across the shores of the Mainland and became masters of so many Men."

"Each sea hierarch considers himself to be next in line to the throne," acknowledged Curubor.

Still examining the eastern embankment, where the sea hierarchs' castle stood, Camatael observed.

"Look at that boatyard. It is empty. The stone shelter there is of a different design to others I know in Elvin ports. With its deep-water access, it can be used as both a wet and a dry dock."

"Some say the sea hierarchs lack softwood lumber for their shipbuilding guilds, and that they now save Tar-Andevar's boatyard for another purpose," commented Curubor, now grim and preoccupied.

"What other purpose?" asked Camatael, eager to know more.

"There are rumours that the sea hierarchs are breeding monstrous marine creatures, captured by their great galleys from the ocean's depths."

Camatael could not suppress a shiver. The vast seas contained many monsters which could now be lurking in that boatyard: Giant Gars, Sea Wolves or even Dragon Turtles.

On the other side of the river's mouth, the residential districts built on the western bank of the Sian Ningy had a bright and cheerful atmosphere. The music of minstrels could be heard at every street corner near the docks. Shops of all sorts offered goods from across the Lost Islands and beyond. Noisy and dirty taverns abounded, out of which sprawled large crowds towards the port. Looking out upon the commotion, the two Elves felt as if they were about to enter a permanent, ever-evolving festival, as if the Men of the city were constantly finding something new to celebrate. Finally, the small coaster from Tios Lleny came to dock alongside the wharf of the western bank.

'The Sian Ningy is filthy,' Camatael noticed, 'dark like a putrid sewer, as if a million crawling creatures have been disturbing the muddy riverbed.'

Those who worked around the pier day in, day out, stopped what they were doing and stared out, curious about the small Elvin merchant ship sailing under the kingdom of Gwarystan's colours. A large gathering of bystanders was forming on the pier. It was not uncommon to see Elvin ships in Tar-Andevar's port, and indeed more and more were coming from different parts of the Archipelago.

But trade was not the only reason to visit Nyn Ernaly during the summer. Elves from distant royal dominions came to this island for an important spiritual reason too. These Elvin pilgrims were setting out to witness the Veil, that mystical manifestation of Eïwele Llyi's power. Each year, to carry instructions, grant favours and deliver revelations, the Deity of Beauty and Arts would send forth the Veil, a vast congregation of butterflies whose colourful flight could restore hope into Elvin hearts and inspire artists and poets.

That afternoon, however, the Nellos commander who came aboard with his troop to inspect the small coaster quickly understood that its passengers were anything but pilgrims. He asked to check the official documentation from the royal administration which would attest to the Tios Lleny coaster's right to trade in Tar-Andevar. The Elvin ship's captain was not used to coming to this great harbour of the Westerners, and he was struggling to find the paperwork that was required. Eager to remain unseen, Camatael and Curubor took advantage of this distraction and descended into the hold, in order to bid farewell to a third Elf, who had so far remained in the darkness of his cabin.

"We will meet again around midnight," said Curubor, hovering at the threshold of the stranger's cabin, "in the wine cellar marked on the map you have been given. That secret cavern is deep underground, far below the old Braglin tower. You will have to navigate mazes. You must follow the instructions written on that scroll to the letter," the ancient mage insisted.

"And if you yourselves fall before you reach our meeting point, I will at least have many fine wines to console me," the Elf replied ironically.

He was wrapped in a long black cloak. Neither Camatael nor Curubor could make out his face through the gloom, from their position by the stairs.

"Rest assured, when we meet again, we will have the crucial information we seek. You will not have travelled so far in vain," Camatael declared.

His voice was firm, though the extent to which he genuinely cared seemed somehow uncertain.

"Then all is well, and I shall enjoy a few sips of the finest vintages while I wait for you. I wish you a safe day," concluded the Elf, his tone nonchalant.

Before heading up to the deck, the two lords returned to their respective cabins, both wrapped themselves in large hooded robes, each a different shade of unremarkable brown, and slung cheap leather satchels over their shoulders. Meeting again in the hold's stairway, they could not resist smiling at each other's appearance. They did look rather like a couple of wine merchants from Tios Lleny. Camatael took the cloak and fastened the brooch. Once on the deck, he walked directly towards the gangway where the Nellos commander stood with his customs officers. Surprising the Man with his sudden appearance, Camatael uttered a few commanding words.

"I suggest you let us pass, Commander, our royal passes have already been verified."

The Westerner hesitated, before he briefly caught the Elf's gaze: full of power and disdain. Without stalling a moment longer, now avoiding looking Camatael in the eye, the Man bowed respectfully, and let them go without a word. The two Elvin lords were out on the docks in an instant, among the crowd, those humble people who together formed the backbone of Westerners' towns.

Amidst the laughter, cries and accusations, the town of Tar-Andevar was bustling, passionately and greedily, with life. The two Elves looked around at the sprawling parade of Men, all from different origins and classes: some were tall and dark-skinned, some were small and pale. There were arrogant merchants, rude thugs, idle drunkards and wicked criminals. Before their eyes and walking all around them, almost grabbing at them was the powerful flow of human life: chaotic, turbulent and unstoppable. Their path led them to the oldest borough, whose narrow pathways, overrun with wild vegetation and bordered by small wooden buildings, formed a complex maze. They walked down a blind alley and found themselves surrounded by ancient houses built on steep slopes. Camatael turned to his mentor for assistance.

"We're nearing our destination. I ask that you please protect me while I ensure that everything is in order."

Curubor acquiesced, as though expecting the request. He stepped to one side, ready to intervene should any threat arise against his protégé. Meanwhile, Camatael selected one of the street's dark doorways, just wide enough to accommodate a single Elf. His hood covered his face. He began muttering words in lingua Hawenti, and soon his eyes turned white. The young lord was suddenly elsewhere; his breathing ceased. A few moments later, the likeness of a sapphire gemstone, as large as a fist, appeared beside him, suspended in the air. Curubor was unperturbed by this apparition and maintained his vigilant guard. The sphere then quickly moved down the street, disappearing through the closed doors of a cooper's shop. The exercise lasted for some time, before finally ending when Camatael broke out of his spell into a coughing fit, gasping desperately for air.

"The way is clear," Camatael announced once he had recovered from his effort.

The two Elves were heading towards the door of the cooper's shop when a feminine figure, in a beautiful, deep-green robe, walked out of one of the alley's gateways. Curubor was unsurprised and seemed to have been expecting the encounter. Calm and respectful as ever, he presented his companion to the charming newcomer.

"My dear Camatael, may I introduce you to Drismile, a talented and highly skilled artist. She is also praised for her silence and obedience."

The graceful Elvin lady responded with a smile. She greeted the two lords ceremoniously, an innocent look upon her face. Her hair was arranged in a wild, effortless style. It partly shrouded her face in a seductive, sulky glow. Camatael, who for his part was somewhat surprised by the encounter, examined Drismile with precision, feasting his eyes upon her lace dress before lingering in contemplation of her delicate gloved hands.

'It was ever thus,' he thought to himself. 'The beautiful flowers, the delicious forbidden fruit, will always spring forth in the wild, never out of pot.'

Inside, the workshop had been set up according to tradition. The cooper was absent, and there was no one else amongst the empty wooden vessels. Camatael examined the artisan's handiwork, inspecting the various casks, barrels, buckets, and hogsheads. Curubor disappeared into the back room. Camatael remained with Drismile in the workshop. There was a silence. The young lord's gaze was once again drawn towards her elegant dress, which brought out the sensuality of her feminine form. He considered her for a moment, wondering what it was that made her so acutely attractive. His attention was suddenly captured by a precious silver bracelet about her wrist, in the shape of a snake. He was somewhat startled and decided to ask more.

"You're no ordinary lady, are you? You are dressed like the finest courtesan of Gwarystan. Your elegance suggest you are more familiar with the royal court than with this filthy harbour neighbourhood. I am surprised it is here, under these odd circumstances, that we are making each other's acquaintance. Where do you come from?" he asked roughly.

"I take that as a compliment, my lord," replied Drismile, smiling timidly. She went on, her voice brimming with innocent charm. "I was born in Yslla, in Nargrond Valley, but I cannot say that I have a home... I do know Gwarystan; back there, I used to follow orders at the royal court. I had to bow to earn my living. Here, in Tar- Andevar, I have no master and no tutor. I write my own story. There, I survived. Here, I live."

Camatael examined her with even more attention; he found her fascinating and could not turn his eyes away.

'Yslla, so that's it,' he thought. 'She must be a Night Elf. I should have known. Her exotic beauty makes her... interesting.'

"How will you let our guests know that we have arrived?" asked Camatael regaining his self-control.

"I have written a scroll to that effect. I ask that your lordships seal it with your personal runes. The children will take it to... your 'guests'. As the king's ambassadors, they dwell a high tower, which is still under construction. It is a round keep, covered in arrow slits, one league north of Tar-Andevar. Some say it will one day be the tallest edifice on the island, and that the top, when it is completed, will be designed to resemble an open hand with six fingers."

"How dreadful! Evidently, we do not share the same taste in architecture... You mentioned children. Why would you rely on them for such an important mission?" Camatael asked.

"There are many poor, abandoned children in this large town of Men. They can prove efficient agents and, more importantly, their minds are easily corrupted. Their memory can be worked at will."

"Ah, I see..."

Camatael did not have time to elaborate further. Curubor returned, satisfied by his inspection of the back room.

"All is in order. We can proceed as planned."

Drismile withdrew the scroll from her pocket and presented it to the two lords. Camatael read the text closely. The writing was that of a consummate scribe, well versed in lingua Hawenti, which none but a few scholars practised across the Lost Islands any longer. The careful wording met all the requirements of Elvin trade agreements. This letter was a proposal; it offered to grant the distributor exclusive rights over Llymar goods across the Archipelago. Camatael was visibly pleased with the work.

"This is perfect. If they have the brains to understand these numbers, they will soon work out what this secret trade monopoly would be worth. Though Llymar Forest and the kingdom of Gwarystan have a tense relationship, we are not yet enemies."

"I agree. This should be tempting enough for them to come and meet us. At heart, these royal servants are courtesans, who will always strive for that extra ounce of power or gold," Curubor concurred. "You have worked with diligence, Drismile. It's almost as if you have carried out all these calculations for your master's benefit," he added, with a smile on his lips.

"I am glad that your lordship praises my work," answered the charming lady simply, her head down.

Curubor then sealed the missive with his four rings. Camatael took the breastpin that held his cloak and left his own mark: the image of the racing unicorn, symbol of his house. Once the formality was completed, the elegant Drismile was on her way. Before exiting the artisan's shop, she turned one last time.

"I wish you farewell, Lord Curubor and... Lord Camatael. Perhaps we shall see each other again."

Drismile bowed, fully conscious of the myriad fleeting emotions she had kindled in the Dol Lewin's mind. After inspecting the main workshop, the two lords decided to withdraw into the back room, where they still had much preparation to do. Neither talked, for both were focussed exclusively on their tasks. It was a large room, albeit with a low ceiling. There were no windows, for this section of the building had been carved into the rock of the hill. Flickers from the fire danced upon the walls, and the corners of the room were shrouded in deep shadow. In front of the hearth, on a dusty rug, was a wooden table, surrounded by eight comfortable-looking chairs. Two were facing the room's only door, while the other six had their backs to it. Camatael felt confident.

"The room is the perfect size for what we have planned."
"It is small enough, yet we will not be overcrowded," agreed Curubor.

He paused to pass his gaze over where their guests would sit, imagining their positions. His eye hardened. When the last of the sunlight was gone, the scene was set; now, it was only the actors who were missing. The two lords lit candles and sat at ease, enjoying the silence in the comfort of their armchairs.

*

Night had reigned for some hours when voices were heard at the workshop's main entrance. Until that moment, the alley outside had been remarkably calm, as was to be expected in this remote part of town, particularly along a path that led nowhere. As the voices became more distinct, the two lords realized that the commotion did not come from any of the cooper's neighbours. Soldiers were taking position and orders were being shouted. The small shop was completely surrounded. They heard several great crashes as the doors of neighbouring houses were forced open before the screams of protest from their occupants as they were violently dragged away. The two Elves judged from all the noise that a full battalion of the city watch must have been rallied to arrest them.

Their attention was then drawn to the roof above their heads in the backroom, above which they could hear footsteps breaking tiles. It was then that the wooden door of the main entrance to the shop was shattered into pieces by a great, fiery explosion.

They were soon struck with the smell of burning wood, and moments later smoke started infiltrating the backroom, seeping through the gap below the door. Strangely, the cloud of smoke seemed to grow denser in the air, before it took the form of an Elf's face, with two burning red eyes.

With a quick movement of his hand, Camatael uttered a short, sacred incantation, calling upon Eïwal Lon's power. The ghostly figure was held for a moment longer in the air, while Camatael repeated his prayers and raised his voice. It finally vanished, disappearing in a burst of flames, sending burnt fumes billowing violently around the room. Curubor let out a quick succession of mysterious words, circling his open palms around his head several times. His features then became placid, his face closed, his lips immobile.

A few moments later, the door was slowly opened, its rusty hinges emitting a long, sad whine, like the faint, night-time whimper of a Chanun Giant slave. Three silhouettes, clad in large red cloaks, stepped into the room. Their ruby-coloured headdresses masked all their features but their eyes. All three wore a gauntlet of rare design on their left hand, the very same as the other members of their order, which could be used as a dreadful weapon in close combat. It was the golden hand with six fingers. Camatael and Curubor immediately recognized the dreaded knights. Norelin had honoured them all with the title of Mowengot. Only three of the king's servants had come.

First Megiöl, the Half-Elf, appeared. He was known as an enchanter of shadows and was feared for the evil influence he held over the king's judgements.

Second came Turang, the Westerner: a schemer and a trader of gold, a master of spies and plots, dreaded for his murderous ways. He had skulked his way to the steps of the throne by supplying the royal court with invaluable stolen information.

Finally, in golden armour, their commander stepped into the backroom. This High Elf was the most powerful knight of their order. Eno Dol Oalin, the cadet of a famous house, had forsaken his family to seek true power alongside the king in Gwarystan.

Eno was the first to speak. Smoke still wisped around the dark red glove on his right hand.

"Good evening to you, Elves of the forest!" exclaimed the tall knight sorcerer with dark irony. "Or what, exactly, should we call you? Perhaps 'dyn Lewin' and 'dyn Etrond' would be more appropriate titles for those who, I believe, are honoured members of the council of the forest."

The spite he put into these last words contained every ounce of the disdain he held for the assembly of Llymar.

"How have you come to this? How could you renounce the power of your former ranks? Do you not envy the other Dol who are masters over others' destiny, and who subdue both Elves and Men to their wills?"

"These are arrogant words, Eno Dol Oalin…" countered Camatael to stop the flow of insults.

He deliberately used the knight sorcerer's former name, knowing full well that Eno had long since cut all bonds with his family, to embrace this very different path.

"Indeed, they are, but my arrogance is not undeserved. I am the commander of the Golden Hand; I can afford to be undiplomatic."

Neither Curubor nor Camatael dared reply to the outrageous boast. Taking their lack of reaction as a sign of weakness, the knight sorcerers stepped into the backroom and up to the three centre seats. Slowly and cautiously, never losing sight of their hosts, they sat down on their side of the table, their weapons close at hand. In an attempt to clear the air, Camatael spoke again. His voice was soft.

"You cannot imagine what it is like to meet Blue Elves from across the Austral Ocean. Those famed sailors believe that the music of Gweïwal Uleydon still lingers in all the world's waters, like an invitation to set sail and discover new horizons. I think that many High Elves, too, are drawn to this music, yet are not able to properly listen to it. The towers of Gwarystan are furnished with thousands of fountains, yet none who lives there pays attention to the message carried in the melodious flow."

"Let the Blue Elves have their superstitions!" responded the proud Eno Mowengot, laughing. "Gweïwal Uleydon, that so-called God they worship, may well be master of all waters. He may well control the breaking of rain and the formation of clouds. He is nonetheless a mere elemental spirit. It is absurd to claim that he has the power to influence our fate," Eno Mowengot exclaimed, his eyes burning with arrogance.

"Remember, Camatael, the ancient songs of yore," he continued, "that tell of the time when the Elves were finally forced to part. The High Elves did not join those who hid, still less those who fled and were lost. And yet now, after all this time, you have decided to side with those cowards. You are following the path of those who have always lost battles and fled. Do you even understand the extent of your humiliation?" provoked the commander of the Golden Hand knights.

"You may be a great sorcerer and a master of war, Eno Dol Oalin, but you should not speak of what you do not understand… Indeed, the High Eves were invited to gather at the knees of the Gods. All the woes that have befallen our kin can be traced back to those dreadful summonses. So, let me ask you: who were proved wisest in the end? Who chose the right path? Perhaps it was those who preferred the wide empty spaces of the Mainland to what the Gods offered us: the glory of immortal life. It could well be argued that the stubborn Llewenti patriarch and the bold Irawenti guide, who chose to reject the Gods' gift and stay behind, made the right choice."

Camatael spoke with passion and conviction. As he preached, he had no illusions about persuading his interlocutors, but he nevertheless felt a profound contentment in proclaiming his faith, in throwing in their faces the beliefs that inhabited him.

By his side, Curubor remained silent, impassive and absent, his gaze empty. The young Dol Lewin continued his passionate declaration.

"You should know that we can learn a lot from those Elves you call simple. Their path took them to Essawylor and ultimately to the shining waters of the Lost Islands. All these years, as we have been striving towards our ruin, they have lived in freedom," concluded Camatael, with utter faith in what he preached.

"We have not come here to discuss history," interrupted the Half-Elf Megiöl Mowengot. "We received your unsolicited trade proposal. How dare you ask us to enter a secret agreement such as this?"

"How dare you suggest we are such low-level smugglers?" added the Westerner Turang Mowengot. "Have you fallen so low that you would expect the Golden Hand to barter with traitors?"

"Did you really hope that we would ever deal with tainted outcasts?" insisted Megiöl Mowengot. "Did you really expect us to abandon our vows for the sake of more gold? On the contrary, capturing you alive and taking you to the royal justice will be a far greater reward. You cannot imagine how eager King Norelin is to watch you kneel before the Ruby throne."

With a malicious look in his eye, Turang Mowengot concluded the onslaught.

"How does it feel to be trapped? As we speak, you are surrounded by our troops: dozens of guards awaiting our order to seize you. You cannot escape."

The knight sorcerer caressed his gauntlet with his other hand, as if the six metallic fingers were already grasping the two rebel lords. Eno Mowengot laughed loudly at Camatael.

"Tell me, my friend. Is it merely for love of this Dol Etrond maiden that you have disavowed your rightful sovereign? Is it possible for an Elf to throw away millennia of tradition for the intoxicating favours of a tempting prey?"

The dreaded Eno was staring at Camatael with flames in his eyes. He continued with a renewed fervour.

"We are the foremost servants of the king in Gwarystan. All kneel, seeking his guidance and protection. For the first time in history, Norelin has united Elves and Men under one kingdom... For more than a century, the Archipelago has seen peace and prosperity, thanks to the strength of the king's army holding all its factions together. With time, the memory of those wars and conflicts shall fade, and the bonds uniting High and Green Elves, Westerners and Barbarians, will strengthen... Look to history. Remember those warring domains ruled by the Elves at the time of King Lormelin. We were easy prey for the savage barbarian tribes, as they sailed southward to seek new lands. When their long ships landed on the Islands to take tribute from our tiny cities, the glorious noble houses of the High Elves also shuddered."

Eno Mowengot paused, looking for the effect that his more pragmatic argument was having on his future prisoners. Then, he went on, unable to resist the desire to mock the rebel lords before him.

"Camatael, I daresay the Ruby College taught you to count with an abacus. If King Norelin had not forged this alliance with the Westerners, the barbarian tribes would have become more numerous and more powerful. They would have ultimately conquered every single island. King Norelin has reversed the tide of history. The years of chaos and destruction on the Lost Islands have been ended."

Camatael was not impressed by this argument. Ignoring Curubor's utter passivity, he fought back.

"A ruler who does not acknowledge his subjects is a wicked sovereign. Norelin ignores his kingdom's population; he is perverse. He has renounced the legacy of his house. Remember how his forefather King Ilorm walked with the Gods, and how he thereby acquired a profound knowledge of all creatures' relative merits. He could speak the least of languages, of birds and of hounds, but also the most complex tongues of the Elves. Where has that wisdom disappeared to now?" Camatael appealed.

Turang Mowengot that cold Westerner with the gaze of a murderer, suddenly understood the purpose of this unnecessary debate. Camatael Dol Lewin was stalling.

Deep in thought, losing the thread of the ongoing conversation, his gaze concentrated on Curubor. Unconsciously, his metal gauntlet reached for the pommel of his sword. Meanwhile, Eno Mowengot, as sure of himself as ever, was embarking on a long tirade, with all his arrogant spite.

"In an effort to preserve its safety, Llymar chooses insularity and therefore paralysis. The kingdom of Gwarystan is doing the opposite. Its ships travel the oceans and establish trade agreements fare and wide. King Norelin shall defeat adversity by claiming all routes across the seas. His ultimate prize will be to link all cities to each other and rule the unified world he shall create," he explained, before launching a final, decisive charge. "Who is your hero? Your Protector of the Forest with his long spear... a mere hunter, a lowly warden charged with defending the boundaries of your woods. Our new allies are honoured with the title of sea hierarch. They command great galleys and travel the vast seas."

Suddenly, Turang Mowengot realized what Curubor had been doing. A small but powerful illusion had been masking the movement of the ancient mage's lips. The Westerner reached for his leader's arm. But Eno Mowengot paid no heed to his companion's warning. He could not resist one final humiliation of Camatael.

"A scribe such as you, Camatael, should stick to writing manuscripts and avoid attempting discourses. You think you are making history simply because you are drawing fine lines of ink on rich parchment... Let me tell you, scholar, it takes far more than that to be a ruler. The knights of the Golden Hand are lords who serve the rightful king. We help him bear the burden of his responsibilities. We truly are the fingers who hold the sceptre."

"I can read your face like an open book," Camatael spat back. "When I look at you, Eno Dol Oalin, I see what I could have become; it makes me nauseous."

Turang Mowengot then saw that Curubor had been patiently uttering long, inaudible incantations, though his lips and body seemed immobile to his inattentive guests. Suddenly, the knight sorcerer stood up.

At the same time, Camatael violently leapt up from his chair, a flash of anger on his face. He struck his hands out towards Megiöl Mowengot and delivered a formidable blast of energy. His nails seemed to multiply and extend outwards towards the Half-Elf's head. In the blink of an eye, the knight sorcerer was flung against the back wall, out of his companions' reach.

Waiting for this moment since their guests walked in, Curubor sprang from his chair, uttering a sudden roar. The formidable energy he unleashed as he stood brought the heavy table flying towards the other two knight sorcerers with force. It came crashing against them just as Turang Mowengot was about to throw a dagger, and just as Eno Mowengot was summoning unnatural fire.

Curubor was standing at his full height in the middle of the room like a God of War seizing the battlefield. From his own hands he sent forth a powerful field of energy, which began forming a wall of unnatural power. Four runes, the colour of gemstones, which had been carved into the corners where the walls met the ceiling and floor, now glowed brightly, strong as the four corners of a dam that holds back a strong river.

Now blocked by the impassable barrier and separated from

their companion, the two Golden Hand knights called upon their powers to break it up. Yet, their joint efforts proved unsuccessful. Meanwhile, beyond the translucid wall of energy, in a concert of horrible cries and terrifying shouts, Camatael's spirit claws were penetrating the mind of Megiöl Mowengot, searching his memory and seeking out his secrets. The Half-Elf lay on the ground, his free hand pulling out his hair, his body convulsing violently and his strength disappearing.

"Quen Asta! Quen Asta!" Camatael repeated like one possessed.

Suddenly, the roof broke in above the young Dol Lewin; cracked tiles and broken timber came crashing down onto the floor. Another knight of the Golden Hand leapt down in the room. This new Westerner, short and agile, landed on the soil floor like a cat. He swung his gauntlet at Camatael who stepped back in panic. This surprise attack freed the spiritual hold Camatael had imposed over Megiöl Mowengot. Almost dying and barely able to move, the Half-Elf reached for a dark dagger hidden inside his cloak. Without hesitation, he gripped the deadly instrument and pierced his own heart. The effect was instantaneous. His body burst into a cloud of vapours, the colour of blood. The nauseous cloud escaped upwards through the large hole in the roof. Only his headdress, clothes and weapons remained on the empty soil. His gauntlet, however, had disappeared.

Seeing that their companion had escaped, Eno and Turang abandoned the battlefield and escaped by the front door, barking orders at their troops. The final knight sorcerer hoisted his muscular body up onto the roof as quickly as he had jumped down from it. The backroom was soon empty. Camatael turned to Curubor.

"Quick, to the trapdoor. They will burn this building to the ground."

In an instant, the dusty carpet was taken away and the floor tiles removed. Underneath was a large opening, leading down into utter darkness. The two Elves swung down into it, becoming engulfed in the shadows, climbing down a ladder for more than several dozen feet. Finally, they reached a level tunnel, and stepped away from the ladder for cover. The air was humid and stale. Camatael turned to run, eager to minimize any chance that their enemies might catch them.

"Wait!" ordered Curubor, as he listened to the sound of a formidable wreckage echoing down to them.

"They did it. They've destroyed the shop," Camatael ascertained.

There was a moment of silence between them, as they watched fiery debris tumble down into the tunnel.

"I suppose that solves the issue of being followed. Now, I believe we have a map to look at, if we wish to honour our arrangement to taste wine with our special guest," stated Camatael. He was already on his way.

CHAPTER 4: Saeröl

2712, Season of Eïwele Llya, 96th day, Tar-Andevar, Nyn Ernaly

The vast wine cellar, animated in the dull radiance of sparse, flickering candlelight, had something of a mystic atmosphere. Stacked about the cave walls were innumerable bottles, carboys, amphorae and barrels. Temperature and humidity were carefully maintained, and the darkness provided protection against harmful external influences. A dozen alleys, each with towering bottle racks on either side, radiated out from a large central room.

An Elf was standing within this room at the centre of the wine cellar. He wore a black tunic and a broad, dark cloak. A silk scarf, the colour of leaves, was wrapped around his head, out from which flowed his long black hair. His face was fair: almost as white as snow like that of a Night Elf. His right cheek was marked with the infamous rune of outcasts. A contemptuous smile crept across his face as he started to sing the melancholic verses of an ancient song. His voice was melodious, almost musical. The Night Elf headed towards a large cabinet and selected seven crystal glasses. He arranged them in a perfect line upon a long table. Still alone, he continued to chatter away.

"Why, after all these centuries, is the tasting of wine the only thing that soothes my soul? I wonder. All that makes up this elixir is a few grapes, mixed with various flowers and herbs, before it is left to ferment and age in oak barrels. Well tonight, I propose a blind test. I will be dead soon enough, so now is the time to confirm whether or not these wines of the Nargrond Valley are still up to scratch. Let's free these precious nectars, allow them to breathe, so that they might reach their full potential!" the Night Elf exclaimed.

With a wide movement of his arms, as if he were passionately conducting an orchestra, he sung out, his pristine voice soon climbing to unnatural heights that only accomplished bards can reach. The notes built in intensity until all bottlenecks exploded under the pressure, sending their waxen corks shooting all the way up to the ceiling. Satisfied after this demonstration of his powers, the extraordinary singer carried out the same careful ritual: first, he would pour the wine into a crystal glass, examined at length its colour, tannins and its consistency. Next, he would breathe in the complex aromas released by the exquisite drink, which he did with his eyes closed in order to sharpen his sense of smell. Finally, he would take a sip of the liquid, swilling it about his mouth for some time, all the while sniffing and emitting odd noises, until he had fully analysed the wine's contents and structure, and understood how its taste evolved over time once taken in.

This ceremony lasted over two hours. As he methodically carried out his exploration, the wine-lover set down many notes on an old scroll with his quill pen and ink, until all seven phials were empty.

"That was quite an experience," he concluded, a feeling of exhilaration overcoming him as he abandoned himself to the inebriating mists. "There is no better way to reach the soul's depths, though I doubt you would agree with me," he added, as he seized his bastard sword, which had so far remained hidden beneath a green blanket on the table.

The Night Elf looked at the dark weapon, delicately caressing its amethyst-encrusted pommel as though it were the gentle skin of a lover. This sword, its blade four feet long, was a powerful weapon designed to be held with both hands at the hilt. It could only be wielded with a particular technique. Its aggressive design had been optimized for thrusting and cutting. The powerful, enchanted black blade gleamed like an agent of pure chaos, a servant of the shadows that could summon the darkest of forces. Its edge looked capable of slicing through any material that was unprotected by potent sorcery. The Night Elf addressed the sharp blade as though some spirit inhabited it.

"I tell you, Moramsing, this 'O Wiony' is definitely the finest. I am not coming to this verdict out of pride, or because I spent my youth walking among those vines. I can feel that you disagree, that you deem me biased. This I freely admit; after all, I have harvested these grapes by hand, at night when the moon was full, as dictated by tradition. I replanted those vines when they reached seventy years of age. With my bare hands, I have ploughed the sandy soil of my family estate… You have now fed upon my soul for so long; you should know that I am able to form a fair opinion on wines! 'O Wiony' is extraordinarily rich with the characteristics of exotic plants, truffles, spices and black fruits."

Looking aggressively at the dark blade with an evil look in his eye, the Night Elf began to raise his voice, becoming increasingly absorbed in the debate.

"You disagree! I can feel that you do not trust my judgement! Well, why would you? Your appetite for controlling me is second only to my own thirst for Elvin wine. Your cursed nature has stolen my life force, sapped every ounce of hope, and made my life into an endless, agonizing journey, with only guilt and self-loathing for companions. Savouring wine is the only pleasure you have not destroyed. Why is that?"

Despite the intense scrutiny it was under, the dark sword remained silent, impassive as the metal it was made of. After a long, tense silence, a strange noise emanated from the depths of one of the cave's alleys, like a cat mewing for a mate. The Night Elf stood, readying his dark, bastard sword. In an instant, the dizziness obscuring his mind had disappeared. Soon, the shadowy silhouette of a black cat emerged from the alley. It rushed to the Night Elf's feet, wildly meowing all the while. As it ran, it felt as if the souls of thousands of flies and spiders were buzzing and creeping all about the cave.

"So, they have finally come," the Night Elf concluded, as the shadowy form of the black cat was absorbed by the dark blade, like a soul returning to its grave.

The Night Elf concealed his bastard sword in its woollen blanket, and then carefully chose his position, selecting a comfortable armchair and settling down with a final glass of 'O Wiony' in his hand. The scene was now set; his expected guests could arrive.

*

A few moments later, the sound of footsteps on the dry floor echoed around the darkness of the cellar. Two High Elves were silhouetted against the weak light of the candles beyond. The young lord Dol Lewin and his mentor, Curubor Dol Etrond, emerged from an alley. They seemed calm as they selected their own seats and sat around the main table. The newcomers behaved as if they had left their interlocutor only a moment before. After some customary words of welcome, Camatael spoke.

"I chose this place for our meeting, Master Saeröl; for I knew that it would meet your high expectations."
"It has exceeded them, Lord Dol Lewin," replied the Night Elf. "I have begun to explore this magnificent cellar; the wines I have found were beyond my imagination. I know of many hidden treasures across the Lost Islands, but I never could have guessed that such a bounty existed so deep underground."
"This cellar is indeed remarkable. Lord Dol Braglin was a wise Elf, well versed in the knowledge of wines and liquors. Some accumulate fine weapons, others amass precious jewels, but Lord Braglin collected rare vintages, of every variety and

from all parts of the Lost Islands. He must have known that this remote place would be ideal for preserving such marvels."

"A stable temperature and appropriate humidity are what's required to preserve the finest vintages," added Saeröl. "However, it's the power of the alchemist's rune that eventually makes all the difference. The wine remains its own master; only it can decide whether to live through the centuries or return to nothingness."

"Lord Dol Braglin was a fine Elf; it seems he has left Camatael precious legacies," said Curubor as he looked around at the cellar, visibly impressed by his young companion's inheritance.

Camatael smiled. "These wines will remain here for the sole enjoyment of those who know of its location. Not a single flask can be removed from this hidden place. The contents could not withstand it."

Saeröl understood that Camatael was sharing his precious secret to help the negotiations that would soon be discussed in this very place. The move was either deeply generous, extremely foolish or, perhaps, highly astute. His own reaction to their offer would decide which. Saeröl emphatically expressed his satisfaction.

"You honour me greatly, Lord Camatael, by granting me access to this shrine and all its treasures."

Visibly enjoying the exchange, Camatael simply nodded politely. He was now curious as to what would happen next.

"Might I suggest," he proposed with some enthusiasm, "that we taste some wine to mark the occasion?"

Slowly, enjoying every part of the ceremony, Camatael drifted towards a remote part of the cellar. He was totally absorbed in his task, as if he were worshipping of Eïwal Lon in the temple of light. Camatael delicately withdrew an old bottle from a dusty hidden corner. He examined the rune impressed upon the cork before announcing, with an unembellished tone.

"An 'O Mento' vintage, marked 'Rowë Dol Nargrond, Year 492 of the Second Age.' What would you say to that?"

"That bottle is over seventeen centuries old! Will it have survived unspoiled from those heroic times?" exclaimed Curubor.

"Let us see whether it is worthy of its reputation. The cork bears the rune of Rowë Dol Nargrond, which should be guarantee enough," replied Camatael, becoming excited.

Saeröl, however, was keeping his distance from the other two Elves. He softly caressed the blanket that covered his sword, deep in thought.

"You've selected that year for a reason, haven't you?" he eventually asked.

There was a silence.

"The year 492," Saeröl continued, "is the last harvest that Rowë could have possibly enjoyed. By the end of that sad year, he had disappeared into the entrails of the Oryusk mines, along with his friend Lon and three other companions... only to reappear before the eyes of the Elves a few days later... However, the lord of House Dol Nargrond was not the same. His head, his arms and his legs had all been cut from his body. Those dark remains, soiled by shadowy marks, had been placed within his large shield, which then floated along the river from the mines of the Volcano and into a swamp, close to the lake of Yslla."

Camatael, unmoved by the horrible description of Rowë's tragic end, replied.

"You are right, Master Saeröl; what we shall taste today is, in all likelihood, one of the last bottles that Rowë ever marked with his rune: a legendary 'O Mento' vintage. Is this not an appropriate homage we could offer to his glorious memory, before embarking on such a dangerous quest?"

Camatael, impassive, continued with his preparations. From an old iron chest, which he unlocked with a small key, he extracted a jug and several glasses of crystal. The carafe's delicate curves, combined with the exquisite precision of the glass, added a considerable elegance to the scene. Meanwhile, Saeröl shared his remembrances, his gaze lost in the shadows.

"Indeed, it is. You should have seen the Nargrond Valley in the last days of the year 492. As for me, I witnessed every moment of the spectacle. I watched the units of the clan Myortilys marching to war for the first time since the battle of Ruby and Buzzards. You should have seen with your own eyes the constant comings and goings of that multitude of Dark Elves, driven on by a common thirst to exact vengeance. Once Rowë and his disciples had been murdered, once Lon's preaching on the Lost Islands had ceased, the clan Myortilys were instigating the war of shadows."

"Your father, Elriöl, was among those assassinated with Rowë," Curubor recalled, carefully but deliberately.

"Indeed, he was. Strangely enough, his mutilated remains were found inside his shield on the banks of the river near our own vineyard, 'O Wiony'. My father considered himself the Nargrond Valley's greatest alchemist, and Rowë's foremost companion. He devoted his life to the realization of their great design. That unshakable loyalty led him to his doom."

"Elriöl was a great visionary who left us the mightiest of legacies. I knew him well," Curubor declared, wishing to pay tribute to the legendary bladesmith.

Saeröl was apparently indifferent to the homage. Finally, in the profound silence that followed Curubor's words, Camatael decided to open the bottle. The young lord, conscious of the importance of that moment, brought the bottle close to his nose. When he spoke, his deep voice was without emotion.

"The wine is… unspoiled."

He then set about pouring the wine from the ancient bottle into the carafe.

"Pay close attention," he suggested as it flowed, "the nectar is releasing some of its aromas already. See how its colour is dark ruby, for now."
"Indeed, the surface of the wine is almost pitch black, as though some wickedness dwelled within it," added Curubor.

Camatael picked one of the large glasses of crystal, so refined that it seemed carved out of ice. He heated it above the flame of a candle. Once this delicate task was complete, he slowly poured the wine from the carafe. It was a solemn moment, and all of them, as if by tacit agreement, stopped breathing. The red liquid, as deep as a dark ruby, trickled into the glass. A magnificent mixture of complex aromas diffused about the three Elves.

"Without even moving the glass, you can already pick up those fleeting, highly volatile elements. See how its colour is turning to a magenta with purple hues," commented Camatael.
Looking at the precious liquid with fascination, Curubor noted, "This is extraordinary. It would seem, from its colour and texture that the wine has lost none of its quality or complexity."
"I shall serve the two other glasses," declared Camatael, seizing the crystal carafe, "with the very same method used by the alchemists in Yslla to get the most from their fairy wines."

With a gesture of his right hand and some quick incantations, Camatael performed a spectacular decantation of the precious beverage. Two thin trickles of the wine flew up into the air from the carafe, like dancing threads of red silk. With incredible dexterity, moving the two crystal glasses with his free hand, he managed to fill them with the precious liquid without wasting a single drop.

"This exercise is extremely difficult, and not without risk," Camatael confessed, "but, according to the alchemist masters of the Nargrond Valley, this is the best way to release all the aromas of the finest vintages. Let us put their theory to the test."

Saeröl, having accepted his glass, moved it far away from the candles, holding it out towards the darkest side of the cellar. He contemplated it for a long time, as if inspecting a precious gemstone. Finally, he expressed his excitement.

"Magnificent!" he began, unusually loquacious in front of company. "The shadow of the reddish-purple mixes is like a perfect dark garnet. Did you know that some of the best vintages from the Nargrond Valley have the power to recount legends? Indeed, it is said that the alchemists of the legendary guild of Yslla used this very method to communicate their final testaments to their families. Imagine the close family members of the deceased sharing the same vintage, all understanding at once what was his will."

Saeröl could not resist any longer. He wetted his lips and took a tiny sip from his glass. The Night Elf was silent for some time.

"It's as if I'm entering a secret vale, surrounded by luscious plants... the multitude of sensations is like nothing I've ever felt."

Saeröl was much older than what his delicate, refined appearance implied. Such was the reputation of his bloodline; time had little influence on the Night Elves. He was born in the city of Yslla, in the Nargrond Valley at the apogee of Rowë's rule. Each gulp of the 'O Mento' transported Saeröl back to his youth, to that land of subtle remembrances where smells, colours and feelings comingle in poetic assembly. The wine's effects started to take their own bewitching course.

"This is a most inspiring experience," he declared. "This moment deserves music. I feel like hearing a moving symphony, with dozens of powerful woodwind instruments. Some wines engender decadent sensuality; others give you a taste for blood, while others still inspire perverted desires. This vintage is unique. It's telling me of the end... the magnificent end of all things."

"As if Rowë knew that his own end was coming..." agreed Curubor.

"What I'm feeling goes far beyond Rowë's destiny. I feel something much wider, deeper, some phenomenon of incredible magnitude; it is far away, yet somehow inevitable, like a great wave rising in the distance, drawing its power from the void. And still it grows, like the just ire of an almighty creator..."

Overwhelmed by the powerful sensations that the wine was provoking in him, Saeröl resolved to seek refuge in his art, the only shelter that could protect him from his extreme anxiety. He seized his flute. The five-holed wind instrument had a v-shaped mouthpiece and was carved from the bone of a vulture wing. Saeröl took a deep breath, brought the flute to his mouth, and began nimbly stopping and releasing the holes, creating rare harmonies with a distinct, bright timbre. He improvised a new piece of music, at once grandiose and terrifying.

Over a long few minutes, he played a powerful lament, which was both intoxicatingly beautiful of unimaginably sad. He then lowered the flute and sang improvised verses of his own dark poetry. Finally, Saeröl declaimed a prophetic tale, whose grandeur amazed his small audience.

"This, I know: the harpists, the violinists, the flautists, the pipers, the organists and the countless choirs of Elves shall come together. They shall attempt to create the most beautiful piece of music ever known; they shall send forth beautiful melodies, which will mingle and dissolve amid the thunder of their harmonies, till the Lost Islands will be filled with music, the echo of that music, and the echoes of its echo. But it shall be to no avail; the roar of the vast seas will not be halted, and the great wave will swamp them all, until the lowest of valleys and the highest of peaks are submerged."

The prophecy's glorious beginning and the tragedy of its end caused both High Elf lords to shiver before Saeröl. When at last he had finished, a profound malaise reigned in the shadowy room. Curubor was speechless. Camatael was silent but, after a while, he could not resist countering the dismal prediction.

"The words of your song are dreadful, though undeniably poetic. You craft verses with the bitterness of one who sees only darkness in the world."
"I am what I am," Saeröl spat back. "Revenge is my sole comfort. The sorrow of my enemies is my only joy, for it feeds my pride."

It felt as if there was no more to say after this violent exchange. Each Elf turned his attention to the contents of his glass... At last the heavy silence was abruptly ended by a dry interruption from Saeröl.

"Lord Curubor, I think that the time has now come for you to explain why you have sent for me?"
"Indeed, it has..." replied the Blue Mage, feeling suddenly under pressure. "First, I must thank you for your patience, and for ensuring through your connections that we reached Tar-Andevar's harbour safely. It was an important first step, and we are now your debtors."

Curubor made a pause as if every word would count.

"The second part of this plan was our responsibility, and I can inform you that it was executed successfully. Lord Dol Lewin and I now have no doubt in our minds that our worst fears were justified... The knights of the Golden Hand have set their sights on the testament of Rowë. Norelin has sent them forth to find the tombs of the four bladesmiths of Nargrond Valley. By way of this supreme blasphemy, the king of Gwarystan intends to deliver a message to the Arkys in the Secret Vale. There is no force powerful enough to resist the king and his Western allies. By seeking to desecrate the graves of the bladesmiths, Norelin is proclaiming the advent of his empire."

Visibly unimpressed by the Blue Mage's uplifting rhetoric, Saeröl replied.

"There are some rare occasions when flowery speeches are needed. I am not sure that this demands such grandiloquence. What do you know, exactly, of the knights of the Golden Hand's plans?"

Camatael stepped in, eager to prove himself.

"We've learnt a great deal in Tar-Andevar; it was a risk worth taking. The clan Ernaly are trying to move the tombs to safety; the Golden Hand knights know of their every move. We have learnt that they are already preparing a trap at the Ningy Pool, which the expedition will have to cross."

"It will not be easy," added Curubor, "to leave the wood of Silver Leaves with such a cumbersome load. Mynar dyl and his troops will have to face the wrath of the Hageyu Falls. The river will inevitably lead them to the Ningy Pool, where the final cascade falls into the Sian Ningy River. It's a wild place, where progress is difficult; any expedition party would get entangled, making it the perfect location for an ambush."

"Who will strike, when, and using what force?" Saeröl inquired impassively.

A long silence followed.

"We were interrupted. We do not know," Camatael finally admitted.

Saeröl laughed. "You do not know... so you are relying on me to find out... It is more than likely that we will never know the truth. It would be a most perilous task to meddle in the affairs of the king's dreaded servants..."

The two lords decided to remain silent. Seeing a weakness in their campaign, Saeröl pressed on.

"One thing I would like to understand is the part you're both playing in all this turmoil. Why, for instance, are you not rushing to alert your friends, the Green Elves of the ancient clans, to tell them of the impending ambush? Would not that be the honest thing to do, and in the best interest of those who are, after all, honoured members of the council of the forest?

This question demanded a certain ability to be creative with the truth. It was therefore Curubor who chose to answer. The Blue Mage spoke with confidence.

"Master Saeröl, your question is legitimate. The truth is that we have not, so far, been directly involved in this expedition. We understand that Matriarch Lyrine organized it in response to a call for help from the Arkys. For her own reasons, she has decided not to involve us. She set up everything in secret with the clan warlords: Tyar dyl, Gal dyl and Mynar dyl. We are not meant to know of their mission, still less interfere."

"Ah, I see!" replied Saeröl, smiling.

The master of the guild of Sana was starting to enjoy these negotiations. He decided to take Curubor's reasoning through its logical next steps.

"You are not meant to know about it, yet now you do. You

have therefore decided to act, but not, dare I suggest, for the sake of a few units of scouts, and neither to prevent the king from getting hold of the precious will. By proceeding in this underhand way... you must want it for yourself. You want Rowë's testament, and I would like to know why. Why is it so important to you, my lord Curubor?"

"How dare you?" interrupted Camatael. "How dare you offend us with such accusations?"

Saeröl now openly showed his disdain. Hatred could be seen in his eyes, as he stood up and reached for the blanket that lay across the table. Curubor made his calm voice heard.

"Peace, my lords! Peace between us! We are not here to fight. The stakes are too high."

He turned to Saeröl and regained his usual professorial tone.

"The testament of Rowë is of considerable importance, Saeröl, as you well know. It is our most important inheritance. We believe it contains divine secrets that were unveiled to Rowë before his death. We believe that the last lord of Nargrond Valley was shown the final challenge that the Gods will impose upon Elvin kind. He then bequeathed that secret in his will. His followers insisted it must not be unveiled until the right time comes."

"As Rowë himself demanded," added Camatael, with utter conviction.

"And why would that be?" inquired Saeröl ironically, his lack of concern apparent.

"We know that Rowë," explained Camatael with fervour, "deliberated carefully on the prophecy that Eïwal Lon had revealed to him. For a long time, he hesitated to share what he had learnt with anyone else, worried about its implications."

This was no longer a lord of House Dol Lewin talking, but rather a high priest of Eïwal Lon. Carried by a sudden rush of enthusiasm, the cleric of the temple of light continued.

"I believe the Demigod's words of wisdom influenced Lord Dol Nargrond as he set down his final testament."

Saeröl smiled sardonically.

"It's as if I'm back at the temple of light in Yslla, listening to one of the clerics who took it upon themselves to educate me, though you yourself have more of a naïve charm... What do you expect you can teach me of Lon, or of the lord of House Dol Nargrond? You must know that my father Elrïol, the first master of the guild of Sana, was one of Rowë's closest companions. You must know that I was raised in the very place you speak of; the Nargrond Valley. Perhaps you are unaware that I performed my first concerts in front of Rowë and his household. Lon the Wise, as we called him at the time, would often congratulate me himself for my virtuosity with the flute."

Curubor, who had also attended some of Saeröl's extraordinary concerts over nineteen centuries ago, acknowledged, with a most flattering air.

"With your art, you illuminated that golden era, when Elves of all origins came together in the Nargrond Valley to pursue dreams of shared knowledge. Free from royal rule, Rowë Dol Nargrond was true master of his fief, where he built a realm for the free among those of us who truly sought the Lost Islands that were promised... I mean for all Elves, whatever their origin. I remember his words: 'The Lost Islands were promised to Llyoriane and to her seeds.' We are all Llyoriane's seeds, for our lives are devoted to realizing the vision of those Deities who forged the Archipelago itself. Rowë was the first High Elf lord to understand this. And it was he who lay the foundations for the realm of Llyoriane's seeds in the Nargrond Valley. Never in the history of the Lost Islands had there been a place which embodied so perfectly this ideal. Do not doubt us, Master Saeröl!

Everyone knows the part you played in the glorious history of the Nargrond Valley; that is why we have come to you."

Saeröl ignored this compliment. It was apparent that he did not share the same noble values. Once again, he resorted to insults.

"How touching! I ought to have spent more time praying at the temple of light. There is little better than children's tales to soothe one's soul."

Curubor placed his hand on Camatael's arm to dissuade him from the temptation of another aggressive and fruitless debate. The Blue Mage suggested, with a polite tone.

"Perhaps you have developed a different theory?"
"Indeed, I have, although my own views are not hypothetical, but rather verified facts supported by evidence," Saeröl stated.

He then expressed his views with great conviction.

"Every Elf has a mother and a father. Nobody reaches this world out of thin air. In the particular case of Lon, I always considered his heritage as the mightiest ever known… I knew Lon's mother well, for it was in the city of Ystanargrond that she gave birth to her fabled son, losing her life as a consequence of her efforts. Meoryne was the noblest, sweetest lady imaginable, a model of wise conduct, true to the House Dol Valra's celebrated values…"

Saeröl paused for a while, as a skilled orator about to deliver the final blow.

"It was a God that seduced her in the end and not some common divinity either, for it was none other than the mightiest of them, Gweïwal Zenwon. Oh! How I would like to have seen him riding that fair virgin, savagely making love to her... I don't doubt he visited her bed many times before she gave him a son."

Camatael, utterly shocked, protested vehemently.

"This is heresy. You blaspheme. How dare you... you degrade everything you come near..."

Now smiling openly, demonstrating the intense pleasure he was now taking from their discussion, Saeröl continued with his argument.

"I said I could provide evidence for my beliefs, hateful as they may sound to your ears."

Saeröl looked with relish at his two interlocutors, already savouring the damage he would cause. Visibly satisfied with their lack of responsiveness, he resumed his inquiry.

"Do you really believe what you were taught at the temple of light? Do you really believe that Rowë, my father Elrïol, the two other bladesmiths, and Lon himself could have been ambushed by a clan Myortilys raid in the mines of Oryusk? That this formidable party could have been defeated?"

Faced with only the puzzled expressions of his tiny audience, Saeröl pressed on.

"Do you really believe that Rowë would have set down so precisely all of his final wishes the day before he was murdered? How could he have known of the danger he would face by visiting the mines of Oryusk, which were after all his own stronghold?"

Saeröl paused to enjoy the sight of his interlocutors. Doubt was creeping into their minds.

"On that very day, I received a letter from my father. I can still remember every word. Elrïol knew that he was not coming back. He had written to entrust me with the custodianship of the guild, he so cherished. Before that decisive moment, the old fool had not cared much for me. I suppose it was my own artistic nature that caused his disdain: such a far cry from the rigour of his alchemist's mind. It must have been a sacrifice for him to write this final message to his sole heir."

Camatael and Curubor held their breath; they knew the worst was to come.

"Lon, son of Gweïwal Zenwon; Lon, so called divinity of wisdom and light, sentenced to death his four companions... I believe Lon killed his companions according to the rites of old, cutting their heads and limbs from their bodies like the priests of his godly father did to those sentenced to death in the days of yore. That done, he let their remains float inside their shields down the stream of the Sian Dorg: as signs to be interpreted. Access to the Halls of the Dead had been denied to the victims..."

Saeröl let these words echo within his interlocutors before continuing.

"The wise among the Elves understood Lon's message. The corpses had been rejected by the river; it meant their souls would be trapped in their corpses until Gweïwal Agadeon, the Greater God of the Underworld, deemed their punishment sufficient. Hence, the remains of the four bladesmiths, who had forged the swords of Nargrond Valley, were buried inside tombs, a completely unprecedented act in the Archipelago's history... Elrian Dol Urmil, Odro dyl Myortilys, Elriöl Dir Sana and Rowë Dol Nargrond did pay for their crimes. They were executed for spurning their divine masters; those who had first offered them their mighty knowledge... Lon could disappear. His task was complete."

Saeröl was finished. He took his crystal glass and emptied it in a single gulp. Curubor was immobile, deep in thought. The vast cellar seemed darker; many of the candles seemed to have gone out. Camatael too was paralyzed, stunned by such an abject distortion of the truth, such a heretical attack against the cornerstone of the Islands Elves' faith. His mind started racing to construct opposing arguments. But his lips remained closed and his face turned pale.

"I see you cannot find a single fact to prove me wrong," rejoiced Saeröl, looking at the priest. "Everything you knew about Rowë and his companions' tragic ending, you learnt at the temple of light: from songs, tales and poems. How many times did you read the great story of the Myortilys raid, of that grim day when the assassins infiltrated the mines of Oryusk to seek murderous revenge for their lost lands? Dark Elves they were called thereafter, for they unleashed a mysterious force, and Oryusk has been shrouded in deadly shadow ever since."

Camatael felt like he was falling from a great height. His senses betrayed him, as a feeling of utter emptiness overwhelmed him.

"What if I am right?" insisted Saeröl with relish.

Camatael began to feel nauseous; the foundations of his faith were being shaken.

"What if all you learnt during your youth at the temple of light was a web of lies, spun to maintain the spiritual power of the Arkys over the credulous Elves of the Islands?

Curubor coughed, apparently unaware of Camatael's turmoil. The Blue Mage was calm and picked up the conversation as if Saeröl's extraordinary claims were a mere academic curiosity.

"And what of the blades of Nargrond Valley, Master Saeröl, how do they fit into your story?" asked the Blue Mage, his tone one of polite interest rather than outrage.

Satisfied with the effect his theory was provoking and seeing that doubt was creeping into his interlocutors' minds, Saeröl continued.

"My father taught me little about the blades of Nargrond Valley, though their grand designer had probably been him: Elriöl's reticence was indicative of the secrecy surrounding their forging and, no doubt, also indicative of his disdain for me. I am neither smith nor alchemist, but I know that Rowë gathered six different metals from various mines across the Islands. He took quantities of gold, silver, platinum, bronze, copper and lead, and mixed them with the meteorite's iron to produce an alloy which held all of its component properties, but also new ones. This new material had an unparalleled hardness and lightness; they say it cannot be destroyed."

Curubor remembered. "This was the time that the greatest deed in the Lost Islands' history took place. Rowë was now at the height of his powers, yet he was filled with a profound new concern. Some say that he was given warning: a dream telling him of a distant threat. He thought long about how he could preserve the beauty of the Lost Islands, how he could ensure this last Elvin haven would last forever."

Saeröl felt encouraged to say more.

"Rowë summoned my father Elriöl to his side, as he knew him to be the ablest alchemist of the Night Elves. The two great lore masters brought two other Elves, of different creeds, to join them in the city of Yslla: Elrian Dol Urmil, son of a shipwright descended from the Blue Elves; and Odro dyl Myortilys, the famed smith of the Green Elves... Together, the four bladesmiths gathered all their skills, and set out upon a rigorous, painstaking task. They made blades of unknown might, unlike anything that Elves had ever seen before: six swords made with the metal from the heart of the meteorite, which had struck Gwa Nyn long ago. They forged the swords of Nargrond Valley with powerful enchantments. Each bladesmith shared every ounce of his knowledge to create these masterpieces, and the blades were each given a name, for each was unique. Their lore is now long forgotten."

Curubor seemed disappointed.

"You provide us with many details about the genesis of the blades, yet you have somehow said very little. The swords of Nargrond Valley are at the heart of the most important myth in the history of the Islands' Elves. Their legend has passed down through the generations; they are the symbol of our independence."

"They were forged before the coming of Lon. This I know." Saeröl insisted.

He hesitated for a moment, but at last resumed.

"Lord Curubor, have you ever considered what makes Elvin kind so unique, what makes our essence so different from Men, Gnomes and other creatures? It is the extravagance we demonstrate in our creations. There are Elves who do not bow even before the Gods. Pride characterises our aspiration to rise up to the level of divinities, which we try to achieve by designing devices mighty enough to bring an end to the chaos of primitive forces. Elves have the potential to bring eternal harmony to this world that was born from the sick imagination of the Gods. This is a supreme offense in the divine powers' eyes. Whatever were the original intentions of the four bladesmiths, forging the swords of Nargrond Valley was another insult to the Gods, another crime which deserved harsh punishment."

Curubor seemed curious. He encouraged Saeröl to say more.

"So, you believe that Eïwal Lon's coming to the Lost Islands was the consequence of the forging of the blades of Nargrond Valley."

There was a silence, but visibly excited, Saeröl expressed further his thoughts.

"It is no coincidence that Lon was born in the Nargrond Valley. The son of Gweïwal Zenwon had one true purpose: to ensure that the lords of the Elves, despite their considerable bodies of lore, do not raise themselves to the status of Deities, that they do not put an end to the cosmic disorder as defined by the divine assembly. I believe that in the eyes of the Gods, Rowë was behaving like a thief. In the early days of his long life, he benefited from their knowledge, living by their side and contributing to their creations. There he learnt to manipulate divine fire, wield the magic Flow and harness the power of gemstones. Rowë then fled along with the High Elves, betraying the oath he had sworn to the Gods…"

For a moment Saeröl's gaze seemed lost, as if contemplating the consequence of such a betrayal. But at last, he resumed his explanation.

"Rowë allowed his pride to pervert his mind, and set about creating those powerful weapons, whose blades could pierce the Gods' armour, thus endowing the Elves of the Lost Islands with near-divine powers. With these new weapons, Rowë shored up the newfound independence of the Elves, thus leading them another step away from the Gods' grasp. Unlike all other species, who obey divine law and limit the purpose of their existence to the role they were entrusted with, Rowë strived to liberate his kin, offering them the freedom to forge their own destinies. The truth is that the Elves living under the protection of the swords of Nargrond Valley threatened the eternal tyranny that the Gods wished to impose on us. This is why Gweïwal Zenwon condemned Rowë and his companions."

These last words sounded like a conclusion, but Saeröl was not quite finished.

"But Gweïwal Zenwon also set up a cruel punishment for the Elves of the Islands so that, once and for all, they would renounce pride. I believe in his mind, their crimes deserved twice the divine retribution: first, executing the offenders and, second, defiling their creations. I believe his son, Lon, cursed the swords of Nargrond Valley with malicious enchantments. I believe the legendary blades will cause the utter destruction of the last realm of the Elves."

Once again, though taken aback by this apocalyptical vision, Curubor managed to remain calm.

"I thank you for sharing your beliefs. Nevertheless, we must be cautious. Most things that are still to come cannot be foretold. Events do not spring so directly from the past. One must always maintain a certain distance when it comes to these visions, though we should undoubtedly pay them heed," Curubor argued enigmatically, careful not to offend their guest.

Camatael had finally regained his self-control, having used Curubor's digression to return to his senses. The young high priest realized that he had almost succumbed to the words of the doom-monger. Camatael now understood that Saeröl was a master of deceit, like one possessed by a demon of the dark. He was a powerful bard whose curses could cause an Elf to renounce his ideals, fall into despair and abandon all strength. Camatael suddenly stood up. A bright light illuminated his face, as if he were attempting to push back the growing shadows that were continually invading the cellar. When he spoke, his voice sounded loud and clear.

"I remember the last prophecy of Eïwal Lon, when he told his followers that a day would come when the threat will be so great that all will look to the wielders of the swords of Nargrond

Valley. If the blades can unite, then the Elves will survive."

Saeröl sniggered, unaffected by the genuine faith in Camatael's plea. Nevertheless, Curubor spoke up after his companion's intervention to further their case.

"Camatael is right. Our strength lies in our faith. We must take courage in the belief, which has been passed down through the generations, that the Lost Islands are our promised realm. The Elves have survived many disasters to conquer it… The Green Elves risked their lives to cross the Austral Ocean aboard their small ships. For centuries, the Blue Elves attempted to circumnavigate the Sea of Cyclones. Lastly, the High Elves incurred the curse of the Gods, to fight for their freedom and make the Archipelago their home… These Islands were conquered only after many noble feats. It's now up to us to keep them safe… Today, the legacy of our glorious elders is being threatened. Our worst enemy, that king who is destroying all we have ever built and letting himself fall into the hands of Men, now intends to defile the tombs of the four bladesmiths, our heroes. He wants to seize our scriptures, the foundations of our common heritage… I will not let that happen. Lord Dol Lewin will not let that happen either… I am imploring you, Saeröl, the legendary bard whose passion for music brought all who witnessed his art to tears. I am imploring the son of the bladesmith Elriöl. The Elves of the Lost Islands need you. The powers you wield are unique…"

Curubor rose from his seat, so as to make his plea even more poignant.

"The clan Ernaly's expedition is doomed to failure. The knights of the Golden Hand will close their deadly trap within the wood of Silver Leaves. They command dozens of units of Men. They will seize the tombs and take the testament… Only you can escape their grasp. Only you can save the will of Rowë. You know what I speak is true."

Saeröl looked at Curubor, wondering if the ancient mage had lost his mind. He answered quickly and said more than he had intended for, once again, a surge of pride had lessened his cunning.

"A master of the guild of Sana does not utter empty words. What he says he will do, he does… However, he never takes unnecessary risks and always demands a reward. What makes you think you can convince me to undertake such a dangerous endeavour?"

Curubor nodded. He could not help but feel pleased at the finesse of his last push, which had set the dangerous Night Elf upon a slight headwind towards the intended goal. Curubor did not remove his eyes from Saeröl's, trying to overpower him with his piercing gaze. The candlelight danced upon his glowing skin. In that moment, the strength and resolution emanating from the Blue Mage was overwhelming.

"I know you, Master Saeröl, more profoundly than you might expect. I have eagerly read all your poems; I have passionately listened to all of your songs. How could I forget a single one of them? I think I even understand a little of your process: how that lightning-flash of inspiration then gives way to inwardness as you compose the subtle movements of your art. The result is magnificent; your audience feels as if they are hurtling through the impossible logic of a night dream… You, Master Saeröl, were an exceptional phenomenon, unique in the history of music. The great artist I know you to be cannot have lost his soul entirely. You will help us in this task because you must."

After a while, Saeröl smiled.

"Is this all you have in your arsenal? Do you think I will partake in such folly, merely for the sake of protecting my father's tomb? In truth, I could not care less for what happens to his remains. My concern is no greater than the love he had for me."

"If that is so," Curubor replied, "I feel sad for you."

"Feel as sad as you wish; it will not change my mind," Saeröl aggressively concluded. Somewhat disappointed, almost ready to take his leave, he added, "Was this all you had to offer?"

A silence followed. Saeröl then moved to rise from his seat when he was suddenly interrupted.

"I will bring you a gift," declared Curubor finally.

"Ha!" laughed Saeröl. "You will bring me a gift? I wonder what present could be generous enough to justify this favour you are asking of me."

"A most unexpected one, I daresay... and probably the greatest gift that the guild of Sana's master, the last of his lineage, could possibly desire," declared Curubor enigmatically.

"Then you must mean the head of King Norelin on a plate... Is that a gift you can offer? Are you suggesting that you could put an end to that traitor's reign, he who brought about the ruin of my guild, who condemned me to an ignominious death, who watched with relish as my lifeless corpse fell from the top of Gwarystan Rock?"

"That is not within my power," admitted Curubor.

"I am not surprised. You also have your limits..." Saeröl said, a sardonic smile creeping across his face. "But, as it turns out, I have already arranged the king of Gwarystan's journey from life into death," he declared, a mad look in his eye.

Both Curubor and Camatael were startled at such an unexpected claim. They could not avoid catching each other's eye to confirm what they had heard. But, like artist under curse, Saeröl spoke on, as though he were alone.

"Great calamities are often brought about by the smallest of causes. Move a grain of sand to just the wrong place, and an ancient dune collapses."

Looking very pleased with himself, Saeröl added.

"I happened to shift that grain of sand to just the wrong place... in fact, to the worst place possible. The end of King Norelin will be the most spectacular conclusion of any reign in history. In ten thousand years, Elves and Men will still allude to that grim day. After it comes, none will dare to wander into Gwarystan again."

Camatael shivered, unable to hide his malaise. He had difficulty coming to his senses. Almost paralyzed, he turned to Curubor, desperate for his mentor to intervene. To his surprise, however, the Blue Mage chose to ignore Saeröl's extraordinary threat, as if they were the words of a harmless lunatic.

"I have offered you a precious gift, and I meant it," Curubor's voice was as calm as a mountain lake; his words were nothing more than the clear expression of a truth.

Saeröl stopped swirling his wine glass. The droplets that had been circling up towards the rim now dropped back down to the bottom... For a long time, Saeröl fixed his gaze upon Curubor without saying a word. An unbearable tension reigned. Finally, the Night Elf broke the spell. His habitual arrogant and uninterested composure had radically changed. He sat forward on his seat.

"How can this be true?" he muttered, now fully convinced that Curubor possessed what he claimed.
"I never pose such questions," responded the ancient mage simply. "Might we say that we have an agreement, Master Saeröl?" Curubor asked.
"In the end," the Night Elf concluded thoughtfully, "there remains only one thing, just one: the legacy one passes on to his bloodline. Lord Dol Lewin, Lord Dol Etrond, you can indeed say

that we have reached an agreement. The guild of Sana thanks you for your trust."

Curubor stood up. "You are to watch the progress of the sacred tombs' repatriation once the expedition has crossed the Ningy Pool," he ordered. "If, as we fear, the clan Ernaly's units are ambushed by the knights of the Golden Hand and are defeated, you are to seize the testament of Rowë and bring it to me, unspoiled."

"Such is my errand, and I accept it willingly in exchange for the prize you have promised," confirmed Saeröl.

Curubor drew from his pocket two small copper rings, encrusted with jewels.

"This first enchanted ring will lead you to the secret place in Nyn Ernaly where Lord Dol Lewin and I will be waiting for you. This second ring will direct you to the place where you will receive your just reward. You are not mistaken concerning what it is... though it will take some time for me to complete my side of the bargain. Rest assured, however, that you have my word."

"I never doubted you, my lord Curubor, and I can prove very patient," Saeröl concluded.

He approached the Blue Mage and looked at the two precious objects for a long time before taking them. Saeröl smiled when he saw that there were two small rubies incrusted within each ring.

"I see your purpose, Lord Curubor; you want me to keep your magic gemstones with me, so that I remain devoted to your endeavour. Well, I accept them, Blue Mage, and bringer of the unexpected gift."

Placing the copper rings in his pocket, Saeröl seized his flute and began playing notes increasing to what felt like an impossible frequency. Shadows began to seep out from underneath the blanket masking his sword, which Saeröl had always kept close at hand. Soon, those ghostly animal forms were gathering around him. Three black cats took shape. A grey owl, with eyes as dark as night, suddenly flew out of one of the cave's galleries before perching on its master's shoulders.

"I bid you farewell, my lords," were the last words Saeröl uttered.

A moment later, he was on his way, surrounded by his ghostly animals.

**

Two days after the secret meeting in the cellar of Mentobraglin, Saeröl reached his destination. Curubor had described how the only possible way out of the region of the Hageyu Falls was at the Ningy Pool, where their chaotic, cascading waters clash with the flow of the Sian Ningy River. This place lay deep within the wood of Silver Leaves. It was very difficult to access through the thick underbrush and dense tree cover.

After considerable effort, Saeröl had finally reached the top of a ravine which overlooked both the final cascade of the Hageyu Falls and the Ningy Pool below. This position provided a superb outlook over the surrounding area and the meandering Sian Ningy River. Saeröl was not alone. He was enjoying the company of the charming Drismile, who had joined him in Tar-Andevar. Indeed, it was this lady who had facilitated his exit from the town of the sea hierarchs. She knew how to leave the city unnoticed; corrupting the city guards was only one of her numerous abilities. The two Night Elves had discreetly left Tar Andevar on a moonless evening, taking advantage of the darkness to avoid the numerous mounted patrols of the sea hierarchs' units. Their night vision enabled them to progress swiftly and unnoticed during the darkest hours. The two Night

Elves had now been hiding in the vegetation atop the Ningy Pool for hours, enjoying the murmur of the forest. They had listened with pleasure to the rustling leaves and tumbling waters below, whilst lying back and taking in the vibrant flowers and wild plants that surrounded them.

Now Drismile and Saeröl quietly sat on the edge of the escarpment, which gave dramatic views over the surrounding landscape. The darkness of the starless night reigned. They did not mind staying on this rocky promontory, despite its slippery surfaces and close proximity to the cliff edge. Their small campsite was invisible from the wild meadows that bordered the Sian Ningy to the south of it. The pool was surrounded by either tall pine trees or vertical rocks faces, and its shallow banks consisted mainly of loose stones and forest debris, constantly wet from the waterfall's spray. The Ningy Pool seemed to be alive with moving sandbanks beneath its surface, as sunken vegetation moved and mixed indistinguishably with the boulders at the base of the fall. The humid air, warm temperature and mist from the waterfall all made it difficult for the two Elves to get an exact picture of the landscape around the pool.

"I almost did not recognize this place," confided Saeröl. "Last time I was here, I remember being struck by the pool's pristine waters. A clear moon had added its own touch of silvery light, which twinkled along the ripples of the surface. Tonight, however, the water seems thick with mud, as if the small lake has slipped into a jet-black cloak."

Drismile nodded in agreement. She was busy sewing runes of dark silk onto canvas, handling a long needle with dexterity. Saeröl also contributed to the work's progress. Sitting beside Drismile, he worked at the black material with a needle of his own. Despite the darkness of night, Drismile was looking at him with passion as she worked, admiring the rare beauty of his delicate features and intelligence in his eyes. An owl came to perch on his shoulder. The night bird's head darted around, as if it were consulting the winds before pronouncing an omen.

"My prince, the cats have returned," advised Drismile, as she noticed the shadowy silhouettes of several lynxes lurking around them, staying nonetheless well away from their camp.

Saeröl, who had spoken little for several hours, decided to share his thoughts.

"I summoned them. My lynxes will be more useful if I keep them close by. We might need their protection. I am surprised that they have found no trace of the ambushers nearby. The closest Nellos units we have noticed are several leagues away, to the south of the wood of Silver Leaves. I do not believe they can stop the Green Elves now. The clan Ernaly reached the plateau above the final Hageyu Fall earlier in the night. As we speak, they are busy carrying timber for scaffolds, a few hundred yards upstream from us. Mynar dyl's troops will commence their work at dawn. They will build a lifting platform in order to cautiously dismount the four small boats that are transporting the tombs. We must be ready. Let us now unfurl our dark sail. The clan Ernaly's birds of prey will soon spread out across the area to search for spies and other threats," said Saeröl.

As if echoing his words, a clap of thunder rang out.

"So, it will happen this coming morning," Drismile understood, suddenly concerned. "This is strange; all is so quiet. Why would Lord Curubor expect an attack in this desolate, inaccessible place? Everything we have undertaken may well have been in vain."

The rain began to fall. Finished with his work, Saeröl stood up and started to unfurl the great sail.

"Hurry, we have already taken too long. We must proceed without delay!" he ordered.

Drismile reacted immediately. She intoned a soft chant. The

sail began to lift up into the air, its dark colours comingling with the night. Soon afterwards, Saeröl started playing his flute, the notes piercing and shrill. Suddenly, like a shadowy firework exploding in the sky, the sail disintegrated. Fragments of the silver runes, which had been embroidered with so much care, began to fall across the camp. The rain, indifferent to the witchcraft of the two Night Elves, intensified. What had started just a moment ago as a gentle shower was now becoming torrential.

"It begins," Saeröl warned. "The Elves of Mynar dyl have not come alone. The power of Eïwele Llya protects them."

Drismile, now anxious, hid behind a large rock, which also offered some shelter from the elements. She called out to her liege.

"My prince, what are we to do with him?" she asked, looking over to the other side of their little camp, where a Man, fully bound from head to toe, was suspended upside down from the lowest branch of a chestnut tree.

Without moving, Saeröl considered the prisoner for some time, an evil look in his eye. The Man was a scout, who belonged to a barbarian tribe that had settled on the island recently. They called themselves the H'ibans. They were foreigners from distant lands, known for migrating in the wake of the powerful Westerners, to seek riches and establish trade. Their reputation was not good; they were widely considered, even among Men, as disloyal, opportunistic and treacherous, thieves who were easily manipulated with a little gold. Their greed made them useful followers for the Westerners.

Drismile had identified the Man for his tracking abilities inside the wood of Silver Leaves. Saeröl had captured him in the middle of the night and offered him a deal. The scout had honoured his side of the bargain but had not been rewarded as he expected by the two Elves. The serpents hindering his movement reminded him cruelly of the danger he now faced. After a while, Saeröl laughed.

"Considering your current position, one could argue that H'ibans are not so good at striking deals after all. What do you say to that, Lokah? Nevertheless, I note that you have served us well by showing us the way to the Ningy Pool. The treatment you have received in exchange might appear harsh, though it was prudence that dictated such a stringent approach. Hanging upside down for three days, without food and water, in the company of Moramsing snakes, is no small feat. If those odd little movements you are making are anything to go by, I suppose you are still alive. Without question, that would be an achievement... You deserve a second chance, Lokah. And I have dreamt up a simple mission for you, a task that will earn you my eternal gratitude."

The Man could not respond to the ironic comments of his captor, muzzled as he was by the shadowy serpents that crept around his neck and head. A sudden command from Saeröl released him from their grasp. His body fell from a height of several feet onto the ground. The dark snakes moved away from him, heading slowly towards the big woollen blanket, which now lay on the floor at Saeröl's feet. They disappeared inside as though retreating into a nest.

A few moments passed before the Man regained his senses. A warm rain fell upon him, washing the dirt from his face and drenching his unkempt hair. His long-hooked nose was bleeding heavily after his fall from the tree branch. The first words he said were to enquire about the safety of his wife.

"What have you done with her? Where have you imprisoned her?"

"Imprisoned her?" Saeröl was surprised at the Man's question. "Oh no! Rest assured I have not confined her in any way."

"So you let her go... Is she safe?"

"Oh yes, she is no longer in danger..."

"What do you mean?" inquired the Man, his worry mounting.

Saeröl raised his hand so as to prevent any outburst.

"I killed her... poisoned her, to be precise."

"No! You miserable murderer!"

"I am not sure 'miserable' is the right word, but 'murderer' is certainly appropriate. You see, Lokah, I did not know her. How could I tell if I could trust her as much as you? Consider my situation: sentenced to death, banished by fire and water, a mark of disgrace upon my cheek, and so on and so forth... I did not have a choice. It was unfortunate. She may have been a good wife, and probably possessed other valuable qualities. No one will ever know now. She has now returned to the anonymity of her birth."

"Why did you come to our home? Why capture me, why hurt her?"

"I deeply apologize for the intrusion into your home. I am a fervent believer in the sacred laws of hospitality. But I was in a hurry, and my errand could not suffer any delay. Funnily enough, when I entered your room, I thought I could hear wild animals frantically enacting some breeding exercise... What a surprise it was to discover that humans do not actually make love but rather mate, like savage beasts of the forest! Now I can finally agree with the matriarchs: Men cannot compare with Elves and should be classified as one of the lowest species of living beings."

"You are insane. I hate you," was all the defeated Man could say.

Indifferent to his despair, Saeröl continued, visibly enjoying his anthropological musings.

"There is one unifying tendency among Men, though they might have different rites around how they go about it. I believe the Mother of the Islands is right to place the blame upon Men. The fewer that live, the better the followers of Eïwele Llya feel. I agree with the teachings of the druids of her cult: human life is resolutely not more important than any other creatures' existence. Plants, animals and above all else trees make crucial contributions to the harmony of this world, to the preservation of the Gods' creations. Men ignore this fundamental law, and instead constantly create chaos… To tell you the truth, I cared little for your wife's life. Putting an end to it meant no more to me than crushing an anthill with my boot."

"You are utterly mad," repeated the Man on his knees, the hammering rain blinding him.

Impervious to doubt, Saeröl continued with his argument.

"Living alone, always hiding from those who hunt you, procures some advantages. One has time to think. It is amazing how you can dedicate yourself to wisdom when you do not have to waste your forces in futile babblings with lesser beings. As a result, I had the time to think about the human problem, and I have reached something of a conclusion. The solution is to trigger a massive war between the factions of Men. One would have to ensure that the forces involved were reasonably well balanced. This war of unparalleled magnitude would have to last a long time in order to rid the Lost Islands of their human surplus."

Lokah tried to stand in a final effort.

"You are mad. But your ideas of chaos and destruction will never come to be, they are empty, like the cursed words of your songs."

Saeröl disagreed. "Ah... It just so happens that I have made some rather special arrangements: carefully formulated plans that might just lead to the spectacular denouement we so badly need."

Lokah remained silent, understanding that his end was near. He was trying to control his fear, making every effort possible to deny the sadistic Elf the spectacle of his complete surrender.

"I mentioned I had a final favour to ask of you, Lokah, before you are dismissed," Saeröl recalled as he seized his strange flute. "Something is hiding around us. Something very powerful has managed to escape the vigilance of my lynxes. This is most frustrating. So I have thought of a better plan. I thought perhaps that you could go down this little hill to cause a diversion... a noise so jarring that it would force our enemies to reveal their position."

Saeröl started to play his wind instrument. Suddenly, Lokah felt his chest tighten, and a sudden giddiness seize his arms. With each step, his uneasiness grew, which soon turned into nausea. If he had been able, he would have fled into the forest, despite the tumbling rain and rolling thunder. But then he imagined an infinite number of shadowy creatures, circling around the grove in the night, watching him from their hideouts in the branches and in the thickets, ready to strike him at the slightest stumble. Each of his movements became more painful. The scout did not understand what was happening to him. The music produced by Saeröl's flute emitted an intense, corrupting force that filled him with utter terror. He suddenly felt incredibly cold and broke out into shivers, before finally opening his mouth to scream like a mad Man. But as hard as he tried, he could make no sound.

At that moment, a bolt of lightning struck so close that the entire vale was illuminated with brutal electric light. Then thunder, loud as a thousand drums beating to the march of absolute chaos, made the hills' very foundations tremble. Saeröl hit the Man with the flat of his dark blade, then forced him backwards towards the cliff edge, which overlooked the river's banks.

"Lokah," taunted the Night Elf, "you have demonstrated a distinct lack of judgement. In the face of such weakness, I, Saeröl Dir Sana, like a gardener for the Gods who aims his silver crossbow at a trespasser in their divine orchards, have but one answer: let the miserable thief go back to where he came from."

The heavy shower, which carried the warm spray of the Austral Ocean, poured down from the heavens as if to cleanse every creature and every plant of their impurities. Saeröl, soaked, his eyes fixed upon the sky, let out a wild laugh as the storm continued to sow its electric seeds farther away, its white fire already reaching the distant Chanun Mountains. He played a few piercing notes on his flute; the sound was confusing, full of distress. With a final silent scream, Lokah threw himself from the top of the cliff, crashing on the rocks a hundred feet below, before his lifeless body rolled to a stop upon the sandy soil of the riverbank.

Drismile carefully approached the cliff edge. She looked carefully out at her surroundings, scrutinizing every rock, branch and tree. Nothing stirred. After a long, still moment, she turned back to Saeröl. A simple flick of her hand told him that the two Elves were utterly alone in that wild place.

"My prince," said Drismile, "if each of us were given the opportunity to choose the way we died, we would choose what is painless. I believe Lokah had better luck than most…"

"I agree," said Saeröl.

For the next hour, the two Elves sat in silence, waiting for the spectacle below to commence. The rain ceased. Dawn came, and the first rays of the sun reverberated on the silvery waters of the cascading river. Suddenly, the silhouette of a great stag appeared right in front of them, on the other side of the Ningy Pool, at the top of the western cliff bordering the final Hageyu Fall. The powerful cry of the majestic animal reverberated through the earth, sinking deep within the mountains, the hills, even to the bed of the coursing river.

As if responding to the formidable creature's call, hundreds of birds came down from the sky like arrows raining upon a battlefield. Hawks and falcons were darting wildly about the entire area, all engaged in a violent, frenzied hunt for any enemies that might be lurking in the forest.

Undetectable and undetected, the two Night Elves remained seated in the shade of a tall pine tree, appreciating the grand spectacle of the birds' wild dance in the sky. Then, as the whirlwind of hawks moved away into the forest, Elvin silhouettes appeared at the top of the cliffs bordering the waterfall. Clad in green cloaks, these Elves were hardly visible, but after a mere few minutes, they had established a great construction site. From the two opposite banks at the top of the cascading waterfall, dozens of Elves started to build a complex scaffolding structure, whose parts had already been assembled in the cover of the trees.

After a few hours, the two sides of the structure met, creating something of a bridge just above the cascading river as it disappeared over the waterfall's edge. The first bold Elves set about scaling up the structure, more than a hundred feet above the pool's seething waters at the bottom of the fall. They worked tirelessly to set up a system of pulleys and ropes at the centre of the structure, like as many sailors working the high masts and long beams of a warship. Looking out at them, Drismile could not help but wonder if that structure, which looked so flimsy, had been put together properly.

"I understand," she whispered, turning to Saeröl. "They are going to lower the boats down the waterfall one by one, from those improvised winches they're setting up now."

Saeröl did not respond. His gaze was fixed downwards, towards the banks of the Ningy Pool. After a while, Drismile realized what was causing his concern.

"The corpse of Lokah... it's disappeared."

"The river has taken it, Drismile. This day might not be as calm as we had thought."

Meanwhile, indifferent to the two Night Elves' musings about the muddy waters of the Sian Ningy, the clan Ernaly's fighters were making good progress. The first small ship was lined up just upstream of the structure, held back against the flow by Elves grasping ropes on either side of the river. Saeröl and Drismile could distinguish the tombstone's edges protruding from the sides of the boat. A chief was coordinating their manoeuvres from a commanding position on top of the cliff. Saeröl recognized Mynar dyl's voice as the warlord of Tios Halabron shouted instructions to his brother.

"Voryn dyl! Take half a unit down to the pool. We start with Rowë's tomb; I am not sure this scaffolding will hold for all the boats. Make haste. There is still much to do."

The youngest of the dyn Ernaly was not one to challenge orders, and he was soon on his way, descending the steep cliff with a few chosen fighters. Unfazed by the danger and impervious to the raging elements around them, his troops abseiled down the taut ropes and, when they neared the bottom, jumped into the pool. When they had all surfaced, Voryn dyl announced that his group was in place and ready to receive their precious cargo.

The Elves at the top of the waterfall began the manoeuvres they had so carefully planned. Those on the banks slowly loosened the ropes which were holding the small ship back just before the waterfall's edge. As the boat neared the void, it was carefully attached to the beam that jutted out over the waterfall, and then slowly released so it could move over the edge of the cliff, all whist staying level. The small watercraft was now suspended above the void.

Three Elves upon the makeshift bridge then took to the winches and started operating its dangerous descent. The boat and its reflection soon blurred together in the wild water's spray;

it looked for a few tense moments as if it had been totally submerged and destroyed in the elemental power of the cascade. However, the boat reappeared near the bottom of the waterfall, intact but seriously flooded. It was becoming dangerously heavy; the Elves had not accounted for so much water being taken on. The scaffolding above groaned and rattled under the strain. The Elves still positioned on the structure to manoeuvre the descent sensed the imminent danger and hurried towards the safety of the riverbanks. They were too late.

Under the weight of the flooded boat, the entire structure split apart at the centre. Its joints disintegrated, and its parts broke off into pieces before disappearing into the wild flood of the torrent and hurtling down towards the pool below. The boat dropped and sank into the waters before immediately resurfacing some distance away, spat back out by the awesome power of the waters. The tremendous noise of the wreckage was followed by a profound silence. There was no sign of the three Elves who had fallen with the structure from its great height. Finally, the voice of Mynar dyl sounded out across the canyon.

"Voryn dyl! Get aboard the boat and confirm whether the coffin is intact."

Answering his brother's call, Voryn dyl, the first of his group to recover, started to swim towards the drifting boat. The current of the Ningy River was strong, and the small vessel was quickly gaining downstream momentum. With powerful strokes and sheer determination, Voryn dyl managed to reach the boat and pull himself aboard. A few moments later, he was joined by another strong swimmer. But Voryn dyl was no longer responding to his brother's command. Rather, his gaze was fixed upon a shadow beneath the water, which seemed to block the way just downstream of the boat. As Voryn dyl leant forwards to get a closer look, his breathing stopped. He was seized with panic and could not even let out a cry.

"Watch out!" a warning was lost in the wind.

Some monstrous marine creature was surging upwards from the depths of the Ningy Pool. The beastly leviathan was armoured with turtle-like scales; its head resembled a Dragon's. Its shell was almost exactly the same colour as the waters around it, and it glistened with reflections of the heavenly bodies above when it broke the water's surface. The back of its neck and tips of its limbs seemed guided with gold. As it reared up high above the tiny boat, it became clear that the beast was over thirty-foot long.

Atop this monster was a Man, clad in scale armour and wielding an enormous war hammer. His head was entirely covered by what looked like a gleaming white octopus with snakeheads at the end of its legs. The freakish mask completely covered all features but his mouth, which now emitted a furious roar as he started swinging his impressive weapon from his golden gauntlet.

The Dragon Turtle he was riding ignored Voryn dyl and the boat, and instead let out several deep exhalations, of scalding, venomous steam, in the direction of the clan Ernaly fighters who were still swimming after the boat. Its breath was devastating; many of the brave swimmers did not surface again.

Meanwhile, the knight of the Golden Hand faced Voryn dyl and his companion. Voryn dyl was finally recovering from the surprise. Just as he was moving to seize the powerful bow strapped to his back, the war hammer flew through the air with tremendous force. It hurtled downwards and struck Voryn dyl's companion on the side of his head, barely slowing down as it crunched through flesh and skull alike, before continuing its course and taking some of the poor Elf's brain matter with it. The dreadful weapon continued upon a curved path through the air before landing back in its master's golden gauntlet.

Voryn dyl stood frozen, paralyzed at the utter horror of the attack, as his companion's corpse collapsed into the water. The Dragon Turtle continued wreaking havoc with its powerful claws, sharp as scythes, among those swimming Elves who had not yet succumbed to its venomous breath.

The knight sorcerer threw his war hammer again, which emitted a horrible screeching noise that tore through the air with it.

Voryn dyl only just avoided the missile's fatal blow. Now feeling utterly desperate, he jumped into the water to gain what little protection it offered. The war hammer once again circled back to its master's gauntlet. The battlefield now cleared of his enemies; the knight of the Golden Hand ordered his monstrous mount to drop him aboard the small boat. The Dragon Turtle's shell seemed almost impervious to the many arrows raining down upon it from Mynar dyl's troops above; with no way to descend quickly, they were trapped, and all but a few of their projectiles ricocheted off the monster straight into the water.

"Fire your bows! Kill that monster!" yelled Mynar dyl, like one possessed

Saeröl had been witnessing this scene with the cold rationale of an Elf who has looked upon many battlefields in times gone by. As the knight sorcerer began directing the boat downstream, fleeing the Elvin arrows' reach, Saeröl reached for the woollen blanket beside him and withdrew his black sword. Drismile was terrified; she could not remove her gaze from the bloody struggle raging between the Dragon Turtle and the clan Ernaly's archers. The marine monster was blocking the way downstream, facilitating the flight of its master. Saeröl uttered a few quick words to Drismile.

"Flee the wood of Silver Leaves. Find pilgrims of Eïwele Llyi and follow them. We will meet again where they gather to celebrate the Deity of Beauty's gift."

Drismile, paralyzed by the events before her, only just summoned the strength to respond. "As you order, my prince."

Saeröl ignored her. Dropping to his knees, he planted his bastard sword down into the soil and started to incant powerful words of sorcery. His voice rose to what felt like an impossible volume, its force and depth like an entire choir chanting a majestic hymn in a vast temple. Before Drismile's amazed eyes, his silhouette began to fade, his body taking on a ghostly form.

CHAPTER 5: Curwë

"We must carry on. I have no more arrows, Master! This is dangerous!" warned Gelros.

"The state of your quiver will be of no consequence whatsoever if I cannot rest this second," uttered Aewöl, before he collapsed onto the ground.

The path along the Sian Ningy had slightly widened; the injured Elf had managed land on a patch of grass away from the thorny bushes. Aewöl let the dark green cloak that covered him slip to the ground. The one-eyed Elf, with dark hair and lunar-white skin, was protected now only by his thin black chain mail. The sun was already up in the eastern sky. Thunder had been roaring all night; a heavy storm had torn through the wood of Silver Leaves. Torrential rain had caused the Sian Ningy to burst its banks. The forest was now severely waterlogged.

The lack of adequate supplies made it impossible to tend properly to Aewöl's injured arm. So as not to aggravate the wound, Gelros removed the light chain mail that had been protecting his master. He then made an improvised sling from the cloth of his own cloak: carefully balanced to support Aewöl's wrist and elbow without covering the wound or applying any pressure to the injured side. This done, the scout set about preparing a concoction of magic herbs. Gelros was still standing by the riverside, carefully watching its flow, when their two other companions joined them.

Roquendagor and Curwë were marching towards the improvised camp with determination. Despite wearing his full plate armour and his helm, Roquendagor moved gracefully and swiftly. The tall knight spoke in lingua Llewenti, the common tongue of the Lost Islands, which he now practised fluently, as did the rest of the Elves who had come from Essawylor.

"You fought like a lion, Curwë! I am proud of you," praised Roquendagor as he dropped his heavy equipment to the ground.

There was soon quite a pile by the swollen riverbank, as he unburdened himself of his two-handed sword and started removing the many parts of his plate mail. He shook off his gauntlets, before unfastening the helmet which also protected the back of his neck, then the gorget that covered his throat, the pauldrons for his shoulders, the besagews for his underarms, the couters for his elbows, the vambraces for his forearms and, finally, his large breastplate. Curwë returned the compliment, his green eyes still sparkling with excitement after their intoxicating battle.

"Without your bravery, we would now be lost. A just cause are not enough to win a battle. Force is the key."

The bard was equipped for war. He carried a light crossbow and a finely crafted long sword. The leather armour he wore was reinforced by a steel breastplate of exquisite design. Beneath his battledress, Curwë had not been able to resist donning his usual flamboyant clothes of multi-coloured silks that had brought him so much fame and admiration in Llymar. But a long green cloak, the colour of leaves, hung about his shoulders, allowing him to blend into the woody surroundings if need be.

Roquendagor was now almost naked as he stepped into the river, indifferent to the cold. His back was covered by a large tattoo. The tall knight felt desperate to refresh himself after the long, exacting pursuit through the woods.

Since their secret landing on Nyn Ernaly's shores a few nights before, their group had spared no effort to reach the border of the wood of Silver Leaves. Their mission had been somewhat complicated when they were attacked by a full unit of cavaliers bearing the arms of Nellos. Aewöl and Curwë's bolts and Gelros' arrows had begun to turn the tide of the skirmish.

But, above all, it was Roquendagor's heroism that had saved the group from a bloody end. The knight had caused great confusion in the enemy ranks by knocking several cavaliers from their mounts. Like any experienced fighter, his tactics were swift and efficient: injuring his enemies quickly to incapacitate or hinder them. It enabled him to move on rapidly to the next opponent. Since the violent encounter, they had run through the night, anxious to put as much distance as possible between themselves and the inevitable reinforcements that would follow their fresh trail.

"The river carries peat," Gelros said unexpectedly, looking preoccupied.

"In last night's storm, the Sian Ningy flooded and ripped up most of the vegetation along its banks, taking up much of the soil with it," advised Roquendagor as he waded further into the river to wash up. "During our flight, Curwë and I remained behind for a while," the tall knight added. "I wanted to check if there was any sign of pursuit. But none of those Men dared to follow us into the wood of Silver Leaves. This is not surprising. The riders are not equipped appropriately, and they will fear us after the routing of their cavalry."

But Gelros contradicted him.

"I believe a spy is after us."

Roquendagor was surprised. "How do you know?"

"He is no common scout, for I have failed to track him down. He is most probably a Green Elf familiar with Nyn Ernaly. I doubt I can catch him," advised Gelros simply.

Roquendagor was not impressed. "Well, good luck to him if his plan is to stop us. His chances of success are low, alone against the four of us."

Curwë noticed that their other companion had remained silent and prostrate.

"Are you severely wounded, Aewöl?"

The one-eyed Elf muttered a few words to reassure his companion. Sitting down beside him on the wet grass, Curwë inspected the bandage that Gelros had made. Aewöl went on slowly. His breath was short, and his body was bruised with many injuries.

"It will never stop. Since we escaped our city in flames, we have not known peace. We were thrust into a devastating series of events that day. When will this journey end? What is the purpose of it all? We only wished to stay at home, back there, in Essawylor."

Curwë tried to comfort his friend.

"Do you remember the life we had? Nothing gave me more joy than to see the Elves of Ystanlewin forming those long queues in front of our lord's hall in the hope of being allowed in to listen to the minstrels' songs. I remember how, inside, drinks abounded on the numerous tables. Guests would sit together in good cheer, enjoying the confusion of the feast. These are the moments in my life I cherish the most. Nothing will ever compare to that blessed time: at home and with friends."

Aewöl winced as the pain in his wounded arm flared up before he turned again to Curwë.

"We are now exiles, far from home."

Curwë, suddenly inhabited with renewed strength, replied, "Like the heroes in the tales of old, Aewöl, we did not choose our fate. Many misfortunes have befallen us, toppling our once peaceful lives into chaos. We must face these challenges if we wish to find peace again. I see this all as our trial. I understand this ordeal as a message sent to us, asking us to renounce our unshakable arrogance and fight for our survival. This trial is not easy, for we must flee both those dark memories of Essawylor in flames and the false hopes we once nourished about the Lost Islands. But, when we step back, there is one salient fact which remains: we are still alive; we have been given the chance to go on."

Surprisingly, Roquendagor intervened. He had taken up his sword once again, washing off the human blood that dirtied it in the river's flow.

"Aewöl is right. Let us face it: we are exiles. Never again will we see those Elves who we loved, for now they haunt the Halls of the Dead. We are far from home…"

Roquendagor bowed his bald head gravely. But soon he raised his strong shoulders again.

"But we must not abandon ourselves to weakness."

The former lord of House Dol Lewin then turned towards his companions. He wished to share his thoughts. This was unusual, so all three paid attention.

"I like walking in the mountains alone. It procures time to think, to seek wisdom, so to speak… My former self died in Essawylor when Ystanlewin fell, when those I loved perished. Once, Aewöl, you told me that I would be reborn into a second life and, when that day came, my destiny would be clear…"

The tall knight took a deep breath.

"Well, now that Roquen Dol Lewin has renounced his legacy, I believe the time for Roquendagor to write his own story has come. I know how eternal glory can be earned: through heroic acts of bravery. By my deeds, I seek to carve my name into an eternity that will survive my own ephemeral life, to become legend, a myth that will be told by scholars in the centuries to come. The name of Roquendagor will either survive the ages or fall into oblivion. This is my purpose, no less... now that I realize that life has an end, even for us immortal High Elves."

Roquendagor was standing straight, his gaze fixed upon the horizon. There was something in the firmness of his voice which demonstrated his inalienable resolution. His friends remembered the fury that had inhabited him in the battle they had just escaped, when confronted with a full unit of Nellos cavaliers who had tried to prevent them from entering the wood of Silver Leaves. Roquendagor had fought like a Dragon, almost claiming victory alone: beheading opponents, toppling horses, ruthlessly slaying his enemies. Somehow, in his macabre dance upon the battlefield, in the countless deadly risks that he had taken, Roquendagor seemed both invincible and possessed by a suicidal madness. Somewhat afraid of these words and what they might imply for the future, Curwë tried to soften their meaning.

"Victory is of little significance if it does not serve a purpose. Glory is all the greater for any hero when it is acquired in the name of a righteous cause or to preserve the world's harmony. Noble deeds such as these are woven into all those songs and poetry of the Green Elves that celebrate their heroes."

Roquendagor was surprised at that, and he could not help showing his frustration at his former herald's words, which sounded too much like a lecture for his liking.

"You are no simple Elf, Curwë, despite your strange emerald eyes. You are an immortal High Elf whether you like it or not. You will not reincarnate into a spirit of the ocean like the Blue Elves think they will, still less as a wood sprite or a tree like the naive Green Elves believe. When your life is cut short by the thrust of a sword or the blow of an arrow, you will join with your anonymous brethren in the Halls of the Dead. The Greater God of the Underworld fashioned that invisible realm within the entrails of world, to which the souls of all High Elves killed in battle must go."

Roquendagor had a lump in his throat and spoke with a more toneless voice.

"One day or another, you will encounter his stately figure. Gweïwal Agadeon will be standing before the great iron door of his underground fortress. In his hands will be his formidable flail, his great globe and his black key. Once you have been ushered in, you will be locked within the Halls of the Dead forever so that you have time to understand what it means to break an oath once sworn to the Gods. You will become faceless, lose your name and become a servant to the stern and unpitying Greater God of the Underworld. Believe me, all that will remain of you will be your deeds celebrated by bards in their songs... or perhaps not."

Aewöl made an effort to turn away, despite the pain in his arm, trying to hide from his companions how distressed he had become at this reminder of their cruel destiny after death. The one-eyed Elf shivered like a leaf in the wind. His silver diadem reflected the pale light of the morning sun. Due to his restless nature, he often appeared ill at ease but, in that instant especially, dark thoughts were torturing his soul. His clear-sightedness defined him, and it often proved a burden too heavy to bear.

Curwë caught his eye. It looked as though Aewöl was drowning in a dull anguish, like he was looking out upon the hundreds of thousands of dead High Elves locked within the Halls of the Dead: a multitude of shadowy forms groaning in confused discord, in which no individual voice could be distinguished.

Curwë, disturbed by the suffering that Roquendagor's harsh words had provoked in his friend, decided to answer his former lord. For once, the bard spoke without the full consideration due to Roquendagor's former rank.

"As for me, I see it differently. Even if things are meant to end the way you describe, I say we can choose a different path. I want to understand what has drawn so many Elves from such different origins to the Lost Islands... Think about it, since the world's beginning, Elves have risked everything they own to reach its shores. They did so to seek safe refuge, yes, but also to embark upon a spiritual quest..."

Curwë's tone changed as he came to focus on his own destiny.

"Believe me, I will explore this fabled archipelago to find answers to my questions; I will take the time to meet with its inhabitants, to learn their customs and to understand their beliefs. Some, I will most probably hate, but others I will love. I do not expect this journey to be without challenges; indeed, I foresee many trials that will push me to my limits. But, in the end, whatever the hardships, I will accept my fate."

There was a long silence, only interrupted from time to time by the sound of the wind through the trees. The four Elves, who had only just escaped death, now found themselves confronting afresh their visions of the afterlife and, with that, their deeply held spiritual beliefs.

*

Events had unfolded quickly once Aewöl and Curwë had met with Dyoren in Llafal under the watchful eye of Nyriele. Ever since, the days had flown by like a sudden gale in the bay of Penlla. Gelros had gathered their horses and the three riders had travelled for several days through the forest of Llymar and the hills of Arob Salwy before finally reaching Mentollà, their community's stronghold. At this time of year, the Elves of the tower had been busy. Master Aertelyr's vessel had been anchored in the bay, and his sailors were loading the summer's harvest into their large ship.

The Breymounarty had a monopoly over trade between the forest of Llymar and the principality of Cumberae, the dominion of House Dol Nos-Loscin, which lay far away to the south of the Lost Islands. Sailors of that merchant guild were famed for their ability to navigate the waters of the Archipelago. Indeed, their navigation skills had earned them an almost exclusive dominance of all sea trade outside of the kingdom of Gwarystan's routes.

The produce that the community of Mentollà sold to the Breymounarty was unique, owing to its tropical origin. The bulk of their exports were made up of fruits, spices and exotic plants: high-value goods for Master Aertelyr. For decades, he had defied the dangers that the royal warships of Gwarystan could pose to his illegal trading activities. That guild master was a smuggler as much as a trader. He had quickly come to an arrangement with Aewöl and Curwë. Against a higher percentage margin of the shipment to compensate him from the risk taken, Master Aertelyr had agreed to take the four Elves from Mentollà aboard, before quietly dropping them off on a remote beach of Nyn Ernaly.

Curwë had been the mastermind behind the expedition, and his two companions, Aewöl and Gelros, had agreed to accompany him. The fourth passenger was none other than Roquendagor. The tall knight, who usually favoured solitude and preferred to cross the pass along the Arob Tuide range, had not been able to resist the petitions of his former herald Curwë. The smell of battle had proven too tempting for him; Roquendagor was eager to prove himself once again.

*

Now they could take a few moments' rest. Certain calm had returned to them and, with that calm, the memory of the deadly fight they had just escaped. It now felt as though Gweïwal Agadeon himself had, for a moment, slightly opened the heavy doors to the Halls of the Dead, inviting them to join their fallen brethren for all eternity. Gelros suddenly broke the silence.

"My lord, get out of the water... now."

Roquendagor immediately stopped bathing, hearing the urgency in Gelros' voice. He knew from experience that the former hunt master of House Dol Lewin was not one to give warnings without reason. All looked to the river, upstream, to where Gelros was pointing. Soon, they saw the remains of a huge wooden structure surfacing along the rapid current. Chunks of broken wood, tied together like the snapped branches of a giant tree, surged down the river before their eyes.

"Look!" exclaimed Gelros, "There are corpses too."

Curwë immediately recognized the many bodies being carried by the current.

"These are Green Elves. They belong to the clan Ernaly. See how their hair is adorned with hawks' feathers."
"It would seem that the fight for the testament of Rowë has already begun," said Aewöl, his tone grim.
"Mynar dyl and his elite units must have been attacked upriver. We must hurry!" Curwë pressed.

But he was interrupted by a deep, intense noise, like the cry of a great wind spirit. It felt as if the Deity of Storms was breaking free from the invisible bonds that chained him beneath the Sea of Cyclones. The atmosphere became filled with a sudden new heat. Dangerous gases seeped down from the lowly clouds, causing all birds in the vicinity to flee. The air was struggling to contain the power of impending lightning. The sky darkened to the north. A black, unnatural cloud emerged over the peaks of the Chanun Mountains.

"Some time ago," said Curwë, looking up at the ominous sky, "I heard the priests of Eïwele Llya say, 'Water is the blood of the Mother of the Islands, the trees its hair, and the clouds its voice.' When I see that overcast sky, I cannot help but fear the worst."

"We cannot linger by the river," advised Gelros. "Quick! Gather the equipment. Please help Master Aewöl while I look for shelter."

The scout disappeared beneath the canopy; his companions still startled by the suddenly changed vista. Nevertheless, they quickly packed their belongings, like Elves living in the shadow of a volcano trained for evacuation. They prioritised protecting the food they carried from the coming rain.

After a while, Gelros returned. The scout had discovered a shelter. Immediately the group departed. They did not have to go very far. Climbing up a hill heading north, they reached their destination after less than a quarter-league.

It was a rough hut made of wood and stone that stood beneath a few willows: a traditional shelter where hunters would dwell overnight. A small stream, a tributary of the Sian Ningy River, bathed the roots and hanging branches of the willows, and split in two just before the hut, enclosing it amidst the reeds and hedges of its banks. All was empty, lonely and desolate.Gelros pulled out his long dagger, cut a willow branch, whittled it into a spear and lodged it between the door and its frame. He pushed with all his weight. The door opened.

Gelros came in. He went about his actions with a feverous determination. The scout urged his companions to join him, and then proceeded to barricade the door with a table and some seats he found near the hearth. Somewhat reassured by these precautions, Gelros placed himself in front of a half-open shutter and began to look out. It was starting to rain again.

A heavy shower soon tore down upon the roof. The sky was low and dark; it seemed to be bursting, emptying itself upon the ground, dissolving and melting the earth. Gusts of winds swept through with unnatural heat. The flow of the two streams bordering the hut became more intense, and Gelros looked at them with concern. Seeing his companion's dark mood, Curwë understood that the weather's sudden turn was now a serious danger to them.

"There is without doubt some unknown threat hanging over these hills," Curwë thought aloud. "Where have the animals gone? What terror caused them to abandon these woods?"

"Listen!" Gelros interrupted.

A moment later, what the hunter's instinct had perceived, the bard began to hear. A long murmur, as if of the wind, arose from different points of what sounded like a semicircle stretching from east to west. It was interrupted only by what sounded like jets of warm air heavy with water, like the sound of the rising tide on a stony shore.

"What is that?" asked Aewöl. "Could it be the wind?"

"No. It's the wind that is carrying the noise. The two are distinct," distinguished Curwë.

"Is that the crackling of some gigantic fire?" wondered Roquendagor before reconsidering his first instinct. "No, the sound is so close that we would see its flames, but darkness is rising all around."

The noise became louder and more distinct: it was the incessant, all-pervading and rumbling roll of a surging wave.

"I see it!" exclaimed Gelros from his lookout. "Like a deathly rope closing in on the horizon above the trees. It's coming towards us from the Chanun Mountains. It is heading towards the sea and will soon be upon us!"

Gelros was still uncertain about the gravity of the unnatural phenomenon, for he had never witnessed such a thing before. When he looked down, the scout saw how all around their shelter the grass was growing heavy with water. The stream was overflowing. It began to drown the reeds which had hitherto contained it.

"We must go!" Gelros cried, now overcome with panic. "We must flee, or we will be swept away! Look! Just look! Do you see now?"

Opening the shutter wide, Gelros pointed to the large cloud, which was whitening on the horizon, roaring as it progressed, like the vanguard of a celestial army. Paralysed in awe, as though already defeated by the demonstration of such strange power, Gelros let out one final murmur.

"This is the Mother of the Islands' wrath."

Roquendagor reacted immediately. He threw the barricading furniture aside and broke the wooden door down with a single kick. Grasping Aewöl at the waist, the tall knight disappeared into the engulfing darkness outside. After a moment of surprise, Curwë and Gelros were on his heels. The four Elves, supporting one another as they went, attempted to reach a large rocky outcrop uphill, which could offer them better shelter. The elements unleashed their fury around them. Trees bent, and branches were torn in the powerful gusts. Debris flew around in the darkness, like ghostly whispers flying past their ears. Their senses were overloaded by the chaotic spectacle that engulfed them.

Then, they heard a crash, and looked back to see the hut they had just left cascading down the slope, overwhelmed by the weight of the flood. The timber frames had given way and the stone pillars were tumbling downhill. Unmoved by the plunging ruins, the rumbling waters rose up in the thicket below; they could make out the top of the cedar tree trembling. Its branches cracked as if a whole flock of birds were storming through its foliage. The four Elves continued their flight uphill, away from the furious new-born torrent. Every few moments, Gelros stopped to wait for his companions, shouting.

"Move faster! Move faster!" repeatedly.

Roquendagor managed to keep up with him, but Aewöl and Curwë were lagging behind. The rain intensified, and now water was pouring down the slope, making the ground muddy and slippery. As the black sky poured, floods of foaming water on the hill's slope drowned everything it touched. Suddenly, Curwë uttered a cry of terror. Just beside him, Aewöl had been caught by a torrent of mud and was being helplessly dragged away in its flow.

"Flee!" the one-eyed Elf cried to his companion, before being swallowed by the dark waters.

But Curwë, as if he were determined to risk his life for him, ran down alongside the torrent, watching for the tiniest window of opportunity to help his friend. Aewöl sank into the muddy water, but then resurfaced. He eventually succeeded in clinging to a tree trunk, around which the torrent still rushed. Curwë was soon by him, attempting to extract him from the raging flow. There was a moment of struggle. Aewöl, clinging to Curwë's, was then struck by a floating chunk of wood. The impact was heavy and, before he knew it, the one-eyed Elf was overcome with intense pain, as now his wounded arm was the only thing Curwë could grasp.

Finally, Aewöl managed to seize a fistful of branches and, in an effort of will procured by sheer desperation, pulled himself up from the muddy water to reach Curwë on the trunk. But the torrent had grown wider and stronger. All across the slopes of the hill, the cascading waters were ripping up vegetation and dislodging rocks. The trunk suddenly shifted and was then being carried away by the current, towards the surging river downhill. The two exhausted Elves just about managed to keep their balance, thanks to their last reserves of agility and strength, upon their unconventional raft.

Just after, the tree trunk collided with a large boulder. The shock was hard. The two Elves were thrown into the dark waves of the Sian Ningy. But, with one last effort, they managed to swim towards the rocks of the riverbank. They found footholds and hauled themselves up. Aewöl and Curwë were saved from the most pressing danger, for the flood, strong as it was, would never reach this new high ground.

Then the sky split in two and the rain fell more mercilessly than ever. Crouching on the rocks, Aewöl and Curwë were severely bruised. Their clothes were thick with water darker than blood. The two bedraggled companions could now contemplate the great fury of the elements around them. Aewöl watched the rapid torrent which had almost swallowed him continue its mad course while Curwë, his face hammered by the rain, raised his gaze towards the tormented heavens. The rain's violence abated as quickly as it had risen. It was soon nothing more than a faint drizzle. The clouds seemed to flee and, suddenly, a broad ray of sunlight struck the devastated hills. The blue backdrop of the heavens soon reappeared: a clear and beautiful azure sky. A fresh breeze drifted around Aewöl and Curwë, like a happy sigh from the earth. The two Elves were safe, but their other companions, Roquendagor and Gelros, were nowhere to be seen.

"We should wait here for them," suggested Curwë, "they will follow our muddy tracks downslope and come to the river."

"If they survived," added Aewöl with his grim tone.

Curwë chose not to answer, but rather focus on his surroundings. He hoped that Roquendagor and Gelros would emerge from their refuge and show some sign of life. He dearly wished to see their faces glow in the warming sun that was now shining on his. A moment later, Curwë caught sight of a bright spot upon the devastated horizon before him: a reddish glow dancing on the river upstream. Despite his aching bruises, the naturally curious bard was transfixed by this phenomenon, separated from them by only a hundred yards.

"Look, Aewöl! There is a wrecked boat upriver. It's blocked by those tree trunks that have fallen across the river."

"I see it," confirmed Aewöl. "But there seems to be someone aboard. No, some kind of creature… a large creature!"

Indeed, an imposing silhouette could be seen above the fallen trees which blocked the river. The figure was wrapped in a red cloak; the being beneath was part man, part beast. Up to his chest, his body was human. But protruding upwards where his neck should have been, was a twisted, interwoven nest of flailing sea serpents, hissing and snapping at the air, as if a normal Man were wearing a mask of living vipers. His great stature meant his monstrous head was colliding with the overhanging branches. A golden gauntlet protected his left hand, in which he wielded, with unnatural strength, a huge war hammer.

The colossus was attempting to destroy a large coffin that had been thrown from the wrecked ship when it collided with the barricade of fallen trees. He brought his massive weapon down upon the casket in a cacophony of enraged cries and frenetic blows. Loud, echoing cracks broke the silence of the forest.

"Stay here!" whispered Curwë, his breath becoming short as he began the perilous journey across the ravaged woodland to reach the river's eastern bank.

The seriously injured Aewöl had no choice but to watch with concern as his friend progressed upriver as discreetly as possible. Curwë's long, greenish cloak did well to camouflage him against the wooded landscape. He darted between the snapped branches and felled trees, heading towards a difficult, steep approach to the site of the wreckage. The more ground he covered, the better Curwë could make out the strange creature, still absorbed in its destruction of the coffin. Curwë recognized the tall Man's order from his blood-red cloak. The bard then noticed the Golden Hand of rare design that the creature bore upon his left hand. The gauntlet had six fingers. These features matched the description Master Aertelyr had given as they had crossed the strait of Tiude. Curwë was facing one of King Norelin's dreaded servants: A Mowengot.

The knight sorcerer started swinging the weapon high above his head. Curwë was amazed how quickly he could manoeuvre the hammer given its size and weight. The fearsome weapon struck the coffin's lid one last time. It crushed through metal and wood, splitting the casket's cover in two pieces. The knight sorcerer immediately reached down into the coffin and grabbed a cylindrical box, the colour of gold, with Elvin runes inscribed across its surface.

"I have my prize!" the knight with the golden hand proclaimed, his gravelly voice rising above the roar of the mountain torrent.

The golden box blazed forth suddenly so that all the shadowy woods was lit with a dazzling radiance like sunlight, but it did not remain steady and passed. It was then that Curwë noticed the shadowy silhouette of an Elf looming in the woods on the other side of the river, as though it had been waiting for that particular moment to make its appearance. The fallen trees, which had blocked the progress of the knight sorcerer's boat, also formed a natural bridge across the river.

The tall Elf dressed in black was now standing still and resolute at the other side of this bridge, stoically awaiting his moment. He had stopped in his tracks forty yards from the knight with the golden hand; there could be no doubt that he was issuing a challenge. Swirling around the Elf were shadowy, spectral duplicates of himself. The dark apparitions were moving with and around him, constantly shifting their positions, making it impossible to keep track of which image was real. Slowly, without a word, this Elf of many shadows drew a bastard sword from a blanket that hung behind his back. He looked down at the fearsome weapon, delicately caressing its amethyst-encrusted pommel. The powerful, enchanted black blade gleamed like a servant of dark forces.

"Die!" yelled the knight with the golden hand.

In a heartbeat, the war hammer was flying through the air. The deadly projectile hurtled downwards, but it was deflected, diverted from its course, with a swift parry of the Elf's sword. The dreadful weapon continued along a curved path through the air before landing back in its master's golden gauntlet.

The Elf of many shadows moved slowly forward, as though utterly impervious to the extreme violence of the onslaught. The knight sorcerer threw his war hammer again, which emitted a horrible screeching noise that tore through the air. The Elf avoided the missile's fatal blow once again, but one of the shadowy illusions around him disappeared. Now readying himself for attack, the Elf moved quickly onto the bridge, closing the gap that separated him from his opponent.

"Return to me!" ordered the knight sorcerer.

The war hammer once again circled back to its master's gauntlet just in time for him to parry the Elf's first blow and strike back. Almost simultaneously, the tall Man counterattacked, neutralising his aggressor before a flurry of new blows. The narrow bridge allowed the Elf to dominate the fight without using undue physical strength. The knight sorcerer therefore chose to retreat. He shook the curls of his snake hair, making them rain their venom down on his opponent. But the poison had no effect. The Elf of many shadows stood strong; he remained valiant and continued his attack upon the tall Man with the serpents' mask, pushing him back with his bastard sword as black as the night.

The fighting was now intense. Several times the Elf charged, responding to any opening with furious thrusts and swipes, but he failed to deliver a decisive blow. The knight sorcerer had so far managed to use his golden gauntlet to parry the dark blade's murderous dance. His plate mail impeded his movement, making him a slow-moving target for the Elf, but penetrating his armour to inflict real damage was no small task. Nevertheless, the Elf's speed and precision gave him the upper hand; he was driving his opponent to exhaustion. It was the Elf who controlled this fight, and he did not intend to leave anything to chance.

"You will never get my prize!" cried the knight with the golden hand, but already he was short of breath.

The Elf closed the distance between them, circled his opponent for an opening, feinted, jabbed, blocked a blow from the golden gauntlet, then leapt to one side and finally connected with a decisive hit. The dark blade of his bastard sword pierced the mail between breastplate and gorget. The knight sorcerer fell where he stood on the bridge in agonizing pain.

In a final effort, he tried to reach for a black dagger hidden behind his steel leggings, but the Elf's sword immediately severed his right hand. Not content with triumphing over his opponent, the Elf flayed the face of the still-living knight sorcerer, to make a trophy of his snake mask, which he stuck to his black sword. With another swift movement, he brought his weapon down upon his foe's other arm, and then yanked the golden gauntlet from his enemy's severed hand.

Finally, the Elf of many shadows seized the cylindrical box engraved with Elvin runes, burying it in an inside pocket of his cloak. Without a word, the Elf left as he had come. He swiftly crossed the bridge and entered the devastated woods. His shadows soon disappeared, flying up through the leaves of the canopy towards the north-west.

*

Still concealed behind a tree trunk, the hood of his long cloak pulled up over his head, Curwë remained absolutely still: almost totally invisible against the wooded surroundings. His breath became short as he tried to process the consequences of what he had just seen. He remained there for some time, unable to come to any decision. There was no sign of Aewöl, or of his other two companions.

After a long, agonizing few minutes, the cries of the knight sorcerer ceased. The servant of King Norelin was dead. Then, only the flow of the mountain stream and the wind through the branches could be heard, as though Eïwele Llya had conquered her dominion anew. Wild animals started returning to the area. The singing of birds and the chattering of squirrels comingled to create a new music in the cool morning air. High in the sky, above the river, hawks were circling.

Curwë spotted a great stag with splendid antlers on the other side of the river, a creature unlike any he had seen before.

"What could this be?" he wondered in awe.

The stag was as big as a war horse, and indeed it was galloping like a loyal stallion returning to its master. The ground was strewn with dampened undergrowth and snapped branches, but the majestic animal was unimpeded as it moved gracefully across that difficult terrain.The great stag neared the shipwreck. Ignoring the flooding caused by the fallen trees that were partially damming the river, it jumped with unnatural agility onto the bridge to reach the wreck.

A moment later, the noble animal's cry reverberated throughout the woods. The majestic animal seemed to be expressing a most profound distress. It was feverishly searching the area, seeking out marks and sniffing for traces, but there was no trail to follow, no clues left by the mysterious intruder for the great stag to follow. It then looked high in the sky at the hawks circling above him, as though they could ease its pain. A moment more and it was gone, towards the north from whence it came. With the straight-legged, bouncing gait of a fawn, it quickly disappeared into the forest.

Curwë could no longer contain his curiosity. He leapt out of his hideout and rushed towards the wreck. Moving upriver along the bank, he quickly covered the forty yards' distance. When Curwë looked down at the macabre scene, his eyes became wide and his face deathly pale.Turning his gaze from the mutilated corpse of the knight sorcerer, he focused on the pillaged coffin.

Curwë saw the elaborate carvings upon the rich woods and precious metals that had made up its lid, but which now lay scattered and broken in pieces. The outside of the broad, rectangular frame was painted on three of its sides, and its inside was covered with white quilted cloth. The structure itself was made of coarse clay, dyed in colours that ranged from emerald to aquamarine. Such luxurious decorations indicated the high status of the deceased Elf. Inside lay a corpse that had been preserved from decay with most sophisticated methods of embalming. Decomposition had been halted by washing out the body with essential oils. The only organ that appeared to have been removed was the heart.

'Elfin tradition holds that the heart is the cradle of the soul,' remembered Curwë.

The corpse still held a broad dagger in his right hand. Its hilt was made of gold and encrusted with diamonds. It was marked with the image of a blacksmith's anvil. When Curwë leant down to seize it, the blade started glowing brightly. Unafraid of its reaction to his presence, and somewhat carried away by the magnificence of the weapon's design, the bard could not suppress his want. He seized the precious weapon, which he found to be unexpectedly light and handy, despite the broad blade. It was balanced perfectly. Trying the tip of the blade on a piece of the coffin's lid, Curwë noticed that it cut through the wood as if it were a much softer material. The bard heard twigs snapping somewhere behind him. By reflex, he hid the dagger behind his back and hooked the hilt to his leather belt. Only then did he turn to face the newcomers.

"Come Curwë! Come fast!" urged Gelros, from his position thirty yards downstream, just at the edge of the woods.

Aewöl and Roquendagor were just behind the scout. Sensing that danger was close at hand, Curwë immediately gave up his search. Jumping nimbly around the debris across the natural dam, he soon reached the western bank of the river. His companions had not waited for him. They were already entering the woods, heading north-west. It took Curwë some time to catch up with them. Finally, he managed to convince them to halt.

They all stopped to rest. Barely visible against the forest, the four Elves, clad in their long green cloaks, sat amongst the aspen trees at the edge of a clearing.

"We need to move on," urged Gelros. "Soon this area will be invaded by clan Ernaly troops. Dozens of fighters are coming from the Ningy Pool. Their hawks are already covering this territory,"

"Gelros' birds have spotted them," confirmed Roquendagor. "No doubt they will soon be on our trail."

"But why should we fear them?" asked Curwë. "Have we not come to these dreaded woods to assist them? This is the very mission Matriarch Nyriele gave us."

Aewöl intervened, his face still strained with pain and exhaustion, "The clan Ernaly's fighters will have questions for us after what happened at the dam. I too saw this fight. We do not want to be scapegoats. It will hopefully require from them many efforts to retrieve the coffin. They will need to secure it as quickly as possible. That will delay them and buy us time."

Curwë disagreed. "But what should we do now? Roquendagor, I am surprised. Do you agree with Aewöl? Shouldn't we rally the units of clan Ernaly and join them in their quest?"

The tall knight hesitated for a moment. Two opposing urges wrestled within his soul.

"Aewöl is right," he finally declared. "The Elf of shadows you both saw at the dam is beyond our power to capture, still less to coerce. Let us leave his fate to that which hunts him, whatever that great stag might be… We must think and act carefully. Our survival may depend on what we decide to do now. I do not trust the clan Ernaly, and I trust its intriguing warlord even less. My orders are that we make for the north of the island, to the barbarian territories. That way, we will escape the wood of Silver Leaves and circumvent the Chanun Mountains on their western side. Our aim is to join the fleet of Llymar. We know that Gal dyl's ships are somewhere up north, sailing off the coast of Nyn Ernaly, waiting for the time to land on the northern beach of the Island to pick up the clan Ernaly's troops."

"We do not even have a reliable map," protested Curwë with a final effort.

But Aewöl concluded the debate.

"Gelros will lead us."

Curwë realised he would never convince his companions. The decision had been made; nevertheless, he had difficulty hiding his disappointment. In an attempt to regain his self-control, he discreetly gripped the hilt of his new dagger. A blast of intense energy swept through his arm, but none of his companions saw the brightness in his gaze that flashed up in that instant.

The four Elves gathered their few remaining belongings and headed north-west into the woods. Gelros led the way, Aewöl and Curwë on his heels with Roquendagor covering the rear. Progress was difficult through the thick vegetation of the Silver Leaves' wood, damaged as it was after the storm. Despite Gelros' tracking skills and the assistance of his birds, the four Elves had to retrace their steps several times after coming across dead ends where steep cliffs stopped them progressing further. Aewöl was slowing down the group. The one-eyed Elf needed regular care, though his condition showed steady improvement. He had already drunk their full reserve of healing plant decoctions prepared by Arwela, the seer of the clan Filweni.

*

Their long day was drawing to an end when Gelros asked the group to stop. He kneeled under the cover of a tall oak tree, taking care to pull up the hood of his cloak. His companions copied him without a word, their gazes fixed on Gelros' next move. When he spoke, his voice was heavy with concern.

"My birds have not come back in time," warned the scout.

All was quiet. The site they eventually reached was sheltered from the elements and, although it had been overcast and windy to the northwest throughout their journey, the group knew that the wind usually died down before sunset in the Lost Islands. On this occasion, however, all was too quiet. Most birds had deserted the area, as if tipped off about some secret threat. Only birds of prey could be seen gliding high above. An eagle stretched its wings against the red sky of sunset as it passed overhead.

"I see a walkway," said Gelros, indicating its direction with a nod of his head, "forty yards west of us downhill, but high up in the trees. See wood hanging from those ropes? It looks like the suspended walkways the Green Elves use in the forest to travel between their settlements."

"I see it too," confirmed Curwë, "swinging slowly in the wind... or perhaps..."

"There are Elves walking that footbridge," added Aewöl, suddenly tense.

A silence followed. Gelros scrutinized their surroundings in every direction. Then, he realized.

"There are Green Elves all around us. We are surrounded."

Gelros revealed himself, stepping up and out of his hideout, throwing his bow and short swords to his feet. Curwë soon followed him, as did Aewöl. Only Roquendagor remained hidden. His long green hooded cloak was wrapped around his entire body, completely concealing his presence. From somewhere in the dense undergrowth, an Elvin voice called out.

"Night is upon us. I love this time of day when the leaves spread out across the expanse of glowing orange in the warmth of summer... You must have travelled to Nyn Ernaly to admire its beauty, foreigners from distant Essawylor."

Voryn dyl stepped forward. His silhouette was long and emaciated. The captain of the clan Ernaly's severe features left no doubt about his fierce nature. An aggressive-looking hawk was perched restlessly on his dark leather glove. The brother of Mynar dyl was trying his best to speak in a friendly, melodious manner, but it sounded forced. Nevertheless, he continued with the same tone.

"The Daughter of the Islands say that summer is getting longer every year. Apparently, warm gusts of wind are coming from far away in Essawylor, causing the land to dry up and the trees to grow weak. I believe they are right. I believe that what comes from across the Austral Ocean is never good."

Voryn dyl 'the Ugly' was progressing slowly through the trees. The dreaded archer held his bow in his left hand. There was menacing intent in his posture and gait. Many other Elves of the clan Ernaly now appeared amidst the vegetation of the woods, creeping between trees and hiding behind trunks. The clan Ernaly's insignia, a grey falcon stalking its prey, was woven into their hair along with their hawk feathers. They gradually positioned themselves at regular intervals in a circle around the four Elves. A dozen fighters, heavily armed with javelins and short swords, were now standing close, ready if a melee broke out.

The Elves of Mentollà were also within range of the dozen archers on the walkway. Their bows were raised and loaded, and their quivers, slung over their fine chainmail, were heavy with arrows. Curwë stepped forward, holding up a silver necklace so that all could see. The ivory-white pearls that adorned it were shining vividly the ambient light of early evening.

"We mean you no harm, Voryn dyl. We come in peace; we come to help. Matriarch Nyriele has entrusted us with a mission. We are here to alert you of the dangers you face."

For several moments, Voryn dyl hesitated. He looked tempted to fire his bow at the bard. Disgust was stretched across his face. The Ugly could not stand the idea that the noblest of Llewenti maidens might willingly give her sacred necklace, the symbol of her rank as Eïwele Llyi's high priestess, to a mere foreigner, a refugee from across the ocean. Blinded by hatred, he raised his bow at Curwë, which sent the hawk on his arm flying away. This treacherous move provoked something that none could foresee.

Roquendagor leapt up from his hideout and stood before all. He was furious to see his friend threatened by one of their own allies. He felt the dishonour as if it were his own. The tall knight was preparing to lead his small retinue into battle against the clan Ernaly's forces.

"This day shall not end until my honour is regained," Roquendagor shouted out.

Burning with rage over Voryn dyl's actions, he was swinging his two-handed sword above his bald head. Taken aback to see the hero of the battle of Mentollà, Voryn dyl lowered his bow. For a moment, it seemed as if he were weighing his odds of winning the fight. His gaze went from the four High Elves, now regrouped in a defensive formation, to the two dozen fighters awaiting his instructions. No doubt his unit would have the upper hand, but at what cost? It was the sudden cry of his great hawk now flying above that seemed to change his mind. Voryn dyl took a further step back, behind the cover of an elm tree trunk.

"You have come to help…" he declared, his tone now full of disdain, "You are naive fools... You do not know the enemy we face. It is beyond your imagination. Go back to your high tower by the creek. You do not belong on this island."

In an instant, the clan Ernaly troops withdrew, darting back through the trees, like as many deer springing away into the depths of the woods. They quickly clambered up the ropes and ladders amid the trees to reach the forest footbridge. Soon, they were gone, running along their passageway hanging high in the trees' foliage, as if they were speeding down any well-maintained track on the ground. Finally, one last instruction could be heard.

"Cut the ropes behind you! I do not want these fools to follow us."

And then, as darkness set in, the forest fell silent again.

"That was a long day," concluded Roquendagor. "We should stay here. Now, we are nothing more than simple travellers under the night's sky, looking for a place to pitch camp and prepare food."

There was nothing more to say.

*

The next day, when the sky was red with sunset, the four Elves left the wood of Silver Leaves behind. Heading north-west still, they traipsed up long slopes, keeping close to the cover of the craggy foothills of the Arob Chanun. They moved slowly and stealthily, like green shadows through a forest, constantly wary of taking wrong turns, for the clan Ernaly's trail was no longer easy to follow.

When dusk deepened, and stars emerged, their progress was slowed when they came across an area strewn with sharp rocks. The western sides of the Arob Chanun were steep and harsh, with many gullies and narrow ravines. Now that his birds were no longer returning to confirm the presence of the clan Ernaly fighters, Gelros was at a loss. The Green Elves seemed to have vanished into the ridge. Bent to the ground, the scout looked out, searching across the nearby hills. Curwë was some way ahead, eager to find the trail. Finally, he reached the crest of a rocky hill, and a sudden breeze blew through his hair and stirred his green cloak.

"Not even my eyes can make anything out at this late hour," Curwë called back.

"Their disappearance is a riddle… to answer it we need the light of day," said Roquendagor. "We're staying here for the night."

"I do not like this place," warned Aewöl. "I don't doubt that barbarians often pass through. We're not far here from the human tribes' seat of power in this region. We may well wake up tomorrow to the company of Men out on a hunt."

But Roquendagor quickly ended the debate: "We have no choice."

A little further downhill, they came across a gorge, through which a tiny stream cut a path down into the foothills. Bushes and patches of grass lined its banks. The four Elves agreed it was a suitable place to camp. Curwë offered to take the first watch. The moon was full, and stars glittered in the sky. While his companions settled down to rest, the Elf with green eyes tried to stay cool by dipping his hands into a small pond near their camp and wetting the back of his neck. When the surface of the pond settled, his face shone back at him in the water. He could not help but smile, proud of how he looked. In his eyes was a very specific form of intelligence; he could look at the world in a way that was both hopeful and realistic.

Curwë was known for being cunning, lively and courageous. His inherent attractiveness, fabled among females of all Elvin origin, he owed to his sharp mind and curious nature.

'Mother used to say I am different, I am an exception,' Curwë remembered as he smiled again at the reflection of his image in the water.

And indeed, he had always felt like it. His rare talents must have come from his bloodline; he was one of the few Silver

Elves who had lived in Essawylor. Perhaps because they were called 'Hawenti' in their language, the Green Elves often forgot that, historically, High Elves were divided into two main groups, each ruled by their own kings: the more prominent Gold Elves, and then the Silver Elves. Almost every High Elf living in Essawylor and in the Lost Islands was of Gold Elf ancestry. Only very few Silver Elves had joined them in their exile at the end of the First Age. Curwë's late mother was one of them.

Since setting foot on Nyn Ernaly, Curwë had felt an indomitable force within him. After the many challenges he and his companions had confronted since crossing the Austral Ocean, he had finally found a new beginning. Over these past few years, Curwë had faced death many times; he had looked it in the eye.

'I am not afraid. I will confront my fate with open arms, however dangerous it might prove,' Curwë deeply believed.

The past few days had been a succession of extreme trials; any one of them could have claimed his life. Even now, his heart rate was too high, his blood vessels too narrow, to release him from the tension that still gripped his body. Looking at his companions who were lying still, quietly concealed in their great cloaks and fully absorbed in their dreams, Curwë began to think aloud.

'This all goes to show that life often hangs by a thin thread, and that sometimes only the help of others can save you. I often wonder if I am protected by the star of the Blue Elves, this heavenly body they call Cil. Thirty years ago, in the jungle of Essawylor, I looked to the Star of the West and prayed that my eyes would one day be able to see the secret of life. Well, it looks as though Cil has fulfilled my wish.'

Curwë smiled happily; he was starting to feel what he called the gift of Eïwele Llyi flooding his heart and soul. This sensation was thrilling, unlike any other. It visited him every night in the moments before he fell into deep sleep. Since his last day in

Llafal, the day he spoke with Nyriele, the bard had been swept up in a wave of intense emotion. Curwë loved poetry, and many of his favourite poems had described how, in those unforgettable moments of great love, one can feel immortal.

'My chosen lady seem elevated above all the others. Each of her gestures becomes a favour granted. Every word she speaks becomes a blessing,' he whispered, thinking about Nyriele.

Breathing heavy with the passion he felt, Curwë now realized how devastatingly powerful that encounter had been. He knew that his life had changed its course forever. Nyriele must have known how she had made him feel. He heard it in her voice, he saw it in her movements, it was written across her face! Curwë wavered where he stood, then staggered around, before he fell forwards, groping his way through the darkness, letting his imagination soar. A powerful and uncontrollable flow of absolute love surged through his veins and flooded his heart. The gentle shock of that exceptional emotion had knocked him to the ground. Curwë smiled, fully enjoying the magic of the moment. Looking at the beauty of his surroundings, he suddenly felt inspired. He raised his voice up into the night.

"I breathe, I live, on the steps to your door,
I breathe, I live, more than ever before."

Suddenly, flying insects were swarming around him, interrupting the song he had composed for Nyriele. But these creatures were not moths, as might be expected at that late hour, but many-coloured butterflies, visiting him on his lonely watch as they had done since he came to Nyn Ernaly. That night, there were a great many of them; hundreds, far more than before. Curwë watched their beautiful ballet; intrigued to notice that white was the dominant colour among the butterflies. Then he had the strange feeling that their slow dance had a purpose; he gradually distinguished the outline of some design within the swarm. Before he knew it, the beautiful body of an Elvin maiden appeared in front him, floating gently above the ground, her delicate movements full of grace. Curwë was blinded by the glory of the maid; he fell, but the beautiful ghost of butterflies caught him before he hit the ground. She placed her divine mouth on his, eating him up with the intense light in her eyes.

*

Sometime later, Curwë slowly regained consciousness. The butterflies were gone. The divine vision had disappeared with them. But, to his astonishment, he was not alone. It was Aewöl who stood in front him, an unforgiving gaze expressing his annoyance.

"The first shift was your responsibility," spat the one-eyed Elf. "Your meanderings could have cost us our lives! We must not rest until we escape this evil island. It's your fault we're here in the first place, Curwë. I need not remind you that you brought us here. What's happening with you? You're not the same anymore."
"And so what?" Curwë replied harshly.

He had raised his voice; the sleeping Roquendagor stirred slightly, turning his head in their direction. But soon, all was quiet once more, and the tall knight resumed his restorative reverie.

"I sent Gelros off to check all is safe" informed Aewöl, anxious to establish again a friendlier dialog with his companion. "You can speak to me. What's made you change since we left Llafal? What's troubling your mind?"

Aewöl's only eye was sharp, his gaze deep and piercing. He was trying to determine what was hiding Curwë. The bard knew that, sooner or later, whether he liked it or not, Aewöl would draw the truth from his veins. Suddenly, like a river bursting its banks, he decided to let the emotion that filled him spill out.

"I have feelings for the young matriarch", confided Curwë.
"What does that mean?" asked Aewöl, now intrigued.

Curwë went on, like he was talking to himself rather than
answering the one-eyed Elf's question.

"In that moment with her on the temple steps of Llafal... it
was like I lived an entire life... like it lasted an eternity. It was a
moment of utter perfection. The Green Elves have written songs
about this phenomenon. They say that, on very rare occasions
during an Elf's lifetime, the sister Deities can make time itself
stop, swell and stretch... I remember verses a bard from Llafal
recited aloud in the Halls of Essawylor. The poet was describing
a special favour that Eïwele Llyi could grant her followers, if she
truly wished to reward them. The Deity of Love would visit her
sister, Eïwele Llyo, in her underground hall and beg her to stop
time, so that the blessed lovers she had chosen could enjoy a
moment of infinite happiness that would remain forever in their
memory. I think this is what I experienced that night with
Nyriele."

"Everything you're saying leads me to believe that you have
'fallen under the spell of Eïwele Llyi,' as the Green Elves would
put it... Curwë, my unfortunate friend, you must immediately
extinguish this flame that consumes you, while you still can."

"You're right. A ravaging fire is burning in my heart. I
fought it with all my strength, but my will cannot triumph. A
higher power is rendering my efforts futile. I would not be
surprised if I have become the victim of what poets call
'Hamel'... How is it that, since that night in Llafal under the
stars, all I have cared about is her fate? I had met her many times
before without coming to any harm. But my life changed
dramatically after that magical instant in Temples Square."

"You must put an end to this dream," insisted Aewöl, now
with all the persuasion he could muster. "Friendship might be
possible... maybe... but love... it cannot be. High Elves are
blessed with the gift of immortality; Green Elves are simple
beings doomed to die. I believe that what the Gods made

different cannot become alike. Your destiny is to dwell with us until the end, whereas Nyriele will one day leave us. Even nobles among the Green Elves, despite their divine blood, must die. So think better of it. Forget this love."

Curwë grew heavy at these words. He reacted passionately, for his mind was tainted with the poison of absolute love; the venom of that all-pervasive feeling was subtle, yet strong.

"What is an eternal life of nothingness compared to a mortal life full of passion? I would rather die six times than renounce my dreams. If it had been possible, I would have already eradicated this folly. I would have cured myself of this madness. But an overwhelming upheaval is besieging my heart, my very soul. I can feel it, and, in the depths of my being, I want it. It's an uncontrollable passion that's driven me to this impasse."

"But why would you want to love a stranger, who does not belong to our world, the descendant of a queen no less? Her family at the very least despise us. Most Green Elves hate what the High Elves represent. Your own kin may well find you a lady worthy of your love. The fate of this young matriarch is not yours to bear."

"But I want this great love to live! I want to make this blessing from the sky last! What crime have I committed? These are noble sentiments; who would dare tell me otherwise? I cannot help it. I have fallen deeply in love with her fragile beauty, her youth, her noble origins, her brave heart and the purity of her soul!"

"There is no such thing as a 'pure soul,' Curwë! You are talking nonsense! The one thing we can be sure of is that this everlasting bond you dream about will end as quickly as it began. Nyriele's supposed passion for you will wane over time; she will soon turn her eyes to someone else."

"Never! She might as well throw herself into a river to find cover from the rain," cried Curwë, his gaze consumed by violent passion.

"These are the ways of the Green Elves," insisted Aewöl,

"above all their most powerful matriarchs. You must have heard, as I have, that their high priestesses select their consorts according to their mood. Some even choose their partners as part of their strategy. I've heard common gossip that Nyriele herself was born from an arranged union without love, when two clans wanted an heir with a rare bloodline."

"I've had enough of your deceitful advice. My fate has not been set by any power, and it will never be. I will be whoever I wish to be. Hear me, Aewöl! Curwë follows his own path. Curwë chooses his destiny. Nyriele's kindness towards me is living proof that Eïwele Llyi has blessed my coming to these Islands. She is the incarnation of tenderness. Nothing can compare to her smile. One day, I will offer her my silver ring... then we will see how she responds."

"Beware, Curwë! You've talked in such extreme terms since we started this conversation. Your obsession is turning into a sickness of the mind. I can well believe you've been bewitched by her power. I read all the myths about her. Eïwele Llyi might well be the divinity of arts and beauty, but she's also the great spirit of lust. Those who operate by seducing others will often resort to all artifices in order to gain an advantage. My view is that Eïwele Llyi's influence, like the powers wielded by her high priestess, encompasses all these attributes: seduction but also lies; charm but also vanity; love but then the inevitable jealousy that follows. The irrational passion she ignites within minds also gives way to deceit. Though you might not think it, love and strife go hand in hand."

Listening to these words, anger was growing within Curwë's mind. He now regretted confiding in his companion. Aewöl embodied the figure of the councillor, which was so different from that of the priest. He did not draw his authority from any secrets that the Gods had divulged to him, but rather from truths which he had come to himself having considered and tested them. Aewöl made his points without the support of occult mysteries; rather, his arguments were based on rational, verifiable reasoning. He would never oppose someone head-on.

Rather, he would reinterpret and repurpose the beliefs of others to his own advantage. He knew the art of reusing the words of those he was persuading, to divert their meaning and offer new perspectives.

Aewöl looked into Curwë's eyes and immediately knew that he had gone too far in his opposition, and that any further attempts would prove counterproductive. The two Elves sat silent for a while. Finally, Aewöl offered to take the watch, which the exhausted bard gratefully accepted. Soon after, Curwë had plunged back into a profound sleep, his mind's eye filled with the image of beautiful Nyriele.

*

The next day, as a red strip of sun emerged over the mountains, they searched everywhere for any sign of the clan Ernaly unit's trail. But all was still, quiet and insubstantial. Colour was gradually returning to the waking woodland. To the west, the meadows of Nyn Ernaly, from where they stood all the way down to the sea, were shimmering with green. To the east, the unlit peaks of Moka Kirini stood blue and purple. The highest mountains at the heart of the Arob Chanun, however, already flushed with the orange of morning. After searching for some hours, Gelros finally admitted,

"Finding this trail is beyond my capabilities."

"Let us continue northwest and find shelter somewhere on the edge of the forest of Mentolewin's border. We can then head to the wild beaches of Nyn Ernaly's northern coast. Perhaps we will see the fleet of Llymar," proposed Aewöl, looking in the direction they must take.

The ridge on which they stood descended steeply downwards in a rugged slope before it ended in a dangerous cliff. This was where the Chanun Mountains ended. Half a dozen leagues away, the green forest of Mentolewin stretched away beyond the edge of sight. All afternoon, the four Elves hardly stopped moving. At times running, at times marching, they followed an invisible track which led straight on, northwest towards the forest. They were constantly vigilant for any sign of beast or Man. Dwellings of barbarian tribes were close by, on the western coast of Nyn Ernaly, and those herdsmen were known to keep flocks in that region. But no movement could be seen in this, the easternmost part of the barbarians' dominion. The land was surprisingly empty. The calm that reigned was not the quiet calm of serenity.

"The barbarians have deserted their meadows and gathered their herds, all along the coastland, as if they feared a large-scale invasion," said Curwë.

"Druids are chiefs of those tribes," advised Aewöl. "They are wise in the ways of the Mother of the Island. They can foresee such threats."

A couple of hours after noon, Gelros suddenly stopped. At his feet, the ground, though still uneven, had become soft, like an unpaved road.

"This must be the old gravel track of the High Elves," the scout said, "which led from the city that was once Mentobraglin to the great fortress of Mentolewin. The path is barely ten feet wide. But see how it snakes through the thickets of ferns."

The ever-encroaching army of brambles and nettles, which would normally have made the path almost invisible, had been pushed back and trampled. The full width of the track, it seemed, had been recently reclaimed by a large group passing through. Soil had been turned up and stones dislodged by a great many feet and hooves. The wheels of heavy carriages had left their own distinctive marks. From where they were standing, they could see the trail continuing northeast towards the dry foothills of the Arob Chanun. Gelros kneeled and examined the tracks with great care.

"Nellos troops from Tar Andevar travelled this path not long ago… I estimate they would have been here just yesterday. The army is large: several hundred strong at least, with cavalry and well-armed infantry. They are carrying significant supplies with them, for their chariots are heavily loaded. They were progressing slowly. If they kept going at this same pace, they will probably still be very close."

"Then we have no choice," said Aewöl. "We must hurry to the borders of Mentolewin forest and seek cover."

Curwë challenged this conclusion, his emerald eyes flashing.

"What if this army is heading towards the units of Llymar? You believe we should move in the opposite direction?"

"I would rather not see that happen. Come, Curwë, in the forest we will have an impassable barrier protecting us. It will give us time to find the information we need. We must first understand the strange events occurring in this land," warned the one-eyed Elf.

Roquendagor gave Curwë a cold glance. "Aewöl is right. The course he suggests is wise. We head to the forest."

His feet were firmly planted on the ground and his hands gripped the hilt of his fearsome two-handed sword: clear signs that his decision had been made. The four Elves set off immediately. They progressed quickly, but stayed stooped low, cautious to remain unseen in the wilderness. They marched without rest for several more hours. Gelros ran ahead, grim and cautious. Aewöl followed; the one-eyed Elf looked weary, perhaps more in heart than body. Curwë, however, showed no signs of fatigue. His pace was light and fast. It looked as if the bard were drawing his energy from a continuous, exquisite daydream, his mind brimming happily with eroticism and beauty. Roquendagor marched at the rear, as tireless and unshakable as stone. The long journey seemed to affect neither his strength nor his will. The sun was sinking when they finally reached the first trees of Mentolewin forest.

*

The next day, the four Elves were marching north along the tree-clad borders of the forest. They saw no sign of fresh trails, within the woods or in the great spaces of Nyn Ernaly's northern plain. The weather was overcast, with low clouds shrouding the sun. At last, they decided to halt in an open glade, just within the edge of the forest. They made their camp beneath a maritime pine. The tree looked isolated in that large forest of chestnuts but, looking at it, the four Elves knew they were not far from the sea, which now lay barely a few leagues to the west. It somehow reminded them of their own situation.

The four companions stood below the isolated pine, feeling troubled by all their ill fortune since setting foot on Nyn Ernaly. Many leagues separated them from the fleet of Llymar, their only hope of returning to their home. They could still find no trace of the clan Ernaly's expedition, their only potential ally in this wild and dangerous part of the island.

Another night passed. Curwë, once again, took the first shift on night-watch. When Aewöl later got up to replace him, the two close friends exchanged only a few words. Gelros took the watch next, before Roquendagor stood on duty until dawn. Like he did every night during those rare few hours of tranquillity, the tall knight performed the ritual of shaving his head. The three others awoke to find a hot sun shining beyond the Chanun Mountains. A morning wind had swept away the last shreds of clouds, which were now retreating towards the south. Curwë, seeing that his companions' moods had turned gloomy, decided to try to cheer them up.

"Crossing the wood of Silver Leaves has proven beneficial in some ways. Several nights have now passed without our mysterious Elvin spy showing so much as a shadow again."

Failing to notice the irony in Curwë's words, Roquendagor spat back a reply harshly.

"We need to stay vigilant if we are to see more of that scout while our voyage lasts."

The first part of the day was dedicated to working on their weaponry. Gelros knew the art of making arrows and bolts, and Aewöl always carried with him a spare supply of arrow heads made with the best alloy. Leaving their other companions to speculation and conjecture, the two Elves focussed on the making a fresh stock of projectiles. Their work was efficient, and, after a couple of hours, their quivers were loaded with a new supply of expertly made arrows. Then, Curwë unexpectedly interrupted their careful work.

"Look at that high mountain, I think it's Eïwal Vars Lepsy!" he cried, pointing up into the pale eastern sky. "I mean the peak that looks like the finger of a God pointing to the heavens. Birds of prey are flocking in huge numbers above it. They are very high in the sky, moving with great speed from the north towards the Chanun Mountains."

"The last time I saw such impressive gathering was the day before the battle of Mentollà," remembered Aewöl.

"Yes. Hawks protected the army of Llymar's approach before it charged and broke the siege of the tower. I wonder what their errand is this time," said Roquendagor.

"They are a dozen leagues east of us at least," added Gelros, "though it is hard to tell. We will need a full day to reach the area, and only if we make haste."

"This means we no longer need to find the track of Voryn dyl and his unit," observed Curwë. "We now know where they are going. Let us head to the paths of the Chanun Mountains with all possible speed. That is where the army of Llymar is gathering."

Leaving the cover of the forest's edge, the four Elves came out onto the grass of Nyn Ernaly's wild meadows. It swelled like a green sea around the foothills of the Chanun Mountains' northern range, dominated by Eïwal Vars Lepsy's peak. On the vast plain, the air was hotter, thick with scents of burnt herbs as if, here, summer was still clinging firmly on. Now that they were travelling fully exposed through those barbarian lands, the anxious Elves progressed in single file, running like a pack of wolves following a fresh scent.

Gelros ran at the head of the pack. The summer sun climbed to high noon, and then dipped slowly towards the sea. During those long few hours, they hardly paused, fighting back against weariness by singing old songs of Essawylor, the war chants of the Northern Province. As the sunlight faded, their green-cloaked figures faded against the background of the empty landscape. A wind arose from the sea, as though urging them on to their destination. As shadows began to loom from the hilltops, still the four Elves ran on.

Finally, they reached the first stony dale of the ridged hills. The sun was now sinking into the evening mists above the sea. When night came, they decided to stop. More than ten leagues now lay between them and the edge the forest they had left at dawn. Though the moon was full, its light was weak, for eastern winds had brought dark, threatening clouds. The stars were fully veiled. The four Elves were alone in the wilderness.

*

They awoke the next day to a cloudy, stormy sky. Like every morning since they had left Mentollà, Curwë was up first, as if he did not need to rest at all. He urged his companions to start moving again, sensing they were getting close to their goal. The trees in the area were knotted and twisted, and the ground overrun with brambles, wild roses, reeds and nettles. No elder trees grew here.

"Let us head up that mountain pass. No army would take

such a difficult route. We will be safe. Once we arrive at the top, we will have a dominant view of the valleys surrounding Eïwal Vars Lepsy's peak," Curwë said, pointing in the direction of a mountain, south of the 'God's Finger' peak.

The four Elves looked around at the faint light of morning, and hope was restored in their hearts. They followed Curwë, climbing the steep mountain's slope, scampering up narrow trails and scaling vertiginous rock walls. Gelros and Aewöl fashioned ladders out of their thin ropes to help them overcome some of the sheerest climbs. Finally, after considerable effort, they emerged at the top of the mountain. It had taken them a full day to reach this high ground, five thousand feet above sea level. The northerly wind brought a chill from the snowy Moka Kirini peaks to the south. The twin white tips appeared to float upon the low clouds. The four Elves halted again and prepared to weather another night away from home.

*

At sunrise, the sky was cloudless. A wind from the north had chased away the mountain mists, as if Eïwal Ffeyn were sending his blessings from his oceanic prison. As they looked down, the harsh light of the morning sun revealed a narrow valley, its sides almost vertical, cutting through the mountain range. In the large gorge was a small river which flowed swiftly towards the vast plain of Nyn Ernaly. To the north, they saw the vertical granite walls of Eïwal Vars Lepsy's peak. The four Elves sat there for a moment, looking at the spectacular view before them in complete awe.

After some time, Gelros spotted movement further down in the valley, just where the river began to trickle down from the higher plateau towards the vast verdant plain. They immediately descended a few feet down the mountain, away from the peak where they would stand out starkly against the clear sky. There was silence between them after this development; the four Elves listened only to the wind whistling through the rocks. After a while, Curwë rejoiced.

"Finally, here are some good news."

Curwë could see far into the distance. He had inherited the rare power from his Silver Elf forefathers, known for their farsighted vision. He described to the others what only his emerald eyes could see. From the tiny moving specs of shadow, he could make out, Curwë detailed with great precision an entire army, the army of Nellos. He saw cavaliers mounted on war horses, archers clad in bright chain mail, spearmen in straight formations and wagons drawn by oxen. All four of them could see smoke rising in large plumes down in the valley behind them. Curwë immediately understood.

"The army of Nellos is on the move. It is entering the gorge of Eïwal Vars Lepsy. But look far away to the other end of the valley! Its rear-guard seems stuck, the units in total disarray. I think it's making an emergency retreat."

"What do you mean?" asked Roquendagor, becoming impatient.

The tall knight disliked any situation he could not fully control. After observing a while longer, Curwë became sure of what he was seeing.

"The army of Nellos is under attack. It explains the smoke we see in the distance. They are seeking cover in the gorge of Eïwal Vars Lepsy. See how their archer units are positioned on either side of the valley. The rear-guard is fighting hard to gain the rest of the army time, to make sure their wagons can reach a safe haven. This is what is unfolding before us... The question now is: what force is pushing that large army into a dead end?"

"I see only one answer to this riddle," said Aewöl, his only eye beginning to shine like a dark amethyst. "The army of Llymar has come."

The four Elves set off down the northward slope with as much haste as the steep terrain allowed. The descent was long and dangerous. Time passed slowly. At last, they began to hear the distant yells of Nellos officers stationing their archers along the valley slopes. Deciding to be as careful as possible, the four Elves drew near the highest positions occupied by the soldiers. They finally reached a hideout a hundred yards uphill, a little above the defensive lines of the Westerners. Wrapped in their green cloaks, the four Elves lay on wet grass behind the protection of rocks.

Now the cries of the Nellos troops were ringing clearly over the hill. Those Men of great stature were organizing themselves calmly. Their exemplary composure belied the fact that their army was retreating. They looked like experienced warriors. Their faces were grim, their hair cut short. In their hands were their long bows. Each of them carried two quivers full of arrows. Their small shields were slung at their sides, painted with the symbol of Nellos: a setting sun upon the ocean. Their navy-blue cloaks were billowing in the wind, revealing the broad swords and daggers hanging at their belts. The archers were running around, carrying out their officers' orders to build stone walls, behind which they would be able to find cover or hide.

None of them noticed the four Elves behind the rocks, watching them from above, barely a few dozen yards up the hill. The archers had almost finished taking their defensive positions when two formidable riders appeared, each leading a unit of elite guards. Both cavaliers were proudly wearing the golden gauntlet of their order on their left hands.

The first knight sorcerer, taller than all the rest, was clad in golden plate mail and wrapped in a broad red cloak. A crest the colour of ruby flowed from his helm. He commanded the strategic disposition of their troops.

The second knight sorcerer followed closely. He was a Westerner, strong and limber. His head was bald, and he was naked down to the waist, his face and torso covered in tattoos and tribal marks. His black stallion was dragging behind him two prisoners, bound in chains and visibly drowsy with drugs.

"The captives are High Elves!" exclaimed Curwë.

The two knights of the Golden Hand checked their steeds and, with masterful horsemanship, turned in opposite directions, set off into gallops, and circled the area several times. Visibly satisfied with their defences and the dominating view the position offered over the valley, the two knights leapt down from their horses. Without a word or cry, dozens of soldiers began setting up what was to become the army's command base.

Meanwhile, the main column of the Men's army continued retreating into the gorge. With ten four-horse chariots and a dozen armoured wagons, they carried enough food and provisions to last the thousand troops of its army several weeks. Each chariot bore three officers and was accompanied by fifty-foot soldiers. Each wagon, stocked with food and supplies, came with twenty-five other workers including grooms, cooks and slaves. Each pair of chariots, therefore, had over a hundred and fifty Men in tow. The army of Tar-Andevar was manoeuvred with discipline; they were wise enough not to move too fast, and not so stupid to take too long in their retreat.

For a long time, Roquendagor looked out upon the scene before him. Now he too could see the army of Llymar entering the vale. The clans of the forest had mustered around fifteen units of light troops, including archers, javelin throwers and sling-wielders. Roquendagor guessed that this was probably as many troops as their fleet, sailing at full capacity, could have carried to Nyn Ernaly's shores. There would be no reinforcements coming. The Elves of Llymar were throwing everything they had into this battle. Roquendagor's sharp, incisive mind enabled him to predict the ebb and flow of any battle before it begun. The former heir of House Dol Lewin had led large armies through many conflicts. He prided himself on his mastery of the art of war. He was equally adept at commanding large numbers of units from a distance as he was at fighting blade to blade in the heat of combat. Roquendagor now understood the Nellos commander's strategy.

"Look! The army of Men is trying to win this battle without fighting. The Westerners are not attacking their enemies head-on, still less attempting to flee. What they're doing is setting a trap, in order to capture the entire Elvin army. If they were to succeed, it would be a martial achievement. This is how they have chosen to fight. Because they outnumber their enemy almost three to one, they will want to surround them. But, contrary to what might be expected, they are hoping to achieve this by retreating, by pretending they are fleeing into that vale to seek the protection of the hills. Their Elvin opponents are resolute and consider themselves to be the stronger side; they will most likely fall into the Westerners' trap."

"I see Gal dyl Avrony, his long spear in hand, at the vanguard of the Elvin army. He is fighting bravely like a hero of yore," Curwë observed in the distance.

"That fool is ordering his troops to advance into the vale and start climbing the hills' slopes," said Aewöl coldly. "He will hobble his army, like tying his horse to a post."

Roquendagor concurred. "Gal dyl is making a mistake even by fighting at the vanguard. He is being reckless and may get himself killed. Even if he is only injured in this useless fighting at the front line, his troops will become vulnerable. He must have been provoked and been unable to control his anger. Either Gal dyl is a kind-hearted Elf who is fighting out of guilt, or else he is a proud fool who has been humiliated. Whatever his weakness is, he compromises his army by interfering with the vanguard's fighting. His actions will bring confusion among his ranks."

Roquendagor considered further the human army's movements.

"On the other hand, the Nellos Commander knows when to fight and when not to fight. He has wisely decided how best to use his larger force against a smaller but fiercer enemy. See how the upper ranks of his units are lying in wait for when the Elves are exhausted. This is a guarantee of success."

Aewöl pointed to the top of a large rocky promontory, down from where the four Elves hid, where the knight sorcerers of the Golden Hand had set up their command centre. The post overlooked the vale the Elvin army was entering.

"That's their commander," Aewöl said, "the one with the golden armour and shining helmet. He's giving orders on the army's movements, which are then communicated in signals by his retinue. He's managing that multitude of Men as if they were a dozen. He's positioned his troops on a gentle slope, with the right flank and rear-guard towards the high ground; death lies before his army, and survival lies behind."

Curwë fixed his sharp eyes on the Nellos army's commander. He added.

"That's no Man commanding the troops of Nellos. It's a High Elf. And that's a golden gauntlet on his left hand... He corresponds to the description of Eno Mowengot, commander of the knights of the Golden Hand. As we crossed the strait of Tuide, Master Aertelyr warned me about him; he is one of King Norelin's most dreaded servants."

Turning away from the battlefield, Aewöl lay on his back, white-faced, beside Curwë. His low voice almost echoed, as if it came from a dark tunnel.

"Roquendagor, you said that Gal dyl must have been provoked to engage in such a dangerous strategy. I believe you are right, and I think I know why. The two Elvin prisoners chained to the bald knight's horse are the answer to that riddle."

Curwë immediately looked in their direction, only a hundred yards down the slope.

"The prisoners' wrists and ankles are tied with chains. A company of Nellos soldiers are standing around them. A few are posted on watch duty, but most of the Men are lying on the ground, looking dispirited. They are probably wounded soldiers who have been assigned the easy task of watching the captives, far from the fray. I cannot see the prisoners' features, for their faces are hidden by red turbans. They are taller than their jailers. I don't doubt they are High Elves, and probably prominent figures at that, judging by the cut of their clothes.

Curwë' gaze was sharp. None of his companions could distinguish such details.

"One is dressed in blue robes; golden embroidery adorns his cloak. The other Elf looks younger and stronger. His silk clothes are some kind of purple, though it is difficult to tell, given the mud and bloodstains covering him. These Elves must have suffered cruelly. They have probably undergone torture at the hands of their captors, and perhaps worse, for they look acutely weary. Look! The older Elf is not being watched. Though his legs are securely bound, his arms are only tied about the wrists; he has just managed to free his hands. He is now removing his turban; he could hardly breathe before. His hair is a distinctive grey, a mess of aristocratic curls. It looks like that ancient lord from Tios Lluin! The one known as the Blue Mage."

"It must be Curubor Dol Etrond," said Aewöl. "That prisoner is Gal dyl's counsellor... and friend. It explains everything... or at least why the Elvin army is so eager to free the knight sorcerers' captives. But how has the ancient scholar ended up in such dire peril?"

Roquendagor seemed to care very little. Since the victory of Mentollà, he had deliberately kept his distance from the other High Elves of Llymar Forest, avoiding meetings with their representatives and refusing all their invitations. The oath of Lormelin remained heavy in his thoughts and, furthermore, he wanted nothing to do with the Dol Etrond lords, old enemies of his own house in the days of the war of Diamond and Ruby.

Roquendagor instead opted to praise the military skills of the Nellos commander.

"Now I understand his strategy even better. This Eno Mowengot is a master of calculation; he is able to monitor both order and chaos. The movements of his carefully assembled formations are drawing Gal dyl's units even further into the valley. At this present moment, he is handing his enemies what looks like an easy victory, luring them onwards behind his retreating chariots, promising them the destruction of his supplies and the chance to free the lordly prisoners. But his best troops are lying in wait. They were probably first to the battlefield within this vale and have now the luxury of waiting for their enemy. The astute knight sorcerer is making his foe's decisions for him, and he is not permitting his foe to do the same back. By dangling the bait of the chained Elvin lords in front of Gal dyl, provoking anger and forcing him to move, Eno Mowengot has summoned his enemy to the precise place he has chosen to fight."

Now fully understanding the scope of Roquendagor's predictions, Curwë could not help but admit to the genius of the Nellos army commander.

"This Eno Mowengot is truly a master of the art of war!"
"War is a not an art, Curwë," disagreed Roquendagor bluntly.

He spoke with passion in his voice when he went on, for he treated all aspects of warfare with reverence.

"I see it as a very particular craft, a series of vital rules and considerations. War is not an art, and neither is it a game, for the price of defeat is too high."
"I know that involving ourselves in the battle should be a last resort," Curwë reluctantly admitted, "but surely now is the time to intervene! We know that this will be a decisive conflict.

We cannot stay here like the audience to some tragic drama. We must help them."

"Curwë," Aewöl intervened, "You are always one for epic songs, but could you really handle the reality of what you are suggesting?"

"There would be nothing noble at all about watching our allies get slaughtered. I will not stand idly by while our units march to their doom."

"Those proud words do you much honour," Aewöl insisted, "but the impending disaster is clear for all to see, even to my paltry single eye. The army of Llymar is about to be defeated. The Westerners are conducting this battle impeccably. They haven't put a foot wrong. Their victory is certain, for Gal dyl has already lost due to his own poor strategy."

Curwë, now on the brink of despair, implored Roquendagor.

"We cannot let that happen. It's never the easy victories that go down in history. Glory is only earned when valour wins the day, whatever the odds before the battle begun. The time to show our immense courage is now."

This passionate plea seemed to have made its mark upon Roquendagor who remained silent. After a while, the tall knight made his decision. His gaze burnt like looming fire.

"To avoid a probable defeat, you need a wise defensive strategy. To achieve an unlikely victory, however, the unexpected attack is your only hope. We will sweep down from this height upon the enemy's reserve fighters and seize what is most precious to him: his prisoners. Then we flee into the mountains. They will have to pursue us, thus disorganizing their ranks and giving Gal dyl's army a chance to escape."

"I fully disagree," countered Aewöl immediately, imploring them to think of their own interests. "This is madness. In the days of Essawylor, we only ever fought when we were sure of victory."

"And we ended up losing Ystanlewin. Our friends and families perished because of our failure," Roquendagor reminded him, hypnotized by that grim memory, which obscured almost every moment of his new life.

"If we want to live a prosperous life on these islands, we cannot act as if we're invincible. I don't doubt that there will be many other challenges to come. Are battles only fought to seek glory? No. The best warriors remain in the shadows, uncelebrated in songs... Let me ask you a question. What do we gain by wading into this conflict?"

Roquendagor, whose decision had already been made, did not even consider answering his former counsellor. The tall knight was already planning his next move.

"We will force this Eno Mowengot to change his tactics. We will win by targeting his weakest points and avoiding his stronger units. We must wait for the moment he decides to unleash his best troops; the moment they charge into the lowest depths of the vale. Then we can launch a surprise attack against his disorganised reserve, which will be caught unprepared. Those weak troops will be prone to disorder."

"This is folly," complained Aewöl, still in total disagreement.

Roquendagor, who was not used to being contradicted, replied sharply.

"On the contrary: we are taking the unwatched road and attacking their least-guarded flank, and we will quickly withdraw with the prisoners. When striking the snake at its tail, speed is the key, for you can be sure that its head will soon snap round. Our attack may well allow the Elvin army to avoid being routed and retreat in an orderly manner."

Curwë then spoke up, attempting to convince his two other companions who remained uncertain.

"I say we have a chance. We are not going up against fresh troops. Our backs are against the hill; we have the higher ground. There is nothing obstructing our retreat into the mountain's rocky slopes after we strike. Our escape route is clear. Most of those soldiers are tired or wounded. Their spirits are low after what they've been through already. If we press them hard, they won't fight to the death."

"Let us show our strength. The sun is in our backs. And we have the element of surprise," concluded Roquendagor simply.

The four Elves resumed their watch. There were many birds of prey perched upon the cliffs and outcrops. Flocks were circling high in the air, black against a pale sky. From time to time, a hawk would plunge into the fight, eager to assist when its master's life was at risk. As the hours slowly passed, the Elves from Mentollà still lay in wait, peering down into the encroaching gloom. They were awaiting their enemy's slow march from afar; they rested while the Nellos reserve laboured hard, busy organizing the withdrawal of the wounded back towards where the captives were being kept. Suddenly, loud orders echoed throughout the gorge, as officers began waving flags of different colours in the evening mist.

"Look! It is starting. These units of Men that were standing in reserve are being ordered to march. They know the terrain around the river, the choke points in the valley and the boggy ground in the lower marshes. They will use this knowledge to their advantage," said Roquendagor.

An imperceptible tension grew amongst the small group, for each Elf knew that the moment to launch their raid was upon them. All looked to Roquendagor. The knight was orderly in the face of chaos, calm in the face of commotion. Such was how he managed his heart.

"We move. Strike like lightning!" ordered Roquendagor.

Curwë repeatedly blew his small horn until the very foothills surrounding them rang out. Many different echoes came back from the gorge, as if dozens of Elvin trumpets were answering Curwë's call. But he was also answered by loud yells in the Westerners' tongue, and the clattering of steel weapons being drawn. The cruel bow of Gelros began to sing. Arrows flew from the Elvin string with an almost impossible frequency. The cries and calls of the Nellos soldiers rang out throughout the valley and, among them, the sharp orders of the knight sorcerers.

"Fire of Narkon!" someone in the bushes suddenly screamed.

Then, just where the reserve soldiers were gathering their equipment, there was a sudden burst of flame, like a blacksmith's forge exploding under too much pressure, which detonated out of nothing with a low roar. The burst of the dark fire released a huge amount of pressure near the prisoners' camp, where their guards stood. Everything flammable in the area was ignited. The heat of the explosion even melted the metal of the guards' armour. Many Men died, others just about managed to dodge the impact or roll aside. The smell of sulphur was thick in the air.

The remaining guards looked around at the terrifying spectacle, paralysed by the prospect of having to join in the fray. Their camp was burning. All around them, hot ashes were still smouldering. By their feet lay broken helms, plate mail, shields, swords and many burnt corpses amid other ruined equipment. Smoke was now raising high in the sky and could be seen by all combatants fighting in the valley below.

A second explosion was heard. A curtain of dark, shadowy fire blazed around the guards: an opaque sheet of flames ten feet high that formed a semi-circle, emanating waves of intense heat. The surviving soldiers drew their swords and daggers but hesitated. All round the small knoll on which they were gathered; fires were springing up, the dark flames moving likes shadows, until a complete ring was formed. Some of the archers shot their arrows at the dancing fire, until they realized it was a waste of their missiles. The swiftly moving silhouettes of two tall Elves could be barely seen in the fire dark's smoke.

Roquendagor rushed forward, his eyes wild. Drawing his blade and crying

"Roq Laorn! Roq Laorn!" he charged down the hill.

His huge two-handed sword gleamed with a singular brilliance, almost a luminescence, amidst the swarm of black flames that surrounded him. Aewöl covered Roquendagor's flanks with his light crossbow, as he chanted mysterious verses. The one-eyed Elf looked as if he himself was on fire. Thin, dark flames wisped around his cloak, giving him the appearance of a demon of the Underworld. None dared approach him and many fled in panic at his coming, overcome with a mystical terror.

Roquendagor rushed down the final section of slope at full speed, slamming into the first lines of soldiers who had stayed with the prisoners. Once his charge had cleaved the unit of Nellos fighters in two, he began a massacre. Arms were cut off, heads decapitated, and limbs split in two, as fountains of blood erupted all around him. The cruelty and ferocity of Roquendagor's attack immediately inspired intense horror in the hearts of all who saw. Some archers drew their long bows and fired at the formidable Elf, but none could pierce his chain mail; the shadowy veil that surrounded him seemed to provide unnatural protection.

In the melee, Roquendagor saw the bald knight sorcerer: a large Man with broad shoulders, powerful arms and a muscular exposed torso. Without warning, the Man sprang forward as a number of his guards began to flee. With a swift stroke of his blade, the bald warrior sliced the head off one of the deserters. The other wounded guards scrabbled away, cursing their commander behind them. There was much confusion.

The knight sorcerer threw his javelin at the tall Elf. The short spear flew over the melee and pierced the Elfin chain mail, burying itself in Roquendagor's left shoulder. Blood spurted out of the wound, drenching the front of the Elf's armour.

But, despite his wound, Roquendagor continued to fight, massacring enemies as he attempted to withdraw from the melee. His blood sprayed out again when he managed to yank the spear from his shoulder. Roquendagor pressed the burning blade of his two-handed sword onto the wound to stem the bleeding.

"Get behind me Agadeon!" he cried with pain and seemed to lose all sense of self-preservation.

Terrified at the Elf's frantic resolution, more guards fled, leaving the bald warrior almost alone with his two prisoners. Roquendagor rushed towards the last remaining soldiers, like a wounded lion leaping into battle one last time. He killed the first Westerner with a throw of a spear he picked up, which struck the Man in the chest. Then he killed a second; Roquendagor literally split the guard in two with the sharp edge of his sword. The blow hit the Man in the shoulder and continued down through his torso in a fresh eruption of blood. His severed bust thumped onto the ground. Such was the atrocity of the scene that three more terrorized soldiers took to their heels.

Only two opponents now separated Roquendagor from the bald warrior and his prisoners. The tall Elf threw a stone at the first, who could not get out of its way before it smashed into his hip. The unfortunate Westerner cried out in pain and fell to the ground, helpless. Roquendagor went to finish him with a thrust of his sword, but the last remaining guard stepped in his way. Carried away by his rage, Roquendagor assaulted the Man with a ferocious swing, which slashed his forearm. The soldier fainted in agony. Roquendagor now faced the bald warrior, the last bastion between himself and the two prisoners. The Westerner did not move, waiting for his foe to attack.

"BANG!"

In that very moment, down in the valley, there was a formidable crash, which echoed long around the gorge. The flash of flame and smoke had been seen by all combatants on the battlefield. A chariot had exploded, killing many Elves. A gaping hole was blasted into the Elvin vanguard. The trap designed by Eno Mowengot was closing in around the army of Gal dyl. The knight sorcerer commander was positioned on the edge of a cliff that looked out over the battlefield, a hundred yards away from Roquendagor's position. Surrounded by his personal guard, Eno Mowengot pointed his golden gauntlet in the direction of the Elvin units, which were struggling to retreat. From the flaming chariot, a rain of fire began to pour down upon the Elves of Llymar, setting their clothes ablaze, burning their flesh and terrorizing even their bravest fighters.

A hundred yards east of the cliff's edge, Roquendagor moved forward, as righteous and noble as the engraved portrait of an ancient Dol lord. The bald warrior waived his golden gauntlet. Roquendagor saw that it only had five fingers; the sixth was mutilated. His naked torso was covered in tattoos, his face in tribal markings. Muscular as a bull, tall as a Giant, his great stature was terrifying.

"Come, Elf warrior! Come to me! Experience the gentle touch of my golden hand," roared the knight sorcerer.

He slowly lifted his scimitar above his head, drinking the blood that ran down the blade. Roquendagor could wait no longer.

Crying, "Roq Laorn! Roq Laorn!" he charged headlong to greet his foe.

Their blades met with a big clash. But the fury of the Elf was greater. His skill with the two-handed sword equalled the bravest knights of bygone ages. Roquendagor clove through his opponent's defences like a scythe through a wheat field. His long blade broke into many shards as he cut the golden gauntlet from the bald warrior's arm. The Westerner was thrown down by the force of the blow. Roquendagor leapt into the air and landed on his wounded enemy. He began hammering at the Man with his fists. They began fighting hand-to-hand on the ground, wrestling and grappling as they stood up, each looking for an opportunity to throw or strike the other.

Both warriors were fighting with everything they had to gain and maintain a superior position. Finally, out of a seemingly unbreakable grapple, Roquendagor executed a ferocious throw. He then pinned his opponent to the ground to ensure his victory. He used his full body weight to contain the Westerner as he choked him with both hands. After a few spasms, the bald warrior let out a shrill cry. The echo of his wailing died in the wind.

"Victory is mine !!!" roared Roquendagor with a gleam in his bloodshot eyes.

Still at the cliff's edge, indifferent to the fate of his companion, Eno Mowengot was now conjuring volleys of flaming arrows against the Elvin army. Nothing, it seemed, could put a stop to the bloodbath he was orchestrating, as he unleashed the full might of his power against the forces of Llymar. The Elvin army seemed like it would be routed any moment, surrounded and outnumbered as they were by the Nellos troops.

"I have no more bolts!" Curwë exclaimed and he threw away his crossbow.

Leaping to his feet, Curwë drew both his sword and Rowë's dagger. At his side, Gelros was still firing his own arrows. Curwë started running down the hill straight in front of him. He quickly emerged out of the cover of the undergrowth. His gaze was fixed on the cairn overlooking the valley, upon which Eno Mowengot stood, summoning a deluge of fire to swamp the Elvin army below.

Each of Curwë steps brought him closer to his target. As if possessed by an indomitable courage, he charged. Curwë jumped over waterlogged ditches, fallen trees and jutting stumps. Impervious to fear, he relinquished all caution in pursuit of this decisive feat. Nyriele's father was about to be defeated, perhaps killed. His body and spirit were enflamed by the oath he had made to the young matriarch. There was no way he would return to Llafal with the mark of failure on his forehead. He would not let that happen. Curwë reached the bottom of the slope and rushed at the first ring of defence around Eno Mowengot. Suddenly appearing in the full light of sun.

"Roq Laorn!" Curwë madly yelled the war cry of House Dol Lewin.

He slammed into the first guards, toppling them with the force of his attack. Curwë lost all awareness of danger, his frantic howling rising up above the murmur of battle below. He was slashing and thrusting at a multitude of enemies: breaking limbs, smashing skulls and stabbing at flesh, until the blade of his sword was broken in the fray. He was terrible to behold, as if protected by a powerful Deity. Combining physical prowess and a fierce focus, Curwë threw his broken sword, which spun in a long arc before striking one of his numerous enemies at a distance. He could see his own blood spilling out of numerous wounds, but the energy and hatred that inhabited him mitigated the pain. Refusing to give up, Curwë was now fighting his way towards the cairn.

Only two guards were between him from the dreaded knight sorcerer. Without thinking, he threw Rowë's dagger straight at the face of the first defender. The soldier's helm did not protect him. The dagger's blade tore through his lips; he had to spit out several broken teeth. The guard fell to the ground with a grim crunch as his neck struck a rock. Taken aback by the violence of the assault, the second defender remained motionless, unable to put his long spear to use, paralysed by his proximity to his doom.

Curwë, now unarmed, leapt at him, seizing his neck with his bare hands, squeezing with murderous rage and then head-butting, smashing the soldier's nose and his lips with his forehead. His hands did not let go until the Man 's vertebrae broke between his fingers. The guard fell first to his knees, his arms motionless, before he flopped down onto the ground, his body convulsing violently.

"SLASH!" A red sword, covered in raging flames, cut through the air.

Curwë rolled to the ground to avoid the deadly blow. The burning blade continued into a guard's corpse, splattering more blood across the ground. Curwë managed to recover Rowë's dagger, but he quickly realized that its short blade would be of no avail against the opponent he was now facing. Standing tall and straight on the cairn above the cliff, Eno Mowengot, in his golden armour, was surrounding by red flames. The Golden Hand commander looked like a statue of the Greater God of Fire dominating the war-torn landscape. He held, in his six-fingered gauntlet, a cylindrical box marked with runes. Curwë recognized it as the same precious box he had seen in the hands of the Elf of many shadows.

"The testament of Rowë," he murmured.

As Eno Mowengot raised his burning long sword in the air, he spoke words of power.

"Astanar Gweïwal Narkon!"

The air around him seemed to rip open, like a silk sheet tearing into pieces, and from the void blew the breath of a volcano. The temperature around the knight sorcerer rose to unnatural heights, and a horn of fire formed along the reddish blade. Curwë knew that his end was near. In a tremendous discharge of energy, fire sprang from the blade in his direction. The blast beat him back down the cairn steps but, in a desperate effort, he just about managed to protect himself with his cloak. Fire was consuming everything around him, burning plants, corpses, weapons and armour to ashes, but to his astonishment his mantle resisted. Scintillating reflections of butterflies appeared over the cloth.

Then, a horrible pain seized Curwë; his boots were on fire. A new wave of hatred flooded his being, rising up in his chest until its power made him find his way to his feet. Now standing, his hair burning and obscuring his vision, he rushed forward, dagger in hand. The blood drained from his face. Curwë pounced up the dozen steps that separated him from his enemy with lightning speed. The red sword pierced his side. His left hand grabbed the knight sorcerer's armour. His dagger pierced through the golden gauntlet, severing flesh and tendons. Curwë pushed his opponent forward; in the tussle, both were set ablaze. Like a flaming torch cast from a fortress wall, the two opponents fell off the cliff, from a great height. Their bodies came crushing into the tree branches below, bouncing on the slope of the gorge, before disappearing into the thick bushes of the pine forest below.

CHAPTER 6: Aewöl

2712, Season of Eïwele Llya, 112th day, the forest of Tios Lly, Nyn Ernaly

When he opened his eyes, Curwë was hit with an intense pain. His body felt extremely heavy; an unnatural gravity was drawing him downwards, beneath the ground, as if Gweïwal Agadeon, Lord of the Halls of the Dead, had judged that his time to pass had come. For a brief time, Curwë thought he had already made that journey from which there can be no return; that he had gone beyond the mirror, after his body had hurtled down the ravine in a deluge of fire. His eyes widened as a stable image of the world formed itself around him. Curwë could scarcely believe what he was witnessing. He was still alive, lying broken in a grove of pines that had saved his life. Curwë saw the distant light of Cil, the Star of the West, piercing the forest canopy, before other stars, less bright, emerged out of the darkness to be admired.

A gust of wind drew his attention to the immediate surroundings to his right. He made out another glimmering ray somewhere in the bushes. This new glow, much closer to the ground, appeared to be dancing in the night. It became more distinct as it approached him. Instinctively, Curwë cried for help. The light moved quickly towards him until it was so close to his face that he felt the burning iron of an enchanted blade. Curwë, utterly helpless, was blinded by the flash, but before his eyes closed out of fright, he recognized the sword bearer's traits. The face of the Elf was painted with many tones of dark green. The clothes he wore blended seamlessly with the forest. His gaze was hard, though his eyes were clear. Reaching for Curwë, the newcomer drew from his pocket a small container of sweet-smelling balm. He murmured mysterious incantations. His voice sounded familiar.

"Dyoren, it is you!" Curwë exclaimed.

And, too weak to talk any further, he fainted, abandoning himself to Eïwele Llyo, the Deity of Fate who, it was said, haunts the dreams of the gravely wounded when their life hangs only by a thread.

*

Two days later, Curwë woke up from a deep slumber. The blood pumping through his veins still carried the residue of powerful drugs, though the medicine's effects were starting to wane. Now he could fully feel the pain that seared through his body. He attempted to bring his hands to his face, to remove the wet cloth that covered it, but he could not manage even this. Curwë felt, beneath his suffering flesh, the agonizing throbbing of his shattered bones and crushed tendons. He shook his head from side to side, wincing all the while, until the cloth slid from his eyes. He could barely make out the room he was lying in.

It seemed to be a small log cabin, constructed with the lopped branches of chestnut trees. There were no windows and the door, a thick wooden board bound with a chain, barred the only exit. Weak sunlight filtered through the gaps of the improvised refuge. The small room was empty but for a leather bag, a hammock of coarse fabric, a few tunics of badly combed wool, and several jugs of water. After a while, Curwë became sure that he was in fact alive, and not surrounded by the hallucinations of some strange dream. He remembered that Dyoren had saved him from certain death. Feeling relieved at last, Curwë let himself be carried away by his emotions. Soon he was asleep again.

*

Several hours later, Curwë awoke to the sound of hail, which kept breaching the leafy roof of the hut. Trenches dug around the cabin were meant to serve as drains, but the rain was so heavy that it was not much help. The site had become a little pool of mud. Curwë could now see much clearer. He discovered he was not alone. Dyoren was changing the dressings on his legs.

"Now I know without doubt that the Deities of the Islands sent their messenger and rescued me from a cruel end," said Curwë, barely audibly.

Dyoren's reply was harsh. "You have not been able to stand, sit, or even feed yourself for three days. Don't think you can just get up and walk out. It will take time for your strength to return."

Nevertheless, Curwë tried to raise his head to look down at Dyoren.

"How can I ever thank you," he muttered with some difficulty, "for what you have done?"

"Drink this beverage," was the only response the Lonely Seeker would give. "It will help more than you can imagine. It will rid your fatty tissues of the drug residues they have absorbed," Dyoren said as he held Curwë's neck, so that the bard could swallow the contents of the wooden bowl. "The constitution of the High Elves is extraordinary," he added. "Your bodies can recover from injuries, even from the most severe. If you do as I say, you will soon be on your feet."

Once he had finished the hot elixir, Curwë watched Dyoren with great attention. He noticed his great stature, broad shoulders and long blond hair, which appeared almost silver in the darkness of the hut. It was difficult to estimate his age, but he clearly appeared to have grown to his full strength. Though his figure was thin, his body was muscular and hard, moulded over many years' worth of difficult workouts and strict diets. The wrinkles around his eyes ran deep. His face told the story of a tough life, spent outdoors in unforgiving environments. Each of his meticulous movements and precise gestures demonstrated his firm will. That day, Dyoren had abandoned his war clothes and was dressed very simply in a brown tunic. He walked barefooted; his toes were marked with the ochre of the earth.

"Take this. You have not eaten for days. You need food to regain your strength," Dyoren advised as he handed over some rye bread. "The air of these woods can heal the pain that life procures. Nyn Ernaly's wine is light and brings joy, while my music will allow your soul to rest and help fight the chimeras of fear."

Curwë managed to shuffle into a more comfortable position, while Dyoren adjusted the tightly packed leaves which formed his bedding. He began to eat slowly, chewing with great care and intense pleasure, as though that brown loaf was the food of the Gods. Once Curwë had finished, his natural curiosity prevailed, and he could not resist asking what had been on his mind.

"Had you been following us all that time? How did you cross the strait of Tiude? Did you stow yourself aboard Master Aertelyr's ship too?"

"I see from all these questions that life has not completely given up on you yet. No wonder the Elf with green eyes is so difficult to kill," answered Dyoren, a wry smile on his face.

"This is just so unexpected. Even Gelros could not sense your presence on our heels," continued Curwë along the same line of questioning. "I do not know your scout companion, but one thing is sure. Whatever his tracking skills were worth back in Essawylor, he cannot rival me here. This was my home. I know every one of its paths and hideouts," replied the Lonely Seeker. "But why did you not simply join us on Nyn Ernaly?"

"Hear me, Green Eyes! I walk alone... as I always have. I chose to cover your backs. What happened to you proved me right."

"Indeed, and for that I must thank you," admitted Curwë once more.

His gaze was filled with genuine gratitude. Curwë asked no further questions. He understood Dyoren would answer only what he wished. There was a lot more he desired to know, but he felt that interrogating the Lonely Seeker further would only provoke his silence. Soon, Curwë was resting again, bathing his spirit in deepest slumber.

*

The next morning, Curwë realized that he had slept in very late. A pleasant dream still hovered at the edges of his memory. White butterflies were greeting him, dancing around patches of sunlight. The sound of a distant waterfall attracted his attention, and he stayed quiet for a while, enjoying this blessed moment of peace. Seeing Dyoren's silhouette wandering through the campsite, he tried to bring his memory into focus. After a while, images of the battle returned to him. Curwë called out so Dyoren could hear.

"Where are we?"

"You are safe, beyond the grasp of those who seek you," replied Dyoren enigmatically.

"That does not tell me a lot, does it?"

"We are in the forest of Tios Lly, on the eastern coast of Nyn Ernaly. It is the morning of the 115th day of Eïwele Llya's season, the year 2712 of the Llewenti calendar. Is that detailed enough?" asked Dyoren with irony.

"What happened to my companions? How did the battle of Lepsy Gorge end?"

Questions were now piling up in Curwë's head as he fully regained his awareness.

"I believe your friends survived. They even managed to free the two lords, Curubor and Camatael," said Dyoren, his voice somewhat neutral."How do you know? They probably think me dead by now. They saw me disappear in a shower of flames. They must have fled into the Chanun Mountains. That was our initial plan, I recall."

"Your friends are not alone, Green Eyes."

"What do you mean?" asked Curwë, now impatient.

Finally, Dyoren relented, and told Curwë what had occurred after his fall, though Dyoren's summary of events was somewhat brief.

"Your attacks send the army of Nellos into complete disarray. It enabled Gal dyl and his troops to flee, breaking the deadly trap that was closing around them. After nightfall, I believe the Elves of Llymar withdrew to an entrenched camp they had built on Asto Salassy beach, north of Nyn Ernaly, where their fleet is anchored. Your friends and the prisoners they freed must have joined them by now. It looks as though your act of heroism saved the army of Llymar."

Curwë, ignoring this last comment, focused on understanding precisely what had happened.

"Do you mean the Nellos troops abandoned their chase?"

"Only three of the kings' servants seemed to have survived the campaign. The remaining knight sorcerers led the Western troops back to Tar-Andevar. I cannot imagine that the sea hierarchs would want to leave their city vulnerable to attack any longer. They have already honoured their alliance with King Norelin beyond what anyone expected, by providing numerous troops to support his servants during their errand here... Remember, there are many barbarian tribes in the north of the island, and their loyalty to Nellos is uncertain. It's the druids who rule those wild Men... But the knights of the Golden Hand have not been left idle. They have sent scouts into the wilderness in order to find... you," said Dyoren, staring at Curwë.

"Find me?"

"Many are they," Dyoren resumed, "who are seeking you at this very moment: your friends, Gal dyl's fighters, the clan Ernaly, and also agents of the Golden Hand knights... When each of these factions reached the bottom of the cliff and looked amid the undergrowth, they found only one burnt corpse... with its left-hand cut. All will be wondering what has happened to the hero who defeated Eno Mowengot..."

"I remember we fell off the cliff together, surrounded in flames, spreading the fire as we crashed down through the branches."

"With your heroic intervention, Green Eyes, you defeated the commander of the knight sorcerers, pushing him into the void, to his doom. That was no small feat, for that Elf was a master of unnatural fire."

A long silence followed. Curwë shuddered, remembering how he had struck Eno Mowengot with his dagger. He could still feel it in his arm, the sensation of stabbing the short blade into the golden gauntlet. After some hesitation, Dyoren spoke on.

"Perhaps I should also mention that all of them want what you now have in your possession. They will not stop until they find you and seize it."

"What do you mean? What do I possess? I see nothing."

"I have put the testament of Rowë by your feet. As you will see, it is still intact, despite what it has been through. As long as the powerful glyphs which protect it hold, it will remain unspoiled. You know who designed those complex runes. That should be guarantee enough."

"You mean... you managed to save the testament of Rowë from the fight?"

"When I found you in the undergrowth, at the bottom of that ravine, you were still holding the sacred box, though your body was broken. In your other hand, you still grasped the dagger which had cut the gauntlet from the knight sorcerer's arm... I destroyed his golden glove. That was no small task, for even Rymsing's enchanted blade had to strike it many times before it was ruined for good. I leave you the precious dagger and the sacred box. These relics are now yours."

Dyoren gestured to the two items, carefully wrapped in a blanket of fine cotton, at the foot of Curwë's bed of leaves. Then, he left the small camp, muttering something about patrolling the surroundings. Curwë now felt safely hidden, deep in the forest of Tios Lly. Being there, under Dyoren's protection, was the perfect cure for his wounds and his weariness. As the evening drew on, Curwë attempted to get up, and he found that he no longer needed to stay completely still.

Now well fed, he turned his mind to the sweet mixture of aromas which his nose had picked up some time ago: a glass of Tar Andevar white wine that Dyoren had left out for him. He brought the glass to his lips, and the refreshing liquid swelled in his mouth with a burst of deliciously balanced flavour. Soon, the bard had a mind for storytelling. He waited for what seemed like hours before Dyoren returned.

*

At their small campsite, there were no tables laden with food, no welcoming fires burning in a great hearth, nor any monumental carved wooden pillars, as there had been inside the Halls of Essawylor in Llafal. Nevertheless, that small glade, with its many tree branches arching like a vaulted stone ceiling, gave them a taste for songs and tales. Dyoren's face was serene, neither weary nor sad, though his gaze belied the memory of the many events he had witnessed, most of them dark and sorrowful. Like an Elf who had celebrated many a festival, inspiration and joy came easily to the Lonely Seeker.

When Dyoren finally decided to sit down and rest, he started humming a simple tune, which Curwë began adding to. A few moments later, the voices of both Elves opened out, their sweet music resonating beautifully with the wood of the glade. The two minstrels sang like their powerful harmonies could reconcile their different cultures. After some time, their singing found a natural end, and the discussion began. Curwë carefully explained everything that had happened to him since they had parted ways in Llafal. Dyoren's interest reached its peak when Curwë described, in detail, the fight at the natural dam, between the knight sorcerer with his war hammer and the mysterious Elf of many shadows. Dyoren suddenly rose from his seat, like a predator ready to catch its prey.

"There is only one way to interpret what you saw. The sword Moramsing has found a new wielder..."

Curwë pressed him in an effort to understand. "You mean that the Elf of many shadows who killed the knight sorcerer with the war hammer is carrying one of the blades of Nargrond Valley?"

Dyoren now sat silent, deep in thought. After a while, he confided in Curwë.

"For all these years, I have been travelling the Islands seeking the other lost swords. But I had no hope of ever finding where Moramsing disappeared to, that dark blade of the East which draws its power from the Amethyst."

"Why is that? What is so particular about that sword?" Curwë asked feverishly.

"Moramsing was last seen in the hands of Saeröl, the guild of Sana master," recalled Dyoren.

Curwë immediately made a connection to ancient tales he had heard.

"Are you referring to Saeröl the Regicide, murderer of King Lormelin the Conqueror? I remember songs in Llafal about his tragic destiny. He was a legendary character, one of the renowned bards of the Lost Islands."Dyoren nodded. "Saeröl lived in the Nargrond Valley with other Night Elves long ago, in their golden age, before any Men set foot on the Archipelago.

The valley leading to the volcano of Oryusk was then ruled by Rowë Dol Nargrond, and his fief remained under the protection of King Lormelin. At that time, war was raging between the clan Myortilys and the kingdom of Gwarystan. After his father was slaughtered by the Dark Elves, as the new guild of Sana master, Saeröl became the natural leader of all the Night Elves on the Lost Islands. He commanded his people to swear the Oath of Shadows, a deadly promise that they would exact cruel revenge against his most-hated enemies, the clan Myortilys. The atrocities and war crimes perpetrated by both sides were too numerous to count, and the upheavals their conflict caused throughout the centuries would become the darkest pages of our history…"

Dyoren stopped at this point, as if focusing on something else than the dark tale he was counting. But eventually, he went on.

"Only a long time after the war of shadows started did the clan Myortilys eventually prevail. The Night Elves who had survived it were now scarce, and they preferred to hide under the protection of the noble houses of the High Elves. Saeröl was consumed by a cold fury against his sovereign, Lormelin the Conqueror, the king who had done very little to protect his subjects against the clan Myortilys."

Dyoren shivered.

"It is said that none can escape the vengeance of a Night Elf. Saeröl eventually had his revenge. Lormelin was found one morning dead in his chambers, his throat cut savagely. The mages of the Ruby College soon accused Saeröl of the murder. A formidable hunt was launched across the Lost Islands until Saeröl was captured and taken to Gwarystan. But the guild of Sana master did not utter a single word in his own defence. His sword, Moramsing, was never found. He was sentenced to death ignominiously but remained stoical throughout. The new king,

Norelin, only son of Lormelin the Conqueror, had him tortured in vain. His cheek was branded with red-hot iron and, as the Night Elf still would not confess, he was thrown from the top of Gwarystan rock. It is said his corpse was burnt to ashes with magic fire by the mages of the Ruby College, so that his soul could never find its way to the Halls of the Dead where the High Elves dwell after death."

Curwë could not believe what he was hearing.

"I laid eyes upon one of the blades of Nargrond Valley. I saw the sword that killed the king of the High Elves!"

A light flashed in the Lonely Seeker's eyes. "My friend, you have done more in a couple of years than the knights of Dyoreni have managed in several centuries. Your coming to the Archipelago must have been blessed by the Islands' Deities."

"I haven't really done anything. I just happened to survive… Who, then, could this Elf of many shadows be, and how did he come into the possession of that legendary sword?" wondered Curwë.

"Moramsing, the dark blade of the East, has re-emerged just as the testament of Rowë is in danger. Its new master has come to protect it. He risked his life by challenging a knight sorcerer of the Golden Hand to a mortal duel. He recovered the precious will," said Dyoren, but his mind was elsewhere, racing to find answers to the unavoidable questions now surfacing.

"But this doesn't make sense. In the end, we found the testament in the possession of Eno Mowengot, commander of the Golden Hand. Why would that mysterious Elf of Shadows kill one of the knight sorcerers and seize the relic from him, only to hand it over to their chief?" asked Curwë, thinking aloud.

Still with warmth towards his fellow bard, Dyoren replied, "There is surely an answer to that riddle, my green-eyed friend. That Elf of many shadows was indeed on an errand to protect the testament. He intervened only after Mynar dyl's troops lost it…"

The moment he pronounced these last words, Dyoren suddenly stopped. His hand seized the pommel of his broad sword. The Lonely Seeker's blue eyes shone with a new brightness.

"A wielder of Moramsing cannot be easily tracked, believe me," he stated, speaking more directly with Curwë now. "If he wants to remain hidden, he can do so…"

Dyoren remained silent for a while. At last, an uncharacteristic smile crossed his face and he said.

"Hope is restored. My sword, Rymsing, can feel at this moment that her sister blade is nearby. Nothing will stop us now. How strange! I had to wait until I was officially stripped of my title to start making progress… and regain the love and trust of my only companion."

Dyoren became thoughtful.

"Compliance with the order of Oron is not always the best way to achieve one's goals," he said enigmatically. "But what is sure is that one must remain pragmatic. Hope is a combination of patience and perseverance. Just as a violin maker will carefully adjust the forty pieces that make up a cithara until its resonance is perfect, a Seeker must adjust the clues, all the elements which constitute the order, until the order is revised…"

"What will you do, Dyoren?"

"First, I must renew my equipment: ensure I have enough supplies for the hunt that is about to commence. I have not given up my quest. On the contrary, I have never been closer to reaching my goal than I am at this moment. Once the blade of the West is reunited with its sister from the East, it will be clear who should have been trusted…"

As Curwë continued listening closely to the Lonely Seeker, he realized that Dyoren was constantly looking ahead: to next moves, plans for the future, and the means by which he would achieve his goals. It was as though he was utterly obsessed with fulfilling the hope that had been placed upon his destiny. In truth, Dyoren's presence at his side was an illusion; the Lonely Seeker's mind was already wandering far, to wherever his quest would take him next.

Curwë could not help imagining what Dyoren's life must have been since he was given his sacred sword. For decades, the Lonely Seeker had devoted his all energy and skills in pursuit of a hypothetical moment of glory: the day he would return one of the lost blades to the Arkys in their Secret Vale. He had foregone both love and friendship. Dyoren had come to see life's simple pleasures as pernicious wastes of time that would only jeopardize the accomplishment of his dream. He voluntarily renounced living in the present moment; he saw it rather as an obstacle between him and his idealized future. His obsession with his quest was making him traverse that veil between present and future; he was almost losing his mind in the process, for he could behold today everything he would have to live through in days to come. Curwë had lost the thread of what Dyoren's had been saying in a flood of uninterrupted speech. He managed to concentrate his attention again as the Lonely Seeker, excited as ever, spoke on.

"Well, it's like I've told you already. You still have much to learn, Green Eyes. Our laws were made by the Deities of the Lost Islands who love to plant their teachings through parables. A priestess of Eïwal Llyo once taught me that, contrary to what the beliefs of the High Elves claim, an Elf's dignity does not depend on talents he receives at birth but rather on what he chooses to make of them. And, in that sense, what you achieved in Nyn Ernaly is of considerable impact, Curwë."

"What do you mean? I am no powerful Dol of the High Elves, still less a dyn of Eïwal Vars' bloodline like the noble Green Elves. And I will never be so!"

"I can see how, to a mind-set still governed by ethics of bloodlines and rankings, my way of thinking would seem like quite the revolution. I believe that across the Islands, all Elves are equal; whatever natural talents they have simply don't come into it. What can earn you dignity and worth in the eyes of our Deities is not the gifts an Elf receives from nature, but how he chooses to use them. In that sense, Curwë, you have already accomplished far more than I have."

"I won't hear that, Dyoren. You saved both my life and the testament. Without you, I would be no more than a pile of ashes by now."

Ignoring Curwë's gratitude, Dyoren went on.

"Believe what you want, Green Eyes. You still have time to understand. But know this: you are now one of us, one of the free Elves of the Lost Islands, true to our Deities' faith. You belong with the Seeds of Llyoriane. It's clear that you have great intelligence and strength of mind, but these are simply the qualities that fate has given you. Your nature is neither good nor bad in itself. But what you have made of it so far leaves little doubt about your virtue."

"I thank you for these kind words, Dyoren. They honour me greatly."

The Lonely Seeker continued his reasoning, almost talking to himself.

"You are different, Green Eyes, very different to any High Elves I have ever met or read about. You have no fear. Almost all heroes, though they would never admit it, refuse the gifts that are granted by the Deities of the Lost Islands. They live in fear. Fear, like any other kind of overwhelming distress, prevents us from living in harmony as was promised to us. Such anxiety stops us thinking clearly. Fear of violent death is so strong among the immortal High Elves that they have become egocentric and paranoid. It is not so with you. You are not afraid of your death, and therefore you can live your own life freely, choosing to get the best out of whatever time you have. You seem to have understood that, in order to learn to live, you must first agree to die. It is this that makes you so strong. How is this so, my friend? Can you explain it to me?"

"Your gentle remarks are perhaps true... but I cannot explain it. All these revelations are so new for me. You would probably find me ridiculous..."

Dyoren looked his new friend in the eyes for a long time. Finally, he concluded.

"Curwë, of all the High Eves I have ever met, you are by far the closest to the Green Elves. If you continue along this path, Eïwele Llyo will bring you under her protection. After your death, you could even escape Gweïwal Agadeon's Halls, and live in joy for eternity, as a spirit of the forest."

The Lonely Seeker laughed: a fresh, generous laughter that he was unaccustomed to.

"You laugh, Dyoren, but you might be closer to the truth than you think," replied Curwë, who disliked being mocked.

When he spoke again, Curwë's tone acquired a new depth, as if he were trusting Dyoren with his most intimate thoughts.

"I know that one day I will die, be it by the sword or by the dagger, because I do not intend to spend my entire life fleeing the dangers of the world. I refuse to sacrifice my passions for the sake of immortality. Furthermore, I do not see death as the end of all things, as an everlasting imprisonment of the soul in the Halls of Gweïwal Agadeon. I see the end of our present life as a passage from one state to another, within a world governed by the Gods and Deities, a world made in perfect balance. I accept the cycle of life. I will one day die, like that apple will one day fall from its branch and decay upon the ground. Though the apple will cease to exist in one sense, the elements that make it up will live on. They will feed other beings, and perhaps one day another apple tree will grow in the very place it fell."

Night was coming. The two Elves had eaten a light meal of bread and fruits, and a white wine, local to the island, had quenched their thirst. Then, without warning, just as Curwë was looking forward to the comfort of his bed of leaves, Dyoren began getting ready to leave, collecting his belongings and checking his equipment. He barely took the time to wish his friend farewell. Curwë, surprised by Dyoren's haste, struggled to adequately express his gratitude for all his effort, support and advice.

"But where should I go next?" Curwë asked, now feeling anxious.

Dyoren was restless, like he was hungering for action.

"If your companions do not find you first, once you fully recover, you must go north to the sea. You will arrive at a vast beach called 'Asto Salassy'. The army of Llymar is waiting for you there."

Dyoren removed the hut's makeshift door and vanished into the night, like an actor disappearing behind a curtain. Curwë felt sure he heard a few words called out, though they were lost in the deep woods.

*

When Curwë opened his eyes the next morning, the hut was empty. The bard slowly removed his bandages and set about getting dressed. Clean garments, including a simple green tunic and soft leather boots, were laid out ready. They fitted him perfectly. The day grew brighter as he finished getting ready. Where all had been so dark, the forest of Tios Llyi now gleamed with a soft green light. The colours and smells swelled about him. Once he had left the glade, Curwë turned back for one last look at the small campsite where he had recovered from his injuries. It felt like, for the first time of his life, he was hearing the sounds of the forest: the silent songs of the Lost Islands. The feeling was so powerful that he had to lean on a tree to avoid falling over. The contact of his hand on the trunk seemed to instil the strength of the woods in his veins. He let that vivid flow flood through his body. The bard did not realize that he was being watched. Then, a voice was heard, its tone neutral.

"Have you lost your way, Curwë of Mentollà?"

The bard almost fainted at the surprise, feeling the shock all the more keenly with his fragile newfound vitality. Two silhouettes emerged from the shadows of the forest.

"Aewöl, is that you?"

In the dim light of morning, the one-eyed Elf and his servant, Gelros, stepped out into the glade. Curwë, overjoyed to see his two companions again, invited them to celebrate their reunion with the traditional ritual of the clan Filweni. Aewöl normally kept his distance from others, staying on his guard to protect himself and so he would not be found wanting. But, on this rare occasion, he felt such profound relief at finding his friend alive that he agreed to join him in this unusual outpouring of affection.

Gelros pretended not to have heard the proposal. He was already busy inspecting the campsite's defences. The scout felt such devotion to his master that, to his mind, it would be inconceivable to act so familiar with him. Aewöl walked over to Curwë. Each grasped the other's left shoulder with their right hand, before the two friends repeated twice, in the tongue of the Blue Elves:

"Mywon tyn!"

Letting his emotions go, Curwë added with a smile.

"This deserves music! I cannot believe it: Aewöl is embracing joyous Irawenti customs!"

Aewöl was highly adaptive when it came to hiding his emotions; in daily life, he could almost always maintain a perfect mask to block others from knowing what he felt. Those who knew him better like Curwë, however, could sense that he was always struggling with many painful anxieties and also with a profound, personal insecurity. The distress he always felt hindered his relations with others and stopped him from enjoying the many gifts that nature had given him. But, in that moment, Aewöl smiled openly. He begged Curwë to return with him to Dyoren's campsite.

"Come, let us remain here. You need more rest. It is far too early for you to be out in the open. Gelros and I travel only at night; we stay hidden during daylight. There are tales of scouts of the Westerners roaming these woods. The forest rustles with rumours of your disappearance. All of Nyn Ernaly is after you, my dear friend. We are eager to hear your news."

Curwë warmly accepted the invitation and walked back into the glade. His strength was still very limited.

"First," he asked, "how did you find me?"

"We hardly stopped looking once we discovered you had survived that dramatic fall into the ravine. But, despite all our efforts, we had no idea where you were hiding. It was Gelros' night birds that found you in the end. As a matter of fact, it happened just this morning, as though the veil which had been hiding you was lifted by a mysterious wizard."

"You could not be closer to the truth," Curwë confirmed. "All this time I have been with Dyoren."

"So the Lonely Seeker joined the battle of Lepsy Gorge?"

"He did… well, in his own way. I believe he was trying to

scale that cliff when I fell from it with the knight sorcerer. He probably had the same idea as me: to put an end to the battle by killing the commander of the Nellos army," Curwë guessed.

"Except you took the deadly initiative first. It could have cost your life," said Aewöl with concern.

"It was worth it," Curwë smiled. "I understand that the battle was won. That's not to mention the testament of Rowë..."

"What are you telling me?" asked Aewöl, totally incredulous.

Curwë shared his story in full. The bard detailed everything that had happened to him with great emphasis and flare, as though he were already composing an epic song that would recount his own feats. He spun the tale with his usual grandiloquence, more for entertainment's sake than to boast. Aewöl usually kept his feelings to himself. But even though he had not yet fathomed everything his friend's tale implied, in that moment he displayed his deep fondness and gratitude with a broad smile. He was now keen to tell Curwë his side of the story.

"I am not sure the Elves can claim victory at the battle of Lepsy Gorge. In truth, when night fell at the end of that painful day, there was so much confusion that both sides were eager to retreat. The Elves of Llymar owe you a lot, Curwë, for, without any doubt, it was the death of their commander that prevented the Nellos army from achieving an all-out victory."

"What of our lord Roquen?" asked Curwë feverishly, ignoring Aewöl's praise. "I saw him locked in furious battle with that bald warrior. Why is he not with you?"

"The being who will defeat Roquendagor in single combat has probably not yet been born. Our lord fought ruthlessly, with all his heart. Having routed the prisoners' guards, Roquendagor then defeated that monstrous warrior in hand to hand combat. This latest deed of his allowed us to free the prisoners, Curubor Dol Etrond and Camatael Dol Lewin. Roquendagor's shoulder was seriously wounded and he was bleeding badly. We all retreated up into the hills to find cover. But, because the sun was rapidly setting, the Westerners did not follow us. We remained hidden in a cave all night," recounted Aewöl.

Curwë interrupted him with a sudden thought.

"So, the two branches of House Dol Lewin finally met? I'm sorry to have missed that! I remember how Lord Roquen never replied to his cousin Camatael's invitations, choosing lonely walks along the Arob Tuide paths over festivities in Tios Lluin's temple of light."

"Roquendagor did not change his position. He said nothing about his origins. I believe he wants to leave behind all vestiges of his former rank. The words he spoke were few; our past did not come up once. We should all respect his decision and stop calling him Lord Roquen, even between ourselves," recommended Aewöl.

"I agree," said Curwë.

With a knowing smile, the one-eyed Elf continued.

"You should have seen the two of them standing side by side in that dark cave, as Gelros attended to their wounds. They looked so similar and yet so different, almost like twin brothers separated at birth. Both are noble and haughty, possessing a natural majesty of their own. Yet while Camatael is thin and diplomatic, Roquendagor is strong and direct."

"One day or another, they will need to have a thorough, open discussion. Rivalry between the two branches of House Dol Lewin dates back several centuries. The two households are now ruined; each of them has now forsaken their vows to their respective sovereign. Both heirs have proven they are bound to the Lost Islands' fate. Roquendagor and Camatael are now truly members of the Seeds of Llyoriane," Curwë mused.

Aewöl nodded. "Time will tell. Remember, the oath of Lormelin stands between them."

The mention of this ancient curse caused them a certain uneasiness. Whenever they referred back to their cruel past, their feeling of isolation deepened even further, and this shadow passed over them now. Aewöl, usually so cold and unfeeling, suddenly seemed vulnerable, his lack of self-confidence unconcealed. Curwë believed that his friend's lifelong quest for an identity was the source of his weakness. Aewöl went on, but his tone was now devoid of all joy.

"The following day, from our vantage point in the mountains, we saw the army of Nellos leaving the gorge. The Westerners were abandoning the battlefield and heading towards Tar-Andevar. We could see them dispatching scouts across the entire region, so we waited for nightfall to make our next move. Gelros informed us that your corpse had not been found in the ravine below. You had disappeared. We quickly understood that those scouts were after you. As a result, we decided to split up. Roquendagor led the wounded northwards. Curubor and Camatael accompanied him to the beach of Asto Salassy, where Gal dyl's army was retreating to, and where the fleet of Llymar is still anchored. The Green Elves had already dug in at the beach. I decided to stay behind with Gelros and look for you."

The conversation between the two friends lasted a while. They were enjoying each other's company even more than they needed to rest. But, when the sun reached its peak in the sky, Curwë felt he needed more time recovering in bed. He was still weak, despite the restorative qualities of the pure forest air. Aewöl composed a short message to be sent to Roquendagor, to inform him that Curwë was safe and that they would soon join him at the Elvin army camp.

Gelros was expert in the ways of birds; he could tame and befriend even the wildest of them. The scout knew some of their simple languages and could charm them with ease. Gelros chose a blackbird which dwelt within range. He persuaded him to visit the northern beach of Nyn Ernaly, find the Elvin camp and look for a crow's nest, set atop a long pole. Roquendagor was familiar with this type of communication, which they had used extensively during the wars of Essawylor. Gelros wrapped the small scroll, which Aewöl had written, around the bird's leg. He guessed that a raven could cover forty leagues in a day. It meant their message would, in all likelihood, reach Roquendagor before nightfall. This task done; the two Elves resumed their activities. Gelros quickly disappeared into the woods.

"Barbarian tribes dwell in the forest of Tios Lly. Rumours of an Elvin army on the northern shore of Nyn Ernaly must have spread. The barbarians will be eager to defend their hunting grounds. We must stay vigilant," he warned before leaving.

Gelros climbed to the top of a tall pine tree that gave him a dominant view over their campsite's boundaries. Up in the air among the branches, the surrounding woods rolling out before him, he could easily spot any potential enemy approaching below, whilst he himself remained completely hidden.

Meanwhile, Aewöl was immersing himself in the study of several small manuscripts that he always carried in his satchel. They included maritime maps, population figures of the Lost Islands' cities and price lists for various products, he had managed to gather when dealing with the clans of Llymar and the Breymounarty company.

Aewöl was focussed on his work, using all his attention to plot out mysterious plans. He was first and foremost an alchemist, always seeking to capture the essence of various forces, from the composition of raw materials to the ebbs and flows of commerce.

Again, a painful awareness of his loneliness threatened to take hold. In order to escape that familiar, oppressive feeling, Aewöl was now fully absorbed in his task. From that point on, the words and numbers flowed, and, after a while, he had amassed several pages that were covered in lines of writing.

*

Eventually, just before sunset, Curwë stretched himself out and arose from his bed of leaves. His dreams had been pleasant, and his bruised limbs showed further signs of recovery. He was soon chatting away with his usual good humour, showing an interest in Aewöl's work.

"This planning is of vital importance, Curwë," replied the one-eyed Elf, his tone serious. "The situation has changed. With our newfound reputation that our latest deeds have earned us, we can now nurture even greater ambitions. Going forward, there is little the clans of Llymar could deny us. Lord Curubor has already mentioned one reward; he made a personal pledge to Roquendagor that the community of Mentollà will be granted one of the swanships in recognition of our actions. It was Feïwal's wish that we could roam the seas of the Lost Islands freely. Do you understand what this means for us? The community of Mentollà can now develop Alqualinquë, its own maritime company. We will finally possess a vessel capable of sailing the high seas. We'll be able to trade the exclusive goods we produce ourselves."

Curwë was excited. "Imagine when the matriarchs hear that the testament of Rowë has been recovered… when they lay their hands on the sacred box and marvel at the beauty of the gleaming glyphs protecting it. I think it's fair to expect their sincere gratitude. The future certainly looks promising."

"More than you could ever hope for, my friend. We control production of rare goods. We have brave sailors to travel the seas and the valiant captain Nelwiri to command them. And, soon, we will have our own ship, the first of the Alqualinquë company," rejoiced Aewöl.

He explained his reasoning further, his sole eye bright as ever.

"The clans of Llymar use no currency. Gold, silver, coins, indeed any kind of money, are prohibited according to their ancient laws. Goods and services are available freely to each individual at the city market. In return, each Elf has to join a particular organization and can be called up to work for the community. Gold, and all forms of currency, are viewed as a pernicious shortcut that some Elves use to elude their duty towards the community and avoid their share of the work. The Green Elves only trade what they cannot produce themselves. Barter between the guilds is the norm. As a result, commerce between the clans across the seas of the Archipelago is limited… at least, it has been until now."

"What do you mean?" Curwë asked.

He had gotten somewhat lost in Aewöl's overture. The one-eyed Elf ignored his friend's question and pushed on, turning now to commercial practice within King Norelin's realm.

"On the other hand, trade within the kingdom of Gwarystan is far less interesting. The only factor that can slightly affect price is your ability to bargain. Outside of the kingdom's boundaries, however, where bartering is the convention, trading valuable goods without exchanging gold may well create considerable opportunities for us. Think of it, the clans of Llymar have no common measure of value between them. Without currency, there is no indivisible unit of worth by which one can value other goods, and that's not to mention the difficulty it causes storing wealth. The conclusion is that the intermediary, whose position enables him to barter with the Llewenti clans, can then smuggle goods into the kingdom of Gwarystan. That participant, Curwë, becomes rich… considerably rich… as Master Aertelyr probably is today. And, with gold, there are a lot of things one can achieve."

The bard smiled at his friend's enthusiasm. Ignoring Curwë's amused look, which he interpreted as naïve candour, Aewöl gestured, with the silver tip of his polished dagger, to two ground beetles, feasting over the remains of a large snail.

"That little scene," murmured the one-eyed Elf, "is a good

summary of what commerce in the Lost Islands could become..."

"What do you mean?" asked Curwë, curious.

"When the main player weakens and decays, there will always be other factions who can partner up and ruin him."

Aewöl always looked upon the outside world with great distrust. He perceived his environment as threatening, and always interpreted any relationship through the lens of conflict. The one-eyed Elf struggled to consider things with any generosity. After some thought, Curwë understood his friend's point.

"Are you referring to what might happen to the Gwarystan trading companies if they become cut off by our alliance with Master Aertelyr?"

"I will let you draw your own conclusions. But, after this new defeat in Nyn Ernaly, King Norelin finds himself in a difficult position. His failed attempt to seize Rowë's testament isolates him further from his Elvin partisans. To the Elves who identify as 'Seeds of Llyoriane,' he now looks like a grave robber. By sending his servants on this mission so directly, King Norelin has openly committed sacrilege against the Lost Islands' history. News will spread among the realm's Elvin communities. Many Elves may well turn away from their rightful sovereign. That is when our merchant company, Alqualinquë, will come to the fore."

"There's still a long way from the cup to the lips," Curwë noted, somewhat dubious.

The bard observed that, as he had been passionately discussing his vision for this new company, Aewöl had been drinking Dyoren's reserve of wine without restraint. Curwë could not resist issuing a gentle reprimand.

"Do not think that you can drown unquenchable longing with draughts of wine. Such a course will only replace your ambitious aspirations with new ones, which would eventually take you to your doom. There are unsatisfied desires dwelling in your heart, my friend, and in no other Elf have I ever seen such thirst for impossible achievement."

"We shall see, Curwë!" countered Aewöl. "We shall both see the glorious future of our company unfold. Concentrate on the sales talk: I will manage strategy."

Curwë smiled and proposed a toast. "Long live Alqualinquë! Long live the Flamboyant Bard and the Merciless Alchemist! Or I should say... Long live the Hero and the Treasurer."

After that improbable boast, the two companions laughed loud and long. A starry sky materialized above them, and Gelros came down from his pine tree. The air was already cool and soft, as if the days of Autumn were approaching. But the scout soon understood that the group would not be leaving the campsite that night. Curwë undoubtedly required more time to heal his burnt skin and bruised limbs and, indeed, another matter played an important part in their decision to stay put. Aewöl and Curwë were laying the foundations of a maritime company. They spoke all night long, until Dyoren's wine reserve had finally been drained.

*

When the morning came, Gelros lay motionless beside the two Elves, his gloved hands clutching his long bow. Indifferent to the noise of their impassioned conversation, his eyes were closed. His mind was travelling through vast stretches of memory, resting quietly in a deep reverie, as was the way of the Elves. The wind was blowing gently through the trees. Other than the chatter of the two recent founders of Alqualinquë, there was no sound in the forest.

Suddenly, Gelros woke up. In the blink of an eye, he was on his feet. Startled by his sudden reaction, Curwë and Aewöl immediately reached for their crossbows. They carefully scanned their surroundings, but did not notice anything out of the ordinary. Gelros did not say a word and made no gesture. He stood still, looking into the deep shadows of the woods, his hand placed on a great tree. Multi-coloured butterflies were gathering around him. Deep in thought, he looked as if he were listening to the silent voices of the forest.

"My birds are gone. Something has drawn them away from us," Gelros finally said.

There was silence. The forest which, until then, had hidden and protected them was perhaps now yet another threat ranged against them. After a while, Gelros spoke again.

"The butterflies tell me of azure shapes flying between the trees, of blue bards roaming the woods, inquiring about an Elf... an Elf with green eyes. They tell me of illusions, like evanescent impressions of..."

A severe voice interrupted him from the depths of the woods.

"Evanescent... the impressions we make upon the world are always evanescent, if not ephemeral, Gelros the Archer. Didn't Eïwal Lon once say, 'By this effort, we put the seal of eternity upon the evanescent moment of our existences."

There, on the edge of their campsite, stood an old High Elf, straight and tall, dressed in fine blue robes, a golden arch embroidered on his shoulder. His grey hair was curled in the aristocratic manner. Everything about his appearance was clean and neat, the expression of unimpeachable self-confidence. The ancient Elf strode forward. The sun was just emerging between the trees, imbuing the air with new warmth. A bright beam of sunlight fell upon his face, illuminating his intense azure eyes.

"Lord Curubor!" exclaimed Curwë.
"Greetings, Elves of Mentollà," the Blue Mage saluted

them, "I am glad to have found you at last. It is good that you are safe."

In other circumstances, they would have greeted him warmly. They had met Curubor several times in Mentollà, for he had regularly visited their community, always offering gifts and words of friendship. A few days ago, too, after being broken free from his captors, the Blue Mage had shown his deepest gratitude to the heroes who had rescued himself and Camatael.

But, in that instant, the three Elves from Mentollà felt strangely anxious, unable to find words of welcome. Curubor was meant to be at the Elvin army's camp with Roquendagor and Camatael, with the wounded, yet here he was, walking alone in the woods. They looked at the ancient Elf, watchful, as he drew nearer, step by step. Finally, Aewöl and Curwë lowered their crossbows, though they both kept the bolts in their hands. Indifferent to their cautious measures, Curubor joined them, his eyes keen and bright, gleaming with satisfaction. The Blue Mage broke the silence first.

"I am glad indeed to see you again, Curwë. I suspected you would be severely wounded, needing a period of convalescence. So, I have brought you some herbs of the forest that the matriarchs of Llymar use for healing."

Without waiting for an answer, Curubor sat down next to where they stood. He lit the fire and started boiling water in a pot. The three Elves from Mentollà stood silent, none of them taking the initiative, as if some spell lay upon them. Unable to stir, they all took a cup of the brew Curubor had prepared. They enjoyed the drink, and soon a pleasurable sensation washed over them. The decoction procured a remarkable feeling of being comfortable and a general sense of well-being. Still feeling in good health and good spirits, they started swapping their stories. They sat on the ground, their hands upon their knees.

Curwë began his tale. He told of their errand after meeting with Nyriele and Dyoren in Llafal. He spoke, as if he were spinning the yarn in a busy tavern, of their perilous crossing through the Silver Leaves Wood, of their involvement in the battle against the Nellos army, and of his rescue by the Lonely Seeker. Despite his apparent naive keenness, the bard was careful not to mention many of the more intriguing details he had discussed with Dyoren. He did not allude to the question of the Elf of many shadows and his dark sword, nor did he share his theories on that mysterious Elf's role in the events that had unfolded. Above all, he did not mention his recent acquisitions: neither the testament nor the dagger.

For a long while, Curubor said nothing, but the ancient Elf's azure gaze was constantly fixed upon the emerald eyes of the young bard. It was as if he could guess what Curwë was not saying. At last, Curubor sighed with relief when he heard of the Lonely Seeker's new errand.

"My heart feels lighter now that I know Dyoren's part in your rescue. His humiliation was a tough trial for such a brave knight. The matriarchs of Llymar told me he was in peril, having refused to obey to the Arkys' orders. The Lonely Seeker chose to follow his own path. I fear for him, but I cannot help admiring his courage. Dyoren continues to fight for the benefit of all, true to his oath, and faithful to the principles of the Seeds of Llyoriane. I personally knew each of the six Seekers who preceded him in his duties. Dyoren the Seventh is without doubt the worthiest of our esteem."

Curubor smiled as a streak of sunlight caressed his face. Having little patience for non-committal praise, Aewöl could not resist a provocation in response.

"I do not think we've heard your story, Lord Curubor. We have all been wondering how and why Lord Camatael and yourself ended up prisoners of the knights of the Golden Hand."

The Elves from Mentollà looked to the Blue Mage. A gleam of sunshine pierced the fleeting clouds to fall upon his hands, his four rings with their different gemstones lighting up as it did so. Eventually, Curubor looked straight up at the one-eyed Elf.

"There is little to say, Aewöl... Lord Dol Lewin and I played our part in the recent events... perhaps even the most dangerous part. We had to rely on our own skills and intuition. But we were not wise enough, it would seem, for we failed to account for all the dangers that beset us. It is a perilous thing, trying to snare the knights of the Golden Hand. They have grown powerful; not only are they commanders who lead armies, they are also sorcerers with the teachings of the Ruby College at their fingertips. Camatael and I did not realize the peril we were in, so eager were we to lay our hands on the sacred tombs. We could not wait, so we came forth to assist the clan Ernaly troops. Such a little moment of impatience can prove deadly. We arrived too early and, before we could return to the safety of our hideout, spies of the Westerners spotted us, and the knights of the Golden Hand surrounded us. The battle was quick; putting up more of a fight would have been of no use."

Curubor nodded, before continuing with a more hopeful tone.

"Nevertheless, our actions were not in vain for, in the end, King Norelin's servants were defeated and the four tombs are now safely within the entrenched camp of Llymar's army, ready to be picked up by our fleet. Who knows? Perhaps this conflict has triggered yet another devastating series of events, like a tiny block of ice breaking off the top of the Moka Kirini's peak, which then tumbles over a cliff and sets off an avalanche..."

Again, the Blue Mage knowingly smiled. Aewöl, without hiding his disappointment, replied,

"You like to speak in riddles, my lord."
"I suppose I do, but I don't even realize it anymore. Perhaps, if you were as old as I, you would understand... But

you must all be weary after so much storytelling. When old friends gather after a long stretch apart, it's quite right that they spend some time musing over the intervening days. I'd say we've done just that. But now you should rest, for we leave at nightfall. It's a long way to the beach of Asto Salassy, and the journey will not be without its dangers. Many are those still looking for you. The first watch should fall on me; it is my duty. I will make sure nothing dwelling in the forest of Tios Llyi troubles us."

That being said, Curubor leaned against a tree and wrapped himself in his blue cloak. He drew a handful of rose petals from his pocket and breathed in their delicious scent. After closing his eyes, his face seemed to relax. In his fingers he rubbed a pitch of fine sand, almost the colour of gold. The Elves from Mentollà also felt weary. They appreciated the Blue Mage's offer. Feeling now at peace under his protection, they allowed themselves to recover from the exhausting few days they had just lived through. Soon, a comatose slumber came upon them, as deep and restorative as what Men call 'sleep'. Though birds returned to the small clearing, even their shrill cries did not wake them.

*

Aewöl had drifted off after a few moments like his companions, his anxious and cautious nature reassured by the sound of their soft breathing. After a while, however, slumber eluded him. Sunlight had pierced the canopy of leaves, and the brightness made him uncomfortable. The sun was high in the sky, red and hot. He tried to lie still, but finally he could put up with it no longer. Driven by some impulse, he sat up and looked around. All about him lay sleeping shapes. Only Curubor was awake. He sat with his back to the one-eyed Elf, extremely close to where Curwë lay. Aewöl carefully approached the Blue Mage and looked down at him. Curubor seemed to be praying. His eyes were closed, but his lips were moving, mouthing silent incantations. The one-eyed Elf crept up to right behind the ancient mage's head. At that moment, Curubor suddenly moved his hands out of sight, as though his rings were embarrassing him. He muttered some incomprehensible words and then woke up completely, as if alerted of immediate danger.

"Forgive me, my lord, if I frightened you," said Aewöl, his tone humble and apologetic, but his glance suspicious.

Curubor gave a gasp, shivered, and then became quite rigid. He could not utter a word. After a moment, visibly embarrassed, Curubor felt the need to share what was troubling him.

"I've been having difficulty finding peace. Recent events have affected me more than I would have thought. There are times when even a wise Elf is dragged by his hair and forced to face the darkest moments of his past. Even worse is the obsession with what the future will bring... I suppose thinking your death is imminent can cause this type of strain."

Aewöl immediately suspected something odd was afoot. He must have caught the Blue Mage in the middle of casting some kind of spell. Aewöl looked down at Curwë, who was still immobile despite their loud exchange, and wondered what Curubor had been up to. Aewöl proceeded as if he knew something was amiss, though he was unsure of what had happened.

"I saw you," he said, his gaze cold and heartless.

Curubor quickly regained his composure. The ancient mage was now standing in the middle of the campsite, his deep azure gaze fixed on the one-eyed Elf. Finding his usual confidence, he made an effort to appease Aewöl with rational thinking and a balanced tone.

"I needed to ensure that your friend had not deceived me. The situation demanded it. These are no ordinary times, and the stakes are high. Unusual times mean unusual methods. But all is now well, for I know that Curwë did not lie to me, though he could have told a lot more."

In his mind, Aewöl was still dubious, though he felt strangely appeased. Curubor's voice was melodious, his words reasonable. The one-eyed Elf then replied, though he had become weak and hesitant, as if some spell were hindering his mind.

"There are powers in motion I cannot completely understand. How is it that a forgotten tomb and an old scroll can create such turmoil? Are they really worth all these wasted lives?"

Curubor smiled. His azure gaze was soft again. He could sense that Aewöl was yielding to his natural authority. The one-eyed Elf's mind was drawn to his by a deep thirst for knowledge. A desire for wisdom had awakened within him. Without realizing, Aewöl now sought to gain a higher awareness of the forces at play. Curubor's low tone gave Aewöl the hope that, one day, the best kept secret of the Islands' power struggles might be revealed to him. The Blue Mage put his hand on his interlocutor's shoulder. His four rings glimmered like as many little candles. Now reassured that he had regained the upper hand in the discussion, Curubor adopted his usual professorial tone.

"The real reason for the king of Gwarystan's fierce determination to capture the testament of Rowë has come to light. Norelin is feeling his weakness. He is trying to prevent a disaster in which he would lose his throne."

"What do you mean?" Aewöl asked hesitantly. "The king has no heir who could challenge his authority."

"I don't mean a pretender to the Ruby throne. It's not the sword Norelin fears the most, but a mighty threat… This menace is more powerful than his armies and more devastating than his high mages of the Ruby College. The king of Gwarystan wants to intervene before what he so fears is unleashed. He tried to hinder change, to halt history itself. After all, an orderly world is what every monarch jealous of his power desires most. The testament of Rowë has the answer to his profound questioning."

"How could that be? How could a mere scroll change the order of things?" Aewöl asked, fascinated.

Curubor laughed, but his laughter was without joy.

"That is what you cannot conceive. But you are young, Aewöl... I witnessed the end of the First Age. I had a close relationship then with the Elvin lords of that heroic time. They were capable of creating artefacts that could free us from the laws inscribed by the Gods. The High Elves of yore rose to inconceivable heights. They developed advanced techniques this world has ever seen, drawing upon their deep knowledge of gemstones. They had a purpose; they wished to become superior beings. With the staggering arrogance that characterizes the High Elves, they made a bid to rise to the level of the Gods. Our forefathers once threatened the harmony of Oron, which Gweïwal Zenwon and his peers had so painfully succeeded in crafting. They created their own destiny and, in so doing, wreaked havoc. There is a price for such sacrilege. Believe me; I have had time to think about the 'order of things,' as you put it. We have not seen the end of what the Gods have in store for the High Elves, to punish them for their mad ambition. Believe me Aewöl! Our fate, as decided by Gweïwal Zenwon and his peers, will be one of spectacular tragedy. There can be no salvation without trial."

Aewöl was lost. "I can't understand what you mean."

Curubor shrugged. "Is this even worth explaining this to you?"

The Blue Mage looked at the fine cotton blanket that lay beside Curwë.

"The testament of Rowë holds the answer to our questions. The answers to all our questions are inside the sacred box wrapped in your friend's blanket. It takes a strong will to resist the temptation to open that reliquary. We must find the courage to keep it closed," Curubor said, a fiery look in the eye. Aewöl was on his guard again. "How do you know what's in there?" he asked, suspicious.

"I have seen it," Curubor replied with his most haughty tone.

Suddenly, he no longer looked the same; there was a restrained but deep-rooted hunger in his voice.

"Why do you think I have come? Do you believe I would leave the sacred will unprotected? I will personally ensure that the testament of Rowë is safely returned to the Elves of Llymar. The warlords of the clans are waiting for your return and, indeed, someone else is expecting you."

A silence followed. Aewöl, looking lost under the Blue Mage's spell, gazed at his two companions still in deep slumber. Curubor suddenly announced that he was heading off.

"I need to go to the forest's northern borders to meet a messenger and hear news. I'll only be gone a short time. I have left our path back to the army's camp unwatched for too long."

Though he spoke these words lightly, Aewöl noticed that he looked tense, as if anxious to be done with something important. It was difficult to tell what the Blue Mage was thinking.

"Be on your guard," Curubor warned. "I leave you with your friends. When they awake, prepare yourselves. We leave at nightfall."

His azure robes had soon swept away into the woods. Aewöl was disturbed by such a sudden departure. He wondered what the purpose of Curubor's comings and goings were. But his uneasiness soon wore off, and he relaxed, for a while forgetting to regard the outside world with suspicion. He was still the only one awake in the camp, breathing in the fresh air of the day, marvelling at the trees laden with fruits. He felt a sense of satisfaction, even of superiority. Everything that had happened since he left Essawylor was passing through his mind. Aewöl recalled the many perils he had lived through, and the fears he had overcome. His new life in the Lost Islands had been filled with victories. Aewöl could now look to the future with greater ambition.

Suddenly, he snapped out of this reverie, as if the light breeze in the trees had spoken to him. A strange gleam appeared in his one eye. He turned his head, but all he saw was his friend, smiling in his sleep. Aewöl stood motionless next to the slumbering Curwë, the testament of Rowë still wrapped in the blanket at the foot of the bed. He could not keep his mind off the precious relic. Looking around, he realized that there were no unfriendly eyes watching him. Only the wind murmured through the branches, as though inviting him to take the next step. Aewöl shivered. Suddenly, his heart turned cold.

'What if I looked at the testament?' he thought, the strange gleam in his eye even brighter. 'It contains great knowledge of events to come. We are vulnerable refugees, far from home, fighting for our survival. If I had such wisdom, I could be rid of my doubt. I could use whatever it tells me... to protect us.'

A fire was now raging in his eye, and the murmuring light breeze willed him on with ever more insistence. He tried to control his emotions and ignore these urges. After a while, however, Aewöl felt overwhelmed by his impulses. Deep-seated aspirations were resurfacing. The feeling became too intense; he could no longer control the flow of his thoughts. A battle between desire and restraint pervaded his mind. Finally, his will was overcome.

"We will need to know," Aewöl whispered.

He looked down at Curwë. The bard was resting peacefully, a little smile forming at the corners of his mouth. Then Aewöl made out the cylindrical shape of the sacred box wrapped in Curwë's blanket. He could see its outline perfectly, like a treasure chest buried only inches beneath the sand. Aewöl knelt down, gasping for breath. He unwrapped the fine cotton cloth. His hands were shaking. At last, he could look upon the precious artefact.

"This is a marvel!" Aewöl exclaimed.

The reliquary of Rowë's will was a box of rare wood, which he could now see was shaped like a smith's hammer. Only one-foot-long, it was decorated all around with little jewels. Affixed to its wooden frame were golden plaques. Unlike the sacred boxes used for rituals in Essawylor, the design on its outside was not the figure of a guardian but rather a series of glyphs, made up of fragments of gemstones. To Aewöl's surprise, these magic markings Curwë had mentioned were no longer shining, as though their protective powers had waned. The one-eyed Elf saw this as a good omen, a sign that he was, indeed, meant to access the secrets contained by the will of Rowë.

Now on his knees, Aewöl sized the box and lifted its lid. It was open. Aewöl gazed inside. He became rigid, as if paralysed by shock, still holding the cylindrical object in both hands. Suddenly, a ray of sunlight pierced through the shadows of the forest, dazzling him. He dropped the reliquary in front of him; it rolled across the ground, stopping when it reached Curwë.

The bard stirred slightly in his slumber. He brought a hand up to his face and, a moment later, the light of day had woken him. Curwë opened his eyes and discovered what had happened.

"What have you done?" Curwë cried in panic. "Do you realize what you've done? Close it… close it immediately!" he urged.

His friend's violent intervention seemed to free Aewöl's mind, as if he was suddenly broken free from the hypnosis that was holding. The one-eyed Elf snatched up the lid and darted for the reliquary. The sacred box was closed again. A tense silence ensued. Finally, Aewöl confessed.

"That was not me, Curwë, I did not mean to do it. The sacred box was just lying there, right next to me. Its glyphs had stopped shining; they were no longer protecting it as if... I was being invited. I do not understand. A strange feeling took hold of me... But I did not see anything, and now the box is closed, as it always was."

Curwë examined the reliquary before wrapping it back up in the cotton blanket. He did not dare look inside, and instead tried to comfort his friend.

"Say no more. None of us have come to any harm, and the box is intact. Although, you are right, its runes are no longer glowing."

Aewöl lay still, prostrate.

"Nothing has changed," Curwë said, trying to reassure him. "Come, let us wake up Gelros. We need to prepare our equipment. We have a long journey ahead of us. We are going back home."

When Curubor returned from his errand in the woods, the three Elves from Mentollà were standing in the middle of the campsite, heavy with troubled thoughts. They stood with their bags ready, as immobile as statues. Ignoring their sullen moods, Curubor declared, his voice as clear as ever.

"You should come now. I have made sure the way is clear. Night will soon be upon us."

And, slinging the small pouch that was his only baggage across his shoulders, Curubor gestured for them to follow him. The sun was sinking behind the western range of the Chanun Mountains when their group set out from the forest of Tios Lly. Gelros went ahead. The others followed him in single file.

**

For two days, they strode under the wheeling stars. First, the four Elves crossed the forest of Tios Lly, heading north, tracing their way through the high ferns. Then, they left the protection of the forest's shadows and, away to their right, they could admire the sea: the strait of Tuide that separated them from their home. When their journey through the wilderness begun, Curubor urged them to make haste, and had they barely exchanged a word since. Tired and uneasy, they rested on the ground, stopping only for a few rare moments to eat food, always on the lookout for danger.

Finally, after another night of running and hiding, they reached the beach of Asto Salassy. The warmth of dawn was approaching. But the morning mist clouded the sand dunes well after daybreak, and they had to wait for the fogs to disperse in order to locate the Elvin army's trenches. A great falcon, the size of an eagle, circled above them. For a moment, they stood still and silent, showing signs of weariness. Nevertheless, they held their heads up high, for they knew they had managed to reach their safe haven. Their way home was in reach. They were relieved.

As the mist lifted, they began to be able to make out the colourful tents of the Llymar units and, eventually, the green banners of the various clans: the white swan of Llyvary; the grey hawk of Ernaly; and the colourful peafowl of Avrony. Birds were flying high above the camp. The Green Elves had dug trenches in the soil around the wooden walls that formed the camp's perimeter; the sea had filled this trench to form something of a moat. More than a dozen warships were grounded on the beach. The bows of these ships were wedged into the sand, while their sterns were battered by the waves. Their masts dismantled, and their keel deeply buried, the Elvin ships lay down on the vast beach like flightless swans. Their colourful sails, beautifully painted with images of birds, had been refashioned into large tents. The shelters were organized in circles around the command post at the centre of the camp, a large construction of wood and canvas as big as any temple in Llafal. This little city of tents was completed by a wooden drawbridge over the moat.

The sound of intense labour reached their ears, carried by the morning wind. The beating of hammers and clinking of trowels sounded out as artisans continued to reinforce their defences, by the dull light of the torches and flares glowing faintly in the mist.

"See! Fighters are positioned along the entire length of the wooden wall," said Curwë.

"It is as though the troops of Llymar expect our enemies to launch a full-scale attack at any moment," replied Aewöl.

The four Elves walked across the long, wide beach. It ran for more than twenty leagues from the forest of Tios Lly to the ocean hills feet. Its sandy dunes served as natural protection for the fields of northern Nyn Ernaly, a collection of fair and fertile lands terraced along the plateau which lay between the Chanun Mountains and the sea. Before reaching the camp's entrance, they had to cross a boggy section of beach, half conquered by the sea, where numerous little pools and streams hindered their progress.

Daylight spread across the sky as they approached the camp's walls. They all looked up at a great bird that seemed to be drawing near. A shaft of light pierced the morning clouds, and the tips of the guards' lances shone as they waited at the gate. A horn was blown; its clear noted echoed long. The four Elves headed towards the drawbridge. The wooden doors of the gate were opened before them.

Several fighters gathered feverishly around them, eager to see Curwë, the Elf with green eyes who had killed the knights of the Golden Hand's commander. The domineering voice of Curubor sounded out above them.

"Move away! Do you not recognize the standard of the Golden Arch when you see it?"

And, the disappointed fighters had to fall back to let them pass. Through the confusion of their welcome, the four Elves attempted find their way to the command post, where the highest-ranking chiefs of Llymar army were expecting them. Curwë had to push his way through the crowd who came swarming around him as soon as he was recognized. He smiled politely, but nevertheless remained stolid. Though he was pleased that the troops appreciated his efforts, his mind was focused on what would be discussed in the command tent. He knew that it was Gal dyl Avrony, Protector of the Forest, who had summoned them. Beneath his cloak, Curwë was clutching the precious reliquary containing the testament of Rowë. He was keen to deliver it without delay.

The four Elves finally saw the command tent's entrance. They walked past the tent of House Dol Etrond, which had been built nearby. Equidistant from the command centre was the clan Ernaly's headquarters and another well-furnished tent adorned with the white swan of clan Llyvary.

Before them stood the six guards of the Protector, the most trusted of his fighters. As news of their arrival had reached the tent before they did, the four Elves were admitted at once into an anteroom. Daylight seeped in through its walls of painted ships' sails. The canvas separating them from the main room was thin and, judging by the loud murmur they could hear, they immediately understood that a large assembly awaited them. Soon, more clan Avrony guards, wearing splendid ceremonial cloaks in the mahogany and beige of their clan, admitted them inside the temporary, but still imposing, edifice.

"All have been convened!" one of the sentries announced, with the official opening cry of the council of the forest.

It was Curubor who stepped first into the great hall of painted sails. The three Elves of Mentollà followed. Aewöl entered last. The one-eyed Elf had to blink several times before his vision adjusted to the intense light that flooded the hall. As he looked up to the white part of the sails, Aewöl realized several mirrors had been placed in the wide aisles at either side of the assembly, reflecting the sun and filling the hall with the brightness he had found so dazzling. The fleet's highest masts stood in a circle to hold up the sails, like tall wooden pillars upholding a majestic white roof. Many Elves were gathered.

At the northernmost side of the hall was a stage, draped in a large white sail. The many commanders and captains of the Green Elves, at least two dozen in number, were standing there. Priests of the different Islands' cults comingled in their ranks. They were easily recognizable by the colour of their robes; the emerald of the forest for Eïwal Vars' clerics, the azure of the sky for Eïwal Ffeyn's priests, and the gold of sunlight for Eïwal Lon's disciples. Runes carved into precious wood adorned their silver necklaces.

Priestesses of the Mother of the Islands were also present. Their robes were the colour of the woods, and were adorned with magnolia flowers, the symbol of their Deity, Eïwele Llya. The redbreasts flying around them brought cheer to the formal scene.

The priestesses of Eïwele Llyo remained apart, at the far end of the tent, amid the orchids that had been planted there. Wrapped in grey ceremonial robes, some were tending to the many ravens that the great tent housed. Others were absorbed in prayer.

Only the white priestesses of the temple of Eïwele Llyi were missing. A herald invited the attendants.

"The council should start!"

From the stage where they were stood, this assembled multitude could scan the newcomers from head to toe as they came in. In his dirty traveller's clothes, Aewöl felt filthy, out of place among such a noble assembly.

In front of the newcomers, a number of illustrious chairs, decorated with figures from the Islands' mythology, had been arranged to face the stage. The clans' dyl were sitting on these seats. Aewöl counted them: sixteen noble Elves in total. They were wearing their ceremonial garments, which comprised long robes of various green hues. Aewöl thought that this gathering seemed just as official as any of the major ceremonies and clan councils he had attended in Llafal. In front of this impressive audience, the stage dominated the rest of the hall. Four throne-like wooden chairs, adorned with feathers, were set down in an arc. They were the symbol of the warlords' power.

Tyar dyl Llyvary sat nearest the centre, representing Llafal; Leyen dyl Llyvary, captain of the fleet of Penlla, was on his right; Mynar dyl Ernaly, the fair warlord of Tios Halabron, was on his left. Aewöl also identified Voryn dyl the Ugly, standing below the green banner depicting the clan Ernaly's hawk, next to his elder brother.

In the middle of the great tent, at the foot of the stage upon its lowest step, there was one more imposing wooden chair, and on it sat a noble Elf with an abundance of blonde hair, which looked almost like a mane. He had a handsome, slightly tanned face and shining eyes. In his hand was a long lance: the fabled Spear of Aonyn. This was Gal dyl Avrony, last scion of the sixth and lowest clan in Llewenti hierarchy. He nevertheless held the most prominent position in Llymar. Gal dyl, Protector of the Forest, was seated on his oaken throne, its back like a colourful peacock with its wings spread. He was surrounded by the other dignitaries of Llymar's army. It was a striking tableau to behold.

Aewöl then looked to Camatael Dol Lewin, former prisoner of the knights of the Golden Hand, who they had rescued after the battle of Lepsy Gorge. The high priest of Eïwal Lon wore purple robes held by a rare buckle in the form of a white racing unicorn. Camatael rose to offer his chair, as Curubor entered the hall.

"My Lord Dol Etrond, it is your honour to occupy the warlord of Tios Lluin's seat," he proposed.

But the Blue Mage politely declined. He preferred to stand by the Protector's side, marking his higher power and influence.

The great hall of sails was crowded and hot. All eyes turned to the three Elves from Mentollà; they soon became the source of many excited conversations. For a moment, they were somewhat overwhelmed by the amount of attention they were receiving.

Aewöl, in particular, felt uncomfortable. He noticed that Curubor took advantage of the momentary confusion to whisper discreetly in Gal dyl's ear. The Protector of the Forest then stood to greet the newcomers with a show of enthusiasm.

"Welcome! Welcome to the true heroes of the campaign!" Gal dyl exclaimed.

All could now see the reliquary of Rowë's will hanging from Curwë's belt. He seemed taller, more handsome than usual, as though he had grown in stature and beauty as a result of his feat. His light clothes hugged his athletic body, toned by its skill and experience in combat. Curwë glanced towards the back of the hall, behind the warlords' seats, where he saw Roquendagor standing proudly among the other noble dyn and captains of Llymar's army. Curubor noticed Curwë's gaze and immediately instructed one of the guards to fetch the tall knight. The Blue Mage raised his voice, so that all under the great tent could hear.

"May Roquendagor the Tireless, who brought countless ills to the Westerners, join his companions from Mentollà. Many Men's souls did he send hurrying down to their doom, leaving their corpses to the circling vultures."

The four Elves of Mentollà were reunited, but this was not the time for effusive greetings. The ceremony was beginning.

"Welcome, Curwë! It is an honour to have you among us," Gal dyl exclaimed rather quickly, as if eager to have the formalities over with. "Your bravery proved most useful. Incredible! You have quite the future ahead of you, I am sure. Really, though, I am deeply proud to call you our new hero."

Gal dyl was no high-born prince, and he did not possess the natural majesty of a ruler. He felt uncomfortable taking on the role at the centre of that noble assembly. By trying to rush through the formal celebration, his speech became awkward and his behaviour inappropriate. With an impatient flap of his hand, Gal dyl beckoned to one of his guards, who approached holding out a necklace of Eïwaloni leaves, which had apparently been prepared for the ceremony. The guard gave the verdant ornament, a symbol of victory among the clans, to Gal dyl. Before the guard had even returned to his position beside his five other brothers in arms next to the throne, Gal dyl was placing the precious award around Curwë's neck. With no further ceremony, the Protector of the Forest declared.

"Curwë, you have emerged victorious after these recent trials. Before now, when you walked the streets of Llafal towards the House of Essawylor, your great hall of music, crowds were already saluting you with respect. Tomorrow, when the world learns of your heroic feats in Nyn Ernaly, you will become famous throughout the forest. All will be grateful beyond measure, for you have kept the testament of Rowë from falling into the wrong hands."

In response, Curwë gestured towards his companions behind him and declared solemnly.

"I am grateful, Protector of the Forest. You honour me greatly. Allow me to share this praise with my companions from Mentollà. They deserve this recognition too."

The bard moved graciously, as if performing on a stage. His poised tone and controlled manners contrasted with the clumsiness of the Elvin army commander. With theatrical flair, he snatched the precious reliquary from his belt, and offered it to Gal dyl with a deep bow.

"I hand you the sacred box of Rowë, Protector of the Forest," Curwë announced, "so that it may return to the wisest among the Elves of the Lost Islands. May you receive it as a pledge of loyalty from the community of Mentollà."

Gal dyl took the sacred box and raised it with both hands. The moment the reliquary was presented for all to see; the assembly's reaction was ecstatic. The Green Elves broke out into loud, enthusiastic cheers, invoking their Deities and shouting out prayers of thanks. This artefact was of great importance to them, for it symbolised a holy message passed down to them through the will of Rowë Dol Nargrond.

The precious reliquary was now in the Protector of the Forest's hand, safe from harm. All felt confident that it would now remain unspoiled until the time came to open it and read its message from centuries ago. All rejoiced. Aewöl began to find heart. With a tap of his finger, Gal dyl motioned for his servants to bring wine, fruits and bread, so that everybody could celebrate. The many mirrors illuminated the scene with golden streaks of refracted light. In the descending twilight, against the walls of quivering sails, each of the party's guests looked revived and cheerful, their eyes sparkling with renewed hope.

This joyous celebration was suddenly interrupted by the echo of a bird's cry coming from the back of the hall of sails, accompanied by an unnatural wind that felt like the very breath of nature. The plants inside the great tent began to quiver with the force of the gust, and then shook violently. The entire wooden structure of the edifice trembled, as if the masts had begun gasping for life, stirred by the sudden force.

A creature stepped inside the hall, a creature that was both Elf and animal. Its thin body was shrouded in a long robe, made entirely of green feathers and foliage. Upon its head were antlers, proudly displayed. Its unnatural eyes were an intense, burning emerald. The arrival of this mighty creature was greeted with silent awe.

All the Green Elves kneeled slowly, in a display of utmost respect. The few High Elves present hesitated for a moment before adopting the same cautious pose. Mynar dyl was the first to catch his breath. The warlord of clan Ernaly recited the verses of Eïwele Llya's liturgy.

"We worship you, O Daughter of the Islands, Envoy of Eïwele Llya Herself. Your power is drawn from the earth, and upon this earth we kneel. We bow before you: we, faithful servants to the Mother of the Islands."

"Rise!" the legendary matriarch spat back aggressively; her emerald eyes ablaze. She thrust her antlers into the air like a majestic stag.

The Daughter of the Islands approached the clan Ernaly warlord and murmured into his ear.

"The Mother of the Islands holds our destiny in her hands," acknowledged Mynar dyl.

The fair warlord moved towards Gal dyl and asked him for the sacred box. The Protector of the Forest granted the request with absolute obedience. Mynar dyl then spoke out for all to hear. His voice was charged with devotion, his speech emphatic and haughty.

"And so, the testament of Rowë is entrusted to Lore, Daughter of the Islands, and Envoy of the Secret Vale. May the precious will be returned to the Arkys and may they protect it until the time of great peril comes."

Mynar dyl then bowed respectfully. His gaze was fixed upon the sacred box. For some moments, he remained still, almost breathless. He seemed to be concentrating particularly hard upon the precious reliquary. Mynar dyl held it up. It showed no sign of breakage or wear. Markings could be seen on its sides, but they were no longer glittering like magic runes. Suddenly and to the surprise of all, Mynar dyl turned towards Curwë, an accusatory anger in his eyes.

"The warding glyphs of the sacred box are no longer protecting the testament. Someone has dispelled their power. Someone has attempted to violate the secrecy of Rowë's will," Mynar dyl declared.

Curwë almost fainted at the denunciation, as though he had been hit by a violent blow. Beside him, Aewöl's face turned ashen, as pale as the Goddess of Doom. Behind them, Roquendagor and Gelros looked astonished. The Daughter of the Islands moved towards Mynar dyl and seized the sacred box from his hands. For a moment, she stood looking at the precious reliquary. Then, the Daughter of the Islands slowly removed its lid and withdrew its contents, taking care not to reveal anything to the assembly. She examined it at length, muttering unknown words of some mysterious incantation. Finally, her face showed relief, even satisfaction.

"The testament is unspoiled," she declared, her deep voice flooding the hall like a torrent cascading down a mountain, "and nor has it been altered. It now comes with me, to the Secret Vale, where it will be kept by the Arkys, until the time comes to reveal its secrets to the true Elves of the Islands, the Seeds of Llyoriane."

The Daughter of the Islands began to withdraw to the back of the great tent from whence she had come. The assembly seemed to shiver with deep emotion. Mynar dyl called to her, his voice calm and measured.

"What is to become of the offender? What must we do with him?"

The Daughter of the Islands did not even turn to answer him but, before disappearing amidst the white sails, she called back.

"The one you call the 'offender' is also he who saved the testament from the Islands' enemies. Elvin kind's thirst for justice can be satisfied by Elves alone; you freely choose your own fair judges. The Secret Vale will take no part in sentences passed by the Elves of Llymar."

Aewöl had a wild look in his eye. He was paralyzed with panic. He stared blankly and appeared not to notice what was going on around him. Suddenly, he spotted Curubor. The Blue Mage was looking at him directly. Aewöl was unable to hold his azure gaze, such was its intensity. It seemed that Curubor was trying to communicate with him mentally, over the few yards that separated them, using an innate telepathic ability.

'Confess! Confess now, and I will protect you! I will save your life!' Aewöl understood.

The Daughter of the Islands disappeared behind the rear facade of the great tent, made of lofty white drapes hanging from above. The air was hot and still inside, as though Eïwal Ffeyn was denying entry to any marine breeze that might purify the stagnant Elvin assembly. Mynar dyl had not forgotten the offence committed by the bearer of the testament. He turned to Gal dyl.

"Protector of the Forest, I suggest you command your guards to seize the offender and send word to the matriarchs in Llymar. They will decide if the prisoner should be sentenced."

Gal dyl, shocked by this suggestion, which had sounded more like an order, spat back a sharp reply.

"Curwë is under my protection whether you like it or not, Mynar dyl. I alone will consider this matter and act as I wish."

Gal dyl's personal guards approached, standing reverently and silently before him. They did not speak a word. The six clan Avrony fighters waited. No order was given, and neither were they dismissed. Before them, Gal dyl sat on his great oaken chair. The seat, backed like a colourful peacock with its wings spread, suddenly appeared much too large for the Protector's stature.

Tyar dyl of clan Llyvary, warlord of Llafal and the eldest of all commanders present rose from his seat.

"Protector of the Forest," he began, raising his hands in prayer to invisible Deities, "I understand your dilemma. Surely Eïwal Vars, who gave us victory in this campaign, must have blessed Curwë to bring him so much glory. But it is not so simple. Curwë has done us a great dishonour by trying to rob the forbidden testament of its secrets."

Still standing straight in the middle of the great tent, like an offender being tried, Curwë spoke out boldly.

"Who, by his brave acts, saved the army of Llymar from ruin? Have I not served you well? Are my deeds not more valuable than cunning words?"

Leyen dyl Llyvary, warlord of Penlla and captain of the fleet, had been silent until now. He usually remained passive, for he was more celebrated for his ability to draw vessels ashore than for his bravery in battle. But the navigator was troubled by Curwë's words, which seemed to be referring to his own ineptitude at fighting.

"Protector of the Forest," Leyen dyl said with his soft voice, "if I have ever done you service, in counsel or in act, heed my advice now. You must honour our clans, whose blood has been shed for the sake of that testament. Curwë has offended our Deities; they have left us a message, and Curwë wished to steal it. Do yourself honour, Protector of the Forest, by arresting the insolent criminal and letting the matriarchs of Llymar do their duty."

At this, Gal dyl looked deeply troubled, his fair brows furrowed. He could tell that the vast majority of the army's chiefs supported Mynar dyl's proposal. Aewöl looked into the Protector of the Forest's eyes and knew that he feared the wrath of the matriarchs. It was common knowledge that Gal dyl avoided quarrelling with the eldest of the high priestess, Lyrine, his former consort and the mother of his daughter, Nyriele.

In that moment, Aewöl understood that Gal dyl's only fear was that Matriarch Lyrine would mock him. The one-eyed Elf could see the Protector of the Forest inclining his head, nodding purposelessly, failing to consider the matter with fairness or resolve. He suddenly understood that the weak commander would go back on what he had just resolved. Curwë was in danger. Aewöl stepped in front of his friend and cried to the vast assembly in front of him.

"Stop blaming Curwë. You are accusing the hero who has saved your lives!

How can you be so ungrateful?

Have you already forgotten what you owe him… what you owe us?"

This sudden intervention shocked the assembly; the numerous captains began to lambaste the arrogant one-eyed Elf at once, the cacophony of their angry cries filling the great tent. Aewöl felt the roar of voices like rams thudding against a weak gate. His face was very white. His only eye blinked in the light of the mirrors. He looked from face to face, like a beast encircled by his hunters. Slowly, Aewöl drew himself up. Clad in his dark clothes, he looked like the embodiment of looming menace.

"Curwë is innocent..." Aewöl declared, knowing he was about to condemn himself. "It was I who looked into the sacred box..."

The anger of the crowd inside the great tent exploded. Aewöl had seen similar outbursts of public anger in the past, but this manifestation of rage was stronger than any other. It risked alienating the Protector of the Forest further. He tried arguing his case, but no one was listening anymore. Only his companions from Mentollà, who still stood by his side, heard his plea.

"The glyphs had already stopped glittering... I was concerned... I opened the box's cover to verify its contents. I wanted to know... I wanted to make sure that the knight sorcerer had not spoiled it. Is that such a crime?"

Realizing that his explanations were falling on deaf ears, Aewöl raised his voice above the thundering crowd.

"Hear me, Protector of the Forest!" he cried, in an extreme exertion of effort. "Hear me, Gal dyl Avrony, who holds the Spear of Aonyn. Hear me with your heart and soul. Ask yourself this: if I had committed any sacrilege, would I be here standing before you, in the middle of your warlords and captains? I offer my sincerest apology. Grant my prayer, Protector of the Forest; leave me in peace, for I am innocent of any crime."

Aewöl thought he had managed to appease the chiefs of the Green Elves with this conciliatory tone. Having spoken these words, he sat down to demonstrate his humility. On this, the rest of the assembly, with one voice, advocated forgiving the one-eyed Elf and accepting his apology. But not so Mynar dyl, the warlord of clan Ernaly spoke fiercely to Aewöl.

"How can we tell you did not commit the mortal sacrilege of reading the will of Rowë?"

The assembly feared Mynar dyl; this fear gave the warlord of Tios Halabron significant influence. The crowd expressed its agreement with an approving murmur.

"No one will ever read the testament of Rowë...." Aewöl replied with a low voice.

"What was that? We can barely hear you. Speak loud, so that all can hear your lies," replied Mynar dyl furiously, his large chair trembling with the rage that inhabited him.

"The testament is neither scroll nor parchment..." said Aewöl, barely audibly. "Rowë's final legacy is distilled into a vial of golden liquid, a precious nectar... that can only be drunk once," he explained.

Rising suddenly from his seat, the high priest of Eïwal Lon, Camatael, intervened.

"So, the testament of Rowë is a potion, and its hallucinatory powers will reveal the message of Eïwal Lon..."

"The Daughter of the Islands did say before leaving," recalled Tyar dyl, "that the testament of Rowë had not been 'altered'. She used that particular word on purpose; she must have been referring to the purity of the golden nectar."

Camatael considered the issue further. "I have heard of certain ancient vintages of the Nargrond Valley that possess similar properties. The Elf drinking such delicate nectars can experience visions of what will come to pass."

Camatael possessed the authority of a high priest of the Demigod of Wisdom, so the entire assembly listened to him with attention. Meanwhile, seeing that Aewöl was turning the crowd, Voryn dyl Ernaly was horrified. Mynar dyl's brother could not control his wrath any longer.

"You will not leave this hall before admitting your crime. You have acted disgracefully. You have insulted us. What! You were welcomed generously by our communities, you pretend to respect our customs and then, at the first opportunity, you ignore our authority and seize forbidden knowledge for yourself. Do you believe that we are powerless, that our strength counts for nothing?"

The violence of the attack surprised Aewöl. Destabilised, he tried to adopt a different stance.

"I ask for equity. And, in accordance with the laws of Essawylor, Feïwal dyn Filweni, my only liege, must administer justice as warlord of Mentollà. This is the principle of the supremacy of Irawenti law over their subjects," requested Aewöl in an attempt to escape the matriarchs' judgement.

Facing this new challenge to his authority, Gal dyl exclaimed.

"I will not hear another word. The community of Mentollà freely choose to live in the forest of Llymar. That means every single member of that community is subject to our ancient laws. Justice among the Green Elves has nothing to do with the merciful whims you call the 'will of your liege'. It is not goodness nor mercy that decides what is just and what is not. Our only judge is the council of the matriarchs."

"I wonder," protested Aewöl, a hateful sarcasm in his voice, "is your ancient justice so very different from that of the tyrannous Gwarystan kingdom you so despise?"

Mynar dyl intervened, mindful to re-establish his supreme understanding of the law. Now that he could anticipate he would eventually have the upper hand, he spoke patiently, with a soft, delicate voice.

"The Green Elves have been organized in a collegial manner from the beginning of time. Its principles are inherently designed to be applied by our matriarchs, the undisputable descendants of Queen Llyoriane. In other words, keeping the harmony of our world is their responsibility…"

Mynar dyl paused at this, before suddenly turning to the accused.

"Aewöl has attempted to breach the order of things. The Deities of the Islands brought harmony to our clans by ensuring that each one of us remained in their proper place. There is a natural hierarchy of Elvin beings. It is the council of matriarchs' duty to bring peace by ensuring that this order is respected within our cities. Justice is not the vague arbitration of some Irawenti guide…" the warlord of Tios Halabron concluded.

Everyone thought he was finished. But using his usual professorial tone, Mynar dyl reminded the members of the assembly of their traditions.

"Equity is when everyone stays in their place. Otherwise, the world becomes chaos. The council of matriarchs edict judgments, for the high priestesses are both wise and knowledgeable. They are the head of our cities. The noble dyn and the warlords defend our territories, for they possess the strength of the heart. The fighters obey, for they know that it is in the best interest of all. Below, the common Elves simply respect the harmony they have inherited from our history. The law is broken when one who was intended to play a specific role within the forest thinks himself different and acts inappropriately. He thus commits a fault by trying to occupy a position other than his own, breaking the natural order of things."

After taking again his breath, Mynar dyl finished by clarifying his accusation.

"Aewöl has committed a great sacrilege by opening the testament of Rowë, by looking beyond the mirror where only the

Islands Deities dwell. For this crime, he must answer to the council of the matriarchs."

Listening to his elder brother's eloquent words and seeing with relish how the crowd was persuaded by them, Voryn dyl rose up, angry and sure of his victory. His heart was black with rage and his eyes flashed with fire as he yelled, staring at Aewöl.

"Evil foreigner, you may well have brought us to ruin with your sacrilegious act. For such a felony, I believe that the only just punishment can be death. Let our matriarchs condemn you, so that we might offer sacrifice and appease the just anger of the Islands' Deities."

These terrible words echoed long in the ears of those present in the halls of sails.

"I have something of a counter-argument," someone in the assembly opposed.

This was Roquendagor, his deep voice sounding out as the tall knight moved towards Mynar dyl, the true master of Voryn dyl. He leant down into Mynar dyl's face, placing his hands upon the armrests of the warlord's chair, before continuing.

"I am not sure I understood that scholarly little speech you just made for us, small Elf with the delicate face. To tell you the truth, I am not sure I care to understand the intricacies of your laws… But what I am sure about is this: if you do not let my friend Aewöl leave this place unharmed, you will find yourself at war."

Roquendagor was furious, unable to control his wrath any longer. His was in two minds over whether to draw his sword and kill the warlord of clan Ernaly on the spot, or to push the crowd aside and attempt to flee with Aewöl. While he was deciding, slowly drawing his two-handed sword from its scabbard, the assembly stood frozen, waiting to see if Roquendagor would pay for his insolence with his life.

Camatael Dol Lewin rose from his chair and stood as a high priest of the Demigod of Wisdom.

"Stay your anger, Roquendagor! And you also, Voryn dyl, control your rage! Eïwal Lon, who inspires me, cares for both of you alike. However angry you may be, I command you to hold your peace, and obey the Protector of the Forest," he said with his deep voice.

Camatael's hand rested on the golden pommel of his rod, the symbol of his power. Roquendagor looked at the lord of House Dol Lewin with all the contempt of a first-born towards his youngest brother.

"Do not think you have any authority over me, priest-lecturer! I am a knight without banner. I answer to no one."

With this, Roquendagor dashed his two-handed sword onto the sandy ground and returned to his former position, while the brother of Mynar dyl withdrew back to the warlord of Tios Halabron as his rank dictated. Curwë used this opportunity to feverishly plead for Aewöl's cause, addressing Gal dyl directly.

"Lord Protector! Will you be swayed by the reason of force? You can decide to maintain harmony by not showing your power. We ask that you be magnanimous!"

Thereon, Camatael spoke boldly.

"An Elf of Llymar cannot stand alone against the anger of a clan warlord such as Mynar dyl, the foremost of the Green Elves who, if he hides his displeasure now, will yet nurse revenge till he has wreaked it. Will you protect Aewöl by granting your forgiveness before all present?"

With these words, Gal dyl sat down, deeply embarrassed. At last, the Protector of the Forest said, with a new sincerity and goodwill.

"Let us hear from Curubor, wisest of counsellors, who knows events past, present and to come. He has guided us well on many occasions before."

The smooth-tongued Blue Mage rose. The consummate orator started to talk, and the words fell from his lips sweeter then honey wine. Five generations of Llewenti warlords born and bred on the Lost Islands had passed by as he counselled them, and he was now advising his sixth. With a calm voice, Curubor addressed the assembly.

"Somewhere, in the depths of the Ruby throne's halls, King Norelin must be rejoicing. His courtesans in Gwarystan, too, would be delighted if they could hear our murderous in-fighting. Trust my experience; I have counselled Elves greater than you, and none ignored what I advised. Never again will I sit beside Aonyn, the Giants' Bane, Rowë Dol Nargrond, the maker of legendary blades, or Yluin, peer of the warriors of yore. These were the bravest Elves to walk the Archipelago's paths. There are none under this great tent to match them, but those ancient heroes all heard my words and listened to them. So be it with you, for this is the wisest choice at your disposal..."

Curubor's voice trailed off. If some had forgotten his value and experience, this introduction stood as a stark reminder. After a moment of calm, the Blue Mage resumed his speech.

"Mynar dyl and Voryn dyl of clan Ernaly, though you may well truly believe you are acting rightfully, calm your zeal. The testament of Rowë is safe, unspoiled and in the possession of the Daughter of the Islands."

Curubor then turned to the tall knight in a histrionic way. His voice was deep and severe.

"And you, Roquendagor, strive no further against the warlords of the clan, for no Elf who wields a sword to threaten them will find grace with the matriarchs. You are brave and have proved your valour on two occasions, but the high priestesses of Llymar Forest are stronger than you, for they have been entrusted by the Deities with the control of the Islands Flow, the mightiest form of magical power.

I implore all of you, therefore, to end this quarrel, this poisonous argument, which in the battles to come would only be a dear comfort to the king of Gwarystan and his human allies."

Having quarrelled so angrily neither Mynar dyl nor Roquendagor seemed inclined to obey this offer of reconciliation. Both looked at each other as opponents eager to fight in close quarters.

Despite this apparent challenge to his authority, Gal dyl ignored the belligerents, and chose to talk discreetly to Curubor. Their conversation lasted some time and, despite the silence reigning inside the great tent, nothing could be heard of their exchange. After a while, Gal dyl put his hand on the shoulder of Curubor and gave him a knowing smile. The grin on the Protector's face made it clear that the Blue Mage had found him the compromise he was looking for. Gal dyl stood up straight and motionless, his hands at his sides, avoiding eye contact with the Elves around him.

"Stand before me, Aewöl of Mentollà," he proclaimed, "and hear my decision."

Aewöl stood up and moved slowly towards the Protector of the Forest. His gait was hesitant, but his gaze was challenging. His only eye showed his silent determination and the cold hatred of humiliation. The voice of Gal dyl rose high; even outside the great tent, all could hear his judgement.

"Aewöl of Mentollà, you are banished from the army. You will not return to Llymar with the fleet, and you will remain outside of the forest's boundaries until the council of the matriarchs has pronounced its sentence upon you."

Aewöl kept his gaze fixed upon Gal dyl, pursing his lips, on the point of an outburst. He became deathly pale. Now a murderous look was in his eye; his vengeful nature was beginning to surface. He could not utter a word of protest, overwhelmed as he was by a deep sense of dishonour and injustice.

The Protector's guards moved forward. Their ceremonial, earth-coloured cloaks fluttered before Aewöl like some awful nightmare. They seized him at the wrists to lead him outside. It all occurred so slowly, in total silence, as if time itself had stopped and all noise ceased around him. Images ran by, one by one, just like in a night terror.

The one-eyed Elf saw distinctly the faces of his executioners as if Leïwele Sysa, the Goddess of Strife and Revenge, wanted him to remember their faces in that instant: the wrath of Voryn dyl; the disappointment of his brother Mynar dyl; the satisfaction of the warlords from Llafal and Penlla; the sadness of Camatael; the coldness of Curubor and the relieved look of the Protector.

Still looking fixedly at Gal dyl, Aewöl murmured incomprehensible words that sounded as dreadful as a powerful curse.

'E ow tumat sur ywlo !'

The nightmare continued. The prisoner left the great tent under the watchful protection of his guards, passed by the ranks of fighters who were all eager to understand what had happened. Through the maze of colourful tents, he walked like a blind Elf, and was soon guided to the gate of the camp. The silence was deafening.

Finally, Aewöl regained some awareness when he was

called by a tall warrior clad in plate mail, offering him a bag of provisions. He recognized Duluin, one of the knights of the Golden Arch, the most trusted emissary of Curubor. The High Elf approached Aewöl to give him a sack and managed to mutter a few words without drawing attention.

"Follow these shores and look to the west. There lie the ruins of the great tower of Mentolewin. The pilgrims of Eïwele Llyi are gathering in that deserted place to honour the Deity of Beauty. There, you will find assistance. Now go, and do not come back."

Without turning back, Aewöl started to walk in the direction he had been given; placing one foot in front of the other was all he could think to do. His feet sank into the beach's soft sand, leaving a clear trail behind him. His gaze travelled across the boundless horizon of the sea.Finally, he broke down, overwhelmed by his emotions, tears streaming from his eye. He continued to walk all day, without taking care to rest, eat or to drink, driven simply by the necessity to flee the place of his degradation. When the sun disappeared on the western horizon, Aewöl collapsed onto the sandy ground, unable to go any further. Just before he fainted, Aewöl almost thought he had heard a familiar voice nearby.

"Master! It is Gelros. I have come to help you."

CHAPTER 7: Moramsing

2712, Season of Eïwele Llyo, 3rd day, the beach of Asto Salassy, Nyn Ernaly

The 'two winds' of the strait of Tuide, one blowing north, the other northwest, were coming in from the ocean. The breeze carried the briny scents of the sea, which mingled on the shore with the sweet-smelling pines. In the first light of morning, just as the first sliver of sun was coming into view, the Elves of Llymar anxiously watched the marine skyline to the south-east.

The mast of a clan Ernaly's hawkship had appeared on the horizon at sunrise. That morning, its single sail was black, the signal that had been established to mean that enemies were near. The hearts of the Llymar troops were troubled, for the hawkship was positioned to watch the strategic channels of the strait of Tuide; its dark sail must have meant a large fleet of Nellos galleys coming from the south. The sea hierarchs of Tar-Andevar had taken steps after the defeat of their army at Lepsy Gorge. The lords of Westerners were now resorting to the power of their navy to exact revenge.

Gal dyl Avrony, in dismay, ordered his guards to call an urgent council meeting in the hall of sails, summoning the noble dyn of the clans, the priests of the cults, the commanders and the captains. Fear, the sister of panic, was fast taking hold of the Llewenti chiefs. They all gathered with haste, eager to listen to their commander. After a brief talk, Gal dyl concluded his short address thus.

"Warlords, noble dyn, and wise counsellors, we are protected by the mighty hand of the ocean. Gweïwal Uleydon gave his solemn promise to our matriarchs that we could sail safely until we return home. He has been true to his word, and now bids us to go back to Llymar."

Tyar dyl Llyvary, the warlord of Llafal, approved. "Eïwal

Ffeyn is with us. The winds are favourable."

"Our swanships are hardy, able to take the worst the sea can throw at them, so long as they have my capable crews," claimed Leyen dyl Llyvary, captain of the fleet and warlord of Penlla.

Mynar dyl Ernaly also tried to reassure the assembly.

"The great galleys of the sea hierarchs cannot match the speed of a swanship over long distances," the fair warlord of Tios Halabron declared.

"Unless the winds change, or the tide turns," Nerin dyl Llyvary contradicted. "We should make haste," he insisted, "for if the war galleys of the Westerners get near our swanships, we will not have the power to fight back against their crews. The great galleys are equipped with rams. When the Nellos warships are moving at speed, those rams can split a vessel in two."

Seeing disorder growing into the ranks of the assembly, Gal dyl finally gave his command.

"We will do as I say and sail back with all possible speed to the forest of Llymar, for we have not the strength to confront the fleet of the sea hierarchs."

The chiefs of the army shouted applause at the words of Gal dyl. The army of Llymar was returning home. The Protector of the Forest ordered the captains to dig out the swanships that were on the beach of Asto Salassy and draw them into the water. The Elves of Llymar had believed the moat and wall around their camp would serve them well. They had counted on their entrenched camp as an impregnable bulwark against a ground attack, a base that could protect their troops and their ships. But an attack from the sea was a different matter entirely.

In the middle of the hall of sails, surrounded by the chiefs of his army, Gal dyl rose from his imposing oaken chair. His abundance of blonde hair had been combed with great care that morning. His shining eyes were burning with strain. He abruptly dismissed the assembly; all could see how much he desperately wanted to leave Nyn Ernaly. While he was speaking to Leyen dyl, Gal dyl took up the Spear of Aonyn that was placed beside him. It was gleaming with the light of sunrise. Gripping the fearsome silver-shod lance in his hand, Gal dyl stepped outside the tent and saw intense activity around the camp. His troops were readying their vessels for sea. Gal dyl kept his eyes on the weathervane.

'The marine breeze is sweeping down in the direction of the south-east. May Eïwal Ffeyn prove merciful,' he prayed.

But deep within him, Gal dyl feared that the fierce winds of the Austral Ocean might suddenly spring upon them. So far, there was a heavy swell upon the sea, but the waves remained unbroken. A quick crossing seemed likely, with the wind coming as it was from the left side. The swanships would be able to make headway against the stiff breeze without flapping their wings of many oars.

Gal dyl's attention was drawn some way up the beach, away from the intensive work of his troops, to the section of shore where they had first landed. The pier that the Elves had built, long though it was, could not accommodate all the swanships. The fleet looked somewhat cramped: in rows, with each nave placed behind another.

'It will take the full morning to prepare the fleet for departure,' he thought.

One of Gal dyl's personal guards approached. His bronze helmet masked his face. Many were those who thought that the Protector's guards were merely a ceremonial troop, mustered only to be paraded on special occasions. In truth, since Gal dyl had inherited the Spear of Aonyn, they had become a hard unit of dedicated fighters. At all times, four were assigned to defend the Protector while the others rested. They escorted him wherever he went, sometimes standing guard as sentinels if he needed privacy.

"Protector of the Forest," announced the guard, "Curubor has decided to embark on the first swanship to depart, the one commanded by Nerin dyl. The Elves of Mentollà will escort him. Curubor insisted that it would be wise to keep them separate from the dyl of clan Ernaly."

Gal dyl, sounding thoughtful, murmured his consent.

"This is sensible indeed, for they have provoked serious discord. Some members of clan Ernaly consider them to be heartless outlaws. Let us hope that this crossing has the effect of cooling their heated tempers. The Deities endowed Mynar dyl and Voryn dyl with valour but not much temperance."

The sentinel nodded. "The warlord of Tios Halabron and his brother confirmed they will be the last to depart. They said that the clan Ernaly's hawkship will form the rear-guard of the fleet. They volunteered to protect the rest of the swanships if the Westerners were to fill the gap."

The guard of the Protector bowed, eager to be on his way, as there was a lot of work to do before they could depart. Gal dyl held him for a moment.

"I will sail with Camatael. He deserves to be praised. Inviting him on board Leyen dyl's swanship, which carries the four tombs of Nargrond Valley, will do him honour. Camatael has demonstrated his loyalty to our cause. In war, his prowess is beyond question and, in counsel; he surpasses many, despite his young years. He spoke wisely during the assembly. His advice is not to be disregarded."

Satisfied with this initiative, Gal dyl smiled and started to think ahead.

'Once we reach the shores of Llymar, I will prepare a feast

for the army to celebrate those heroes we had to leave to Eïwele Llyo's care. It is right that I should do so. There will be an abundance of wine and plenty of music to entertain our brave troops.'

The sentinel, clad in his light armour, went out, bidding the other fighters of the Protector's guard to join him. They formed two ranks of three, equally distanced from their commander, and escorted Gal dyl to the tent of the high priest. They wound their way around the many alleys of the camp, like as many forest pathways, bordered with small tents made of sails with single poles for support. These were fragile constructions for the common fighters. A few pits, ten feet deep, had been dug into the sand and covered with fish nets. In them were live fish being saved for meals.

Soon, the group reached Camatael's shelter. A picket of spears with feathers of various birds stood by the entrance. The high priest lived in a kind of hut: a series of oars and poles, standing together to form tent twenty feet wide. The structure was strung with fish nets and was covered in white sails that had been taken from the swanships.

When they entered the tent, they found Camatael playing on a silver harp of exquisite design. He was playing soft music and praying to Eïwal Lon. The high priest sung a beautiful chant, which filled the tent. The air was thick with the smell of incense. Camatael was alone but for one servant, who was sitting opposite him and saying nothing, absorbed as he was by the melody. Camatael was dressed simply, wearing only a purple gown and sandals the colour of gold. His austere expression, together with his icy-blue gaze fixed on his instrument, revealed his unwavering devotion to the Demigod of Wisdom.

The newcomers waited until Camatael had finished singing. The calm of his dwelling contrasted with the turmoil in the camp. It was as though outside events could not affect the high priest of Eïwal Lon. Camatael sprang from his seat with his harp still in his hand. He greeted Gal dyl and his guards, stating.

"Welcome, Protector of the Forest! It is an honour to have you here."

With this, he led his guests further inside the tent, inviting Gal dyl to a chair covered with purple rugs. He then asked his servant to give every Elf a drink, as was the custom when welcoming visitor under one's roof. Soon, a large bowl was set upon the table. Elixirs of flowers were mixed with wine.

Gal dyl took his seat facing Camatael, the entrance to the tent in front of him. The two Elves laid their hands upon the exquisite delicacies which remained before them. When he had made sure that both Elvin Lords had drunk as he was minded, the servant left the tent. Gal dyl made a sign to his guards. The sentinels took their watch outside. There was plenty to eat and drink, but the thoughts of the two Elves were elsewhere. Gal dyl started.

"I would like to invite you to join me aboard Leyen dyl's swanship. It is the largest of the fleet. It carries the tombs of Nargrond Valley and will enter the bay of Llafal first. I want you at my side as a token of appreciation. When the crowds in Llafal cheer you for your words and deeds, I want you to feel rightfully proud."

Gal dyl had spoken unusual words of gratitude and honour. This pleased Camatael, who appreciated the trust that had been placed in him.

"I am anxious to thank you," the high priest started, "for the confidence that you have always showed me. You have my allegiance."

After these words of thanks, however, Camatael, though grateful, could not resist laying his mind before Gal dyl. He responded with complete sincerity and goodwill, though he chose his words carefully.

"Most noble descendant of Avrony, I speak with all due respect, for I know you are the ruler of many Elves. The council of the forest has entrusted you to wield the Spear of Aonyn. Everything hinges on what you decide, therefore I will say what I think is best. You did mention that my words of council have been of some use to you…"

Camatael stopped for a moment to catch his breath and clear his thoughts.

"Earlier today, in the hall of sails, no ruler could have come to a wiser decision than yours when confronted with Aewöl's sacrilege. Now that your judgment has been rendered, however, as high priest of Eïwal Lon, I urge you to reconsider the decision and to find forgiveness for Aewöl's crime."

Camatael paused at that, and looked intensely at Gal dyl as if he wanted to see through his guest's mind. Encouraged by the passivity of the Protector, he carried on.

"In the absence of a fair trial, the sentence you passed has angered Roquendagor. You have banished his companion and friend from our army. That knight without banner yielded to his own pride and felt humiliated. It is dangerous to offend a hero whom the Deities themselves have honoured with great victories… Yet you still hold the power to appease him. When the time comes, you should show your mercy to Aewöl and recall him to Llymar. Thus, by your first strict judgement, you have fulfilled your duties towards the most intransigent of warlords. But in the days to come, in a fair speech before the matriarchs, you can also placate the community of Mentollà by pleading for leniency."

Gal dyl stepped back, surprised by the proposal. The expression of sympathy on his face disappeared. His response was abrupt.

"I was right in my decision, and I am glad you understand why. You rightly condemn Roquendagor's folly. The knight without banner was blinded with passion and gave in to the basest part of himself. I might reconsider my opinion of Roquendagor if he makes amends, in public before me. If he forgets his anger, I can forgive him. I want him to yield before the matriarchs, who he implicitly insulted with his rashness. He should know that our high priestesses can prove ruthless."

Gal dyl's features in that moment betrayed his fear of the matriarchs' power.

"As for his companion Aewöl," the Protector resumed, "it is beyond my power to forgive him for his sacrilegious act. That dark figure should be thanking the Deities for their mercy. His fate would have been tragic, had he been taken to Llafal."

Gal dyl stood still, clearly pleased with his resolution. Camatael understood that the Protector of the Forest was concluding the debate. Surprised by this sudden stubbornness, Camatael felt that the Protector was making a great mistake by not taking this opportunity to ease tensions between the forest's communities. Aewöl's banishment would undeniably create a divide between the migrants and the old clans of the forest, thus adding to the existing rivalry between the High Elves and the Green Elves of Llymar. Nevertheless, eager not to lose the influence he had recently acquired, Camatael decided to completely change the topic and cease any escalation in tension.

"When you came in, Protector of the Forest, you saw me praying to Eïwal Lon. We were faced with great disaster and, with his help; we will finally save both our army and our fleet."

"The sea hierarchs will not catch up with our fleet. They might roar commands like maniacs, drive their slave rowers with endless lashes of the whip, but they won't reach us before the approach of night. By then, we will be far away," Gal dyl agreed, sure of his case.

Camatael shared what was troubling him.

"I know the Westerners' allies, the knights of the Golden Hand, have vowed to hew the high sterns of our swanships into pieces, and wreak havoc among our troops. Once our fleet is out of reach, I fear they will only seek new opportunities for vengeance."

Now somewhat concerned, Gal dyl responded.

"Who do you think should fear retaliation from the knights of the Golden Hand?"

"I worry for the safety of those Elves who are making the pilgrimage of Eïwele Llyi. I saw many of them in the harbour of Tar-Andevar. The worshippers of the white Deity have come to Nyn Ernaly in great numbers this season, sailing in from different parts of the kingdom of Gwarystan to look upon her divine apparition. Lord Curubor advised me yesterday that, as we speak, they are gathering in Mentolewin, on the western shores of the island. The ruins of the great fortress lay barely sixty leagues from here. The pilgrims would make easy prey for the surviving knights of the Golden Hand and their allies. If we do not help them in time, we will regret it bitterly thereafter. Once the damage has been done, there can be no cure. I would hate for us to be too late to save the pilgrims of Eïwele Llyi from retaliation."

"My good friend Camatael, when Curubor spoke to you of the pilgrims in the ruins of Mentolewin, did he not entrust with you what he was planning?" wondered Gal dyl, visibly satisfied to see that Camatael had not been informed of all of the Blue Mage's scheming.

"Lord Curubor only said that he was confident the pilgrims would be safe," the young Dol Lewin responded. "He was being rather evasive. He made some reference to history: 'Never, even in the kin-slaying wars of old, did an enemy, be they Men or Elf, succeeded in attacking the pilgrims of Eïwele Llyi."

Gal dyl nodded in agreement.

"I may not be as erudite as the Blue Mage, but I do know the legends about the Deity of Arts and Love. My daughter Nyriele made sure of it... To protect her followers from strife, Eïwele Llyi can send forth 'The Veil', a vast congregation of butterflies. Its flurry of intense colour can instil fear into the hearts of those who would do her worshippers harm. Several times in the past, its enveloping cloud has protected her helpless pilgrims by suffocating those who hunt them with its own unfathomable mass. Barbarians and Westerners alike fear this phenomenon; it fills them with dread, even more so than the cyclones of Eïwal Ffeyn."

Gal dyl was speaking with a reassuring tone.

"I am sure none of them would dare approach the worshippers of the white temple as they undertake their pilgrimage. Besides, most of the pilgrims come from the kingdom of Gwarystan. They are subjects of Norelin and travel under his royal protection. The king might despise the old faiths of the Lost Islands and hinder their worship, but he cannot afford to openly attack their followers. Rest assured: the white pilgrims will be safe."

Camatael seemed appeased by this.

"Curubor has organized the white priestesses of Llafal to join the pilgrims of Eïwele Llyi. During the gathering to honour the Deity's apparition, they will circulate the rumour about the knights of the Golden Hand's sacrilegious acts against the tombs of Nargrond Valley," explained Gal dyl.
"I see. The white priestesses of Llafal will condemn the servants of Norelin... they will declare that this desecration of tombstones was overseen by the king himself. Many of those pilgrims might be tempted to flee the kingdom and seek a place of refuge with the ancient clans of Llymar," Camatael guessed.

"We hope so. The forest will need many more Elves if we are to confront the challenges to come," confirmed Gal dyl, still embarrassed by the naïve way in which he had let slip his primary counsellor's plans.

Outside, the troops were still busy packing their gear and dismantling their tents, retrieving masts, poles, oars and sails that were required to equip their swanships. The noise made in the camp by their work contrasted sharply with the calm atmosphere inside the Dol Lewin's tent. Gal dyl showed some signs of impatience. Cries announced that the first of the swanships was setting sail. Soon, their turn would come. Camatael perceived the distress in his interlocutor's mind.

Suddenly, there was a noise outside, and the guards of the Protector appeared at the tent's entrance. They advised their commander that it was time to go. Leyen dyl's swanship would be among the next naves to leave. Gal dyl rose and saluted Camatael. He thanked him for the kind reception. The Protector was soon on his way.

Camatael remained alone, thinking. It did not take him long to gather his few possessions: the silver harp; two books; a few scrolls that he folded into his purple cloak's inside pocket; his long sword; and, finally, his golden rod, the symbol of his power as high priest of Eïwal Lon.

At the tent's entrance, an Elf asked to enter in order to start dismantling the shelter. His tan-leather coat, weapons and helmet were all adorned with the yellow flower of Nyn Avrony. Camatael admitted the guard of the Protector inside his modest dwelling, declaring that he was now ready to leave.

To his astonishment, the guard shoved him bluntly to the back of the tent. He stood tall and straight at the entrance, blocking any possibility of escape. His naked broad sword was in his hand. Slowly, he removed his bronze helmet that had been masking his face.

"Dyoren!" Camatael exclaimed, his breath short. "I do not know what you have in mind but your presence here is…"

"Unwanted," the Lonely Seeker cut in.

Dyoren seemed to be even more tanned than before. His stolid face expressed fierce resolution. Dyoren had not lost his mind. He knew what he was doing. Camatael remained silent, on the defensive, waiting to learn more before deciding how to act.

"I will not bother you long; you will soon be able to join your new friends aboard the great swanship. I have come to ask you a few questions. The quicker you answer, your lordship, the sooner you will leave this soil."

Camatael felt furious. Never before had anyone showed him such disrespect. He was determined to show this unsolicited intruder what it cost to insult a lord of House Dol Lewin. Holding his golden rod firmly, he started drawing strength from his inner self.

To his surprise, the area was deprived of any source of the Flow. He soon realized that he was powerless. Camatael's eye fixed the bare blade of his opponent's broad sword. He recognized Rymsing, the famed sword of Nargrond Valley, which the Lonely Seeker always carried with him. Indifferent to his prisoner's anger, Dyoren proceeded with his questions, with all the authority of one who has nothing to lose.

"What have you done, your lordship? What strange course of action did you and Lord Curubor embark upon?"

Camatael hesitated for a while. He needed to clarify Dyoren's question.

"Do you mean you would like to understand what happened before Lord Curubor and I were captured by the knights of the Golden Hand?"

"Yes. That is exactly what I mean," said Dyoren, unwavering.

Camatael nodded his head before responding.

"You step into my living quarters without being invited. You ask questions with the authority of one acting within his right. This is a surprising course of action… for a fugitive."

Unmoved, Dyoren did not react to this hidden threat, but the bare blade of Rymsing seemed to oscillate with the sea breeze in his hand. Camatael noticed the sword's odd vibrations and looked into Dyoren's eyes without any fear. A cold resolution emanated from the Lonely Seeker's gaze. The young lord raised his voice, now determined to show his authority.

"It is no small offense to threaten a high priest of Eïwal Lon. Furthermore, I would add it is bold to show such disrespect in the middle of Llymar's army camp. I understand that you are upset after your degradation, but that gives you no recourse to insult the very basis of our laws. I believe you leave me no alternative but to punish you. I could call my guards. They stand but a few yards from the tent's entrance."

Dyoren, still stolid, replied. "You could, but you have not yet. And I know why. Of course, you have already calculated that, by the time your guards, as you call them, could be of any assistance, you would have had to parry half a dozen of my attacks with your rod. You will know from legends celebrated by the clerics of your own cult that Rymsing was forged to harm the Gods themselves. Nevertheless, I do not believe that it is fear that prevented you from defending yourself. It is most probably curiosity. The questions raised by my presence at your side are numerous. You are intrigued. It frustrates you that you cannot control the situation, does it not?"

Camatael remained motionless. Nothing in his face or stance revealed his thoughts.

"Allow me to clarify how the sacred box ended up with Eno Mowengot, the commander of the knights of the Golden Hand," offered Dyoren.

He continued without waiting for a response.

"You know as well as I that, before Eno Mowengot recovered the testament of Rowë, another knight sorcerer, the one bearing a serpent's mask and wielding a war hammer, seized it from the tomb of the Dol Nargrond lord. Clan Ernaly's units were attacked as they tried to pass the last of the Hageyu Falls. They lost the coffin. All were made to believe that the knight sorcerer with the war hammer, who had led this attack at the Ningy Pool, took the precious reliquary and then remitted it to the commander of the knights of the Golden Hand before the battle of Lepsy Gorge."

"That is what I heard the noble dyn of clan Ernaly recount," confirmed Camatael, without going into too much detail.

"Oh, you simply heard, did you? It just so happens that I have come to learn that the knight sorcerer with the war hammer, that master of the draconic turtle who attacked Mynar dyl's fighters at the Ningy Pool, was killed just after he broke into the tomb, and that he lost the sacred box to his victor."

"Who told you that? How do you know this is true?" Camatael asked.

For the first time, the young Dol Lewin showed difficulty concealing his surprise. Dyoren did not answer these questions, but rather continued his story.

"The knight sorcerer with the war hammer had fled down the Sian Ningy on board the small boat which carried the coffin of Rowë, but a sudden storm hit the wood of Silver Leaves. The river flooded. It caused landslides and many trees fell. Eventually, the Sian Ningy was obstructed by a natural dam, and the boat was blocked. A mysterious Elf used this opportunity to attack the knight sorcerer with the war hammer. He wielded a great sword: a dark blade of shadows. He eventually prevailed and defeated the knight of the Golden Hand, claiming the sacred box. Based on the account I heard, I concluded that this mysterious Elf with great powers must have wielded one of the swords of Nargrond Valley. I believe he carries Moramsing, the dark blade of the East that holds the power of the Amethyst. I seek that sword. Indeed, I have spent my life seeking it. Tell me that I am right."

"This is a bard's tale. Why should I believe such a ridiculous story?" immediately mocked Camatael.

Dyoren ignored his sarcasm, and continued his narrative, increasingly convinced by his theory as he formulated it aloud.

"I believe that this mysterious Elf of Shadows was an envoy sent to protect the expedition. He intervened only when clan Ernaly lost control of Rowë's coffin. Someone must have feared that the convoy carrying the tombs, led by clan Ernaly, would be attacked in the forest. The six knights of the Golden Hand were watching the surroundings of the wood of Silver Leaves. They benefited from considerable assistance from the sea hierarchs of Tar-Andevar. Dozens of units of Westerners, scouts and cavaliers were patrolling the region, ready to obey their orders."

Dyoren was becoming excited, talking almost frantically.

"Someone must have anticipated the attack. Someone sent a secret envoy, not only powerful enough to defeat the knight sorcerers, but also capable of escaping any pursuit. And this is exactly what happened. Mynar dyl's fighters were eventually deprived of their precious shipment, and this Elf with rare talents succeeded in saving that which is essential for the Islands Deities' cult. That secret envoy managed to preserve the sacred box and, eventually, deliver it to his backer and primary instigator of the plan."

Camatael frowned at this. He now understood what the Lonely Seeker was trying to get at. Dyoren finished his reasoning.

"I believe that the mysterious Elf of many shadows answered to two lords: two allies of the Llymar clans, but who had not been involved in the matriarchs' plan to recover the tombs. Unfortunately, the two lords' hideout in Nyn Ernaly was being watched by the knights of the Golden Hand. After their secret envoy delivered them the sacred box, they tried to leave, but the two lords got captured, and Eno Mowengot reclaimed the prize and took them prisoner..."

Camatael interrupted him, "Your reputation as a storyteller is not undeserved, Dyoren. Your fairy tale ends well, just like the very best stories of the late-night taverns..."

Dyoren was quick to note the irony but remained impervious. He concluded by approaching the matter he was really interested in.

"Still, we are neglecting what has become of the mysterious Elf of shadows... and his dark sword. But I now have a starting point for my quest."

"This very tent, I presume?" guessed Camatael. "You thought that I knew much more than I had been letting on. And you anticipated that I would be more talkative than my mentor, the Blue Mage, when confronted with Rymsing."

"Ever since I worked it all out, I have been tracking you down, for I know Curubor lets you in on his little schemes. I have been waiting for the perfect moment. It was looking likely that you would not sail back to Nyn Llyvary without finding out what happened to the sacred box, which had been thrown down the precipice in a deluge of fire," said Dyoren.

A silence followed between the two Elves. At last, Camatael responded.

"Well, Dyoren, I thank you for explaining to me in such detail the reason for your presence in my tent. But this does not change our situation. Those I do indeed call 'my guards' are still standing a few yards from us, behind the thin fabric of that tent, ready to intervene at my first call. The sharp blade you call Rymsing is still in your hand, beautifully bare, ready to pierce my flank. We still do not know what your next move will be."

Dyoren was puzzled at that, somehow surprised by how calm the young Dol Lewin was proving. He decided to change his angle of attack.

"Let me tell you the story of Dyoren the Third," he said unexpectedly. "He was born a noble dyl, for his bloodline could be traced back to Eïwal Vars. He came from clan Llorely. I remember he earned his reputation during the first barbarian invasion, thanks to his prowess with the sling. It does not really matter, though."

Feverish, Dyoren paused as if he needed to collect his thoughts.

"This brave fighter was one day summoned by the Arkys to their retreat in the Secret Vale. The quest to find the lost swords of Nargrond Valley was entrusted to him, and he started travelling the Islands with Rymsing hanging at his back. Years passed, and Dyoren the Third went missing, before the Secret Vale's envoy, the Daughter of the Islands, found that Lonely Seeker at last…"

Dyoren shook his head sadly with a look of poignant regret on his face.

"The unfortunate knight was hiding inside a deep cave, somewhere in the southern mountains of Nyn Llyandy. Alone, confronted with the perils of the wild, that former wielder of Rymsing had lost all faith; without any more confidence and hope, he simply had ceased his quest. Fear was in his eyes when the Daughter of the Islands found him. The coward thought he could escape the just ire of the Secret Vale when he revealed that Rymsing was safe. This Lonely Seeker had been terribly afraid of losing the Nargrond blade to the enemy; he had buried it deep in that very cave. He now gave it back intact. The Daughter of the Islands took the magic glaive... The poor Elf was then fed to her wild hounds."

Camatael marked his disgust, "That punishment was surely disproportionate."

"I have retold this tragic tale for one reason. Disobeying the Arkys has consequences...

I chose to rebel against their decision to strip me of my duties. I know the risks I am taking. Nevertheless, I have faith in my destiny. I could become the first Seeker in history to ever recover one of the lost blades of Nargrond Valley. Camatael, you know who that Elf of many shadows is, and you know where I can find him. This is why I insist you answer me without delay."

Heavy footsteps were heard outside. The loud cries of nearby Elves, busy preparing for their departure, filled the small shelter. Then, guards entered the tent without warning. They looked eager to dismantle the small hut quickly and started examining its structure made of poles, oars and sails.

"You should be gone by now, my lord Dol Lewin," muttered one of the workers as they set about their task, otherwise ignoring the two Elves who stood frozen in the middle of the tent.

There was a long moment of hesitation as the two Elves stared fixedly at one another. Finally, Dyoren broke the silence.

"Accept my sincere apologies for this unexpected visit! I wish you a safe journey back to Llymar."

With this excuse, Dyoren put his bronze helmet back on his head. He was on the move, about to disappear out of the tent, when Camatael spoke back.

"You are already pardoned for your intrusion, valorous Elf. May the grace of Eïwal Lon be upon you and may the lord of wisdom enlighten your path and favour your actions."

Camatael hesitated, but finally went on.

"If you seek further assistance, it is to the grace of Eïwele Llyi you must now turn. I am helpless in these matters that trouble you... But I hear the followers of the white temple are gathering in the ruins of Mentolewin, praying that their Deity appears to them."

Dyoren heard these last words, but he did not turn. He was already on the move.

**

2712, Season of Eïwele Llyo, 4th day, forest of Mentolewin, Nyn Ernaly

"Hurry! We have to reach the cover of Mentolewin forest!" urged Gelros almost begging his master, Aewöl. "I feel uneasy. That hawk has been following us since dawn. It's killed several of my birds, and the others have fled."

The two outcasts were progressing along the foothills from the beach of Asto Salassy. They ran as fast as they could, through the thick, wild vegetation and tangled thorny bushes. The terrain was rugged, but the path they had chosen eventually took them out of sight, away from the open spaces of the lowland. The cliffs around them echoed with the deadly cries of scavengers. The wind, which had been blowing from the sea ever since they left the beach of Asto Salassy, now seemed dead. The rugged tops of Nyn Ernaly's northern hills protected them from the breath of the Austral Ocean.

Their progress had been difficult. For two days, they had

been stumbling and scrambling among rocks and bushes, moving slowly westward. The sky was pale. They could see the ridges and chasms of Nyn Ernaly's northern ranges turn a fiery orange in the midday sun.

The two Elves were constantly checking over their shoulders, to see if they had been traced by enemies. If they were spotted by a sentry or a scout, a hunt could begin at any moment. Earlier in the day, they had already heard the tramp of iron-clad feet and the swift clatter of hoofs. Horns had sounded out as they were crossing an old abandoned road, and a chorus of cries had answered from the thickets of the foothills. They had not seen anyone or anything, but they had heard the rush of horsemen sweeping over a small wooden bridge, and the rattle of barbarian warriors running up behind them.

"Quick! We are almost there," Gelros urged.

He was leading the way; Aewöl followed behind. Gelros never exposed his pale skin to direct sunlight; his face looked almost bloodless. His dark grey eyes gave his gaze a deep, mysterious aura.

The only reply Gelros received from Aewöl was a low growl. The one-eyed Elf was walking with difficulty behind his companion. He was exhausted and would stop every now and then to rest. Suddenly, Aewöl fell to the ground, his strength utterly spent. He pulled back his hood, revealing his straight dark hair, pale face and single sharp eye. His behaviour showed signs of severe mental strain. His banishment from the army of Llymar had deeply affected him. The injustice he felt was obscuring his thoughts.

Aewöl had barely spoken since Gelros had found him on the beach after he had collapsed, his heart barely beating. The hopeless and dejection had been all-consuming. Since then, the one-eyed Elf had been struggling to concentrate, and seemed unable to remember details of the past few days. He had completely lost his appetite and was unable to slumber.

Gelros felt worried for his master. Nevertheless, despite his master's condition, he needed to concentrate on their current situation.

"There is an open area stretching approximatively fifty leagues from the beach of Asto Salassy to the borders of Mentolewin forest. Only there will we find shelter," said Gelros, trying his best to instil motivation in his master.

As often as they could, they circumnavigated crop fields and pastures, keeping low along their hedged borders, but sometimes there was nothing else but to run across long, open stretches. Thanks to the provisions that Duluin, the knight of the Golden Arch, had given Aewöl, Gelros did not have to worry about finding food.

'We have plenty of bread and dry fruit inside the bag. And we will not die of thirst. The streams of northern Nyn Ernaly provide an abundant supply of water. Still, I will have to go hunting as soon as we reach the forest of Mentolewin,' the scout was already planning.

Gelros, when he had rifled through the supplies, had also noticed a small copper ring, encrusted with tiny gems, at the very bottom of the small satchel. He thought it an unlikely place for a jewel, but soon forgot it. Gelros' priority was to put as much distance as possible between them and the army of Llymar. He also feared unexpected encounters with Men of the tribes who populated the northern stretches of the island. The barbarian territories, a succession of rocky slopes and steep peaks, spread out into the distance. The two Elves scrambled out from the thicket, its thorns like talons. Gelros looked towards that small mountain range to the north. The scout shared his concern with his master.

"At a time like this, it is instinct that keeps an animal alive. And mine is telling me to reach the protection of Mentolewin forest as quickly as possible."

The scout was now using the language of the Night Elves to communicate with his master, which they seldom had the opportunity to do. Gelros was known as a character of few words, not the kind of Elf to get carried away with long speeches. His few companions had always known him as quiet, feeling more at home with the birds of the forest. That day, however, Gelros felt he needed to talk, to talk as he had never done before, in order to hold the attention of his master. He needed to prevent the destructive emotions circling madly in Aewöl's mind from totally consuming him. Gelros realized that speaking incessantly was a way to keep his master's head above water and prevent him drowning in evil thoughts.

"Have you noticed, master, how the Green Elves almost never call me a Night Elf? They simply see me as an immortal High Elf, foreign to them. They are, of course, mistaken. Us, Nigh Elves, are very different to the other High Elves, even though we were originally a subdivision of Silver Elves. We belonged to Nel Anmöl in the starlit woods and, in truth; we are more akin to Gnome folk than other Elves."

Aewöl had to stop and sit down for a while. He shivered, not from the cold of the air, but rather the dreadful anxieties chasing one another through his mind. Gelros unclasped his dark cloak and cast it about his master's shoulders. Aewöl looked at him with indifference. He did not respond. Gelros nevertheless continued his babbling.

"Unlike all other Elves, in fact, we have never worshipped any God. We trust only in our own skills. To my mind, the Green Elves are at their weakest when they are performing their naïve rituals to those, they call the Deities of the Islands. If any of this was of any use, this supposed last refuge of the Elves would be... a refuge for the Elves."

Aewöl kept his head down. They had been trudging for more than six hours when they heard the sound of scavengers' cries that brought them to a halt. Aewöl could go no further.

"I must rest."

"We must keep moving!" urged the scout, as he scrambled to his feet.

"I cannot go all the way at a run, Gelros, I do not know what's come over me," Aewöl said with grimace.

Gelros was struggling with his own weariness, but nevertheless he tried to comfort his master.

"I know exactly what is happening to you! This overwhelming weakness was caused by the pain you felt after that unjust condemnation. You might as well have been stabbed in the back with a poison dagger. This is some wickedness... But we escaped the fall of Ystanlewin, we crossed the Austral Ocean, and we survived the battle of Mentollà. We will get through this ordeal, I promise you," said Gelros, as he turned to lead the way among the stones and boulders.

"I can't go on," murmured Aewöl. "I'm going to faint."

He had drunk from the pools in the vale several times, but he was very thirsty again. Aewöl sat silent, deep in his dark thoughts. Gelros tried to encourage him.

"You should have an obsession for survival."

Aewöl managed to utter a few words back, barely audible.

"I am tired and weary; let us stay here a bit longer..."

He seemed utterly devoid of hope.

"That would not be wise. I will carry you on my back. We must go," urged Gelros.

But Aewöl threw off his cloak and unclasped his light chainmail.

"This weight is too cumbersome for me," he complained, shivering again, though the temperature had not dropped.

"Let us stop and have a rest then. We will move a little farther once we've had something to eat. Take a bite of that bread. It will give you strength."

Gelros reached into Duluin's satchel and broke off a piece of bread for his master. Aewöl chewed it as best he could. A sea of grey clouds coming from the ocean started to form a striking backdrop behind the mountains. The hawk that had been following them all day was still circling above them, high in the sky.

After a while, they started off again. The light of day was now low, and the hills were once again covered with clouds. Through the grey dusk, they could just about see they were emerging from a valley between the hills. It sloped down towards the west, and a lively stream traced its way through the valley's centre. Beyond its course, they saw a path that wound around the foothills. After much wondering and searching, they found a safe route they could climb down. Below them, at the bottom of a ravine of some four hundred feet, was the valley stretching away to the gloomy borders of a vast forest. Far to the south, some thirty leagues away, they could still see Eïwal Vars Lepsy's peak, its thin finger rising to a great height, its pointed tip swathed in cloud. They had not gone far when Aewöl paused again. Daylight was growing weaker.

"I did not know you were so well versed in the history of the Night Elves. Only my mother's bloodline was Morawenti. My father was a Gold Elf. I felt closer to him. That is to say until he was found dead... in my early youth," Aewöl said.

Gelros' spirits were sinking. They were not making much progress and, again, Aewöl needed to stop. He looked at his master anxiously, wondering how he could convince him to push on. Finally, Gelros dropped the idea, and sat down on a boulder. What Aewöl needed most, perhaps, was conversation.

"Your mother taught me a lot," admitted Gelros."That is a surprise. I didn't know that," Aewöl replied.

This sudden interest in Gelros' past animated him somewhat. A mist seemed to clear from his eye. Satisfied with how their dialogue was picking up, Gelros continued.

"Before you were born, your mother dedicated significant time to my education. It's because of her that I know the history of our forefathers."

Aewöl was hearing one surprise after another. He passed a hand over his aching head.

"How could that be? She never said a word to me about our history! I know nothing of her heritage. Indeed, I have no knowledge of my Morawenti origins at all. It's as though I was raised as a High Elf of pure golden blood."

"She did what was best for your future, I suppose," said Gelros.

"I doubt it," replied Aewöl, before deciding to entrust his companion with something of his miserable youth. "My mother was cold-hearted and stern. She never showed any kindness to me, obsessing only over my future. My father had been one of the founders of the Crystal College, a distinguished scholar holding a prominent position at the court of Essawylor. My mother always insisted that I should benefit from the same privileges. Wherever we dwelled together after my father's death, she sought to dominate other guilds in Essawylor, using my rare abilities as a craft master for her own benefit. Her overall goal, I believe, was to accumulate as much wealth as possible, by exploiting any opportunities she could find in all kinds of trades."

He realized this was the first time he had told anyone of this painful memory.

"Whatever you might think, your mother was acting in your best interests. You are a true Night Elf, though you may not consider yourself to be one. Our hearts are dry, and we are impervious to love. The feudal tie to our own community is the only bond that matters. Night Elves see parenthood as a duty to perpetuate our kindred. We do not believe that there is life after death. What we want most, therefore, is to create a material legacy for the generation that survives us. We have a cautious nature. The life of the Night Elves is dedicated to accumulating wealth, which can then be traded off in times of peril. We pursue this obsession without dignity. So, whatever you may have felt at the time, in your mother's eyes, you were the person who mattered most."

"If that is so, why was I raised like a pure Gold Elf? Why would she put so much effort into erasing my Morawenti origins?"

"Back in Essawylor, under Queen Aranaele's reign, the few surviving members of the Night Elves were considered gloomy. We were barely tolerated by the other High Elves, for they believed our nature to be treacherous. But some of us were exceptionally adept at learning, mastering great crafts as smiths, alchemists or rune masters, hence they managed to preserve some influence among the kingdom of Five Rivers. But, regardless of their bonds to the guilds of Essawylor, they owed their true allegiance to your mother."

"They owed their true allegiance to my mother? What is that supposed to mean?" inquired Aewöl, now paying very close attention.

"Morawenti rulership has always been dynastic, since the earliest days in the starlit woods, when Sindöl was our undisputed prince," said Gelros.

"I do not understand. What has this to do with my mother?" asked Aewöl, agitated.

There was a long silence. Gelros looked at the trees in the vale, thinking. The scout pondered whether the time was right to reveal to his young master what he knew about his origins. Finally, he spoke.

"Your mother belonged to the bloodline of the Dir Sana, the princes of Nel Anmöl. Until the day that she perished in the flames of Ystanlewin, when the northern province fell, she was secretly considered by all Night Elves of Essawylor as their rightful sovereign, their absolute ruler."

Aewöl remained quiet. Somehow, though he could not explain it, this revelation did not surprise him.He had always wondered what had caused that bitterness within his soul which, throughout his youth, had propagated only indifference and mistrust towards others. The one-eyed Elf now understood that it was never too late to find answers.

Aewöl often wondered how he had escaped so many perils, how he had developed such a distinct aptitude for survival even as he despised life with such ferocity. For a long time, he had thought that his blood, his origins, were the cause of his fate. He was born a High Elf in the kingdom of Essawylor. It should have meant that a life of influence and power would open up before him. No such thing had ever come to be, for the blood of his mother flowed in his veins and he had always been considered a Night Elf by the elite in the kingdom of Five Rivers.

A grim, tragic history had befallen House Dir Sana and, likewise, the fruit it had borne to the world of Elves. But Aewöl had never committed any crime, nor betrayed his brethren, nor caused any mischief. Nevertheless, he too had suffered the fate of his mother's kin: ostracized and unwanted by other High Elves because of his ancestors' deeds and reputation. His companions' malevolent behaviour, their snobbery and hypocrisy, had gradually consumed him. His anger had grown and threatened to push him into darkness.

But Aewöl was considered a talented alchemist, and a great caster of spells. He had taken refuge in his work as a scholar and earned the confidence of House Dol Lewin. Now that he was aware of his true heritage, he felt fortunate to have benefited from the protection of Roquendagor's family. House Dol Lewin had helped him find his way. Aewöl looked at Gelros with compassion, his spirit rising a little.

"Your attitude towards me has always shown great respect, a mysterious devotion."

"I have dedicated my life to your service," Gelros confessed, "and every single one of my actions has been guided by the orders your mother gave me. Even now, as we speak, as this unjust condemnation separates us from our companions, my loyalty remains with you."

"And to think… I had always believed I was protecting the lonely Gelros, guiding him to excellence among House Dol Lewin," Aewöl smiled. "I always thought you owed your achievements to me, and that you were dedicating your life to your benefactor's service. But I see now I was mistaken. You have chosen a life of duty, Gelros."

"There was no other life available to me. I am a pure Night Elf, dedicated to my kin."

"Has it all been worth it?" Aewöl asked frankly.

"Do not worry about me. I am not one of those who live in the past, consumed by regret. I do not care much for the turmoil of the mind. I worship no God; I am inhabited by no particular faith. I reckon I am closer to animal than to most Elves. I find happiness in the simplest of situations when I am communing peacefully with nature. I suppose that, now we are outcasts, I will come to enjoy many more of those blessed moments in the wilderness."

Aewöl and Gelros gazed out in wonder at the beautiful landscape of Nyn Ernaly. Between them and the Chanun Mountains, all seemed green and fertile. It was a large plain of rich meadows and fruitful orchards. As far as their eyes could see, trees collected in small groves, or immersed themselves in larger woods. Far away to their left, an abandoned wide road ran from the Chanun Mountains to join the northern range, and along it several dark shapes were hurrying.

"I do not like the look of things. Unless my eyes deceive me, those are Men running along the old road" said Gelros, "if we go now, we might reach the borders of Mentolewin forest by nightfall," he pressed.

Aewöl had by now regained some measure of strength.

"We will depart, do not worry! But before that," he asked, "I want you to tell me what you know of my family: the truth that has been hidden from me until now."

Gelros initially refused, crying, "That would take so long! Our history goes back to the council of the elder kings, almost five millennia ago."

"Tell me what you know," ordered Aewöl, now utterly insistent.

His uncompromising stance demonstrated that he would not leave their hideout until he had learnt what he wanted.

"I am no scholar," Gelros winced. "My memory can hardly keep hold of details of those ancient times. What's the use of it, anyway?"

"Tell me what you remember," repeated Aewöl with a softer voice.

Gelros remained silent for a while, hesitant as ever. Finally, he nodded, understanding that his master would not change his mind. He might as well provide him with the knowledge he sought.

"Your mother read me passages from the manuscript of Sana, the book which tells the history of the Night Elves. Long ago, along with the High Elves of the surviving royal houses, the Night Elves traversed the Anroch Desert. Finally, they reached the edges of the forest of Essawylor and were welcomed by the clans of the Blue Elves. The royal houses of the High Elves ultimately divided and waged war against each other during the war of Ruby and Diamond, until King Lormelin led the majority of the High Elves across the sea. Most Night Elves accompanied Lormelin the Conqueror, on his journey across the Austral Ocean. Only very few Night Elves remained behind in the kingdom of Essawylor and entered into active service under the sovereignty of Queen Aranaele. Egalmöl, the second son of Princess Sana, was counted among them."

"I know that name. Egalmöl was the first master of the Crystal College in Essawylor. If I remember correctly, my father was once his apprentice," said Aewöl."Egalmöl was your grandfather. Your mother was his only daughter, though this was known only to the Morawenti community. For reasons unknown, he did not follow his elder brother, Elriöl, the master of the guild of Sana, across the ocean. But what I do know is that you are Aewöl Dir Sana, son of Espa, grandson of Egalmöl and direct descendant of Princess Sana," pronounced Gelros. "That is why you are my master."

Aewöl remained silent for a while, lost in his own thoughts, as though he were gazing, for the first time, into the deep void of his soul.

Gelros decided not to disturb him. The scout watched the sky with attention, preoccupied by the hawk which still drew circles above them. The two outcasts sat under the cover of the thorny bush, while the light of the sun faded slowly behind dark clouds. There were only a few hours of daylight left.

Meanwhile, in the cool dimness of the late afternoon, the one-eyed Elf sat absorbed, still enthralled by this tale of ancient Night Elves: of Princes Sana, her two sons Elriöl, the master of the guild of Sana in the Lost Islands, and Egalmöl, the founder of the Crystal College in Essawylor. And Egalmöl had been his grandfather, whose only daughter was Espa, the mother he had disliked so much, if not abhorred.

"And only you know of this?" Aewöl asked abruptly.

Gelros took some time to answer, pondering long before sharing his thoughts.

"I have never discussed your origins with anyone, nor has anyone ever questioned me about it."

"But..."

"But I believe that Lord Roquen knows. All his family knew, when they were alive," Gelros admitted.

"That would make sense," agreed Aewöl. "The Dol Lewin family agreed to welcome my mother and myself. Despite her undeniable ability to manipulate, even Espa would have had difficulty hiding her parentage from the third most powerful house of Essawylor. They must have known that she was the secret daughter of the mage Egalmöl."

Eager to reassure his master, Gelros added.

"Lord Roquen has never talked. I trust him. He can be as silent as a Night Elf when he wants."

"What makes you think so? No one is to be trusted," replied Aewöl bitterly.

"The secret of your bloodline has been kept strictly confidential, I am sure," Gelros said. "Not so long ago, on one of his numerous visits to Mentollà, Lord Curubor made many enquiries about our community's past, and the latest events that had occurred in Essawylor. I remember that he spoke for a long time with Lord Roquen about the northern province, Ystanlewin, and the Dol Lewin family. More generally, the Blue Mage asked many questions about the origins of the High Elves who had come to the Lost Islands; the Unicorn Guards, Curwë and also... the two of us."

Aewöl remembered. "I attended that meeting. Roquendagor proved very evasive and did not give anything away, unreadable as a stone. But you are right to mention that encounter, for Curubor did ask me about your Morawenti roots. The Blue Mage knew that our community considered you part of the Night Elves, and that you were my devoted servant. I can still picture that scene when I answered him. Lord Curubor's inquisitive look kept leaping from me to Roquendagor, as if he wanted to check the truth of my words in our lord's eyes."

The One-eyed Elf could see the scene unfolding before him. But Gelros had stopped listening to his master. His attention was distracted by the hawk's flight, which seemed to be coming closer and closer to their hideout amid the boulders on the hill.

"Come closer, evil bird of prey!" the scout whispered. "Let me show you what a true hunter is."

Aewöl looked up in the sky. In a flash, Gelros notched an arrow and flexed his Cruel Bow. His arrow flew, whistling through the wind.

"You pierced one of its wings!" Aewöl cried.

But the damage was limited. The bird of prey had barely lost a few feathers. Immediately, it dove at full speed, seeking shelter behind the hills to the east.

"That evil beast must have returned to its master. He must be just behind us, probably on the other side of the hill. We must run... we have already waited too long."

Gelros covered his head with his hood and leapt out of their hideout. He rushed down the hill as if he were fleeing a demon. Aewöl seized the supply bag Duluin had given them and ran after his companion.

The two outcasts set out on the most dangerous stage of their journey yet. Abandoning all caution, first they tore down the hill, completely exposed. They ran around rocks and boulders towards what they thought were an ancient path, curving west towards Mentolewin Forest, which now only lay a couple of miles away. It was not a wide trail, and thorns and ferns spilled out from either side. The two Elves could still not hear any indication that they were being chased, and after listening carefully for a while, they set off westward at a quick, though more measured, pace.

After a couple of miles, they halted. A short way in front of them, the track bent a little southward, and beyond that the path became lost as it met the edge of Mentolewin Forest. At last, they could catch their breath and rest a little. In the stillness of dusk, they could hear the many noises of the woods, sounds they had been secretly hoping for all this time. They had only taken a few steps when Gelros realized that it would be difficult to make their way into this northern stretch of Mentolewin Forest, for there were no paths in sight. In the end, they were forced to walk along its edge, looking for a way in. After half a mile, they saw a glade, hidden deep within the woods. A dozen blue jays were circling in the air. These birds were most active at nightfall and were found in mixed forests dominated by poplar and birch trees. They usually liked to nest near clearings or logging areas.

"We might find a way there. Birch trees often line paths that break into the forest," Gelros declared as he picked a fresh walnut from a branch. "Eat it, for it brings joy to the spirit. It is also a good antidote for many types of poison."

Gelros also discovered a colourful plant with purple and azure leaves.

"This is purslane. We can use this plant for ointments. It will be good for your wounds."

Finding no sign of any other movements, the two outcasts crept into the woods cautiously, avoiding as best they could the thorns that seemed to reach out from all angles. They had hardly gone two hundred yards when they heard the voice of a Man, harsh and loud. The two Elves quickly reached for their bow and crossbow. They hid behind a large, strong oak tree. The voice drew near.

A Man with a grey beard came into view. He was clad in brown and green robes and used a stick to walk. His appearance was unkempt and filthy. Aewöl guessed that he was of barbarian breed given his large size, dark hair and tanned skin. His big nose and wide, sniffing nostrils made him look like a bear. He carried a short lance at his back. It appeared he was a hunter of some kind. The barbarian tracker stopped ten paces from the two Elves. To their utter amazement, he used a form of Llewenti language when he called out.

"Leave, trespassers! Sacred is this grove! This is the territory of the bear wild, of the wolf ferocious!"

Aewöl was unwilling to wait and learn more about this new threat. Reaching to his belt for a bolt, he immediately cried a powerful incantation.

"Yego co Narkon!"

The missile's tip turned red, like molten iron from a forge's fire. The smell of steel and metallic dust filled the air. But before Aewöl could lift his crossbow and impale the tracker, Gelros shoved him to one side, nearly knocking him down. The bearded Man took advantage of this unexpected diversion to flee. He leapt from a boulder and scrambled up a hill. The barbarian disappeared into the woods as mysteriously as he had come.

"What have you done? Have you lost your mind? I could have dispatched the savage with a single bolt! That wild Man will now raise the alarm," shouted Aewöl, furious.Gelros was distraught. "I apologize, master."

Aewöl could not control his wrath. Now moving into the open, towards the centre of the glade where the barbarian tracker had stood, the one-eyed Elf continued admonishing his companion.

"You made a mistake, Gelros. We will soon have dozens of barbarians hunting us down. Don't you think we have enough challenges already?"

The scout tried to explain his reaction.

"I apologize, master, but that wild Man was a druid, one of the Mother of the Islands' servants. He's a holy figure in these woods. The Green Elves always showed great respect to the human Druids. They saw them as priests of Eïwele Llya."

"And so, what? Does that make him any less dangerous to us? Why should I care?"

"Master, the druids control unnatural forces within the forest. Attacking one of them could put us in serious danger. Woe to us if we persecute them!"

"I just see this latest encounter as an illustration of the misery to which we are condemned..."

But Aewöl was interrupted. Out of the cloudy sky, a winged shape tore down like a thunderbolt, sundering the air with a ferocious shriek. The bird of prey burst through the dark foliage and attacked Aewöl, its sharp talons drawn.

Gelros leapt at his master, knocking him to the ground. The scout protected his master from the ferocious bird but received a devastating wound himself. The hawk ripped Gelros' ear from his head with its beak. A silver powder was suddenly all over him: his clothes, cloak and hair. Gelros screamed in pain as the bird of prey spread its wings. But the scout reacted before it could take flight. With a quick strike of his dark blade, he cut through one of its wings.

A bloody melee ensued between the Elf and the hawk. Struggling, yelling, striking, cutting, Gelros could not overpower his aggressor. Aewöl, as soon as he could get a clear shot, ended the combat by shooting a fiery bolt from his crossbow straight into the bird's head. The hawk was killed instantly. It fell to the ground at Gelros' feet.

The scout had barely survived the fight. His wounds were

devastating: an injured leg, a nose broken, a severed ear and bloody scars that covered most of his face. Unable to stand any longer, Gelros collapsed at the foot of a large plane tree.

"What is that on your clothes? Some silvery powder... it covers your hair too!" warned Aewöl.

Gelros did not have enough strength to answer him. Aewöl turned to the bird of prey's carcass, immediately recognizing it from its unusual size and the characteristic white feathers at the tips of its wings.

"This is Voryn dyl's hawk," Aewöl cried in disarray.

The sound of an arrow whistled in the wind. Dropping from the sky like hail, it hit Gelros straight in the shoulder, piercing through his light chain mail. Gelros screamed out in pain. The shaft of the war arrow was brushed with the same metallic powder that covered the scout's clothes and hair.

"Gelros, remove your cloak! Discard your clothes, quickly!"

Translating words into action, Aewöl cast his companion's dark mantle away from him. A second arrow came down from the sky, flying between the branches. It buried itself in Gelros' abdomen, just as he was trying to remove his clothes. The scout cried out in pain again.Aewöl managed to get him out of his tunic, stained with the silver powder. But his hair remained covered in the magical dust.

A third arrow flew towards them. It seemed to weave around the natural obstacles of the forest, drawn as it was towards Gelros. It struck the scout in the top of his back, just shy of his neck, where his hair ended. Screams of pain sounded out through the forest. Aewöl saw no other option than to destroy the magical dust that was calling the deadly arrows. He quickly incanted some strange words.

"Narkon Forya hryd!"

A sudden fiery explosion blinded Gelros for a moment. The flash came into contact with the silver powder and negated its unnatural twinkling. A fourth war arrow pierced the canopy above but was deflected by one of the lower tree branches. Aewöl understood he had put an end to that dreadful spell. He bent down towards Gelros to examine his wounds. The scout was bleeding severely, his condition critical. Gelros could not resist yelling out in pain, such was his suffering.

"These arrows are poisoned... This is why you suffer so much…" Aewöl said.

"Flee, Master! Flee!" Gelros managed to shout through the agony.

"I cannot leave you here," Aewöl refused.

"Flee! He is coming for you!" insisted Gelros, sinking slowly to the ground before rolling over and curling up such was the pain the poison caused.

Aewöl hesitated for a moment, seeing that Gelros was now shaking violently. He threw down his two scabbards and crossbow and ran away, towards the depths of the woods, without turning back. He was torn apart by Gelros' cries. Aewöl was heading in the direction the barbarian druid had fled. He was going deeper into the forest, rushing through the branches. He came up to a small stream, barring his passage. He took a moment to stop and reflect, working out how to cross losing as little time as possible.

But finally, Aewöl waded through the small river on foot before rushing on. A trail of mud marked his path through the trees. After a few dozen yards, the ground rose sharply before it met large rocks blocking the way. Before him were innumerable dramatically scattered boulders, surrounded by steep slopes with colourful patches of heather. The tight passages between the large stones formed a maze. Aewöl stopped to catch his breath. He could still hear his companion's cries of pain behind him in the woods.

"I cannot leave him behind! I just can't!" Aewöl realized.

It was not yet quite dark. Aewöl fell to one knee. He drew from the inside pocket of his cloak a piece of coal. Murmuring words of sorcery, he pressed the dark carbon to his eye patch. A mist spread out from his face. Darkness grew around him, consuming the feeble light of the stars. Even with his night vision, he was barely able to see through the obscurity he had just created.

Aewöl set out on a long detour, hoping to find his way back to his fallen companion. The darkness emanating from his eye patch seemed to move with him. The one-eyed Elf now hastened towards Gelros' continuing cries, which covered the rustle of his passage. Speed, not silence, was his priority. It was difficult and dangerous, moving through the darkness of those pathless woods but, as quickly as he could, Aewöl found his way to the northern edge of the trail they just walked to enter Mentolewin forest. He covered several hundred yards, making sure to avoid the clearing where his companion had been wounded. At last, Aewöl caught the first hint of a presence under the canopy of shadows.

"There he is! I will make that murderer pay for his felony," he whispered, overwhelmed by a cold hatred.

Aewöl hid himself behind an overhanging stone. He sank to the ground beneath the wall of rocks and bowed his head. Gelros' cries of distress were still filling the night with despair. Slowly, cautiously, he looked in the direction of the glade where Gelros lay dying. A strong breeze from the north was driving away the shadowy fumes the one-eyed Elf had conjured. A moment later, Aewöl identified the source of that unnatural gust. He made out the shape of an Elf a dozen yards before him. Wrapped in his cloak, a javelin in his hand, the hooded figure progressed carefully through the night mist, keeping low, like a hunter fearing a deadly trap.

It had been hard for Aewöl until this moment, exhausted as he was. But now, finally confronted with his enemy while his companion was dying a few yards away, his struggle became a torment, worse than a nightmare. Aewöl tried to stop his mind from racing. He could feel the sweat on his neck. He suddenly realized how thirsty he was and began to gasp for air. Aewöl bent his will to control his breathing.

'I need to perform a single decisive rush. There is no hope of approaching this Elf unseen. If I...' Aewöl did not dare consider further the consequence of a failure.

He drew his two daggers, their dark blades not even reflecting the light of the rising moon. Only a dozen steps separated him from his target. The distance was short but, at the same time, seemed impossibly far.

Swift as the wind, silent as a ghost, Aewöl rushed forward. He closed the gap in the blink of an eye.

Aewöl stabbed the Elf with his two short blades. Hit twice in his spine, the hooded Elf fell to his knees. With a quick thrust of his daggers, Aewöl slashed at the back of his victim's feet, aiming for the junction of the tendon and heel muscle.

The Elf dropped his javelin and swayed helplessly, like a dislocated puppet. Aewöl removed the Elf's hood to unmask his face. The mad eyes of Voryn dyl glittered with terror. Aewöl drew a small metallic flask from his cloak pocket.

"The... only... just... punishment... can... be... death!"

Aewöl mouthed each syllable slowly, deliberately drawing out this moment between them. These were the exact words Voryn dyl had uttered in front of the entire assembly in the great hall of sails. As he sentenced his enemy to death, the one-eyed Elf tipped his flask and let a tiny drop of its translucent pearly potion into the eyes of the treacherous archer.

Aewöl began pronouncing incantations. The evil poison seared in the dyl Ernaly's eyes, before passing into his bloodstream. For as long as he could, Voryn dyl contained his groaning, thanks to his formidable courage. But when the excruciating pain triumphed over his resolution, he filled the forest of Mentolewin with appalling cries. The acidic poison devoured his face, and his cranial bones began to show through his skin. At the same time, a fire erupted in his internal organs, and a black sweat poured out from his whole body.

"Watch my face, cursed defiler!" Voryn dyl cried out in a final effort. "May you die in this same pain!"

Aewöl spat upon the corpse of the dead Elf before muttering a final tribute.

"I do not accept your judgment, Voryn dyl the Ugly. I'm no worse than you. I am not responsible for the tragic outcome of our conflict. There was no way we could have ever found peace, for I would never have forgiven you for what you've done. Consider your death a just retribution… a punishment for your harsh words. This is a just vengeance."

The wind had ceased. Slowly, the darkness faded, and the woods were bathed again in the light of the stars. The silence was deafening. Aewöl realized that Gelros' cries of pain had ceased.

Leaving the face of Voryn dyl to be consumed by the self-propagating acidic poison, the one-eyed Elf rushed forward. He quickly reached the glade. The distance between the two casualties was no more than fifty yards. To Aewöl's utter surprise, the glade was empty. Gelros had vanished. Only some of his equipment could be found: Gelros' Cruel Bow and two quivers, his own swords and crossbow, and also Duluin's sack.

Aewöl retrieved the gear. It was growing darker; clouds now obscured the moon's beam and the sparkling of the stars. Nevertheless, Aewöl's night vision enabled him to pick out evidence of movement on the soil.

'Gelros must have crawled to seek shelter,' he deduced, judging by the numerous marks the scout had left through the bushes and earth.

This trail stopped suddenly at the edge of the glade, but new tracks appeared. Large footprints were sunken into the soil, like that of a bear. Aewöl started to follow this path into the woods. He retraced the steps of the big animal along the trail to the maze of rocks that he had found earlier. There was no further sign of his companion's presence.

'Gelros must have been carried away by a savage beast,' was the only explanation Aewöl could think of.

This finding filled him with dread. He drew his light crossbow, readying himself for a fight. After several hundred yards, Aewöl reached an area of dense boulders. Large rocks blocked the passage. These boulders looked like the remnants from another geological age. Their appearance was that of sandstone, forming large nodules that had resisted erosion. It formed a maze of scattered boulders and tight passages, amid trees of different species such as oak, pine and beech. Mushrooms covered the soil.

Still following the tracks of what he guessed was a bear; Aewöl discovered the entrance to a cave. Between two large boulders was a grand gateway, like that from some ancient temple, with a clear floor of crystal water which welled up at the back. Great stones had been laid at the mouth of the cave. The entrance was only slightly lighter than the total pitch blackness that engulfed the passage beyond.

After twenty steps into the cave, around the first curve, Aewöl felt a distinct temperature contrast between air in the tunnel and night sky outside. He shivered as he progressed into an even darker cavern, beset with many jagged and slippery dangers. The darkness utterly enveloped him, while the sounds of the forest remained some distance behind. His night vision allowed him to distinguish the numerous pitfalls and traps that this rough underground cavern held.

Going down even further into the pit, Aewöl noticed that he could no longer see the tracks left by the bear.

"Damned!" he cursed "The ground is made of limestone. The bear must have walked the calcareous soil without leaving any residual moisture behind. The surface of the ground is dry to the touch."

Aewöl stopped as he reached a larger underground chamber. Stalactites of various shapes adorned the cave's ceilings. Five different tunnels sprung out into the depths from that centre point. Alone in the dark, in total silence, the one-eyed Elf realized that there was no hope of ever finding his companion. Overcome by a dreadful feeling of loneliness, he sat on the ground, his back resting against a stalagmite. In the face of his desperate situation, his whole body seized with anguish.

"I am cursed," he thought. "I will no doubt be in pain and distress for my entire life."

Aewöl mechanically reached into Duluin's satchel, looking for some food. He had no strength left. His hand blindly groped about in the small bag. Surprisingly, he came across the cold touch of metal. Aewöl withdrew the small object. It was a small copper ring, encrusted with tiny jewels.

**

2712, Season of Eïwele Llyo, 5th day, Nyn Ernaly, Mentolewin

The pilgrim of Eïwele Llyi looked at his small ring. It was encrusted with various tiny jewels. Little shards of aquamarine, ruby, sapphire and amethyst were visible on its surface. The ring was solid copper, with scratches, dents and signs of wear.

"Do you see?" The white pilgrim asked, turning to the beautiful Elvin lady who stood beside him.

There was excitement in his voice. She drew closer to examine the ring which he held out in his open palm, her thin brows furrowing with attention. Her dark, pinned-up hair, delicate features and elegant neck radiated a warm glow. The slight tan of her soft skin contrasted with her white ceremonial garments. There seemed to be nothing unusual about the ring.

"I see no change, my prince," she concluded at last.

"Well, my dear, you wouldn't have lasted long in my father's guild with an answer like that," teased the white pilgrim. "Try again!"

"I cannot, my prince. Tell me what your eyes see," replied the lady. She frowned so graciously that the white pilgrim, under her charm, could not help but marvel at her beauty.

"These amethyst splinters," he explained with a smug smile, "are glowing an unnatural deep purple. This is a good omen, my dear, a very good omen indeed. The conclusion to this tale is upon us. He is drawing near."

The lady could not suppress a shiver. Her delicate face was marked with sadness. As she glanced at the white pilgrim's right cheek, which was marked with the infamous rune of outcasts, she seemed to be holding back tears.

Unaware of his female companion's turmoil, the white pilgrim rejoiced openly. A smile of satisfaction crept across his face. This dark-haired Elf was tall and thin, dressed in a magnificent white robe which entirely covered his rich, dark clothes beneath. His face was partly hidden by a large hood. There was nothing warm about his fine features, particularly when his icy gaze became lost in deep contemplation and his lips twisted into a contemptuous smile.

The white pilgrim placed a mask over his face. It had been made with leather and porcelain. The design was simple, and its gold-leaf surface gave it a symbolic look. Natural feathers and small gems added to its other decorations painted by hand.

"Do you know that, since ancient times, masks have been used by Elves across the Lost Islands for storytelling or musical performance," he recalled.

Leaving the discreet alcove where they had been standing, which had kept them away from the crowds, the white pilgrim returned to the central nave of Mentolewin's ancient temple. It was a place of power, the embodiment of spiritual and political authority, both religious and secular. Throughout the centuries, the white temple of Mentolewin, the main shrine dedicated to Eïwele Llyi in Nyn Ernaly, had been the birthplace of many communities who worshipped the Deity of Love and Arts. The white pilgrim breathed in deeply.

"It is the smell of violets which fills the temple. It is a delight for the senses!" he rejoiced, visibly enjoying the moment.

Emerging from the shadow of the alcove, the lady put on her own mask, securing it with a ribbon behind her head. Hers was a half-mask, which only covered her eyes, nose and upper cheeks. It was highly decorated with silver and crystals. The mask seemed to have been designed specifically for her, as though she were an actress who did not wish to have her beautiful face covered completely.

All around them within the temple, other pilgrims were also masked. This ancient custom encouraged freedom and creativity and was thought to protect Elves from anguish. During festivals such as this, anonymity allowed for short periods of intense artistic invention.

The white temple of Mentolewin was a ruined monument which owed its beauty to the simple architecture and absence of all superfluous decoration. The love of detail, technical precision and beauty had made this ancestral place outstanding. The ruined remains of the colonnade and dome left no doubt in the pilgrim's mind about the power and beauty of their original design. The stained glass had been utterly destroyed and the marks left by a devastating fire could still be seen on the cross-vaults which covered the nave's ceiling.

The ruined walls of the edifice gave the temple's visitors a panoramic view from within: over the surrounding fortress, the island's coast and then the ocean. The beauty of Eïwele Llyi's ancient shrine in the glow of sunset promised a bright new day to come.

"Today, I will sing," the white pilgrim suddenly declared.

A silence followed. The lady knew her advice would be ignored but nevertheless tried to persuade him otherwise.

"This is not wise, my prince. You could be recognized. It was dangerous enough for you to join this pilgrimage, surrounded as we are by so many Elves from Gwarystan. Why take such risks now?"

"I have been hiding for too long. Now that the end draws near, the time has come for the followers of the Deity of Arts to hear my compositions once more: The Songs of the Lost Islands, the greatest music that has ever been. This place, ruined but magnificent, inspires me. My performance will be such that Eïwele Llyi herself will appear to celebrate my art. I have always wanted to honour the divinity of beauty."

The white pilgrim drew from his cloak a statuette. The small, feminine figurine, carved from precious ivory, was sublime. It seemed to have an identity of its own. It was endowed with a grace, a charm, which demonstrated the unquestionable talent of its maker. A light dress with a low neckline barely covered her captivating shapes. Her bust was adorned with a white pearl necklace. The white pilgrim kissed the statuette several times before putting it back in his pocket. He looked at the vastness of the ocean before him.

The Sea of Cyclones filled the vast bay, reaching all the way up to the cliffs upon which Mentolewin stood. The edges of the bay softened into a vast sandy coastline. The beach upon the western shore of Nyn Ernaly thronged with Elves, dressed in white robes, forming a great crowd. The cry of gulls above them was unceasing. Marching to the sound of many pipes and flutes, they walked in great numbers along the beach, eventually climbing the slopes which lead to the formidable tower in ruins, upon the Cun Kangna. This imposing hill, rising from the strait of Oymal's waters, was considered the westernmost point of the Archipelago, and therefore the closest shore to the Mainland. Beyond, others great rocks surged up from the sea, forming a natural defensive line, curving gently to the north.

On Cun Kangna's slopes stood the ruins of the great fortress of the West, Mentolewin. Its lower walls had been stained a dark purple after many centuries of the gloomy sea lapping at the stones, the waves relentlessly challenged its foundations. This strategic place had been chosen long ago by the High Elves to build the formidable stronghold of House Dol Lewin. Its highest tower had been the largest edifice ever built on the Islands. The silver searchlight at its top had shone far out into the mists of the dangerous strait. No longer could it watch for the ships of the Austral Ocean entering the Sea of Isyl.

That day, the pilgrims walking the alleys among the fortress' ruins were encouraged to reflect upon the Elves that had swelled around these walls: the skill with which they had built their home, the noble origins of the fortress' defenders and the joyful lives they had lived there.

"Let us follow this parade. It will lead us to the amphitheatre where artists will be playing music," suggested the white pilgrim to his female companion.

A small group of Elves, led by white-robed priestesses of Eïwele Llyi, led the parade, accompanied by the delicate notes of the musicians' harps, which made the air hum most sweetly. After them came many Green Elves with fair hair, males gently comingling with the females. The cortege was progressing according to the music of their violins and wind instruments, which inspired joy and admiration in all who heard. This small group then gathered before the great terrace that looked out over the sea. The procession burst into the Song of Beauty in perfect unison. It was said that the chant had been written by Eïwele Llyi herself.

After the light of the moon had gone and the rays of the sun eventually made their appearance, the pilgrims were all ushered onto the vast terrace to contemplate the silvery waves of the sea at dawn. The entire procession flooded onto the terrace. There, they were met by other priests of Eïwele Llyi, who glided between the different rows of pilgrims, letting the travellers know that the Deity of Arts bid them welcome.

Hundreds of followers of Eïwele Llyi then sat in the great ruins of the amphitheatre, filling its numerous alleyways. They had fashioned many beautiful objects. Colourful paintings, delicate woodcarvings and beautiful embroidery adorned the empty walls; the ancient, cold ruins of Mentolewin had grown fair beneath their skilful hands. The hearts of these Elves were glad, and they marvelled at the grassy glades and crystalline waters of the creeks.

Some sat on dark and lonely rocks to contemplate the tumultuous waves. Many Elves had cast flowers into the sea, and their fragments glittered in the moonlight, filling the rock pools of the coast with what looked like shining jewels. Their robes were sewn with pearls, and their clothes were adorned with a great wealth of gems, gold, silver and other precious items. All were wearing masks of beautiful design. The ruins of the ancient fortress' amphitheatre, once dominated by the desolate sound of the wind, were now filled with the voices of the crowd. The carved marble that remained told of the days of glory and happiness. The music they played sounded like the most enchanting sound ever to be heard.

"This moment will be the pinnacle of my artistic life," murmured the white pilgrim as he looked at the audience.

All around him were Elves of all origins. They had come from all the corners of the Lost Islands to this place for a single purpose: to celebrate the gift of artistic creation. More than a thousand Elves were seated in the amphitheatre: artists, musicians, each possessed with that dual obsession for beauty and art. He could not have hoped for a better audience.

The white pilgrim invited his female companion to sit down. He shared a handful of exotic chewing herbs with her. A few moments later, several carafes of golden liquor were brought to them, and it soon became clear that they would need several more to quench their thirst. For a long time, the couple listened with relish to the music, nobler and purer than any they heard for many years. It was full of longing and exquisite poetry. It was as if pipes of silver and flutes of gold were sending forth crystal notes, forming the richest harmonies beneath the rising sun. The closing theme retreated from the tumult that had been gradually building, humming rather with a profound serenity that defined the very essence of music. The white pilgrim longed for the days of his youth. He plunged into a deep reverie, delicately caressing the hair of his female companion.

*

When he awoke from his dream, the sun was high in the sky. There was no more music, save for the myriad sea birds above. Pleasant fragrances seemed even sweeter than before. The light struck his face and he shivered. The white pilgrim arose quickly, seeking the protection of a ruined wall adorned with tapestries.

"My time has come!" he decided.

There, in the shadows of the white linen flapping in the wind, he was protected from the sun. The white pilgrim seized his flute.

The five-holed wind instrument had a v-shaped mouthpiece and was carved from the bone of a vulture wing. He began to blow. The sounds that came out were sensual, exciting, and almost brutal. The audience, caught off guard, immediately applauded, surprised as it was by this music like no other.

Soon, the rhythm carried away everything in its passage, like a wind sewing chaos as it crosses the land. A low melody was then heard, its indistinct elements concealing from the listeners whatever dark pattern created them. The white pilgrim bullied his audience with his frenetic music, like riders charging on a battlefield. Everyone in the crowd felt the growing sense of power, lust and ego being communicated by the artist.

The entire audience was lulled into a chaotic trance. The symphony was a succession of wild sounds in which nothing complied with classical principles. This music had a depth like no other. It plunged the listener into the realm of instincts, the universe of primal passion, a world of intoxication and almost madness, where nothing is sacred. This music shattered all rules and traditions, arousing that dark pleasure that can only be found in annihilation. It surpassed everything, expressing the power of elementary impulses through the overwhelming violence of the sound.

The voice of the white pilgrim rose. The singer was telling of events from long ago, heavy with regret. He was using his art to make keen sorrows both poignant and remote. Alternating singing and the flute, he also improvised passages of poetry, denouncing the tyranny of fate. His poetic lyrics and distinctive voice made an amazing impression on the audience, who reacted to his wild performance with frantic yells and wild cries. His apparent recklessness, his air of subdued menace, the way he improvised poetry, everything about his stagecraft beat his audience into submission.

It led to excesses among the crowd, dancers abandoning themselves to wild performances which in turn lead to further bursts of energy from the artist. His raw talent had unleashed a surge of freedom of expression among the crowd, which was now culminating in outbursts of violence, as though Leïwal Baos, the God of Frenzy, had bewitched these Elves with intoxication and dissipation. Emerging from the crowd, the artist looked overwhelmed by his own performance. He failed to recognize he was out of his depth; the chaos he had created was beyond what he could have imagined. He spoke out to the audience he had conquered with his art.

"Hear me, Elves of Mentolewin! My talent as a musician surpasses that of any other artist who has trampled the soil of the Lost Islands!"

Screaming towards heaven, he went as far as to call upon Eïwele Llyi herself.

"O Lady of beauty, I pray for your apparition. I feel more inspired than ever before, and I wish to pay homage to your benevolent presence."

But another Elf was angry to hear that pretentious bard of chaos command the Deity of Arts. He descended through the amphitheatre, breaking the crowd's ranks.

Until then he had remained unobserved, so he fought his way down the amphitheatre steps through the assembled pilgrims and priests. He reached the stage with difficulty, for in the confusion no one moved out his way to create a path. His face was not hidden by any mask, nor did he wear the white garments of Eïwele Llyi's followers. The bare sword on his back left no doubt as to his identity.

His name was Dyoren. All in the assembly knew him from the many music festivals he had participated in. All acknowledged his reputation as the greatest living bard in the Lost Islands. He carried in his hand a small harp, which seemed to be made of a tortoise shell, inside which strings had been stretched. It was a sophisticated music instrument with a delicate and soft design.

Without pausing, Dyoren crossed the esplanade, coming to stand before the masked bard of chaos, the hero of the crowd. He brandished his stringed instrument forward.

"I will put you in your rightful place!" Dyoren defied the bard of chaos in his turn.

The pilgrims hushed for the newcomer, knowing they would soon hear his music. This celebration of Eïwele Llyi was turning into an unexpected battle between two great artists. From the very first notes, true and clear, Dyoren's music proved to be the opposite of what the audience had just heard. His harp sent forth a harmonious succession of beautiful melodies. The listeners immediately understood that his marvellous instrument allowed him to perform harmonic structures from chord grids with a highly sophisticated technique.

With his quasi-divine music, in which righteous sounds blended with luminous lyrics, Dyoren brought gentleness, peace and serenity to all those who listened. His melodies and chanting fascinated the pilgrims. He delighted their minds by letting them glimpse the endless possibilities born of their musical heritage.

What Dyoren proposed was a penetrating and extremely personal interpretation of the spirit of Llewenti music. It drew its inspiration from the full diversity of the different clans' heritages. Dyoren succeeded in inventing a technically complex tempo, which endowed his music with an extreme sophistication. His harp let the listener believe it was capable of an infinite variety of harmonies and balanced chords. His musical style consisted of excellence through simplicity. All his artistic power was focused towards this aesthetic and technical goal.The harmony of his music seemed to respond to the calm and serene faces of the many statues that adorned the amphitheatre of Mentolewin. The gestures of his fingers on the strings of the harp were incomparable, both elegant and simple but also inspired and powerful. The flow of his music reflected an innate greatness.

When Dyoren finished, there were no wild cries, nor any savage dancing. The unanimous audience simply stood and applauded for several minutes. There was not one voice in the amphitheatre that did not salute his harmonious performance.

However, the masked bard of chaos remained seated, motionless. He murmured something to the lady that was by his side. She handed him a blanket which seemed to hold a heavy object over four feet long. The bard of chaos began to remove his white toga, revealing his fine tunic of dark and grey beneath. He kept the mask on his face.

Dyoren had not missed any of these movements. Indifferent to the applause of the crowd, his gaze was fixed upon the bard of chaos. When the Lonely Seeker saw him leaving the amphitheatre prematurely, he was on the move. Ignoring the supplications and congratulations of the Elves who surrounded him, Dyoren moved through the crowd with authority, pushing aside admirers and pilgrims without a second thought.

"Let me pass!" he repeated harshly several times.

Soon, he had left the amphitheatre and entered a long hallway. The bard of chaos was in sight, moving quickly, though not quite fleeing.

Walking at a good pace, the two Elves passed through a collection of old galleries, ruined gatehouses and obscured passageways. The ruins of Mentolewin were vast. A constant distance of a dozen yards was maintained between them. As the two Elves walked away from the shore, they came across fewer and fewer pilgrims. Before long, they were alone.

At last, the bard of chaos entered a ruined temple. Ravens soared from the edifice into the sky. This ancient shrine had been plundered by armed bands of barbarians and had lost its original splendour. It had been left since then in a state of abandon. That round structure was eroded and falling away in places. The once holy edifice, built upon a rocky outcrop of the Cun Kangna, looked out over the Mentolewin gardens.

Dyoren followed the bard of chaos inside. As he crossed the threshold, he noticed a large iron structure covered in pentacles, which lay broken at the foot of the large opening. The round stone walls were broken by windows shaped like orchids. The roof of the ruined temple resembled an open, jagged mouth. Only one arch remained intact. Its stones were carved with lava markings. The north-facing edifice was shaded, protected from the sun. The two Elves faced each other. Ten yards separated them. Dyoren' voice was deep as he started.

"What type of necromancy made that possible? You can take off your mask, bard of the curse. I know who you are. There is only one artist in the whole Islands' history who has ever been capable of such music, and he never passed on his heritage. Isn't that right, Saeröl?"

The bard of chaos did comply, and his face remained hidden under the white mask. He responded in a cold, haughty voice.

"It is a surprise to see you here, Dyoren the Seventh. It is a dangerous thing to walk in the steps of your predecessor. I believe I was the last to see that reckless Dyoren the Sixth alive."

"How dare you?" challenged Dyoren.

But Saeröl interrupted him, "The scrolls of the Seekers seem to lack some rather important knowledge about my sword. Moramsing wields… considerable power. Rowë Dol Nargrond forged it, and my father Elriöl enchanted its blade with the power of the Amethyst, that dark Flow which Gweïwal Agadeon controls. Moramsing is a keeper of souls and a trusted companion. You should know better, Dyoren the Seventh…"

"For all those years, as the history of Elves has unfolded across the Islands, you had utterly disappeared, remembered only as a regicidal criminal sentenced to death for his wrongs. How have you remained hidden? What dark magic does Moramsing hold?" asked Dyoren.

"For a long time, my soul remained with Moramsing as its only companion… But, slowly, life flourished within me once more, and I gradually awoke, surreptitiously sapping power from the Flow of the Amethyst through its numerous wells. When I was ready, my corpse was given back to me, and I walked again upon the land, though my cheek remained degraded by that infamous mark, as if my soul itself had been soiled by the king of Gwarystan."

"You walked again the paths of the Islands, but death was your only purpose. I imagine it was you who has been relentlessly, almost indiscriminately slaying all those who to some degree had taken part in the fall of the guild of Sana."

"This is true, Dyoren. Forgiveness does not come easily to me. The might of Moramsing and my thirst for vengeance drove many of my enemies to their funeral pyres," admitted Saeröl.

"I sincerely pity you. After all, your fate has been worse than mine, though surely as lonely," Dyoren confided. "The completion of my quest has always guided my actions. It has given my life a purpose. My goal will always remain within reach, no matter the difficulties. Success depends upon me alone, upon the hope I keep in my heart, upon my own abilities. My courage is the only thing I question."

Saeröl laughed aloud. "The Seventh Seeker seems as naïve as his predecessors... You are doomed to spend your life chasing an illusion created by your mind. When you dream of glory, it's because you feel undervalued. When you hope for gratitude, it betrays your guilt. Whatever you wish to accomplish, Dyoren, you are the living proof that hope is a lie. It is evil, for it creates need and loss. Worse, it arouses lust. You will soon see the signs of new and serious disillusions," he promised.

But Saeröl was not finished. For once, he had an opportunity to dump his anger on an opponent worthy of him.

"We all seek to pursue our dreams, Dyoren. We all seek to find harmony, forget about guilt and be released from our duties. But these noble goals are unreachable. You are the Seeker, but what should we seek? Power, gold, love, pleasure? I wonder. All these temptations were created by the Gods to divide us, to play us off against one another. And even if we succeed for a time to form ideals, they will never be fully realised, for our deepest aspirations will always interfere with the state of the present world as it evolves. Yearning for peace is a losing battle, for it will always be temporary. It is an inaccessible gift in and of itself. One is much better off focussing on drinking the best of the Nargrond Valley's wines."

Dyoren was unimpressed by this sarcasm.

"You have possessed the sword of Amethyst for too long, Saeröl. It is written in the scrolls of the Dyoreni that the wielder of Moramsing will know neither peace nor harmony, still less happiness, beset as he shall always be by the pernicious influence of his dark blade. That is your curse, is it not? To fight, day after day, against the despair that Moramsing instils in your heart, to renounce the infinite facets of desire that pervade your twisted mind. Am I not right?" asked Dyoren.

Saeröl remained silent so the Lonely Seeker carried on with his reasoning.

"I have chosen a different path, though recently it risked becoming as harsh as the one you were forced to take. I no longer expect the world to adapt to my expectations. Instead, I have changed my view on others: on every other being. I chose loneliness and I chose to love the life I have been offered, despite its upheavals."

Saeröl smiled at this.

"I am glad we have met after all, Dyoren the Seventh. You appear to be worthier of my esteem than that other Seeker I regretfully had to slay…"

Saeröl voluntarily insisted on that last word before unexpectedly changing his tone.

"Are we not the two most fabled artists of these times? Our performances today proved it again, if such a test was necessary. It is a comforting thought indeed that a privileged audience has borne witness to our battle in music. Unfortunately, however, your teachings reach their limit when applied to my own destiny. Perhaps, as you suggest, I have walked with Moramsing for too long. Nevertheless, I will never believe that one who became an orphan at a young age, who was raised without the example of his father, who inherited the responsibility to lead his people in a dreadful war against the Dark Elves, who witnessed the genocide of the very household he was meant to protect with his own eyes, I cannot believe that this character could possibly 'love the life he was offered despite the upheavals,' as you so elegantly put it. I prefer to leave you to your blindness. If the Gods had wished to grant us peace of mind, Elves would not have been given brains."

Dyoren nodded, almost defeated, but in a final effort he tried to avoid the inevitable duel which he could now feel looming.

"Saeröl, I know your life has been an unceasing river of despair. I am giving you a chance, one final opportunity to surrender your sword. Let me return it to the Secret Vale where it belongs. Choose to kneel and give away the pain that Moramsing has imposed upon you for so long. Abandon your folly and try to redeem your soul before it is taken to the Halls of Gweïwal Agadeon. I am begging you."

Saeröl said nothing. In response, he took a few steps back and unfurled the blade of Moramsing from the blanket that hid it. Saeröl seized the dark weapon, four feet long, at the hilt with both hands. He delicately kissed its amethyst-encrusted pommel as though it were the gentle skin of a lover. The enchanted bastard sword would gleam like an agent of pure chaos when Saeröl wielded it, thrusting and cutting through the air. Finally, he rested the long blade nonchalantly on his shoulder, like a weary worker might do with a heavy tool. He raised his left hand towards his opponent and started to sing verses, his voice guttural.

A dozen yards across the esplanade, Dyoren grasped his broad sword with his right hand. The shining blade of his glaive was much shorter, barely thirty inches long, but it looked quicker and sharper. Rymsing was double-edged for cutting and had a tapered point for stabbing and thrusting. A solid grip was provided by its knobbed hilt, which was decorated with a green rune and many precious emeralds.

The Lonely Seeker knew how to use his legendary glaive for cutting or slashing; his deeds had been told of many a time in accounts of the Centenary of War, when barbarian warriors had looked on in horror at the dismembered bodies of their comrades strewn across the battlefield. Dyoren began a sidestepping movement, his left hand raised, as though it possessed the power to oppose Saeröl's sorcery. Neither of the duellists was protected by any armour. The first hit would prove deadly. Dyoren's voice rose, high and clear.

The two Elves circled round each other, their backs against the walls, keeping the same distance between them. Dyoren's azure gaze was fixed on his opponent's dark eyes, which were challenging him, threatening him. Flowing through these two Elves was a battle between two formidable powers: the verdant forces of the Emerald against the purple Amethyst. Behind them, the energy of the Islands' Flow unleashed its power.

Leaves were flying, blown all over in a nameless wind, wild vines were uprooted by an invisible hand, and the stones of the building were shaken, some falling to the ground. The ruined walls of the edifice shook violently in the power struggle; the temple threatened to collapse.

Suddenly, Dyoren rushed forward, his glaive raised high. Saeröl immediately charged, unleashing his bastard sword. Rymsing met Moramsing. The two blades collided but were then deflected from their course. Both pierced through flesh. Saeröl screamed, bringing hand to hip.

Dyoren made a few steps back and fell on the ground, his right leg severely wounded. He was bleeding profusely. He could not stand up, despite his desperate efforts.

Limping badly, Saeröl approached the Lonely Seeker. With a swipe of his sword, he eliminated the threat of Rymsing, which was thrown against the wall out of Dyoren's reach.

"How did you find me, Lonely Seeker?" Saeröl asked with a threatening tone. "There must be a reason for your presence in Mentolewin. Tell me who betrayed me! Tell me now or die!"

Dyoren did not utter a word, his eyes expressionless. Defeated, without any hope left, he seemed to accept his fate, ready to die with honour.

"Give me that name, fool! Or I will feed you to my sword. Do you want your soul to be confined to the metallic hilt of my blade for eternity? You know what I am talking about... Don't you?" Saeröl shouted, losing all control.

The sharp blade of Moramsing slowly sliced Dyoren's tendons above his two ankles. The Lonely Seeker cried out, overwhelmed by pain. Terror was stretched across his face, as though the voice of the Morawenti bard had opened the gates to Gweïwal Agadeon's Halls before him.

"Give me that name! I ask you again," yelled Saeröl, like one possessed by the fury of a demon.

Dyoren closed his eyes, waiting for the deadly blow that would end his life.

"Lord Dol Lewin," he whispered with a last breath.

There was a long silence. At last, Saeröl left the ruined temple with a heavy limp, leaving his opponent helpless, bathing in his blood.

**

2712, Season of Eïwele Llyo, 6th day, Nyn Ernaly, Mentolewin

Aewöl had been climbing a long, rocky plateau ever since dawn, amid wild vegetation and thick bushes. The forest comprised of deciduous trees that shed their leaves during Autumn, and thorny woods with strange tentacle plants, adapted to the dry conditions of Nyn Ernaly hot summers. Aewöl had progressed with difficulty up a steep and treacherous footpath before eventually reaching the edge of a rocky plateau overlooking the strait of Oymal cliffs.

From this high viewpoint, he spotted the ruined fortifications, winding alleyways, the remains of barracks, and an upper fortress with the remnants of a keep perched at the edge of a rocky plateau. In the light of midday, the waters of the forest's streams comingled in a great waterfall, emptying themselves into the sea over a rocky shelf.

"This scenery is breath-taking," Aewöl reckoned.

In front of him stood the ruins of Mentolewin, the ancient home of House Dol Lewin, and the great fortress of the West where the flag of the White Unicorn had flown in the wind for so long.

Aewöl came out of the woods and entered Mentolewin's garden. The ancient yard, of magnificent design, had been based on eight grass triangles. In its centre stood an ornamental fountain representing Gweïwal Uleydon, God of all Waters. The majestic bronze statue had been defiled by human invaders, its arms and head cut off.

However, to restore beauty to this marvellous place, the white pilgrims, after their arrival, had planted flowers to honour Eïwele Llyi; bulbs, violas and daisies were scattered across the gardens' alleys, while a bed of petunias and dahlias complemented the decoration. Further away, towards the fortress, the garden featured an avenue of orange trees, climbing rose trees and more flowers bordering the edge of the moat.

Trying his best to walk with confidence, Aewöl progressed like an Elf who did not know where he was going. He took a narrow, deserted alley that ran for several hundred yards and ended at the back of the former gardens. He had to climb several steps to finally reach a higher viewpoint. The place was surrounded by wild plants of great size, and it offered a magnificent view of the strait. Shady alleyways rustled with pilgrims' cries, along with traces of music and joyful singing.

Young Elvin maidens walked the driveways, their feet covered with the dust of the paths. Artists and poets attempted to seduce them with improvised verses of burning passion and rhymes of delicate conception. This fair scenery impressed Aewöl beyond measure. Leaving behind him the violence and dishonour of the last few days, he tried to feel the full benefits of this completely new atmosphere.

'It is as if I just crossed the ford of a magical river and reached a wonderland where all is elegant beauty and divine music!' he wondered, completely taken aback.

Aewöl stood silent, his hands on the rusty iron railing above the cliff, looking at the ocean in front of him. Waves sent rolls of white foam crashing against the rocks at the bottom of the cliff. Though his weak eye could not see it, he could imagine the shores of the Mainland, twenty leagues away, hidden by the mist of the sea.

Aewöl's air of extreme pensiveness and his great pallor gave him a sinister look. The memory of burying the corpse of Voryn dyl in order to conceal it irremediably, was still in his mind. His sole black eye was, at present, animated by an expression of the deepest sadness. The loss of Gelros was cruel. Nevertheless, Aewöl did not remain idle long, for he needed action to avoid being driven to despair.

'What if Gelros managed to flee into the cave? Maybe I did not find his corpse because there is none to find,' he hoped.

An idea came to him. Aewöl set about making a nest for blackbirds. Cutting a narrow young trunk with his sword, he tried to clear it of its branches to make a long pole. After several unsuccessful attempts to fix an improvised bird's nest at its tip, he gave up realizing that Gelros' expertise in such matters had been precious. Feeling weary and downhearted, Aewöl decided to sit down and eat some food.

"Duluin's supplies are growing thin," he noted.

Aewöl heard footsteps down in the garden's alley. An Elvin lady was coming to greet him. She had an ingenuous look in her eye. The one-eyed Elf held his breath for few moments. He had normally few dealings with females, and always felt uncomfortable in their presence.The newcomer looked charming and beautiful, her hair as dark as a crow's wing, her soft skin delicately tanned: unusual for a High Elf, but nonetheless beautiful. She immediately offered him a pipe stuffed with delicate herbs.

Aewöl declined her offer without even a smile. Her carefully sculpted mess of hair made her look very seductive. Her elegant lace dress and gloves of the finest silk left little doubt that she was a member of the higher circles of Elvin society. Indifferent to her interlocutor's cold attitude, she lit the pipe herself and, after contemplating the first smoke rings being dispelled by the ocean breeze, she spoke in an enigmatic voice.

"Quite the scenery for what is to come!"

Gold and silver adorned her neck, waist and hands. Her robe was pure white, as befitted the formal attire of her cult. She looked like the priestesses of Eïwele Llyi that Aewöl had already seen in Llafal. His discomfort grew. There was, in the lady's manners and languorous poses, a formidable seductive power. He felt terribly attracted. Aewöl had never felt any love in his heart, but he knew the sensation of lust, a primitive force that could take control of the mind. Carnal desire was a force with which his will was often fighting. Apparently unaware of the inner turmoil her arrival had provoked, the lady continued.

"May I help you? I could see from a distance you were having some difficulty with that pole. What is it you were trying to achieve? It looked as though you wanted to set a nest at its tip."

"That is correct," Aewöl replied, somewhat bluntly. "My

servant used to take care of such tasks."

"What an odd place to try to attract birds: on the top of the cliff, out in the open, exposed to the ocean winds. No bird would want to settle here. That being said, I am no expert with falconry," the lady admitted in all candour.

"I do not expect any bird to settle here. I merely want one to deliver a message," explained the one-eyed Elf.

Aewöl started to realize that he had reached a place of civilization. He was emerging from what seemed like a long nightmare. After all, there were Elves on this island that you could speak to, even ones who might want to help you.

"Do you know the art of communing with birds? I have heard the Green Elves of the ancient clans are very skilled at that."

It seemed that nothing would stop the lady's joyful chatter.

"My servant... did," answered Aewöl briefly, still looking at his interlocutor as if she were a wonderful apparition from the isle of the Gods.

"You keep referring to your servant. Why is he not with you?"

Aewöl hesitated. He examined the beautiful priestess of Eïwele Llyi, still on his guard. Defeated and lost, the one-eyed Elf now had very little of his former strength. But, after weighting up the risks and benefits of his situation, he finally decided to be honest.

"My servant and I were ambushed as we entered Mentolewin forest. We were separated in the fray. I managed to flee. Since then, I have received no news from him," he confided, still marked with the seal of unhappiness.

The lady immediately showed compassion.

"It is as painful as it is sad to hear that pilgrims of Eïwele Llyi have been attacked on their way here!"

Aewöl felt encouraged to explain his objective further. "Since the ambush I have heard nothing. That is why I started to make this nest. If my servant has survived, he will try to send a blackbird to Mentolewin. I hoped it might see that nest in the open and be attracted by the lure I will place there."

"I understand. What a sad story!" she deplored. "But why did you travel on your own? Did you not know that these northern parts of Nyn Ernaly are full of danger? Barbarians roam these woods and I have heard tales of druids leading entire tribes of those savage Men. You should know that the white pilgrims travel in large groups, under the protection of priests of Eïwele Llyi and knights of the Jasmine Flower. They always have done."

"It was not Men who attacked us. It was an Elf, a renegade..." said Aewöl, his tone now bitter.

"Was he an outcast without rune, one of the wild Elves? I have heard of their reputation back in Gwarystan. How sad, that one of our kin should threaten us! Let me help you then, for we must do everything we can to establish contact with your servant. He might be seeking your assistance as we speak."

As good as her word, the lady started to put together a comfortable-looking nest. She added small branches and a pile of dry twigs. Soon after, she was halfway up the long pole Aewöl had made to plant her nest. Her robes slipped as she climbed, exposing her breast.

Suddenly, Aewöl saw that the lady had a small copper ring hanging around her neck. It hanged between her breasts at the end of a long necklace with three butterflies-shaped pendants. The lady noticed Aewöl's sudden interest in the jewellery. Once the nest was secured, she climbed down and opened up her robe from the front, along a seam running down the middle that was invisible when closed. She took the small copper ring and showed it to Aewöl.

"This is my favourite piece of jewellery. It brings protection and good fortune. It is a gift, from a powerful mage who lives far away in the forest of Llymar. His name is Curubor of House Dol Etrond, but many simply call him the Blue Mage."

Aewöl looked at her with suspicion. Ignoring his searching gaze, she went on, eagerly describing the ring.

"See the fragments of gems that decorate it. There's sapphire, which is the gemstone of Gweïwal Zenwon, the amethyst of Gweïwal Agadeon, the aquamarine of Gweïwal Uleydon and the ruby of Gweïwal Narkon. They are the four main elements which compose the Flow. Do you know what? I believe my ring is magic."
"What makes you say that? Is it one of a kind?"
"Oh no! There are many other Elves in Gwarystan who were given rings like this by the Blue Mage. They are magic, though I doubt their power will change the course of history. I believe they provide comfort and fill one's heart with hope. Some even believe they have the power to summon Blue Bards, those evanescent illusions that sing tales of distant lands and provide wisdom," explained the lady.

His curiosity now piqued, Aewöl changed his attitude, leaning forward and speaking with emphasis.

"I have heard of this Blue Mage. He lives in Tios Lluin, at the centre of Llymar Forest, where I myself come from. Have you personally met other Elves who've been honoured with the Blue Mage's token of friendship?" he asked insistently, willing the truth to emerge from within.

The lady seemed particularly excited to meet a resident of the fabled forest of Llymar.

"Is this true? You come from Nyn Llyvary! Elves far and wide sing the praises of the ancient clans who dared to defy the king's authority. I do indeed know Elves who received gifts from the Blue Mage. Most of them suffered persecution in Gwarystan. King Norelin and his human allies, the Westerners, are responsible for widespread injustice. So many Elves are persecuted for their faith. Most fear what the future holds."

"Is that what happened to you?" enquired Aewöl, curious as ever, "Were you persecuted in Gwarystan for being a priestess of Eïwele Llyi? Is that why the Blue Mage gave you one of his gifts?"

Aewöl wondered if these were truly the questions on his mind, or if he was looking for the story he wished to hear.

"Oh no!" she laughed. "I am no priestess of Eïwele Llyi! I wish I was… but it takes a lot of devotion to enter the white temple! What made you think I was? You honour me greatly with your kind words."

Aewöl was utterly captivated by her deep eyes and radiant beauty.

"I suppose, well, I thought, I assumed, looking at your ceremonial clothes…" he said, stammering a little.

It was obvious from the way Aewöl looked at her that her delicate features and charming attitude possessed a power of their own. Feeling comforted by the obvious charm she exerted, the lady revealed a little more of her own story.

"Unfortunately, the truth is very different. This is actually my first pilgrimage. I had my doubts about the undertaking. I longed to visit Nyn Ernaly, I think, in the same way one longs for a faraway, unknown land. That is why I came with the white pilgrims to Mentolewin. And reaching its shores has not diminished its charm. With each step I take, a new vision appears, just out of reach, something extraordinary which calls me onwards."

Aewöl was becoming more and more fascinated by this encounter.

"I have heard that the Elves of Gwarystan have abandoned the old cults of the Islands' Deities."

"That is quite true. But the remnants of the old faiths have proven difficult to eradicate, even for those whose alliances and actions have defiled the ancient traditions. Any Elf of the kingdom, whatever their allegiance, must, at least once in their life, watch with their own eyes the manifestation of Eïwele Llyi's power. Many are those who say it is the most beautiful sight in the world. That is what most of the pilgrims are here for," the lady explained.

Aewöl, intrigued, asked, "So if your faith was not the cause of your misfortune, what bold deed earned you the support and the gratitude of Curubor Dol Etrond?"

"I am not sure it is something I should be proud of. You see, I used to be a lady-in-waiting at the royal court. I served the noble Elves of Gwarystan, living amongst them in a permanent atmosphere of luxury. Sometimes, the temptation proved too great, and extra gold was always welcome..."

"Do you mean to say you had some side trade of your own?" guessed the one-eyed Elf.

"I did," she admitted, "and I can tell you it proved rather lucrative. I would smuggle out bottles of ancient Nargrond Valley vintages, the favourite nectar of the lords... But eventually I got caught and, of all my secret customers, only one helped me: The Blue Mage of Tios Lluin..."

"Now I understand why you wear that ring so... beautifully..." and for the first time Aewöl smiled.

"Now you know my story... and now I am alone. I do things by myself and for myself; No longer do I live my life for the comfort of my mistresses! Besides, they never gave me the attention I deserved. Now I walk freely, where and when it pleases me."

The lady gave him an embarrassed glance, as though she had revealed too much of her past life. Aewöl was feeling better; it was as if the dark days he had lived through recently were finally coming to an end. For the first time since his degradation in the hall of sails, he allowed himself to relax. As enthusiastic as ever, the lady suggested.

"If you want to celebrate the apparition of the Deity of Love and Arts, you should be in the right clothing! Didn't you bring traditional white garments with you?"

"No," mumbled Aewöl, before he came up with an excuse. "I mean, we did, but we lost everything in the ambush."

"How sad! I do not blame you for being embarrassed. Perhaps I could lend you my robes? The weather is mild, and my dress beneath will do. They will not cover your travelling clothes entirely, but at least you will blend in with the crowd. By the way, I must admit I took a couple of those bottles of Nargrond wine with me, hoping to trade them during the pilgrimage. But how about celebrating our new friendship instead, perhaps at the performance in the amphitheatre? The crow's nest is now in place, and we need only wait for news from your servant. Have you ever tasted Nargrond Valley's ancient vintages? You need something to restore joy to your heart, after what you have been through."

The offer was tempting. Aewöl hesitated, feeling guilty about Gelros' sad fate. A few moments later, however, he decided to accompany the lady. There was nothing else he could do for his companion anyway, except waiting for this message which may or may not ever come. He decided he would return to the crow's nest at nightfall. It was also important that he seized all opportunities to make new allies. He was now an exile, with no resources or influence.

The two Elves started to walk along the alleys, enjoying the views. They crossed the vast garden where citrus trees and orchards grew along the sandy paths. The scent of orange flowers mingled with the jasmine. They met with many groups of joyful Elves. One was the Gwarystan revellers, a band of twenty violins. They played a merry tune to welcome the two pilgrims.

"You should have been here a few days ago. The celebrations were on an even larger scale. Many pilgrims have now gone. We heard rumours of war in the east of Nyn Ernaly, and just yesterday there was a duel between two bards. A lot of pilgrims believe that, after such bloodshed, the Deity will not reveal her presence," said the lady.

Aewöl was intrigued. "A duel? What happened exactly? Why would Elves fight in the middle of this celebration dedicated to Eïwele Llyi?" he inquired.

"It surprised everybody. It started in the amphitheatre with a challenge between two marvellous musicians, who both amazed the crowd. It ended in the ruined temple of Eïwele Llyo where Dyoren, the fabled bard, was found dying. Fortunately, the priests of Eïwele Llyi tended to his wounds. His life is no longer in danger. The other duellist fled."

Aewöl was puzzled at this news. Absorbed in his thoughts, he did not notice that, just a few hundred yards away, a raven had landed in his improvised nest. The two Elves were making significant progress as they talked, and they were now coming up to the ancient fortress' compound.

The lady led them to the main gate of Mentolewin dungeon, the gate of supreme vigilance. Many Elves were wandering in the area, waiting for the afternoon's musical performances in the amphitheatre to start. At the gate, the remains of a large sundial could be seen in front of the entrance. This particular piece featured a round, white marble dial with graduations carved on both sides, an iron gnomon, which was still upright, and a square base supported by four stone pillars. Seeing that Aewöl was paying a special attention to the large device, the lady shared what she knew.

"The architects placed this sundial here on purpose, so that it faced the kingdom of Gwarystan. It symbolized how, long ago, the Lord of Mentolewin granted time to all Elves in the Islands, as he was their first defender against the threat of Men."

With a smile, she added, "I did not work that out by myself. A priest of Eïwele Llyi explained it to me. Wait here, I will be back in a moment, with a bottle of the precious nectar."

The lady disappeared into the ruins of the great fortress dungeon. The remains of its ceilings reached surprising heights. The vast entrance room was split down the middle by broken stairways of white marble, which granted access to the lower levels.

Aewöl stood alone in the open, looking at his surroundings and breathing in the ocean air. Without thinking, he reached into his pocket for his own copper ring. He brought it up to examine it further. The one-eyed Elf could identify the same fragments of gems that decorated it: the sapphire of Gweïwal Zenwon, the amethyst of Gweïwal Agadeon, the aquamarine of Gweïwal Uleydon and the ruby of Gweïwal Narkon.

'The four main elements which compose the Flow... the ring is magic,' as the lady had put it.

Aewöl suddenly realized he did not know her name. It was odd that they had not even introduced themselves. Everything had happened so quickly. He looked at his copper ring even more closely, looking for any trace of magic. After a while, the unnatural glittering of the Amethyst fragments caught his eye. He moved sidewise and observed that, every time he shifted towards the dungeon's entrance, the sparkle of that particular gemstone was more intense, as though it were attracted to the lady's presence or, perhaps more accurately, to the lady's ring proximity.

Stunned by what he just discovered, Aewöl stood immobile in front of the dungeon, as motionless as the statues of the Unicorn Guards which still guarded the entrance. Slowly, he unrolled the thread of his reasoning.

'These copper rings given out by the Blue Mage are indeed magical. They possess the rare power to attract each other, like magnets. It was no coincidence that this charming lady stumbled upon me. She came to assist me on purpose. How could I have been so naïve? Nothing can be taken for granted in this world. I should have known better.'

Aewöl was sure that the mysterious lady had uttered no lies. Very few Elves had ever managed to hide their deceptions from his insight. But that did not mean she had told the full truth.

'I won't let her get away with this. I certainly won't be drinking her fine wine, which is probably drugged, if not poisoned,' he decided.

Aewöl looked around him. There were many pilgrims walking inside the courtyard, most of them drunk and fully immersed in the celebrations. But guards of Eïwele Llyi's temple, dressed magnificently in white cloaks and silver mail, were also stationed nearby, commanded by knights bearing the symbol of Eïwele Llyi, a jasmine flower.

'This is no place to force her to talk. I need to get inside the dungeon. There, I will interrogate using my own means,' he decided coldly.

Aewöl felt angry as he crossed the gate of supreme vigilance. The dungeon was dug into limestone. A long gallery running from east to west gave access to a number of smaller corridors leading to cellars and storage rooms.

"I should not have hidden my weapons near the crow's nest. Now, I have only my dagger to defend myself," Aewöl regretted.

He had decided to remain inconspicuous, dressing like a pilgrim of Eïwele Llyi and avoiding drawing unnecessary attention in his war attire.

A few muttered incantations were all that was needed to summon the glow of dark fire upon his blade. Its weak light was enough to guide him. In his left hand, he held the copper ring of the Blue Mage. By the variable intensity of its glow, he could choose the route that would lead him through the underground maze to his prey.

Before long, he arrived at a doorway to a cellar. It was a cramped, humid room of roughly two hundred square feet, with stale air and no ventilation. Sneaking silently into the dark, empty room, he noticed that an object lay at the far end.

It was a heavy book bound in leather. A few pages of parchment had fallen out on the sandy soil of the cellar. The tome contained several hundred pages. Looking more closely, he noticed that a copper ring had been placed on top of the book. He could not be completely sure, but this new ring resembled the one the lady had shown him.

"This looks like one of Curubor's gifts. And my own ring has stopped glittering now that he has found its twin. What could this possibly mean?" he wondered.

Aewöl looked around anxiously and inspected the area. He strained his ears to the silence of the dungeon for several moments, confident that his keen hearing would pick up any suspicious presence. No noise could be heard. Somewhat reassured, he returned to the book, and risked conjuring more light to read by. He could not help shiver when he discovered the title on the cover.

Written in ancient Morawenti script were the words: 'The Manuscript of Sana'. His surprise was so great that he had to sit down. A strange dizziness overcame him, and he felt confused and disorientated. His vision became blurred. After a while, he tried to order his thoughts.

'Someone wanted me to come into this cellar. It is a trap. But why then have I not been attacked already? Unarmed, underground, far from help and desperately alone, I would make easy prey. Yet I am still alive...'

Aewöl could not make sense of all the issues his predicament raised. Giving up on thinking any further, he looked at the few slips of parchment that seemed to have fallen from the ancient manuscript. He started to examine the material. The writing looked recent. The finely crafted words in lingua Morawenti seemed to have been written with a trembling hand.

When Aewöl pressed his finger to the ink, he became sure that these pages had been written barely a few days ago, if not that very same day. He seized one of the pages at random, bringing his glowing dagger up to the parchment. The last line immediately drew his attention.

'And for the crime of treason, there can only be one sentence. The Guild of Sana hereby sentences Camatael Dol Lewin to death. It falls to the Master of the Guild to decide how this sentence shall be carried out.'

Aewöl could not believe his eyes. Confused, almost panicked, he seized several other pages which appeared to come before this first. He started reading the language with difficulty. It was apparent that the lingua Morawenti he was trying to decipher differed significantly from the form it took in Essawylor, which he had learnt in his younger years.

'From the very beginning, I was extremely ambitious. True to my bloodline, I soon demonstrated a desire to act. My father was my constant inspiration. Elriöl represented strength of character, boldness and success. I wanted to be like him. Elriöl had developed a mythical vision of our household's history. He possessed great knowledge and the gift for creation.

The young bard I was truly admired his father, despite his scorn towards me. Elriöl had emerged from the humiliation caused by the fall of House Dir Sana, rising to an even higher rank due to his craft. My father had paved the way for me. But, due to my lack of proficiency in alchemy, he only ever showed me disappointment and disrespect. Elriöl also despised me for my passion for letters. Nevertheless, I dreamt of achieving what my father had failed to do, despite his great reputation. I wanted to prove myself. In pursuit of our common goal, I, unlike him, chose to rely on my ability to conceal, deceive and manipulate.'

'This text has been written by Elriöl's heir! What did Gelros tell me? This Elriöl was the first son of Princess Sana, and the elder brother of my forefather Egalmöl…' Aewöl muttered to himself. He plunged back into the script.

'Dreams of glory fed my ambition. For that reason, early on I began fighting against the supremacy of the High Elves, and more particularly against the haughtiness of their lords. I always believed that I alone could improve our condition. But ambition was not all. I was also an extremely gifted and skilled individual. The contempt my entourage showed never altered my determination.

I was the son of the most illustrious Night Elf. This meant influence and wealth. Nevertheless, I revolted against the mediocrity of my position and I wanted to fight for my place at the head of the kingdom. I secretly planned an unprecedented rise; I wanted to integrate into the nobility and re-establish House Dir Sana with all its prerogatives.

Despite the honours, I never developed a true sense of belonging. I was torn between the pride of playing a role at the top of the kingdom, and the desire to be my own master, to write the story of Saeröl Dir Sana.'

Aewöl stopped reading.

"Saeröl! The author of these lines is the murderer of King Lormelin!" he exclaimed.

Now, avid of knowledge, Aewöl immersed himself in Saeröl's account.

"Unsatisfied as I was with my fate, I then entered into a relationship with Lady Nuviele Dol Ogalen. The heir of House Dol Etrond, the young Almit had also developed a passion for her.I knew how to seduce and succeed in getting myself noticed by the noble ladies. In trying to charm one of the most praised maidens of the nobility, I knew I was playing a very dangerous game, for it was inconceivable that anyone, still less a Night Elf, would try to court the favours of a lady to whom everyone owed only their deepest respects.

The nobles in Gwarystan believe that any common Elf who looks at one of their ladies lustfully has already committed a crime in his heart. In their eyes, it means he desires a home which is not his to claim. I must admit I agree with them. Pining for the consort of another, even only desiring her, means thinking that the institution of nobility could fall. If a Night Elf can seduce a noble lady, it means their higher position counts for nothing. This is exactly what I had in mind.

For me, the conquest of Nuviele's heart was revenge, a campaign against the High Elves and their great noble houses. I must admit, I took delight in seeing this lovely lady breaking every custom and rule of her caste to become the mere mistress of a steward without land.'

Again, Aewöl listened with attention to the silence surrounding him. All was still quiet. He was alone.

'Why has Saeröl written such things down? Is it a testament, a confession? I have heard about Nuviele Dol Ogalen. She eventually became the lady of House Dol Etrond after she married Almit. She was Loriele's mother but, I think... she died... or rather went missing...'

Aewöl was extremely interested by genealogy and since his arrival in the Lost Islands; he had learnt the family trees of all houses of the High Elves. He resumed his reading.

> *'At that time, the kingdom of Gwarystan was under the undisputed control of Lormelin the Conqueror, but the balance of power was changing fast.*
>
> *We were on the eve of clan Myortilys' revolt and the fall of Nargrond Valley which followed. The assassination of my father in the mines of Oryusk, followed shortly after by the fall of Nargrond Valley and the destruction of Yslla, pushed me to adopt the attitude of an extremist. My hatred was concentrated above all upon the clan Myortilys, who had committed genocide against the Night Elves of Nargrond Valley. I called upon the survivors of my household and urged them to swear the Oath of Shadows. I remember confiding to them in that ceremony: 'I have no honour.'*
>
> *Thus, in order to satisfy my thirst for revenge, I suddenly refused to collaborate with the houses of the High Elves, who had remained impassive after the conquest of Nargrond Valley by clan Myortilys. The court of Gwarystan had barely mourned the death of Rowë Dol Nargrond, still less that of my father. The king himself had shown no compassion following the extermination of the Night Elves, and I could not help but think that the ruin of the Nargrond Valley's guilds was not such a bad development for our sovereign.*
>
> *Putting my personal dreams of glory aside, like an Elf who voluntarily asks for his own imprisonment, I committed myself to the rise of the guild of Sana...'*

Aewöl was suddenly interrupted in his reading. A deep voice came calling through the shadows.

"You are not the first Elf to follow Drismile underground; nor the first brave enough, or should I say foolish enough, to descend towards the Halls of Gweïwal Agadeon!"

The silhouette of a tall Elf appeared at the cellar's doorway, blocking all escape routes. The newcomer was clad into a long black cloak. His face was masked by a hood. He was using a long blade, the colour of dark iron, as a walking stick. He seemed to be limping badly. The glowing amethysts on his sword's pommel diffused a weak light that illuminated his steps. A silver pendant necklace was tied to his left wrist. A jewel of unusual size, the form of a complex rune, hanged from it. The tall Elf was holding a glass of wine in his left hand.

A single glance was all it took to send Aewöl's dagger flying away to the opposite corner of the cellar, out of his reach.

Aewöl quickly reacted to the threat. He called upon his inner power, trying to reach for the Flow of the Ruby, that strong fiery energy which was the basis of his alchemy. To his surprise, the area was totally deprived of any source of magic. He soon realized that he was powerless. The one-eyed Elf fixed his gaze upon the bare blade of the dark bastard sword. He soon understood that its metal somehow distorted the circulation of the Flow, preventing anyone around from casting spells, making its wielder impervious to their effects. After watching Aewöl's pitiful attempt to defend himself, the tall Elf rejoiced.

"Good! This is extremely good! I see that, despite all your anguish, you have not yet quenched your thirst for survival. You must have already known that only one of us will leave this cellar alive. You already thought it through."

The newcomer raised the glass to his lips and drank a long gulp, before taking a deep breath.

"418 was a very good year for O Wiony, without doubt the finest of that vintage. It is extraordinarily rich, powerful and concentrated, with traces of exotic plants, truffles, spices and black fruits."

Aewöl stood defenceless against the back wall of the cellar, petrified by fear. Without warning, the dark sword flew through the air, its range extraordinary. It slashed Aewöl's right arm, wounding him badly. Before his other hand had even reacted to control the bleeding, the dark blade was back in the tall Elf's glove. Pain was stretched across Aewöl's face. Indifferent to his prisoner's suffering, the tall Elf licked the edge of his blade, tasting Aewöl's blood as though it were precious nectar from Nargrond Valley. Finally, he gave his verdict.

"I was not deceived. The blood of Sana flows in your veins."

Aewöl's attitude had completely changed. He realized that he would never get out of this cellar. Pride, hatred, and murder were now in his eye. If he was destined to fall, he would make his ending spectacular.

"Give me a weapon, master assassin!" the one-eyed Elf ordered.

The tall Elf looked at him with surprise, as though he had finally seen Aewöl's true nature.

"You act with bravery for one in such a hopeless position. I see in you something exceptional that offends the mediocre, younger offspring of Sana. I can see that your life has been full of pain. Your companions must have looked upon you with hate. They made you pay for your presumption. I see it in your eye, you have already found it by yourself. There can be only one remedy: have trust only in yourself. I am sure your conduct is ruthless. For us, Night Elves, our merciless nature is the only resource available."

Aewöl spat in his direction in an attempt to provoke his anger. Now only a mistake of his jailer could save him. Indifferent, the tall Elf continued with his reasoning like a scholar to a student.

"We were born alone, we live alone, and we will die alone. Only through our family can we create the temporary illusion that we will escape the anguish of solitude."

There was a long silence. Finally, the tall Elf resumed.

"I have only one regret. Maybe I should have mentioned it in the few pages I wrote hastily today. It deserved a better place in my memoirs..."

There was a silence. Aewöl now understood who he was facing Saeröl, son of Elriöl, the author of the last few pages of the manuscript of Sana that he had just read. After drinking another sip of his exquisite wine, Saeröl spoke like one needing to share his inner turmoil.

"For us Night Elves, carnal relationships do not always have to be about satisfying lust. When it comes to marriage, our nature tends towards maidens of noble blood. The history of House Dir Sana illustrates it well. High Elvin ladies are perfect, without fragility; their beauty is eternal. It will not fade. Their perfection and immortality make them utterly unique. They are irreplaceable, and therefore guarantee the perpetuation of the lineage of House Dir Sana. Conquering creatures who represent the summit of grace to perpetuate our race... this is not only our pleasure, but above all else, it is our duty..."

Saeröl took another sip of wine before continuing.

"Our existence should stay governed by a balance between destiny and freedom, between unavoidable fate and conscious choice. But this balance has always seemed tipped in the favour of destiny. Such was the case with beautiful Nuviele... The Night Elves, with their blind devotion, gave the Dir Sana the right to decide the life and death of their consorts, and also of their children. It guaranteed loyalty within the community. Unfortunately for Nuviele I made use of that prerogative..."

The master of the guild of Sana continued as if he were talking to himself.

"My heart was pure. My life goal was to be worthy of her love. But, in the end, she turned me down and married another. She would not give me an heir. I made her die miserably, like a wild animal, throwing her like a doe to the wolves.... I now realize... That was a crime."

Silence endured. Aewöl stood still, unable to decide what course of action to take, faced with this Elf who he now thought mad. Saeröl seemed to be lost in a world of mourning and regret.

"I finally understand the paradox that has obsessed me for my entire life. When the High Elves of yore accepted the gift of immortality from the Gods, they dug their own grave. Remember those songs from our infancy, with their constant references to Gweïwal Agadeon and how he forged the great Halls of the Dead, where the souls of those High Elves who died in violence would forever remain. In the early days of the world, only very few of us were supposed to end up in those Halls, but things have turned out quite differently, and now the majority of us have been deprived of the night sky's beauty."

Despair was etched on Saeröl's face.

"In truth, the Gods had other precious gifts for the High Elves. Pride, jealousy, greed, ambition... all bestowed to ensure that Gweïwal Agadeon's great cathedral of the Underdark would not remain empty. It was a fool's bargain from the beginning. True immortality belongs to Gods, not to Elves. The glory of immortal life was merely bait, set to trap us into a hopeless destiny. Accepting death is the only solution," the Night Elf lord concluded.

Saeröl raised his sword Moramsing threateningly. His voice was strained with the madness that seized him.

"In that web of lies the High Elves call history, House Dir Sana's origins and its secret guild remain veiled in legend, like the Amethyst Magic we wield, the secret rules we obey and the ancient traditions we live by."

With the sharp tip of his sword, he sketched a complex rune onto the wet soil.

"This marking," he explained, "is full of ambiguity. It represents the House Dir Sana, of course, but these diacritical marks also indicate the idea of 'eternity'. While its main scriptural element can be translated as 'revenge', the symbol of the dark moon here suggests secrecy and darkness."

The dark blade of Moramsing drew a regular triangle around the rune.

"Later, when our bloodline was almost spent, and our noble status was denied, we became a secret guild, and completed our mark with these three equal lines, creating a new rune. The triangle evokes the three powers, a concept as old as the world, one that can be found in all Elvin cultures. For members of the guild of Sana, the three lines of the triangle represent the three fundamental values that guarantee unity among our ranks: eternity, secrecy and revenge."

"Why are you telling me such things?" Aewöl asked, with a deep sense of unease. "I have nothing to do with all this. I am Aewöl of Mentollà, nothing more, nothing less!"

Saeröl smiled, as if out of pity.

"That is not so, and you know it. The Dir Sana have language to hide what we feel and to disguise what we mean. The truth is too precious; it must be protected with a retinue of lies until... revenge can be exacted. This is how we think. This is who we are. We have no freedom to decide our fate. I even believe that, in the depths of our souls, there is a need to have every thought dictated by the law of House Dir Sana."

Saeröl smiled, but his smile was grim. He continued.

"Today is a new page in the infamous manuscript of Sana. And we are writing it together, for our two fates have become entwined. The manuscript is usually more concerned with sordid considerations about honour and revenge, but its ruthless principles also apply to other fields, including family affairs…"

Feeling threatened again, Aewöl made another attempt to escape his fate.

"I do not want to have anything to do with the Night Elves. Long ago, I renounced my mother's legacy. I am simply a member of the community of Mentollà."

After a final gulp, Saeröl sent his crystal glass shattering against the cellar wall. He started to move forward, gently stroking the rune of Amethyst, the jewel hanging from the silver necklace around his wrist.

"Why do you think your forefather, Egalmöl, fled to Essawylor away from his elder brother Elriöl, instead of crossing the Austral Ocean with him?" Saeröl asked. "There is an answer to that riddle: there can be only one master of the guild of Sana."

With a quick gesture of his hand, Saeröl pressed the Rune of Amethyst onto Aewöl's shoulder. The effect was immediate: the one-eyed Elf stood frozen and convulsing, paralyzed by a higher power.

"Now hear the Oath of Sana," Saeröl cried.
"I will not swear. I want nothing to do with your sect!"
"Do you think my father Elriöl left me a choice?" said Saeröl before striking him violently across the right cheek. He began reciting the Oath with his deep voice:

> *"So O gomy o tortry*
> *So O wenti, O morawenti*
> *E rayu E souy*
> *Narabety Nel Anmöl*
> *O deyroh da Sana"*

Saeröl released his grip. Aewöl's tunic was torn apart below his left shoulder, just above his heart. The mark of the rune of Sana was burning into his flesh. The one-eyed Elf fell to his knees, utterly helpless.

"Remember our words!" Saeröl shouted.

"DOR will not be, DOL will not deign, DIR SANA I am."

With this, Saeröl slapped Aewöl's left cheek with considerable force, causing him to fall to the ground. In the darkness of the cellar, the one-eyed Elf just about glimpsed the master of the guild of Sana step back, pick up his sword by the blade, and press its pommel against the wall.

Saeröl leapt forwards. The dark blade pierced his abdomen.

He collapsed onto the ground, dead.

For a moment, Aewöl's body betrayed him. It was refusing to get up from the ground. He could not work out if what he was seeing was a vision or a hallucination. A shadowy form, the colour of crimson, seemed to be leaving Saeröl's corpse by his mouth. It rose in the air before disappearing into the pommel incrusted with amethysts of his bastard sword. Terrified by what he had seen, Aewöl rushed out of the cellar.

EPILOGUE

2713, Season of Eïwele Llyi, 1rst day, Nyn Llyvary, Llafal

Marwen, one the young priestesses of Eïwal Lon's cult, opened the temple doors. Overwhelmed by emotion, her sapphire eyes blazing, the maiden, her hair in long, dark curls, could not hide her excitement. It was she who had been chosen for this symbolic mission.When Marwen was done with her task, Camatael and Loriele exited the nave of Llafal's White Temple and appeared before a vast crowd under the sunlit sky. Light shone about them as they walked hand in hand. The couple stood high upon the steps of Eïwele Llyi's shrine, overlooking Temples Square and the Halwyfal below. They could see many of their followers parading among the dense crowd gathered before them on the esplanade.

A guard of honour was part of the cortege. Camatael took Loriele's hand and kissed it before the eyes of the many. Though it had not been planned and went against protocol, the young Marwen could not resist shouting out to the crowd that had gathered on Temples Square.

"Here stand Lord Camatael Dol Lewin and his bride, Lady Loriele Dol Etrond! And they exchanged their silver rings before the altar of Eïwele Llyi!"

There was on the esplanade in front of them a great concourse of Elves, thousands in number. Rumour had spread across the forest that the Blue Mage, Curubor, was preparing the greatest feast ever seen in Llafal, to celebrate his grand-niece's betrothal. From all parts of Llymar, from Tios Halabron to Penlla and the far coast of the bay, all Elves who could make the journey to Llafal had come. The city was filled with the joy of the revellers. The colours of their festive garments comingled with the decoration of the houses, laden with flowers.

Descending the temple steps, Loriele came forward to the crowd. Her smile was dazzling, as bright as the light of day. Her noble and seductive face expressed amusement. When the Elves of Llafal saw her coming to meet them, they cried out in amazement and began congregating around her, full of admiration. With her noble gait and her long, almost iridescent hair flying in the wind, she seemed to float above the ground. The elegance of her tight-waisted azure dress was enhanced by a fine golden girdle. She wore a few jewels without ostentation: a bracelet on each of her wrists and a necklace of marine pearls, a gift from Fendrya dyn Feli.

Music started. Harpists had come all the way from Tios Lluin for the occasion. They were soon joined by flautists and horn-players from the clan Ernaly, fabled for their skills. The clear-voiced singers of Llafal answered them, singing the couple's praises. A group of dancers from Mentollà pushed its way through the crowd, getting the audience to sing along with their exotic chants. The Blue Elves wore wigs of green and blue feathers, which they had attached to their hair with gum. They had stuck large wild goose feathers to their foreheads. On their arms, they wore nacre bracelets decorated with marine pearls of various colours.

When at last Camatael walked down the temple steps to join his bride among the throng, all the bells of Llafal rang out, announcing the start of the feast. The banners of Dol Lewin and Dol Etrond flowed in the wind. The White Unicorn and the Golden Arch were rising above Temples Square for the first time. At that very moment, the trumpets of Llymar guards were blown.

Benefiting from the confusion, the young Mayile, another maiden from Llafal, came to the steps of Eïwele Llya's temple. As she ran, her blonde hair, tumbling wildly about her head, marked each of her movements with a natural beauty. Amid joyful singing and music of the harps and flutes, Mayile passed to the other side of the esplanade. She had finished her duties at the white temple, where the couple had performed the rituals of betrothal. Mayile was eager to admire the city in all its flower-laden glory from its very best viewpoint. Llafal was filled with many trees and luxurious plants. The numerous fountains and statues were wrought of marble. Its streets were filled with the laughter of Elves. The sun-tanned Blue Elves, the blond Green Elves and the tall High Elves of Llymar forest celebrated together this new age they were building together. Overwhelmed by excitement, Mayile called to witness an elegant lady beside her, who was dressed in light blue robes.

"Today is a good day for all the Seeds of Llyoriane. The communities of Llymar, each in their own way, are joining together to celebrate the love of these two Elves. That is the very pinnacle of the Islands Deities' teachings. Tolerance of all and harm to none. This day is full of promise."

Her long dark hair flowing in the wind, the elegant lady could not resist smiling before such candid enthusiasm. Her name was Arwela. She was the elder sister of Feïwal dyn Filweni, the warlord of Mentollà, and considered by many to be the wisest of her community.

"What is your name?" Arwela asked. Her voice was melodious and gentle.

"My name is Mayile; I am an apprentice at the temple of Eïwele Llyi. I answer to Matriarch Nyriele," responded the maiden with pride.

"Listen, Mayile, only time will tell if what you hope will prove true. If this crowd were condemning the betrothed, we would want to understand why. If, as it seems, the crowd is applauding them, we must seek their reasons for doing so too."

SOLI

JOIN
The Songs of the Lost Islands
COMMUNITY
AND SHARE YOUR THOUGHTS

Thank you for reading *The Lonely Seeker*. If you enjoyed this book, you might want to **post a review on Amazon or Goodreads**. Your feedback is very valuable as the *Songs of the Lost Islands* series continues developing.

Songs of the Lost Islands website

To enhance your reading experience, visit the 'Legends and Lore' section of the website.

www.songsofthelostislands.com/

ANNEXES

The Llewenti

One of the seven nations of 'free' Elves, they are called 'Llewenti' in their language, 'Llew' meaning 'Green' and 'Wenti' meaning 'Elves'. They were so named, because their first Patriarch's attire was green. They are counted among the nations of Elves who refused the gift of immortality offered by the Gods. Llewenti enjoy much longer life than Men, living for five to six centuries depending on their bloodline. Their race is similar in appearance to humans, but they are fairer and wiser, with greater spiritual powers, keener senses, and a deeper empathy with nature. They are for the most part a simple, peaceful, and reclusive people, famous for their singing skills. With sharper senses, they are highly skilled at crafts especially when using natural resources. The Green Elves are wise in the ways of the forest and the natural world.

The Irawenti

One of the seven nations of the 'free' Elves, they are called 'Irawenti' in the language of the Llewenti, 'Ira' meaning 'Blue' and 'Wenti' meaning 'Elves'. They were so named, because their first Guide's eyes had the colour of the tropical seas and azure reflections emanated from his black hair. They are counted among the nations of Elves who refused the gift of immortality offered by the Gods. Irawenti enjoy much longer life than Men, living for four to five centuries depending on their bloodline. Their race is similar in appearance to the Green Elves but darker and wilder, with greater physical powers and a closer empathy with water. They are for the most part a free, joyful and adventurous people, famous for their navigation skills.

Having sharper connection with rivers and oceans, they are at their strongest and most knowledgeable when aboard their ships. The Blue Elves are wise in the ways of the sea.

The Hawenti

The High Elves are called 'Hawenti' in the language of the Llewenti, as opposed to the 'Wenti' who identify as 'free' Elves. The Hawenti accepted the gift of immortality offered by the Gods. They are immortal in the sense that they are not vulnerable to disease or the effects of old age although they can be killed in battle. They are divided into two main nations: The Gold Elves (the most prominent) and the Silver Elves. The Hawenti have a greater depth of knowledge than other Elvin nations, due to their natural inclination for learning as well as their extreme age. Their power and wisdom know no comparison and within their eyes the fire of eternity can be seen. This kindred of the Elves were ever distinguished both by their knowledge of things and by their desire to know more.

The Morawenti

The Night Elves are called 'Morawenti' in the language of the Llewenti. The Morawenti are a subdivision of the Silver Elves, the second of the Hawenti nations. They are therefore counted among the High Elves as they accepted the gift of immortality offered by the Gods. Morawenti are immortal in the sense that they are not vulnerable to disease or the effects of old age although they too can be killed in battle. Morawenti tend to be thinner and taller in size than other Elves. Their very pale skin, almost livid, characterises them while their gaze is deep and mysterious. They all have dark hair while their eye colour varies between grey and black. They favour wearing dark coloured tunics with grey or green shades and robes of fine linens, cotton or silk.

MAIN ELF FACTIONS AND CHARACTERS

KINGDOM OF ESSAWYLOR

The Royal House Dor Tircanil

The High Elf ruling house of the kingdom of Essawylor
~ **Aranaele Dor Tircanil**: Queen of Essawylor

The Clan of Filweni

One of the twenty-nine clans of Blue Elves in the kingdom of
Essawylor
~ **Feïwal dyn Filweni**: Guide of the clan of Filweni, Captain of the
Alwïryan
~ **Arwela dyn Filweni**: Seer of the clan of Filweni
~ **Nelwiri dyn Filweni**: Pilot of the Alwïryan
~ **Luwir dyn Filweni**: Oars master onboard the Alwïryan

House Dol Lewin – Elder branch

One of the five noble houses in the kingdom of Essawylor, High Elves
banished by the Queen

~ **Roquen Dol Lewin**: Lord of House Dol Lewin elder branch
~ **Curwë**: Bard of House Dol Lewin
~ **Aewöl**: Counsellor of House Dol Lewin
~ **Gelros**: Hunt Master of House Dol Lewin
~ **Maetor**: Commander of the Unicorn guards

THE LOST ISLANDS

The Royal House Dor Ilorm

The High Elf ruling house of the kingdom of Gwarystan, principal realm in the Lost Islands

~ **Norelin Dor Ilorm**: King of Gwarystan

House Dol Lewin – Second branch

One of the twelve noble houses in the kingdom of Gwarystan, High Elves originating from Mentolewin

~ **Camatael Dol Lewin**: Lord of House Dol Lewin, Royal Envoy
~ **Aplor**: Steward of House Dol Lewin

The guild of Sana

Secret guild in the Lost Islands

~ **Saeröl Dir Sana**: Master of the guild of Sana
~ **Drismile:** Illusionist, member of the guild of Sana
~ **Nuriol**: Servant of the guild of Sana, spy in Tios Lleny

The clan Llyvary

Clan of Green Elves, principal and historical members of the council of
Llymar Forest

~ **Lyrine dyl Llyvary**: Elder Matriarch of the clan Llyvary
~ **Nyriele dyl Llyvary**: Matriarch, High Priestess of Eïwele Llyi
~ **Myryae dyl Llyvary**: Matriarch of the clan Llyvary
~ **Tyar dyl Llyvary, 'the Old Bird'**: Warlord of Llafal
~ **Leyen dyl Llyvary**: Warlord of Penlla and Commander of Llymar
fleet
~ **Nerin dyl Llyvary**: Captain of Llafal

The clan Ernaly

Clan of Green Elves originating from Nyn Ernaly, members of the council of Llymar Forest

~ **Mynar dyl Ernaly, 'the Fair'**: Warlord of Tios Halabron
~ **Voryn dyl Ernaly, 'the Ugly'**: Captain of Tios Halabron
~ **Yere dyl Ernaly**: Matriarch in Tios Halabron

~ **Lore, 'the Daughter of the Islands'**: Envoy of Eïwele Llya
~ **Dyoren, 'the Lonely Seeker'**: Knight of the Secret Vale, wielder of Rymsing

The clan Avrony

Clan of Green Elves originating from Nyn Avrony, members of the council of Llymar Forest

~ **Gal dyl Avrony**: Warlord of clan Avrony, Protector of the Forest

House Dol Etrond

High Elves originating from Ystanetrond, members of the council of Llymar Forest

~ **Curubor Dol Etrond**, 'the Blue Mage': Guardian of Tios Lluin
~ **Almit Dol Etrond**: Lord of House Dol Etrond
~ **Loriele Dol Etrond**: Lady at the court in Gwarystan
~ **Duluin**: Commander of the Golden Arch knights

PRINCIPALTY OF CUMBERAE

House Dol Nos-Loscin

High Elves originating from Cumberae

~ **Terela Dol Nos-Loscin**: Princess of Cumberae
~ **Alton Dol Nos-Loscin**: Ambassador of Cumberae

GENEALOGY HAWENTI
ROYAL BLOODLINES

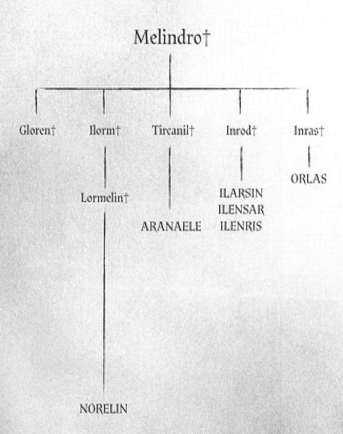

Melindro†

Gloren†   Ilorm†   Tircanil†   Inrod†   Inras†

ORLAS

Lormelin†

ILARSIN
ILENSAR
ARANAELE   ILENRIS

NORELIN

† Dead

GENEALOGY HAWENTI
DOL NOBLE HOUSES

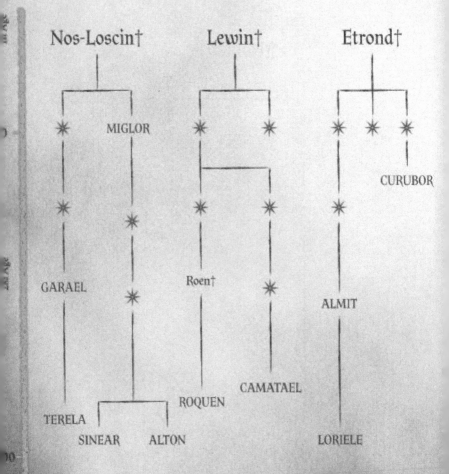

Nos-Loscin†

MIGLOR

GARAEL

TERELA

SINEAR   ALTON

ROQUEN

Lewin†

Roen†

CAMATAEL

Etrond†

CURUBOR

ALMIT

LORIELE

† Dead

✳ Father

GENEALOGY
LLEWENTI CLANS

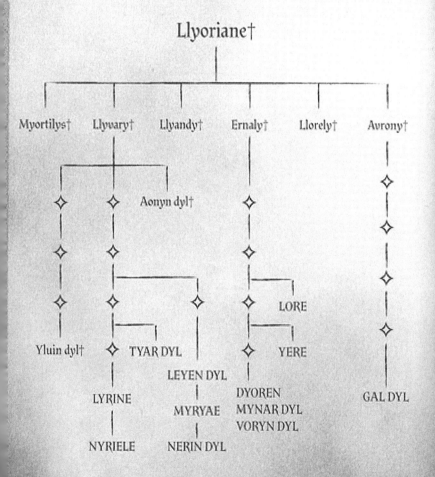

Llyoriane†

Myortilys† · Llyvary† · Llyandy† · Ernaly† · Llorely† · Avrony†

Aonyn dyl†

Yluin dyl† · TYAR DYL · LEYEN DYL · LORE · YERE

LYRINE · MYRYAE · DYOREN · MYNAR DYL · VORYN DYL · GAL DYL

NYRIELE · NERIN DYL

GENEALOGY IRAWENTI
FILWENI CLAN

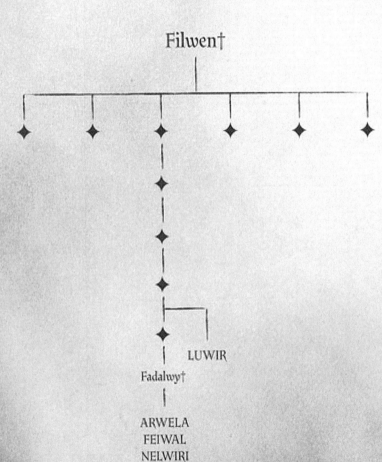

Filwen†

LUWIR

Fadalwy†

ARWELA
FEIWAL
NELWIRI

† Dead

◆ Father

TIMELINE

-5000 LC: Six Deities (Ffeyn, Myos, Vars, Llyi, Llya, Llyo) rebel against the Gods and are banished. They choose a lost archipelago at the boundaries of the Mainland for their Realm. They name it 'The Lost Islands'.

-3000 LC: The Elves awaken in the Mainland by the shores of the Inner Sea. They form nine different nations. The Assembly of the Gods offer immortality to the Elves should they accept their summoning and pay allegiance.

-2979 LC: The Deity of Storm, Eïwal Ffeyn, opposes the Gods about the future of the Elves. Along with the five other Deities of the Lost Islands, he secures the Archipelago as the last refuge of the Elves.

-2970 LC: Two Elvin nations (the Gold Elves and the Silver Elves) accept the gift of immortality and heed the Gods' call. They become the immortal High Elves. The Green Elves and the Blue Elves, along with the five other Elvin nations, refuse the summoning of the Gods and remain mortal. They are thereafter known as the Free Elves.

-2950 LC: Scions of the Greater Gods, the Dragons and the demons, the giants and the gnomes, roam the Mainland, terrorizing and enslaving communities of Free Elves. The migrations of the Green Elves and the Blue Elves begin.

-2810 LC: Eïwal Ffeyn enslaves the Giants on the Lost Islands to build the City of Stones, which one day will be known as Tios Lluin.

-2808 LC: The Green Elves settle in Essawylor by the shores of the Austral Ocean.

-2804 LC: The Blue Elves settle along the torrents of the Ivory Mountains, north-east of Essawylor.

-2800 LC: Eïwal Ffeyn, provokes the fall of a star from heaven. The meteorite hits the Lost Islands. The legend of the fallen star tracing the way to the last refuge of the Elves is born.

-181 LC: The High Elves rebel against the Gods and provoke their wrath. Despite the threat of divine retaliation, most of the High Elves return to the Mainland.

-151 LC: Victims of the Gods cursed manipulations, the High Elves are divided. The 'kin-slaying wars' begin.

-132 LC: An army of Men, the Desert Horde, attacks the Green Elves who dwell in Essawylor.

-16 LC: A navigator called Llyoriane, discovers the Lost Islands beyond the Austral Ocean. She is soon proclaimed Queen of the Green Elves.

0 LC: Queen Llyoriane leads the Green Elves to the Lost Islands. Their crossing of the Austral Ocean marks 'Year 0' of the Llewenti calendar (LC).

141 LC: Queen Llyoriane dies giving birth to her sixth daughter. Her ultimate consort, the Deity of War, Eïwal Vars, buries her in a tomb, concealed in 'The Secret Vale'. The Green Elves divide into six clans ruled by Queen Llyoriane's daughters, the first Matriarchs: Myortilys, Llyvary, Llyandy, Ernaly, Llorely and Avrony.

251 LC: The Blue Elves conquer Essawylor from the Desert Horde. The clan of Filweni's dwellings extend to the southern beaches bordering the Austral Ocean.

<u>508 LC:</u> The last kingdoms of the High Elves in northern Mainland are ultimately destroyed by a mighty flood. The survivors flee the North.

<u>517 LC:</u> The exiled High Elves reach the edge of the woods of Essawylor. The Blue Elves welcome them warmly.

<u>521 LC:</u> Conflict rages between the princes of the High Elves. Aranaele, who wishes to settle in Essawylor, opposes Lormelin who aims to cross the Austral Ocean and find the Lost Islands. The war of Diamond and Ruby rages.

<u>528 LC</u>: Aranaele becomes Queen of Essawylor and rules her vassals and the 29 Blue Elves' clans. Lormelin is proclaimed King of the High Elves by the majority of the noble houses. House Dol Lewin splits into two branches, the second one bowing to King Lormelin. Lormelin pronounces a terrible oath of revenge against those High Elves who fought him.

<u>529 LC:</u> The High Elves led by King Lormelin leave Essawylor onboard the clan of Filweni's fleet and cross the Austral Ocean to find the Lost Islands. They defeat Eïwal Ffeyn and imprison the Deity of Storm in the Sea of Cyclones.

<u>531 LC:</u> First war between the High Elves and the Green Elves: The armies of Lormelin the Conqueror defeat clan Llorely at 'the battle of Seagulls and Ruby'.

<u>555 LC:</u> Second War between the High Elves and the Green Elves: The armies of Lormelin the Conqueror defeat clan Llyandy at 'the battle of Owls and Ruby'.

<u>591 LC:</u> Third war between the High Elves and the Green Elves: The armies of Lormelin the Conqueror defeat the combined forces of clan Myortilys and clan Llyandy at 'the Battle of Ruby and Buzzards'.

640 LC: Fourth war between the High Elves and the Green Elves: The armies of Lormelin the Conqueror defeat the combined forces of the three clans of the west (Llyvary, Ernaly and Avrony) at 'the Battle of Ruby and Hawks'.

707 LC: The construction of the tower of Mentollà is achieved by the High Elves. The fortress controls the northern sea routes of Nyn Llyvary.

730 LC: Lormelin the Conqueror, founds Gwarystan, the capital city of his kingdom.

739 LC: Fifth war between the High Elves and the Green Elves: The armies of Lormelin the Conqueror defeat the combined forces of the three rebel clans of the west at 'the Battle of Ruby and Swans'. Lormelin is crowned King of Gwarystan and receives the tribute of five of the six Llewenti clans. Only the clan Myortilys refuses to bow.

1426 LC: Human barbarians of the Three Dragons' cult launch a first attack on the Lost Islands. Their raids are annihilated by the combined force of the King of Gwarystan and the five lesser clans of the Green Elves.

1677 LC: Human barbarians of the Three Dragons' cult launch a vast invasion of the Lost Islands. The great fortress of the West, Mentolewin, is burnt to the ground by a coalition of barbarian tribes. Men settle in Nyn Ernaly.

1785 LC: Human barbarians of the Three Dragons' cult launch the second invasion of the Lost islands. Men settle in Nyn Avrony.

<u>2425 LC</u>: King Lormelin the Conqueror is assassinated. The master of the Guild of Sana, Saeröl, is found guilty and sentenced to death. The young Norelin is crowned King of Gwarystan.

<u>2509 LC</u>: Human barbarians of the Three Dragons' cult launch the third invasion of the Lost Islands, 'the Great Conquest'. Nyn Avrony and Nyn Ernaly are utterly conquered by Men. New human settlements are founded on Gwa Nyn and Nyn Llyandy.

<u>2511 LC</u>: The last Elves of Nyn Avrony abandon their island. Gal dyl settles in the forest of Llymar.

<u>2514 LC</u>: Global conflict between Elves and Men across the Lost Islands. 'The Battle of Llymvranone' marks the beginning of 'the Century of War'.

<u>2610 LC</u>: Curubor and the last survivors of House Dol Etrond flee to Llymar Forest.

<u>2611 LC</u>: Tios Lluin is destroyed by the Barbarians. Death of the Protector of the Forest, Yluin dyl, father of Lyrine. Clan Llyvary, reinforced by clan Avrony and House Dol Etrond prevails and sanctifies the forest of Llymar.

<u>2675 LC</u>: Curubor Dol Etrond settles in Tios Lluin and starts to restore the ruins of the antique City of Stones.

<u>2688 LC</u>: The refugees of the clan Ernaly are entrusted with the government of Tios Halabron in the forest of Llymar.

<u>2705 LC</u>: King Norelin refuses to marry his cousin Terela Dol Nos-Loscin and denies his support to her house in the conflict against the Dragon Warrior Ka-Blowna. House Dol Nos-Loscin withdraws to its Principality of Cumberae.

2707 LC: The province of Ystanlewin in Essawylor is invaded by the Desert Horde. After the fall of his city, the heir of House Dol Lewin is banished by Queen Aranaele for rebellion.

2708 LC: A ship from Essawylor is cast upon the isle of Pyenty. The Blue Elf, Feïwal, and his crew reach the Lost Islands.

MYTHOLOGY

The Assembly of the Gods

~ **Ö**, Supreme Being of the Universe, Creator of the world and of all existence, "The One Above"

The eight Greater Gods

The Greater Gods are the eight mighty spirits who entered 'Oron', the World in lingua Hawenti, to begin its shaping. They completed its material development after its form was determined by Ö. Each of the Greater Gods added his or her own part to the Flow creating the world incarnate.

Their vision of what 'Oron' should have been was different. This led to a long conflict, called 'the War of Elements', between the four Gweïwali which caused many ills. The final shaping of the world and the geographical distribution between lands, mountains and oceans results from this terrible ordeal.

The Greater Gods dwell in their respective realm but frequently meet in the Island of 'Nol Gweïwali', 'the Gods' Isle' in lingua Hawenti, which is hidden at the centre of Inner Sea, a beautiful land set around an extinct volcano, highest mountain of Oron. The Greater Gods include four sisters, named Gweïwely: Lyfea, Inatea, Menea and Kerea, as well as four brothers, named Gweïwali: Zenwon, Agadeon, Uleydon and Narkon. They refer to one another as brother or sister.

*

Each Gweïwal rules a specific realm of the world. Zenwon received the sky, Agadeon received the underworld, Uleydon received the seas and Narkon received the fiery inner core of Oron.

~ **Gweïwal Zenwon**: Greater God of Air, the heavenly King and Lord of thunder

~ **Gweïwal Agadeon**: Greater God of Earth, the Halls of the Dead King and Lord of the underworld

~ **Gweïwal Uleydon**: Greater God of all Waters, King of oceans and Lord of tidal waves

~ **Gweïwal Narkon**: Greater God of Fire, King of volcanoes and Father of dragons

*

After the War of Elements had ended, the Gweïwely set about the conception of the world. Kerea governed chronological time, Menea ordered the movements of the moon and stars and thus created the seasons, Lyfea gave life to nature and last Inatea organized the settlement of Oron by the animals.

~ **Gweïwele Kerea**: Greater Goddess of Time, Queen of the celestial wheel and Lady of doom

~ **Gweïwele Menea**: Greater Goddess of Weather, Queen of the moon and Lady of stars

~ **Gweïwele Lyfea**: Greater Goddess of Plants, Queen of trees and Lady of flora

~ **Gweïwele Inatea**: Greater Goddess of Living Creatures, Queen of animals and Lady of fauna

The twelve Lesser Gods

The Lesser Gods are the twelve spirits who entered Oron after its creation to give order to the world. The 'Leïwali', as they are called in lingua Hawenti, were powers created by Ö, to directly intervene in the world's course of events. They are part of the hierarchy of spirits that is predominant in Hawenti Mythology. The Lesser Gods' influence greatly affected the destiny of Elves.

~ **Leïwal Kor**: God of Strength, Master of bravery

~ **Leïwal Vauis**: God of Discernment, Master of crafts

~ **Leïwal Nelo**: God of Charm, Master of arts

~ **Leïwal Sorm**: God of Agility, Master of physical prowess

~ **Leïwal Ceres**: God of Ruse, Master of oratory and wit

~ **Leïwal Baos**: God of Frenzy, Master of unforeseeable events

*

~ **Leïwele Sa**: Goddess of Wisdom, Mistress of just cause and balance

~ **Leïwele Layi**: Goddess of Beauty, Mistress of seduction, love and pleasure

~ **Leïwele Vha**: Goddess of Loyalty, Mistress of honour and duty

~ **Leïwele Sysa**: Goddess of Strife, Mistress of retribution and affliction

~ Leïwele Wia: Goddess of Harmony, Mistress of peace and fulfilment

~ **Leïwele Mnye**: Goddess of Memory, Mistress of patience and commitment

The Deities, Demigods and other divine creatures

The term 'Deities' or 'Demigods' refer to minor Gods and Goddesses, who can be mortal or immortal. Deities are the offspring of a god and a goddess, while Demigods are figures born from the union of a God with an Elf and who attains divine status after death. Both are referred as Eïwali.

The earliest recorded use of the term 'Eïwal' in the Lost Islands is by authors such as Curubor Dol Etrond and Sinear Dol Nos-Loscin. In late Second Age, they proposed a hierarchy of divinities as follows: the Greater Gods proper, or Gweïwali; the Lesser Gods, or Leïwali;the Deities and Demigods, or Eïwali (who dwell alongside the Elves in Oron); and the underworld-dwelling divinities like giants, demons and dragons.

The Deities of the Lost Islands

The Deities of the Lost Islands are part of the divinities worshiped by the religious Elves of the Archipelago (the Seeds of Llyoriane). They are considered as a fellowship of Elves' protectors who defend their last refuge against the outside world. Their most sacred shrine is located in the Secret Vale of Llyoriane where their Archpriests ('The Arkys' in lingua Llewenti) dwell.

~ **Eïwal Ffeyn**: Deity of winds and storms, Divinity of freedom, rebellion and anger, the son of Gweïwal Zenwon and Leïwele Sysa and the historical leader of the Lost Islands Deities during their rebellion against the Gods.

~ **Eïwal Vars**: Deity of hunting, Divinity of war and strength, the son of Leïwal Sorm and Gweïwele Inatea, and the second consort of the Llewenti Queen Llyoriane, father of five of the daughters of Queen Llyoriane: Llyvary, Llyandy, Ernaly, Llorely and Avrony.

~ **Eïwal Myos**: Deity of illusions and shadows, Divinity of art, poetry and pleasure, the son of Leïwal Baos and Leïwele Sysa, and the first consort of the Llewenti Queen Llyoriane, father of her first daughter Myortilys, the ruler of the Dark Elves

~ **Eïwele Llyi**: Deity of fountains, Divinity of love, beauty and the arts, the daughter of Leïwal Nelo and Leïwele Layi

~ **Eïwele Llya**: Deity of nature, Divinity of fauna, flora and fertility, the daughter of Leïwal Nelo and Gweïwele Lyfea and the most prominent of the Lost Islands divinities. She is also known as 'the Mother of the Islands'.

~ **Eïwele Llyo**: Deity of starlight, Divinity of dreams, fate, death and reincarnation the daughter of Leïwal Nelo and Gweïwele Kerea

~ **Eïwal Lon**: Demigod of sunlight, Divinity of wisdom, born from an unmarried lady, named Meoryne Dol Valra
Eïwal Lon is a mysterious demigod, born in the Valley of Nargrond after 800 LC. His divine origin was consecrated after his disappearance in the mines of Oryusk in 1000 LC.

Made in the USA
Middletown, DE
26 August 2021